DEBT OF FEAR

Michael Reid, Jr.

Debt of Fear

Interior design and layout: a.r. merlo.

ISBN 9780997350029

DEBT OF FEAR

Michael Reid, Jr.

First edition, edited by:
Annmarie Klyzub Ruggiero
and Heather Schild

*Thanks to John for
telling me it was good;
to Heather for reading
past the first chapter; to
Annmarie for getting rid
of the thousands of typos;
and to my wife for telling
me to quit being lazy.*

*But most of all, thank you
to all who are in the armed
services. You truly are the
most underappreciated and
selfless individuals I've had
the opportunity to know.*

CONTENTS

PROLOGUE

The glass building glistened like a waterfall reflecting hues of orange, red, and yellow in the early morning sun. The eastern side of old hotels came to life revealing details that had been painstakingly completed by artisans long since forgotten. Streetlights adorned with Saint Louis Rams' banners danced slowly to the inaudible melody of the morning breeze. The American flag at the Edward Jones Dome was also dancing unpredictably, quickly whipping up into the air on surprise gusts of wind. A man jogged past the stadium and crossed the intersection without looking for traffic. The white cord from his headphones bounced up and down as sweat accumulated on his shirt.

In his hotel room, Amir allowed himself to look away from his small, focused world through the rifle's scope and check his watch, 0800. *Like clockwork,* Amir thought, as he looked down the street at the man barely visible without the scope's 10x magnification. Amir placed his head back down onto his rifle, looked through the scope, and focused on the runner. The rifle muzzle was eight feet from a window that stretched from floor to ceiling. He had the shades drawn back just enough so the main entrance of the Edward Jones Dome, as well as the street leading south from the stadium, could be seen without obstruction. Amir used the beanbag he bought two days earlier to support the rifle's forearm. Pillows weren't allowing him to pivot the gun side to side or up and down. The new rig was working perfectly as he continued to track the jogger. The man turned south and continued running after he glanced left and right to mind the traffic. Amir placed his finger on the trigger watching the man coming closer. The jogger bounced all over Amir's field of vision through the small scope with each stride. "Boom," Amir said softly just before the man left his field of vision continuing his morning workout.

Something about the last week had not felt right. Amir had learned long ago to listen to his sensations. He was waking up several times a night with a nervous stomach. Even in his hotel room he tiptoed around methodically making sure every moment was consciously thought out. He went through the operative plans in his head several times a day. The plan was flawless and thorough, just as all his missions were.

Amir began prepping himself by taking slow, controlled breaths. Looking down the scope he felt the stress melt down into the bed, his breathing became more regular, his shoulders relaxed and the world shrunk down to a small, defined area. He was myopic, focusing only on the current task. He observed the American flag at the Edward Jones Dome and gauged the wind speed. He checked his range and scope calibration one last time. Amir purchased his M24 sniper rifle from a local who "knew a guy" and loved the extra cash Amir gave him. The rifle came with ballistic tables and a data book of every cold bore shot it had ever taken. Amir had studied the book for the last two days and knew how it should respond. The rifle had a bolt action so he needed to make the shot count.

Click, the safety was toggled off. He continued to breathe and watch. He scanned the area knowing that soon he would see his special operations team enter the event. Several moments passed and the first of four team members went through the gates. Amir glanced at his watch. Then a second, third, and fourth team member entered the venue. He took a few mental notes of individuals who seemed to stand out. The most noteworthy was a wide, muscular man who was wearing a brand-new Saint Louis Rams' hat and hoodie.

An hour passed and Amir found himself blinking hard and rubbing his eyes repeatedly. He tried to keep himself looking through the scope but eventually he would pull back and reset himself behind the scope. Suddenly his body sharpened. The blurring was gone and his hand was steady. The hum of the air conditioner and the smell of stale cigarettes were no longer perceived. All his cognitive force diverted toward what he was seeing. It was the muscular Rams' fan.

It would have been insignificant if he'd seen the same man for a second time any other day. He focused on each detail in the target, from his Rams' hat that still had a shiny sticker on it, to the small white blemish on his cross-trainers. Amir slid his shooting finger from the gunstock down into position at the curved, worn trigger. Tracking him for 30 seconds the fan made two distinct and calculated directional changes in order to follow Amir's accomplice. The Rams' fan was singled out. Amir took one long breath in . . . then out.

The target paused. For the briefest of moments Amir lay prone, subtly bouncing on the bed to the rhythmic *lub-dub* of his heartbeat. He extended the trigger finger and began to put it back onto the stock of the gun. His eyes blurred again as his focus changed to his inner doubt. His body stiffened as he blinked several times trying to clear his eyes. Amir pivoted the barrel away from the target to see what caught his focus. The large man turned and began walking toward a cab arriving just outside the venue. A man in jeans and a black shirt came out of the cab and walked quickly toward the large Rams' fan. The man from the cab turned around looking high into the buildings all around him, motioning with his hands he told the large Rams' fan to run.

Amir wasn't sure who to shoot. He lost control of his breathing and his hand began to sweat. It was obvious he had two targets and a cumbersome bolt action. He scanned left to the man in black and then right toward the muscular fan. Back and forth he scanned as they approached each other more quickly. Amir's heart raced. A car's horn from the street startled him, causing him to slightly squeeze down on the trigger. The world was coming back full scale and he felt the air conditioner turn on bringing a slight chill to the room. The smell of stale cigarettes returned and a solitary drop of sweat accelerated down to the tip of his nose.

Boom! Amir's finger acted on what his mind was so hesitant to do. A concussive wave vaporized the bead of sweat and the rifle kicked back into his right shoulder. The smell of gunpowder quickly filled the room as hot, humid air rolled in from the broken window. Amir cycled the bolt and looked down the barrel at the venue below for his second shot. He looked down the scope, past the broken glass and into the face of the man with the black shirt. People were running in all directions crossing in front of his targets at unpredictable intervals. Amir was shaken. The man in the black shirt stared directly into his room through the broken glass, between the curtains and completely ignored the chaos that was surrounding him. The hair stood up on Amir's arms and a chill went through his spine. He fought off his body's urge to shudder. The man in the black shirt then scrambled to pick up the large Rams' fan.

Boom! A second shot rang out splintering concrete and ricocheting toward the stadium, missing its mark. Quickly the man in the black shirt ran east with the large man on his shoulders, and out of Amir's shooting view. Amir was frozen. For the first time, he was not in control. He continued to lay on the bed and allow his thoughts to overwhelm him. He no longer looked through the scope but at the white linen bedding and a bullet casing that had been expelled from the M24. His thoughts were coming fast and furious and it was impossible to process them all individually. One common theme began to emerge: to run.

His heart raced and he became lightheaded as he leaped up from the bed. He dashed over to the desk as he fumbled with the rifle, trying to break it down and place it into a case but his hands were shaking uncontrollably. Emotions that were foreign to him began to take over, frustrating him even more as a tear fell from his eye. A knot in his stomach became crippling as he reached for the door. Not knowing what would happen or if he was making the right choice caused him to pause. Fear aggressively shook his entire body. For the first time in his life he was on the other side of terror.

He ripped open the door and ran to the stairwell.

chapter
ONE

"Why would you want to be in the Army young man?" the recruiter asked.

"I want to do my part as an American," responded the confident Pakistani teen.

"Good enough for me. Why the Army?"

"I'm talking to all the branches. I just want to serve. Whoever wants me can have me."

"Why so eager to serve?" The recruiter looked at the young man with a smirk.

The teen sat for a moment fighting an internal battle, trying to hold back the real reasons. He felt embarrassed, he felt anger, he felt nobody would understand the real reason why he wanted to wear a uniform. He didn't want pity, nor did he want yet another racist comment or obligatory apology from a white American. He wanted a uniform so people would see him as an American hero, not a first-generation Pakistani, or worse, a "terrorist."

"It's a good opportunity to travel the world for free," responded the teen.

"Well I'm looking at your ASVAB scores here and I must say, you could probably choose your branch. You scored in the top one percent.

Have you thought of going to Army, West Point or the Naval Academy? I feel with these scores and a senator's letter of recommendation you could get into any of those schools. Wow . . . your GPA was a 4.3. Is that accurate?"

"Yes sir. I just want to enlist and become a member of the armed service now. I'm ready."

"Well Sumeet, we'll just read through all this paperwork and get you going. Do you have any more questions I can answer?"

"How soon till I go to boot camp?"

"It will likely take a few weeks to months."

"The sooner the better."

Sumeet went back out into the parking lot where his father sat waiting for him in the car. "I still don't understand why this is so important for you Sumeet," his father said, staring at the steering wheel. "Son, I love you, but we moved to this country so you have more opportunities than I had. I wish your mother was still here, I think she would have been able to talk sense into you—"

"Don't say that!" Sumeet said sternly, cutting his father off and turning to face him. "Nobody would have stopped me. She understood what I wanted. She had the same vision as me. She blessed it last year before she died—you were there." Sumeet rounded his shoulders and melted into the seat.

Sumeet and his father sat in silence. In their minds, both had gone back to the moment they said goodbye to the most important woman in their lives as she lost her battle with cancer.

"I support you, son," his father said as he started the car. "I just can't imagine losing the only thing I have left."

Fourteen weeks passed quickly for Sumeet as he went through basic training. There was no racism here. Everyone was being broken down equally and Sumeet had an unfair advantage. He'd already dealt with verbal assaults for years. He excelled in every way. He was always in the top five percent for physical readiness training. He even received top marksmanship awards and was asked about sniper school. He turned it down because he wanted to stay in the infantry. For the first time, he was part of a brotherhood: Army 25th Infantry Division, Second Battalion, 27th Infantry Regiment, the Wolfhounds.

Sumeet knew their deployment must be on the horizon. The training had morphed from being generalized and mundane, to a more focused approach with each passing day. They had traveled to Georgia for the most difficult training to date. He was confident in his abilities as a leader, but something was draining him. He was sick of not knowing what was coming next. Daily time seemed to go by slowly, but soon a month passed, still with no hints at where

"Listen up," Sumeet said smirking at the squad. they would be going. He wanted an assignment soon, and so did the men of his squad. Whenever Sumeet walked into the barracks, conversations stopped and everyone sat still in anticipation of possible news. Often, he was disappointed having nothing to say to them, but this time he was excited. "We got news. Debrief at 2100 hours in the mess hall." The men all quickly jumped to their feet yelling and giving high fives. The long, dark faces the men wore for weeks had tightened up and seemed alive again. They were laughing, joking, wrestling; for the moment, it was great.

The mess hall was standing room only. Tables were folded up and stacked in straight columns against the wall and hundreds of seats were all lined up facing the front of the mess. Every seat had filled in 30 minutes ago. A few stragglers jammed themselves in against the wall, creating a rippling effect of other soldiers moving to accommodate them. The yellow glow from the lights above gave the men a green hue as they all talked and joked before the colonel entered to address them.

"Listen up men!" Lieutenant Colonel Hardy said as he addressed his regiment. The colonel began speaking as he entered the room with large, powerful strides. "We'll be deployed, and we'll see action. We're going to war; in Afghanistan. We WILL be fighting on OUR terms, on their land. We know quite a bit about the terrain, we know very little about their alliances with local communities. Your training will get you through this, and we already have some men on the ground gathering more intel as we speak. Trust your leaders, leaders trust your men. We WILL succeed, and we WILL come home. Our deployment will be six to nine months, but count on it being longer if needed. We've got a job to do so let's all get that job done right and come home." The colonel saluted the men and they all stood and saluted at attention while he left the mess hall.

Colonel Hardy made eye contact with Sumeet and called him over with the slightest head nod. Sumeet caught up to the colonel as he was exiting.

"Sumeet, I'm trusting you will continue to impress me son. I think you've got a rare gift and a need to prove something. Prove it to your men. Prove it to us all." The colonel finally stopped and faced Sumeet looking him in the eyes. For Sumeet it wasn't common to look up in order to see a man's eyes, but Colonel Hardy was an exception. A heavy hand slapped down onto Sumeet's shoulder and a moment later the loud thud of Colonel Hardy's boots pounded down the smooth concrete outside in the humid Georgia night. Thunder echoed in the distance, but for the moment the sky was clear, and little twinkling lights in the heavens acted as confetti for the twisted celebration of going to combat.

Paktika Province, Afghanistan

The assigned location for 27th Infantry was the Paktika Province along the violent border of Afghanistan and Pakistan. Sumeet had mixed feelings about this. It was the first time he had ever set eyes on his parents' country and it was during an act of war. He knew that someday, and possibly soon, he would have to fire upon Pakistanis. He didn't know that it would be less than a week before his first live fire action.

Afghanistan was a dream. Sumeet felt at home in the rolling hills and short vegetation his dad had often described when talking about "home." The wind was a mix of sensations, mainly warm and constant, but occasionally with a brisk shot of air. A fire burning in the distance rode on the wind and Sumeet was reminded of a few long-forgotten memories of youthful naivety. Conversely the smell of rotting animals and dung brought him back to reality. He was here to fight. The smell of death could become all too familiar.

His squad was tasked with taking a ten-kilometer hike to patrol the most northern edge of the 27th's post under cover of darkness. Prior to the Infantry's arrival, it had been a highway for terrorists traveling through small towns that harbored and supported them. The area had been dead for a few days, but a recent upsurge in vehicle traffic, as well as aerial night reconnaissance has indicated possible border jumping from Pakistan to Afghanistan.

"OK guys, it's 2300 hours. Check your gear. Leaving in 15. Make sure you have your NVGs, water, and stripped packs. We're gonna' be

12 hours. You'll have second squad relieving your post tomorrow. I want radio checks every 30 minutes for location and intel. Sumeet, first squad is yours. Let's see you take care of business. Your call sign tonight is Lone Wolf; we're Big Dipper. Anything suspicious is a shooting star."

"Yes sir, Lieutenant," Sumeet said saluting. "Alright guys gear up. Face paint on tonight. Check your mags, and bring some for your brothers. Let's get it on."

The moon was full, and straight up in the night sky and air was calm and quiet. Everything was visible, so first squad needed to be as stealth as they could be. Sumeet made quick work of navigating the terrain and within two hours they had reached the ridge-line overlooking a dirt road into a small city just on the Afghani side of the border. It was their location of interest.

Sumeet had his men lay prone for the moment as he worked out the landscape and quickly determined the most strategic formation to take. He had one LMG, an M249, and the rest were riflemen carrying M16A4s, two of which had M203 under slung grenade launchers. In total, there were ten men. Sumeet set the LMG on top of the hill at the L-shaped turn in the road that entered the town. He placed two riflemen with the LMG looking down toward the town and called them Alpha team. He placed the remainder of the force looking down the other side of the L-shaped road that led toward Pakistan, and called them Whiskey team. Sumeet decided he would rove between the teams making sure their backside was watched.

"Big Dipper this is Lone Wolf checking in, over," Sumeet said into the radio. It was 0400 and there was no sign of anyone entering or leaving since they had arrived.

"Go ahead, Lone Wolf."

"No sign of shooting stars tonight. I have the kids all tucked into bed."

"Roger that Lone Wolf."

Sumeet decided to take a patrol. He knelt down as he reached Alpha team. "Stay alert, make sure you are scanning the horizon, too. Look for silhouettes. They probably won't be taking the roads in and we have to expect that." Sumeet then went back down the hill and into the shadows. He moved quickly to Whiskey team to relay the same message. Just as he finished the message, he heard footsteps.

"Ramirez, White, on me," he said to two of the men in the rifle squad. Sumeet had heard the noise coming from the shadows about 40 meters behind the LMG location with team Alpha. The three men all moved methodically through the light vegetation trying not to make a sound. The rubber on their boots was softer in the heat, so they seemed to gently kiss the ground rather than scrape against the rocks and hard earth beneath their feet.

"Sims, this is Sumeet. We heard a noise about 40 meters to your six o'clock and are investigating. Stay put, but you may want to have one of your riflemen turn around."

"Copy that sir, already doing it," Sims replied as he signaled his rifleman to turn.

Sumeet halted the other two men. He had heard a rock fall across the ground and roll down the hill in darkness behind Alpha team. Sumeet's hair stood up on his neck. He heard a whisper.

"Alpha group I'm hearing whispers 20 meters behind you, turn your second rifleman. First squad double check safeties are off."

"Big Dipper this is Lone Wolf, possible shooting star, over."

"Lone Wolf, we hear you, any chance you caught the color?"

"Negative, we are looking into it. Stand by."

"Do you need us to send another set of eyes? Over."

"If there are some in the area it would be appreciated. Over."

"You'll have them in two minutes."

Sumeet's heart was pounding. He signaled Ramirez and White to continue to follow. The three of them were now 30 meters from the noise. "NVGs on, first squad."

As Sumeet placed his NVGs on, it was immediately apparent that these noises weren't friendly. He saw four men carrying AK-47s, and they were in two-by-two formation. They seemed to be making a direct line toward Alpha team.

"Big dipper we have four confirmed red shooting stars. Over."

"Roger that Lone Wolf, handle at your discretion, we have our own eyes on location as well."

"OK. Out."

"White, Ramirez, double back and get around behind them. I want them in the bottom of the ditch between you and Alpha team. I'm staying here. We'll have them in a three-way cross fire. You've got one minute." The two men moved like ghosts in the night.

"Whiskey team stay put, we're about to make a tactical takedown on four tangos approaching Alpha squad. Two of you watch your flanks, one watch the town, and one watch behind you to the west. The other three will continue to look down the road to Pakistan. Sims, you stay focused on the city."

"We're in position," said White into the receiver.

"OK, we're gonna' mark up. Sims has the man at rear and east, Ramirez, you have rear and west, I will take front west, and Alpha you have front east. All copy, over."

"Copy. Sims, over."

"Copy. Ramirez, over."

"Copy. Alpha, over."

"On my count," Sumeet said. "Three . . . two . . . one."

Pop, pop, pop, pop, pop! Five shots rang out into the night. It took less than two seconds.

"First squad eyes on your positions. Ramirez, White, up to Alpha and support Sims. Alpha stay in your current configuration, Ramirez and White are moving up to your position. Whiskey I'm coming to you."

"Big Dipper shooting stars are down. Four confirmed. Over."

"Lone Wolf we have second squad coming to you now for assistance, over."

Sumeet looked up toward the road leading to Pakistan. A truck was racing down the road emitting flashes like a strobe and deep guttural booms from the back. It was the unmistakable sound of a 50-caliber machine gun.

"We are being fired upon!" Sumeet exclaimed into the receiver.

"First squad, open fire!" Sumeet yelled into the night air.

"Three tangos in the truck, one on the gun!" yelled Sims as he turned his LMG in the vehicle's direction and began to clink off rounds.

"We have tangos coming out of the village!" yelled White. "I'm counting ten!"

"Alpha team fire down on tangos in the city, Whiskey team take out the truck!" Sumeet yelled to the men.

The truck was driving erratically and the gunner was firing wildly into the hills where first squad was buried. Sumeet was trying to get his 4x scope fixed on the shooter but the driver was so erratic he couldn't keep him in the reticle. Sumeet set his M16 to single shot and laid prone. He took two deep breaths and held the third. *Pop, ping!* One shot fired, and one shot deflected by the steel shield at the front of the 50-caliber. Two more breaths. *Pop, ping!* again. Sumeet blinked heavily, took one more breath, *pop!*

This time he hit. He saw the machine gunner's head immediately snap back, opening his forehead wide as red mist filled the bed of the truck. Sumeet then turned his attention to the driver, *pop!* again it was a hit with immediate results. The truck slowed to a stop.

"Whiskey team fire on town!" Sumeet said taking quick mental note of all four tangos dead at the truck.

"Lone Wolf this is second squad, on your site approaching from the south over."

"Second squad is coming up from the south! Alpha team everyone shoot down onto the city!"

"Second squad we have ten tangos engaged into the city to the north. Alpha squad has best line-of-sight and are at the crest of the hill. Recommend getting up and fire down toward the city!" Sumeet yelled into the radio.

"Copy that Lone Wolf. I see Alpha squad. We'll be there in ten, over."

"Can we use part of second squad to set a perimeter watching our east, south and west? I don't want these assholes creeping up behind us! First contact was from the south!"

"Lone Wolf, copy that. We'll take six guys and set that up. Over."

Time stood still as tracers danced through the night toward the town. It only took a few moments for first and second squad to eliminate the ten tangos that emerged from the city.

"Lone Wolf this is Big Dipper. Over."

"Big Dipper this is Lone Wolf, haven't seen any more shooting stars in the last hour. Still fully aware, perimeter set and holding."

"Lone Wolf we need first squad to come back in for a debrief. Third platoon is coming out to relieve you. They will be onsite within the hour. Set your IR beacons on so third platoon sees you. Over."

"Will do."

"First and second squad, we need IR beacons on. Third platoon is coming to relieve us for a debrief. Watch for friendlies coming in, they'll have IR on."

The hike back was uneventful and numb. First squad was silent as they entered camp. Lieutenant Colonel Hardy was waiting at battalion headquarters to talk to Sumeet directly. "Corporal," Colonel Hardy said to Sumeet as he entered the HQ. Sumeet stood at attention and saluted. "At ease son. You're going to debrief me directly. I want to hear all the details. We're going to record it. Have a seat son."

The sun was rising quickly over the horizon as Sumeet walked back to his barracks following the debrief. He began to shake and feel lightheaded. His pulse raced and darkness began to close in around him. He took off his gear, his clothes, and wobbled his way into the bathroom naked. He nearly fell over and caught himself several times along the way on bunks. Eventually he collapsed on his knees face first over the toilet. He began dry heaving until his abdominals began to cramp. With each heave, he closed his eyes and saw the faces of the men he shot. He became so frustrated with the cycle he squeezed the rim of the toilet with all his remaining strength. Somehow it helped stop the dry heaves and his breath leveled. He stood up and washed his face with cold water, walked back into the barracks, and crawled into bed.

He wrote his father a letter with shaking hands.

Dear Father,

As I sit here looking upon the country you knew so well, I am distracted by the overwhelming urge to hear your voice. I miss you, Dad, and hope to make you proud. I unfortunately stand united with my brothers against the enemy near a place you so recently called home. I'm afraid I'll achieve the goals I set out to do by joining the military, but it will leave me scarred in deeper ways I never imagined. I pray to see you soon. Pray for me.

Sumeet

chapter
TWO

Logan Falcone sat on his bunk cleaning his pistol for the third time that day. Before that, he had gone to the gym with Sherman, his sniper teammate. The two of them had been inseparable since Logan enlisted after the attacks on 9/11. They went through boot camp together, both qualifying as sharpshooters, then into the sniper school. The instructors saw how close the two of them were, so it was natural to place them together as teammates in the squad.

Logan was frustrated. It had been three years since his enlistment and the anger still burned strong within him. To date, his recon company had been deployed twice, and balked at two additional times. None of which allowed him to face the enemy. He was like a hungry tiger in a cage ready to kill; but there was nothing to eat.

"Looks like we're shippin' out," Sherman said while standing in the doorway of the barracks, catching Logan off guard.

"About time," Logan responded, still cleaning his pistol.

"You gonna ask where?"

"Don't care. I'll believe it when I see it."

"Fuck off little man, you care. It's Iraq. We're leaving tomorrow. Let's hit the bar," Sherman said and threw a clean shirt at his scout, Logan.

"Ooh Rah!" Logan yelled as he pulled the slide back on his pistol and took a dry shot.

The bar was full. It had reached capacity an hour ago and the foot traffic had spilled out in to the parking lot. "You need one yet?" Logan asked Sherman as they stood talking to a group of recon men.

"Might as well," Sherman said looking sideways at his beer, then raised it to his mouth and chugged the rest.

"Be back in a minute," Logan said and walked toward the bar through the gravel parking lot. "Hey! Stay the fuck away from the sluts while I'm gone!"

"I'm good man. Just get me a beer," Sherman yelled back and pointed to the bar. On more than one occasion, the handsome, drunk Sherman was approached by a young woman and he had given her a bit too much attention for a man engaged to a girl back home.

Logan came back out, beers in hand, and quickly spotted the group of recon men; minus Sherman. "Where the hell is he, guys?" Logan asked annoyed as he reached the men.

They shrugged, gave each other looks, and smirked. "I'm not gonna sit here and beg, assholes."

Logan searched for Sherman through the large parking lot full of people. It took close to 30 minutes, and two beers, but Logan eventually found him checking under the hood of more than a car. Logan pulled Sherman away from a young woman and pushed him onto the ground. They wrestled in the parking lot for several minutes while the young blonde screamed. Sherman struck Logan hard on the face and then, somehow, Logan turned Sherman. Logan was now straddled over the much larger Sherman. He grabbed Sherman by the shirt with both hands and lifted his torso off the ground bringing Sherman's bloodied face close to his own.

"What's that black ink say on your chest?" Logan spat through his teeth. Sherman softened. Ashamed, he wouldn't look Logan in the face. Logan shook him once. "What's it say?" he asked more loudly. This time the young blonde heard what Logan said and adjusted her purse, bit her lip, and snuck away to her car.

"I love you brother," Sherman said. "Fuck, I'm so stupid." He wiped his hands over his buzzed head and down his face. "Let me buy the next one man. Seriously, you're my brother. I never had one . . . I'm so hammered."

"Damn straight," Logan said finally dropping Sherman to the ground and walking back into the bar.

"I miss Heather man. I don't know why I do that shit," Sherman said as they supported each other, arms slung over shoulders.

"At least you have someone to remember you when we're out in the shit," Logan said smiling."

Sherman stumbled away from Logan, punching him on the shoulder as he did it.

"Oh shit. Maybe we're done. Come on buddy let's call it."

"Ooh Rah, Marine," Sherman said and collapsed to the gravel below, laughing uncontrollably.

Mosul, Iraq

Iraq was a difficult country. They spent hours looking over aerial reconnaissance photos and talking to SEALs who'd been on the ground in their next hot zone, Mosul. The target was an Iraqi colonel set on murdering anyone, including his own men, who opposed Hussein. The colonel had already murdered hundreds of civilians, as well as five of his own soldiers he suspected of giving information to the Americans. His assumptions were right, all five soldiers had been giving the U.S. intelligence, and now it was getting harder and harder to find Iraqi soldiers who were willing to help.

Sherman and Logan were dropped at a location 20 kilometers northwest of the city. They spent two days infiltrating the city and setting up a shooting nest high in an abandoned building the SEAL team had secured earlier that week. Sherman and Logan were just within 1,000 meters west of where they suspected the target would be.

"Target acquired, mobile on foot. Range 850 meters," Logan said looking through the spotting scope. "Wind . . . five knots right to left."

Sherman turned the dial on his scope three clicks for distance, and two clicks for wind-speed to calibrate for the shot based on shooting tables. Sherman had logged thousands of cold bore shots with this rifle. He didn't need to reference the chart anymore. Sherman began to take long breaths in through the nose, out the mouth as he lay prone in the back corner of their hide.

"Exterminator two this is the Roach Motel, how copy?"

"We hear you. Got our target in sight. How would you like us to proceed?" Logan said into the radio, with his range finder raised to his eye as he tracked the target.

"You have a green light. Proceed as indicated."

"Roger Roach Motel. Exterminator two out."

"OK, fire when ready," Logan said as Sherman turned off the safety on his M40. The target stopped and turned around, walking at a much faster pace.

"Breathe Sherman, wait for a steady shot."

Sherman slowed his breathing once again. The target continued walking for several seconds then paused just before leaving the sniper team's narrow visual window.

Sherman let out a long breath and held it. One . . . two . . . three seconds. *Boom!* A shot rang out as Sherman pulled the trigger and the M40 pushed firmly into his shoulder. The recoil caused him to lose sight of the target for a moment, but Logan had seen everything. Just as Sherman shot, the target moved. By the time the round traveled the 850 yards, the target had taken one step forward and the projectile screamed as it hit the concrete walkway. The target heard the shot ring out and echo through the street.

The pedestrians were still active. It seemed as though nobody else heard the shot. Time was moving slowly and the target looked from building to building trying to see where the shot came from. In that brief period of time, Sherman had targeted and sent another round down range striking the man in the face.

As the echoes from the second shot left his ears, Sherman heard a woman scream in the distance and the metallic clacking of guns being snapped to attention. A storm of voices—yelling, shouting—thundered as he watched the life drain out of the man and onto the street.

"Targets on the rooftops," Logan said as he picked up his rifle.

"Call 'em out," Sherman said with his eye still frozen on the crosshairs. It was odd how calm Sherman was in the situation. Typically, it was Logan who was collected.

"Right side of the street, rooftop. 500 yards. Wind five knots right to left. Don't fire, they have no idea where we are. We're dug in well here. Don't think they'll see us. Just take it easy, don't get trigger-happy and stick our ass out," Logan said.

"Roach Motel, this is Exterminator two. Target's down. We've got too many secondary targets. Unsafe to fire. Requesting air support. Over."

"Uh, that's a negative on your Bug Bomb, Exterminator two. We cannot afford to put birds in the air. We have no intel on enemy anti-air equipment in the area. Sit tight in your hide. Let the situation die down, we'll pick up and rally point Bravo at 0100. Over."

Logan looked again into the range finder. "Sherman, we are still looking good. They have no idea where we are. HQ wants us silent then exfil at Bravo 0100. That's nine hours, and ten klicks. Rah!"

"Ooh Rah," Sherman said not looking away from the scope.

Three hours passed. "They're starting to put shit together Logan," Sherman said as he looked down on the dead target. "They figured out the direction the shot came from. We're in the tallest building. Only a matter of time before they get here and go room to room. I think it's time to move."

"OK," Logan said. Sherman drew back the M40 and retracted the bipods. Logan continued to scan the streets, buildings, rooftops. Logan saw a flash from a rooftop.

Crack! A bullet came ripping through curtains veiling the window then back into the wall behind them. Then, a second muzzle flash from a different rooftop.

"Move!" Logan yelled to Sherman.

The second shot came ripping through the curtain but this time with a much different sound. It was more of a thump as the round entered Sherman just below his eighth rib on the right side of his body. Sherman let out a low involuntary groan and took three steps toward the door feeling no pain for the moment.

Logan quickly ran to his teammate. He threw Sherman, their weapons, and packs over his shoulder. He immediately began the descent down six floors and out the back of the building into a much quieter street. Logan made no attempts to check his corners and ran as fast as he could through the alleyways.

Without warning, a small group of Iraqi soldiers burst through a door. Logan dropped Sherman to the ground with a groan and raised his M4. He quickly emptied his clip into six hostiles. *Click,* he heard the heart-stopping sound of the end of the magazine. He reached for his Glock and felt a sting in his left shoulder. He reached toward it instinctively and saw blood on his hand.

Pop, pop, pop! Gunfire immediately toward his right made him fall to his back as he panicked, searching for the source. It was Sherman. He'd placed several precision shots down range, eliminating the last three combatants before passing out. Logan now had five hours to move ten kilometers with Sherman on his back.

As the time passed the shadows became longer and Logan was able to hide better. He ran into little resistance and was about two kilometers from the exfiltration site Bravo.

"Ahrg," Sherman said as Logan lowered him down to the dirt as gently as his exhausted muscles would allow.

"Damn it Sherman you better make it. I'm not doing this shit for nothing," Logan said as he opened Sherman's field kit and began searching for the bandages.

"Grrrrr," Sherman grimaced as Logan applied the dressing to his wound. "Shit that's a lot of blood Logan." Sherman's head dropped back onto the dirt as he took deep, calming breaths.

"It ain't so bad," Logan said as he reached back taking his own pack off for more dressings. Logan's entire pack was sticky and red. Sherman had been bleeding out onto Logan as he carried him for the last several hours. Logan didn't allow himself to think about it. Maybe it was the training, but he stayed calm and focused on the task at hand. He placed the second bandage on the wound.

"I'm never gonna drink again Logan. They got my liver. Haha," Sherman said deliriously as Logan picked him back up.

"Quit being a pussy. We are almost there."

Logan arrived at Bravo with 20 minutes to spare. He began hearing the rotors in the distance. The sounds were bouncing all around the hills and he could barely make out which direction they were coming from. "Hang on you bitch. We are almost there," Logan got no response from Sherman. "Did you hear me? Come on asshole not now they're here!" Still no response.

He quickly lowered Sherman down to the ground. Logan didn't need the faint light that was cascading from the moon, he could tell the bandages were no longer white. They were dark red, and saturated. He checked for a pulse. He checked for breath. Neither was present.

"Damn it Sherman you better start breathing," Logan said through clenched teeth into Sherman's lifeless ear. Logan began performing CPR compressions for two minutes then rechecked the vitals. Still nothing. This went on for what seemed like an eternity. Logan's whole body was numb and he could no longer lock his elbows straight but he continued to try and depress Sherman's chest.

Logan was grabbed from behind and lifted off Sherman. "Get the fuck off me!" he yelled and threw an elbow into the face of the Marine who grabbed him from behind.

"Settle down Sarge. We got it from here," the Marine said. Two other Marines got to Sherman and put his limp body into the helo and they took off.

The flight team worked with Sherman and placed an AED on his bare chest and abdomen. "Clear!" one of the medics said as they shocked him over and over again. There was no saving him. They turned their attention to Logan who sat in the helo, numb to his surroundings, entering shock as he stared blankly at his teammate. The medic took Logan's arm and struggled to find a vein. They poked Logan several times but he didn't care. It wouldn't have bothered him to die with his partner.

Logan sat alone in the medical tent for two hours before a lieutenant came and got him. He was no longer in shock and drank water sip by sip. He was allowed to see his partner. Sherman was no longer bloody and his once bronze skin was now rather pale. The dark tattoo on his chest, "Heather," was contrasted by his pasty skin. Logan touched Sherman and he was cold and tacky. He moved the sheet to look at the wound. The entry wound was smaller by tenfold compared to the exit wound on the posterior side of the torso. Hard to believe Sherman was able to hang on for five minutes let alone six hours.

"Sergeant, the captain wants a debrief," the lieutenant said placing his hand onto Logan's right shoulder blade. Logan nodded, placed his own hand over the tattoo on Sherman's heart, then turned and walked away.

The days passed slowly following Sherman's death. Logan was a shell of himself and rarely said hi to people he typically spent hours socializing with during the many down times. Now, most of his time was spent in his bunk staring at the ceiling, or cleaning his pistol when he couldn't sleep. His eyes would often refuse to shut. It became motor memory just to snap his eyelids open as soon as his head hit the pillow because whenever he closed them, he saw Sherman. In the rare moments when he did sleep, a running loop of the events following Sherman's last shot played in his mind.

Logan would talk to one person, his commanding officer Captain Stevens, who sat, listened, and rarely spoke. When Stevens did speak, he didn't try to comfort Logan. Instead he always gave the same party line of "you've gotta get back out there." Stevens had been there once before. He lost a few close brothers-in-arms on a previous tour. His own survival had showed his leadership potential and earned him his captain stripes.

One afternoon Captain Stevens felt as though he had nothing left to say to Logan. Options were thin and Logan continued to fall further and further into his depressive state. "Logan, I'm going to have to talk with Colonel Jenkins back stateside. See if he has any options for you. I think of you as a younger brother and I'm concerned."

Logan rubbed his eyes and remained focused on the floor for a moment while he slouched deep into a wooden chair. He sighed, sniffled, and looked up at Captain Stevens. With desperate eyes Logan nodded, yes.

Camp Lejeune

"Logan. How are ya' son?" Colonel Jenkins asked as he stood up from behind his desk at Second Battalion Headquarters at Camp Lejeune.

"I'm good sir," Logan responded. Logan was pristine from head to toe, shoes shined, buttons and fly all in line, and corners crisp on his pants and shirt.

"You can relax Logan. Have a seat." Both men sat down. "I've heard differently Logan. Your CO says you have not been able to perform well at all this last month. We've paired you with several other members of your sniper platoon and you just, well, fuck it up son. We're looking out for everyone here, your platoon, your battalion, and you yourself Logan. If we can't trust you to do the job, then we can't have you out there."

"It's different working with anyone other than Sherman. He was me, I was him. All the simple nuances I look for are gone. I can't get a good read on anyone else," Logan said looking down at the colonel's desk.

"Well I have given it some thought. Captain Stevens will keep me informed and depending how the next few weeks go, we have a couple options. Option one, you get folded back into Marine Recon and step away from the sniper post. Option two, you work for me and run some covert black ops recon. I was damn impressed at how you got outta' there with Sherman undetected and hotfooted it to the pickup point. That's exactly what I need. You take these next few weeks and let me know."

Logan walked out of the office and looked at his watch. It was 1500 hours and he decided that he was going out tonight to Hooligans for some live music and to clear his head.

chapter
THREE

Hooligans was busy for a Thursday night. Logan spotted a stool near the back wall and decided that was home base for the night. It had a great view of all the people he had no interest in talking to and the acoustics in that area always seemed good to him. He quickly walked up to the bar, grabbed a Corona, and went back to the open stool.

The night was relaxing. Logan was taking in live country music being sung by average singers at best. He saw a few couples dancing, more than a few singles mingling, and one verbal altercation that was settled over a few beers. The two arguing Marines were familiar, but he never met them. He realized it was because the men reminded him of Sherman and himself.

"Excuse me," someone asked Logan from his left. It forced him out of his reminiscing.

"Uh, hi," Logan said as he turned toward the woman with a smile he still carried on his face from recent thoughts.

"Is someone sitting here?" she asked with a smile.

"No, no. Go ahead and take it," Logan said getting off his own stool to pull out the seat which had been empty right next to him. She took the stool from him.

"Thank you," she said pushing it down firmly into the worn hardwood floor. "But the chair is fine right here." She sat down and stared at him, again, smiling.

Logan sat uncomfortably, matching stares with this beautiful brown-haired, brown-eyed woman.

"My name is Samantha," she said reaching a hand toward Logan.

"Logan," he said returning a smile.

"So, what do you do?" she asked in an excited voice, almost as if she had never actually asked the question before, but rehearsed it in the mirror.

"I'm a Marine."

"OK, Marine, what do you do?" Samantha said taking a drink of her Captain and Coke through the tiny straw.

"I'm with Marine Recon. I'm a sniper."

"Interesting. You must have good eyes. Do you like my dress?" she asked standing up and turning around so Logan could get a good look. It was forest green with white flowers all over, big ones, with no real pattern to them.

"Yeah, it's a good dress on you." He noticed how soft her skin looked. The sun had clearly kissed her quite well making it a lovely rich olive tone. Logan looked down to the floor and started sweating a little.

"What's your story?" Samantha asked sitting back down and turning toward him. Logan was genuinely moved by the question. Something inside Logan was stirring. Something he hadn't felt in a while. He felt like he mattered, like someone might still be on the planet he could connect with. He looked back up, meeting her eyes. Logan was full of confidence.

"You're gonna be here a while?" Logan responded playfully.

"I've got all night, Logan." He loved the fact that she said his name out loud. It was magical, it was direct, it was warming.

Logan and Samantha talked till the bar closed. They swapped stories, flirted, drank, and she even dragged him onto the dance floor, but that didn't last long. Eventually he told her about Sherman.

"Logan, I really liked talking to you. I didn't expect you to be so open about what had happened. I had no idea when I asked you your story you would be so transparent. I really appreciated it," Samantha said as they walked out of the bar.

"Well you made it easy. I hope it helped you decide what you want to do with your career."

"Oh, it did. I think I'll try to work for the government, just not as part of the Armed Forces. I think my criminal justice degree will be best served locally. Maybe Department of Homeland Security, or some local PD."

"Well, good luck Samantha," Logan said reaching out his hand. "I hope we can get together again. I never do this, but I'd like to call you sometime."

Samantha looked around the parking lot and laughed. "Ummm. Can I get a ride home? I actually came with a few friends, but it looks like they left me."

"Yeah I can give you a ride. If you give me your number."

"We'll see how the ride goes."

The time had flown for Logan as he leaned full force into his new relationship. His loneliness, his sorrow, his regret had all slowly crept away. In return, he gained self-confidence, self-will, and confusion. Logan and Samantha had spent nearly every evening together eating out, walking, or just talking till the early hours of the morning. Monday morning was coming and it had been just over two weeks since Colonel Jenkins had called him into the office and laid Logan's options on the table. The options had been keeping him up all night.

He looked lazily up from a piece of paper he laid on the table and saw that it was only 0530. Logan began to make a pros and cons list of Marine Recon versus covert ops with Jenkins. As the sun climbed over the horizon the list grew longer and longer. After two hours of trying to weigh it out it appeared that covert ops were the way to go. The decision came down to the fact that it would allow him the greatest possibility of being stateside—with Samantha. The satisfaction of having a decision seemed to be the cure for the sleepless night and he lumbered back toward his room. He dropped down into bed and closed his eyes and he almost immediately fell asleep; but, then his phone rang.

"Hello," said a cute, gravelly voice.

"Hey girl," Logan said smiling and using his free hand to rub the sleep from his eyes. "You just getting up"

"Yeeessss . . . wanna' go get some breakfast with me?" Samantha asked while stretching.

"Yeah, I've got no plans."

"Leave your place in 30. I've gotta throw some clothes on."

"See you soon."

Logan had decided not to tell her one way or the other what decision he had made. As far as she knew, he was just a jarhead who could shoot.

chapter
FOUR

Sumeet was home, stateside. He sat in his father's living room with his feet on an ottoman and his body sinking low into a blue couch. He wore a smile when talking to his father, but it was empty. His thoughts were of men thousands of miles away. He trusted nobody but himself to lead the men into the hot zones and what good was he here? He was finally accepted by his peers and he was excelling. Nobody questioned what he said. His commanding officer often came to him to run plans by him before any other squad leaders. He was going crazy sitting still, but it was nice seeing his father so happy.

"What are we doing tonight dad?" Sumeet asked as they sat in the living room.

"I don't know. You always want to be doing something. I cannot keep up with you."

Sumeet laughed. "How about we get some food. Let's do . . . Olive Garden!"

"I think that you are Italian, not Pakistani," his father said as he raised an eyebrow up and smiled. "Well let's go already."

The night was mild for late July, but they still drove with the windows down. Sumeet loved driving his father. It was gratifying to see his father relaxed.

"Dad, I always appreciated you coming to my soccer games. I'm not sure I ever told you that."

"I loved watching you. I can work the rest of my life. Soccer was not going to last forever. We both knew you were just average." They laughed.

Sumeet and his father were seated close to the bar where a few loud men watched the Cubs' game and drank beer. At first, they were a bit distracted and slightly annoyed by the bar crowd, but it slowly became background noise. They ordered their food and settled in for what would likely be an hour or so of pleasant conversation.

Sumeet caught the group of loud men looking at his table a few times throughout dinner. For some reason one of the men's looks became longer and longer. There was apathy and hatred in his eyes. Sumeet was familiar with that look.

"Dad, get the check from the waitress. I'm gonna hit the head then we can get outta here," Sumeet said as he got up from his chair and went toward the bathroom. He wanted to get away from these men quickly. He didn't trust himself around conflict while he was stateside. Since he had been deployed his fuse was much shorter. He was still not acclimated to civilian life.

He entered the bathroom and made quick work of it. He washed his hands and looked up into the mirror. It was the first time he'd looked into this mirror since being overseas. His face was much more chiseled and drawn. He was leaner and wider across the shoulders. He stood there for a moment wondering how this one mirror seemed to have captured his change so dramatically. His mind drifted back to Afghanistan and his men for a brief moment.

"Ahhhhh!" a woman screamed. Sumeet ran out of the bathroom leaving his thoughts behind, turned right, and headed back toward his table. He saw the men from the bar standing near his father's table. A crowd of people were pushing past Sumeet toward the door. His heart raced and his senses heightened. He saw his father on the floor, he saw blood, and he saw the man with hate in his eyes standing over him.

"That's where terrorism gets you people," the man said as he pointed the remnants of a broken wine bottle at his father.

Time stopped. Sumeet walked toward the man without thinking. He grabbed the man's hand and twisted it behind his back. The man yelled but Sumeet didn't hear. The broken bottle fell from the man's hand and Sumeet caught it with his own left. He then drove the glass deep into the side of the man's neck. Blood ran through the bottle top as if it was a funnel. The three men that accompanied the perpetrator came at Sumeet but he fought them off with ease. He threw the first one into the bar, the second, he threw a jab to the face, a heel to the outside of the knee, and a punch to the throat crushing his trachea. The third man ran out of the restaurant. Sumeet bent over the man with the bottle hanging out of his neck. He grabbed him by the collar and reached down his own shirt removing his dogtags. He pressed them hard into the man's forehead.

"I am an American and I killed for this country you son of a bitch! You owe me some God damn respect!" He then dropped the man leaving oval indentations in his forehead. Sumeet checked his father. He had no pulse and wasn't breathing.

"You call 911!" he said pointing to the bartender. "Get me a damn AED!" he then yelled in general to anyone who could hear. He began performing CPR on his father. "Where's the AED damn it!?" he yelled after the first minute. Moments later someone threw an AED in his direction. Everyone who remained stared, frozen with fear.

Sumeet placed the shock pads.

"Analyzing patient . . . shock advised please remove hands." The AED shocked his father. "Shock advised please remove hands. Continue CPR."

Sumeet continued to monitor his father as the police and paramedics arrived. His father left with a pulse; Sumeet left with handcuffs.

Sumeet sat in his holding cell staring down at the blood that had dried at the base of his nail beds. Over and over the events played in his head. He couldn't make out the faces on the men he killed. No matter how hard he ended up squeezing his eyes shut he couldn't quite get that memory back. The one image etched into his mild was how his father's face had looked: lifeless.

Sumeet had seen death so many times before. He was finding himself reliving the moments in Pakistan where he had to kill. The thoughts began to flood in and he became overwhelmed by the urge to scream. He reached up and grabbed his head pressing down so firmly that the tips of his fingers turned white. His entire life was flashing in front of him. He realized no matter what he did for this country, no matter how many people he killed in the name of America, it would mean nothing. His own father had just been assaulted and possibly murdered by the same Americans he tried to connect with, to stop being alienated by, and for whom he was fighting. He had enough. He was done with this country, ashamed with his decisions, raging because of his father.

His internal distress was interrupted by the metallic sound of the jail cell door unlocking.

"Sumeet Patel. Come with me," the nameless policeman said as he stood at the door. Sumeet stood up slowly while maintaining eye contact with the man. They walked down the hallway to a small interrogation room roughly 10 by 14 feet. "Have a seat," the policeman said. Sumeet did as he was told. "Hands on the table please." As Sumeet placed his hands on the table the officer placed handcuffs on his wrists again. The policeman walked out of the room closing the door.

A short while later a plain man walked into the room. He was wearing a different type of uniform, navy blue, and had MP written in large print on his upper arm. "Corporal Patel. You are being charged with murder. You are active duty and will be requiring representation. The Army has capable attorneys you may use. If you chose to use our attorney, you may accompany me to Great Lakes Naval Base where you will be detained in our custody."

Sumeet sat there for a moment in silence, staring at the military policeman.

"Corporal, it's in your best interest. You'll not be photographed by newspapers or put in front of the TV for the news. I would suggest you come immediately so that you can avoid the publicity that will certainly be coming any minute."

With that statement Sumeet stood up and the men walked out together.

Several days passed at Great Lakes Naval Base and he had little contact with anyone. An Army lawyer had come and gone twice. The first time he gathered the story from Sumeet and the second time he came with several questions after he talked to witnesses, read testimonies, and had looked at the police report.

Sumeet was unimpressed by everything. The clothes he wore and the bedding were musty. The food was bland and it made his already limited appetite worse. The first couple of days sitting in his cell were dominated by thoughts of the Olive Garden. Every time he envisioned the scene, he saw his father's lifeless body morph into the lifeless bodies of Pakistani men he killed. It was confusing, nauseating, seeing his father's assault merge with events that happened so far away.

These last two days had been a gradual progression from trying to understand why things escalated so fast that night, to how poor an example he had been to his men. Certainly, by now word had spread and he would no longer be on the fast track through the ranks. Sure, some of his closest men would understand but that wouldn't help his case. His dreams of respect, of being a leader of men, were essentially over. He'd never lead again.

"On your feet!" the jailer said. Sumeet stood and turned toward the gate. The unmistakable sound of a jail door being unlocked followed, and the door slid open. Sumeet was confused as he stood looking out the cell at a Marine Corps Colonel.

"Corporal Patel," the Colonel said.

"Yes sir," Sumeet responded hesitantly.

"We're going for a walk," the Colonel said glancing haphazardly back toward the jailer. The colonel then motioned Sumeet to follow. The two men walked out of the jail, down a hallway, and out into the sunlight. Neither man spoke the entire time.

"Sumeet you really fucked up. You're aware of this, aren't you?"

"Yes sir," Sumeet was watching the colonel suspiciously.

"I know you're confused. Why would the Marine Corps care about you? Well, I want you to think of me as someone who can help. This uniform just gave me access to you. You're guilty and no court will ever find you innocent. As far as you're concerned it's just a question of how long will you survive in prison. How much bullshit you will be able to deal with. A good-looking Pakistani boy in prison has no chance, no matter how much hand-to-hand combat training he has. It's only a matter of time."

The men continued to walk for a while in silence, the sun hot on their skin. Sumeet was thinking about how right the colonel was. There truly was no chance. He had terrible representation, so many people witnessed the events, and he still had blood at the base of his nails.

"Do you enjoy this Sumeet? The sun on your face? Walking without anyone watching you? The freedom?"

Sumeet was defeated. The thought of freedom was something he never truly had. He had never been free from discrimination and that was what had caused him to enlist. He realized in the jail cell during the last five days that he wanted to be a leader. Freedom was a side effect of leadership. He wanted to be trusted, listened to, believed in.

"I can give you that freedom. I can help you get away from this without looking back. You'll work for me, but in a very different and discreet way." The colonel stopped walking and turned toward Sumeet. "You may or may not like the work I will give you. But no matter what I ask of you the word 'no' cannot, and will not ever, be your response. These are the only conditions that'll work."

"When would I get my freedom? How will you give it to me? How can I trust you?" Sumeet asked.

"I need an answer."

Sumeet paused for several moments staring at the grass. He hadn't seen grass in days.

"Listen kid, you're smart, well respected, and a leader. It's why we're having this conversation. You don't have another play."

"OK . . . I'm in," Sumeet said quietly.

"Very good then. My name is Jenkins. You are no longer Sumeet Patel," Jenkins said reaching into his jacket pocket. "You are Amir Qasmi." He handed Amir a passport, a driver's license, and $1,000 cash.

"What do I do with this?" Sumeet asked grabbing the items. Jenkins looked at the main entrance.

"We walked this way for a reason," Jenkins said as he nodded toward a sunlit street. "You're to walk out that main gate. Here's a cellphone with 200 minutes on it. The number one is programmed for my number. You'll call me in five days. You have $1,000 dollars to spend till then, and you have to get to Camp Lejeune before you call."

"What about the jail? How will you get out of this? Why are you helping me?" Sumeet rattled off confused.

"I'll handle the jail. You will have more answers and fewer questions soon. Five days Amir." The men parted ways.

Amir was a hundred yards away when Jenkins yelled out to him.

"Amir!" Jenkins yelled. "Amir!" He yelled louder. Amir turned around and jogged back to Jenkins. "You had better figure out who you are pretty damn quickly. I have to tell you one more thing. I am not all good news. Your father died last night. So, don't think of visiting him. He's gone."

Nothing else was said between the two men. Amir turned and walked the quarter mile west out of the main gate. He was free.

chapter

FIVE

Logan was on his first covert op with Jenkins. His mission was to be dropped into the Baghdad hot zone and "sit on it" until he saw a drop that was supposed to be made between rebel forces and their supplier. He was instructed to determine the identity of the supplier who provided them with armor piercing artillery and RPGs by the truckload. Logan was going to be alone. He could take a firearm, small caliber that would go on his leg holster, an MP5 with a suppressor, a water canteen, and a pair of binoculars. The binoculars had a ten-megapixel camera that sent real time pictures taken by the Logan back to base where persons in higher positions could see what was going on and which, if any, known players were present.

Logan was briefed by Colonel Jenkins before the mission. The few others in the room included: the driver, Smith, who would drop Logan off, the radio operator, and the computer tech in charge of receiving the image files.

"There's really nothing to it, Logan," stated Jenkins as he stood at the coffee pot pouring himself a cup and taking the whole thing down in one gulp. As he extended his neck back to get the last bit of coffee, Logan could see several hairs between the colonel's ear and jawline that were missed by the morning shave. "You get in, you take a few pictures, you get out. Make it fun, play hide-and-seek with these assholes. Half of them don't even know what they're doing. I want the damn pictures as soon as they are sent. That's it. Let's get it done!"

"Alright man here's the drop," said Corporal Smith as he pulled up two kilometers south of the hot zone. There wasn't a soul to be seen. It was hard to believe that just a few thousand meters from this spot there were hundreds of Iraqi soldiers aching for American blood. "Good luck dude," the driver waved at Logan and sped away. Logan was alone with his weapon, binoculars, and water.

Logan snaked his way through buildings, around cars and through the filth of the streets. He saw no one in the brightness of the summer day. Logan placed his hand onto the trunk of a rusted old Toyota and immediately pulled his hand off, shaking it trying to cool it down.

The street was full of remnant cars that had been burned, crashed, and picked for valuable parts. There were brass shells from a variety of weapons, .45, .233, 9mm, .50 calibers scattered all over the intersection. He squatted down behind an upturned Iraqi military vehicle and used the buildings and the layout of the streets to orient himself to the aerial photos he had studied. There was a building that had the entire front blown off allowing him to see into the apartments. Some of the square units had bathrooms blown in half and shower stalls sitting suspended in open air, while others had rugs cascading into the environment like clothes hung to dry. The building was perfect and he could focus on nothing else. The vantage point was elevated, there was limitless cover, and he could hide deep within the rooms.

Logan negotiated his way north through the street and approached the building, still not seeing a soul. As he reached the building he noticed that the first three flights of stairs had been completely blown out and there was no way to reach the higher levels. Logan knew there must be another entrance so he began to methodically creep around the east end of the building, hiding in alleys of neighboring buildings and behind several cars.

As he approached the northeast corner of the building he saw a poorly covered tripwire between a 1979 Mercedes 240D and the wall. He carefully followed it and discovered an IED nestled against the adjacent building under a large bag filled with sharp, rusted metal pieces. Making careful mental note of exactly where the wire was, he stepped over it and continued around the building finding the front entrance and a wide staircase leading inside.

Logan could hear whispers and echoes as he entered. His heart quickened and he paused. He was not alone in the building. Logan decided to move quickly and quietly to a dirty emergency sign that had the escape routes drawn on it. He noted the location of the blown staircase and got his bearings. Within moments he found the second set of stairs and quickly moved toward them. The whispers grew silent by the time he reached the stairs in the southwest corner. His soft-soled boots helped him silently climb the stairs up to the fifth floor where he decided that was high enough.

Logan walked to the southeast corner. It would give him the best vantage point of the two streets that led into the area. The streets formed an "L" in an opening surrounded by several buildings including the one Logan was in. He began to see into apartments that had damage as he moved down the hall. The best option was the third apartment from the east end, which was missing its entire outer wall. The kitchen, however, remained intact. He could use a table, a couple chairs, and some remnants of the curtain to cover himself. He quickly crawled under the table and threw the curtains over himself in a very unorganized fashion. He silently sunk into position for what would possibly be 24 hours or more. He grabbed the binoculars and waited. Nobody truly knew when these meetings would take place. Often, meeting times would change because the Iraqi were so worried about American spies and false intel.

As the afternoon passed Logan occasionally heard faint chatter but nothing seemed close. He saw several pickup trucks speed through the gauntlet of broken vehicles as the driver and the gunner in the truck bed screamed orders to each other. Logan began to sweat. Not the kind of sweating you do with exercise, although that had happened earlier, but the kind you feel dripping down your skin while sitting poolside where the stagnant air leaves little relief. He needed something to drink. He had just reached his hand toward his canteen when he heard someone running down the hall in his direction.

The single pair of feet turned into two, then three pairs as he began to hear outbursts of yells and crackling of radios. Logan lay down flat, quickly brought his hand back into a comfortable position, and froze.

In they came, four in all. Logan couldn't see them because he had maximized his position for seeing outside, not behind. The men were laughing and Logan knew his hiding spot would work for the time being.

Hide and seek right Colonel Jenkins? His knowledge of a few Iraqi words helped him understand what was happening.

Soon . . . RPG . . . Truck . . . many men . . . security . . .

It was obvious that something would be happening soon and Logan guessed these were just a few of the men making sure things went smoothly at the drop. So, he lay and waited. He could still see the street from where he was, but couldn't move to get his binoculars in position. After some time, he heard the radio chatter start up again.

No truck . . . Americans . . . later. . . All the Iraqi men in the room groaned in unison. However, this was short lived. An eruption of laughter and high fives sprung forth from the men. Logan laid in his position confused at what was happening not more than ten feet from him. Then he heard it. Cards shuffled and within seconds the men all pulled up chairs around the table Logan was laying under.

The cards were U.S. military-issued Iraqi most wanted. The Iraqis hooted and whistled when they saw a face on a card that they knew personally. Poker was the game. Each one took a turn at dealing, except one. He also seemed to win more often than the rest. He was the most robust and homely of the group. Clearly, he was the leader. He often snuck a card down onto his lap after a hand, discarding it when a better one came along.

Logan stayed as calm as he could and began thinking of scenarios if he was seen. *I can't have anyone fire their weapon or throw anyone from the building. I could surprise them with an attack, which would give me a one- or two-man head start. But, that wouldn't work either if they did radio checks on their position . . .*

He thought a little more into radio checks and realized that none of the men had spoken into the radio during the two hours they had been in the room with him. Showing his cards early may just be the answer. Logan began to factor the odds of him overtaking the Iraqis with a surprise attack when—*boom!*

Logan snapped from his brainstorm as one of the men slammed his hand onto the table in disbelief, losing the hand. A few yells and the dispute was over and they were all laughing again. The leader had shown too much. He was so upset with losing the hand that he revealed he had extra cards that he pulled from his lap. Logan could smell the cigarettes and marijuana the men had begun lighting and it seemed as if they planned to be there all night. Logan stayed put. The leader may have other cards he hasn't revealed for Logan just yet. He needed to let the game play out.

Get as high as you can jerkoffs. It can only help me, Logan thought as he reached down to his leg slowly and grabbed his military-issued 9mm Beretta with suppressor, and slowly dragged it to his chest.

As he lay there he began to gather information about the group dynamic. He knew the guy to his left was the leader. He also knew that the guy behind him was feeling the effects of the drugs most because he had fallen out of his chair twice. The other two were just there. The order he chose to attack them was: leader first, the guy behind him last.

He had just started killing men in close quarters. It used to be from 1,000 meters not 1,000 mm. He felt the sweat begin to secrete out of every gland in his body and he could feel the pulse of his heart in his chest, forehead, and hands due to his sympathetic nervous system blasting him at full force. At any second his body was going to explode into action; muscle memory was taking over and his brain was about to turn off. The only job he had now was controlling the fact that he was now a coiled spring: *three . . . two . . . one.*

"Truck! Truck coming!" Logan heard one of the men yell and they all jumped up from the table and took station at the openings in the wall.

Logan's vision blurred and he became lightheaded as he took several huge breaths. His adrenaline rush had left as swiftly as it began and it hit him hard. He began to wonder how he would complete the mission. On top of this, he couldn't get his binoculars into position without being seen. The sun was beginning to set and his view was becoming overwhelmed with sunlight. He was hoping that the truck wouldn't come till night. Five minutes later, a truck came.

The truck was black and had a large cargo hold on the back. Logan assumed this was the merchandise, but surprisingly there were few guards. From what he could make out there were two people in the cab. Two minutes passed and the cavalry came rolling in: Five trucks with machine guns mounted in the bed, as well as another three trucks full of dozens of men.

Logan decided to try to grab his binoculars. He reached down toward his combat belt where the binoculars were sitting in their case with the button unclipped. He grabbed them and slowly pulled them out, dragging them toward his face a centimeter at a time.

Click-clack the sound of a firing pin being locked into position. Logan's heart froze. He waited for several seconds and nothing. *Click-clack*, two more times.

He laid motionless under the curtain, beneath the table. *Should I jump them before they realize it is someone under this table?* Logan thought as his heart beat so hard that he thought the Iraqis might see it through the curtain. He waited several more seconds, then minutes, and after ten minutes he knew he was OK. He looked down at the street scene and realized why the guns were readied.

A slim man dressed in bright white was shaking hands with an Iraqi soldier. Logan brought the binoculars up to his chin and prepared to take a few pictures. Both of the men proceeded to the back of the cargo hold of the first truck. The driver came out and opened the back. He shook hands with the man in white, raised his AK-47 in the air, and pumped it up and down for his fellow soldiers who began to cheer. Logan could barely make out individuals, let alone details, he was so frustrated that he was stuck in the same room as these Iraqi.

The man in white gestured to someone in a Land Rover and she came running up. Her blonde hair was easy to pick up against the dirty street scene littered with blown up buildings and cars. She reached the back of the truck and the Iraqi with a Nike shirt handed her a briefcase. Logan pulled up the binoculars for a few quick snapshots.

Beep. The binoculars made a quick noise as he took the picture. He felt the Iraqi looking around the room now. Usually they were very loud and obnoxious and now he heard them tiptoeing toward him.

I got one damn picture for all this?

Logan shot up through the table launching it into the air and smashing one Iraqi in the face knocking him instantly unconscious with the tabletop. He looked right and saw another soldier two feet away and kicked him through the hole in the exterior wall sending him 50 feet down to his death. He turned left facing the two remaining men. One man was trying to raise his AK-47 rifle while the other stood stunned with an RPG lazily grasped in his hand, the tip resting on the floor. Logan quickly shot the man with the AK in the forehead twice then moved to the second man. The four shots were quick and precise. Logan then moved to the man who was unconscious and decided to leave him where he was.

He quickly grabbed his binoculars to take several more pictures but it was too late. Everyone was fleeing, so he decided to focus on the man in the white shirt. He was the supplier and the primary target. He snapped picture after picture listening to beep after beep from the binoculars. He could not stop wondering about the man in the white shirt. Suddenly, the man ran awkwardly to the Land Rover and jumped into the back seat, failing to make it all the way inside. His legs were hanging out of the car and a dark, red stain began to spread across his pants. Logan scanned the scene below and saw a small group of men running toward his building, while the remaining few were laying fire down onto the Land Rover.

Logan once again heard footsteps running down the hall. They had seen the body fly from the room. He quickly grabbed the curtain and wrapped it around an exposed beam. He placed his Beretta in its holster, clipped the binoculars in his belt, and rappelled down to the fourth floor. He swung into the room and quietly went to the door. He paused for a moment and listened, heard nothing, and entered the hallway. As soon as he closed the door, a snakelike hiss grew loud before—*bang!*

An RPG ripped into the apartment he exited, throwing debris into the hallway. His hearing was gone, but his head was ringing. He crept methodically down the hall checking each entryway for possible Iraqi. Finally, he reached the staircase. Logan opened the door to the stairs and a loud squeal from the metal on metal hinge echoed through the stairwell.

Bang! The door from the fifth floor flew open and slammed into the wall. A dozen Iraqi came charging down the stairs. Logan began to run down knowing it was his only escape. He heard voices echoing all around him, screaming, radios crackling. Footsteps seemed to come up from below, and down from above as he began to scan wildly for another way out. Suddenly he ran into two Iraqi who were running up. He grabbed the first man's arm and struck him behind the elbow shattering the joint. Logan grabbed the other man's throat, crushed it, and kicked his knee hyperextending it, destroying all his ligaments. Logan threw them both backward down the staircase and jumped over the railing to the floor below.

Logan burst through the door he had entered through several hours earlier and turned left toward the alley retracing all the steps he took on his approach to the building. He didn't care who was around the corner, he just needed to get out of there fast. His legs were aching and his chest was burning. As he neared the Mercedes 240D, he remembered the tripwire and leaped into the air just as the Iraqis turned down the alley in hot pursuit. He estimated it would be ten seconds before the explosion would nail all the Iraqis. He had to get somewhere outside of the blast radius.

Boom! The buildings shook as one of the Iraqi caught the tripwire and instantly his pursuers were no more. He didn't look back; he just kept running toward the neutral zone where he would be safe.

He still had five kilometers to navigate the streets. He stopped for a moment and gathered his bearings. He dove in and out of building avoiding Iraqi as they ran through the streets screaming into radios. Logan assumed all the chatter was directed at finding him. At one point, he had to hide in the rear seat of a Land Rover for 30 minutes while a group of eight Iraqi blocked the only road in the area that led south. Eventually they dispersed. It was the last snag Logan ran into on his escape.

When Logan reached the safe zone he quickly hopped into the Hummer. It was the same driver with a large grin. "Glad to see ya' buddy," the driver said as he hit the gas and headed for the colonel's location in the temporary intel office. Logan just stared forward out of the window still gripping his Beretta prepared for anything that may come his way.

Upon reaching the colonel he found that a lot of the photos that he took were of no great use. Most of them were blurry because of the targets moving, Logan moving, or a combination.

"At such a high magnification, any sudden movements make it hard to get a clear picture," said the computer tech as he moved his thin straight hair off his forehead and in line with the rest of his comb over. Two photographs came out. One was the first picture he took where the blonde had greeted all the men, and the other was as the man in the white shirt was getting into the car. The second picture showed that the man getting into the car was possibly wearing a wig.

Logan sat on a bench in quiet reflection while the late afternoon sun bounced off a sea of metal rooftops at the forward operating base.

The subtle angles in the metal acted as prisms bending and distorting the sunlight creating an infinite number of hues. The wind blew gently, rhythmically across his sweat soaked clothes he still wore, giving him a slight chill and reminding him how close he was to death.

As the sun began creeping under the horizon the round robin of thoughts speeding through his head began to concede to one another leaving only two. He first realized that no amount of training or experience could shake the absolute fact of mortality. Sherman had revealed that a few months earlier. His second realization was that another person had found a way to connect with him in a way he never felt before. He knew he had to stay alive; he had to be with her.

chapter
SIX

Logan had a long flight back to the U.S. He rehearsed repeatedly how he would talk to Jenkins. The only thought that distracted him was Samantha. The Iraq trip could have ended any future with her. Logan had dated a few times, but always focused on his future. Samantha was able to get him thinking in the present. Logan had decided he would go back to a recon battalion for the remainder of his three-year enlistment. At least he would be around other men—men he could trust.

The plane bounced as the wheels hit the tarmac. Logan shifted in his seat. He was nervous to talk to Jenkins, and excited to see Samantha. The plane taxied to the hanger, the door opened, and he saw a black SUV running in the hanger. Logan grabbed his rucksack, brought it up onto his shoulder, and headed toward the SUV.

"Afternoon," Jenkins said as Logan entered the right rear seat. "We're going to debrief you again right now. Shots were fired. We need to clean this op up quite a bit."

"OK sir," Logan said pausing for a moment. "Sir, I want to go back to recon. I know it's sudden but I figured there was no time like the present. I didn't want to keep wondering how to say I'm done."

"I can't say I'm not disappointed Logan. But, I can get you back with recon."

"Thank you, sir. It means a lot."

It took a few days but Logan was reassigned back into Bravo Company Second Battalion. He was welcomed back after his short absence. Nobody asked questions, nobody cared. Logan was happy. He was just another jarhead with no special expectations. Nobody was asking him how he was doing, where he came from, or why he left. Men came and went occasionally and recon men didn't gossip. The lack of empathy and intrigue allowed him to blend in.

"Falcone," the range master said as Logan set his beanbag down in the dirt.

"Sergeant," Logan responded with a nod and rolled up the sleeves of his BDUs. He laid down prone, nuzzling his M40 sniper rifle into his left shoulder. The metallic sound of the gun made as he slid the bolt back made him forget about Samantha. He placed a round in the chamber and slammed the bolt home. One breath in, he focused on the 1,000-yard target. One breath out. Second breath in, he read the wind. Second breath out. Third breath in, he moved his finger onto the trigger. Third breath out. *Boom!* Just over a second later the round hit on target.

Logan took out his shot table book and recorded the cold bore shot. He loved shooting cold bore and felt it was most appropriate to know how your cold rifle shots come out. It was the same reason why he liked loading one round at a time; better make it count. Logan waited in that spot barely breathing and living in the moment. He could stay in this position forever. He finally reached for another round, slid the bolt back, slammed it home. 1,500-yards. Breath in, on target, breath out. Breath in, read the wind, breath out. Breath in, massage the trigger, breath out. *Boom!* Moments later, target down. He reached for his shot table book, recorded the number.

chapter
SEVEN

Several years later. Camp Lejeune

0500 is when the alarm goes off. It was 0456 as Logan laid in bed, staring, just like he had done every morning for the last three weeks. As Logan lay in bed for the last three minutes before the alarm went off, he thought about how many men had complained about the morning PT he put them though. Logan didn't care. In fact, he liked hearing it. "It meant we were getting shit done," he said on several occasions. Logan knew, however, for this latest group of students, the workouts were just maintenance.

Click, Logan turned off the alarm clock at the strike of 0500, stopping the annoying beeps before they began. Life was much different now than it used to be. He was currently instructing special operations groups as an independent contractor. He was doing what he wanted to do, when he wanted to do it. There were no long-term commitments, no real danger, no reason to be scared to lose anyone; not on his short watch, if it could be considered that. He was surgical, in and out with no liability or ownership of the men before or after he worked with them. If he was ever able to commit and allow himself to stop guarding against getting close to someone it would have been Samantha, not another soldier.

Logan was 24 days into a two-month contract with ten Marine recon men. Of those, maybe six would "graduate" and by day three he already had them figured out.

The sun was coming up as he left the bare studio apartment the USMC offered him at Camp Lejeune. He didn't even bother locking the door as he headed straight for the PT field. He hated the jingling sound keys made while he ran.

"Morning Sergeant Falcone," Gunnery Sergeant Ryan McElroy said with a bright smile.

"Logan, gunny. It's Logan."

"Just trying to keep it professional," Ryan said as he finished putting sunscreen on his pale arms. Ryan was as white as a ghost and learned his lesson more than once about the sun.

"Hey gunny looks like it's gonna be a bright sun today," Captain Martinez said as he strode up to Logan and Ryan. Ryan tried to sneak the sunscreen back into his pocket before anyone else arrived.

"What's on the itinerary Logan?" Migs said crossing his heavy, bronze arms.

"Five miles. Then we'll see from there. Got some special training for you guys."

"Oh yeah? Can't wait," Corporal Aaron "Dubs" Egan said approaching with lengthy strides. He towered over the four other men.

"Dubs can you ever be serious?" asked Ryan as he smacked Dubs on the back of his knobby head making everyone laugh. Some of the younger Marines said that Dubs used to play jokes in boot camp which caused his platoon to do extra PT, and Dubs would laugh the whole time. It wasn't hard to believe.

Five minutes later the remaining group members arrived and they started their run. Leading these men was not an honor, but an accomplishment. They were all very competitive and all pushed each other to run harder. Logan just wouldn't be overtaken. He was now 34 but didn't look a day over 25, which happened to be the age of Dubs, the youngest member of the group.

"Alright guys that's it for the morning. Grab a shower and meet in the

BB-5 building at 1200 hours." Logan said before walking off the PT field.

"Hey Migs what you think about Logan?" asked Brian, one of the shorter men among the group.

"Hard read Sergeant. Don't want to try either. I have respect for the man though. I don't wanna go ruining it by digging around."

"I heard that," said Ryan as he looked over his arms, pressing into them to see if the color would turn indicating the beginning stages of sunburn.

"You're such a pussy, gunny," said Dubs as he laughed. "You could get moon burn." The men had a good laugh and continued to joke as they headed to the barracks before grabbing chow.

The cafeteria was brightly lit and the low rumbling of conversation welcomed the men as they entered.

"What'll it be gunny?" asked the large black man who stood behind the skillets as they approached the counter.

"Grilled chicken sandwich," replied Ryan as the rest of the men jockeyed for position behind him.

"Hey Dubs, what's happenin' man!" exclaimed the chef when he saw Dubs in line.

Dubs pointed at the chef with both hands as he looked at the special for the day.

"Philly-cheese huh LeRoy?" Dub's said to the chef. "You're from Milwaukee. You sure you can handle making something like that?"

"I don't come in your barracks askin' you if you know how to turn the safety off on your gun," LeRoy shot back with wide eyes pointing a bread roll in Dubs direction. Both men stared at each other for a few seconds. By this time all of Logan's men were standing around. They quit their own conversations and listened to Dubs and the chef rib each other. The group took careful note of how large LeRoy was and thought Dubs may have met his match. They knew Dubs had never backed down from a confrontation in his life. He called them "life's little pleasures."

LeRoy had Dubs by a few inches in height as well as biceps and didn't seem to be afraid to use them. Just as Logan's men started to become uneasy Dubs and LeRoy started laughing and finished it with a fist pound.

"I woulda' whooped yo' ass Dubs," said LeRoy in a low booming voice. "Are these all your new friends for that class man?"

"Yup," said Dubs as he stepped to the side motioning with his hands as if he were a magician revealing his assistants.

"Ya'll don't know Dubs like me. This man saved my life a couple times growing up. He's the reason I'm here. If you get on his good side, there's nothin' he won't do for you. That's a promise. This Philly's on me," LeRoy said to Dubs.

Dubs looked at the floor. It was the first time anyone had seen him experience a real emotion. The moment didn't last long.

"Well I guess he isn't the Terminator after all," Migs said breaking the short silence. "LeRoy I'll have one of those too."

"Comin' up, Cap. But you're paying for it. I can't feed you all," LeRoy said laughing and slapping the spatula against the skillet.

All the men grabbed their meals and headed to BB-5. They walked up the stairs to the eighth floor, down the narrow hall toward BB-5. Logan stood inside the conference room behind a wall of glass. Upon entering the room each man looked left toward a two-way mirror as if it was uncontrollable. The men always wondered if someone was hiding behind it. Directly opposite the glass wall stood three floor to ceiling windows through which you could see the entire PT field, as well as much of the base toward the south.

"Alright listen up," Logan said as they took their seats in their leather chairs surrounding a cherry stained table.

"We're gonna discuss tactics when feeling tailed both on foot and in the car. Then we will talk about tactical maneuvering and observing your surroundings. So, who knows how to get rid of someone who's tailing you while you drive?"

"Call for assistance," Migs said.

"Drive somewhere familiar to you or a safehouse and try to lose him," Lonnie said.

"Stop and whoop his ass," Dubs said with his mouth full of food, causing Ryan to nearly choke on his lunch as he began laughing.

"All decent answers," stated Logan. "However, if you whoop his ass then you blow your cover. Two, calling for assistance may work, but you're going to be moving while backup is coming so it's hard to give them a good idea where exactly you will be. You never want to stay on the same road too long when being tailed. I like Ryan's idea. Driving past the safehouse."

Migs raised his hand. "Yeah Migs."

"What if they have a couple different cars following you and they keep switching?"

"Pretty good question, that kind of stuff happens often. You want to do the same evasive maneuvering that you do if it's just one car, however, you want to double back onto locations you believe the cars made a switch. By doing this you may catch a visual of a driver, or scare one or both of them off. You also want to call the safehouse earlier because often the more cars that are involved, the more aggressive the tails can be. There is safety in numbers everyone knows that. Calling the safehouse earlier and letting them know can get more men on the job. Occasionally, small tracking devices are given to field agents. If you have one of these devices and you double back noticing one of the chase cars, then you can plant it. That way we can track your tail afterwards. The tracking device is extremely small and magnetic. You just throw it out of the window and it should stick right to the car. I admit it's hard to throw one of these out the window without anyone seeing. It's obvious that they are watching every move you make. Any other questions?

"Good. I think the second part of the evasion plan is obvious. We would rather capture the tail than kill him or her. We are in the intelligence business and if someone is following you then you need to know who, what, when, where, why, and how they found you. Often this will lead you to leaks through our contacts and affiliates.

"Moving on. The next topic I want to discuss is evasion on foot. First of all, when you are under cover you do not want to walk like you normally would. That is one thing that most people forget to change about themselves. People think changing their appearance is all they need to do but I'll tell you what, nine times out of nine I can tell you who you are just by the way you walk, move, hail a taxi. If you're looking for someone focus on the way they move not what they look like. Let's watch some examples."

As Logan hit a button under the table a screen came down on the wall opposite the double-sided mirror and a projector descended from an opening in the ceiling. As if by magic all the windows in the room gradually became markedly darker. The room went black except for the glow of the screen.

"What do you notice about the way he is moving?" asked Logan as a video of a man walking down a busy street began to play.

"He's walking faster than everyone else," said Migs.

"What else?"

"He doesn't swing his arms at all," said Brian.

"Good observation, most people do swing their arms. For someone not to it's a huge anomaly. Anything else?" Nobody said a word. It was tough performing gait analysis for the first time. "I'll help you out," Logan said as he paused the lesson. "The man demonstrated several oddities or abnormalities. I'll try to teach you a few then we'll watch the video again so you see the problems. First, as Brian said, he doesn't swing his arms," Logan demonstrated both walking with arms swinging and without to show how it may look different in the same person. "A second main flaw is that his heel leaves the ground early as he extends his leg back behind him. Normal gait patterns say that the heel should remain in contact till terminal stance, or the most extended position of the hip is achieved. His heel comes up much earlier than that." Again, Logan demonstrated the difference. "Lastly he takes small quick steps. He is moving fast but there are two kinds of fast. Long strides, and short, quick ones. Short and quick tends to mean someone is in a hurry, and long and normal cadence is natural." Once again, Logan demoed the difference.

"Pay attention to the differences I pointed out," Logan said and played the video again. They all saw right away the three deviations that Logan had described. "Now watch closely."

"Whoa. What the hell was that?" Dubs said as he went from sitting back in his chair to leaning forward. "Rewind that?"

"Yep," said Logan who was surprised at Dubs' observation skills and the fact that for once, Dubs was being serious.

"Hey, boss I think this guy is definitely faking something. For a couple steps, there his heel stayed down and he started swinging his arms. He kept walking fast but the other things seem to be falling apart," Brian said.

"Good job. I'll tell you now this was a former MI-5 who was caught working for the KGB back in the 70s. At this moment, he was being followed by British and CIA and he was trying to maintain cover to get away. He lost concentration at that point and that's when they knew it was him. The quick cadence was a sign he was in a hurry." Sure enough, 20 seconds more into the film and he was apprehended by British police and put into a squad car.

The men went through several more examples, and their ability to decipher subtle flaws in gait patterns improved. Logan drilled more details into their heads as the afternoon progressed; they were like sponges.

"Alright men that's it for the day. We went a little more detailed than I thought we would but that's OK. I'll see ya' out on the PT field tomorrow morning. Have a good night."

The next morning was drizzling, cold, and demoralizing but they had agreed to meet at the PT field early.

"Great morning huh Captain?" Brian asked sarcastically as rain spat down in small beads while he stood on the sidewalk next to the PT field.

"Yeah it's pretty nasty out here. I've always thought it was weird when it rained in the morning, kinda' like the weather should still be sleeping as early as we get up."

"No kidding. You think Logan's gonna make us run in this shit? It don't really matter to me either way. I'm already wet. I bet he's got some excuse or experience for running in the downpour."

"Haha, yeah no kidding. Here he comes anyways. I'm sure he'll get right to it."

"Where is everyone?" Logan asked when he approached Brian and Migs.

"Traffic," said Migs jokingly.

"Well, I don't want to wait in this downpour all morning so let's just head toward the barracks. We'll do PT this afternoon."

"You're the boss Logan," Brian said and they headed toward the barracks.

"There ya' are, you bunch a knuckleheads," said Brian as they all ran into each other.

"OK, guys the plan is to get dry and get to the meeting room ASAP. We're gonna have a classroom morning and afternoon PT," Logan said before anyone else spoke up.

"OK, bossman," said Dubs and they all headed back to the barracks and Logan to his place.

An hour later and the men were all dry and wide eyed for their classroom session. BB-5 felt cozy with the rain hitting the large windows and the screen gave a warm fire-like glow.

"OK men, today we're talking about observing your surroundings. Basically, you want to analyze every location you enter and take note of exits, and people.

"Yesterday we went over what you should look for during your pursuit of a target so I believe that also told you how to act when you are undercover. Change your dress, your look, and don't forget the way you walk. I think that's about all the time I will spend on that. We're going to do scenarios again today."

Logan hit a button under the table opening slits in the cherry wood allowing 20-inch flat screen computer monitors to come up. From under the monitor a laser projected an image of a full keyboard, and to the right, another laser projected a square for a touch-pad. The men could have watched this happen a hundred times and they wouldn't be any less impressed. Even Logan was amazed at the technology in this room.

All the computers had the same start screen. Special Training for Covert Operations: Session nine Scanning for details, was the title. In the background was a man sitting at a restaurant booth with an exit sign behind him.

"Alright. You'll be graded on how many questions you get right. You have 30 seconds to survey the scene once you enter the location. After that the test will begin. I'll receive the results. Don't be nervous. It'll show what I need to focus on the most with you men. There's so much I could teach you and two months isn't enough time. I want to focus on the weaknesses. OK, three . . . two . . . one. Begin."

The scene was a hotel lobby. Upon entering through a set of stairs the lobby opened wide into a large foyer with ten-meter high ceilings decorated in Greek mythological paintings and large golden chandeliers. To the right was a long open hallway that led to the elevators and to the left was the check-in desk where a man and two women were assisting four businessmen. Directly in front were several leather chairs sitting on a floral print rug approximately 30 by 30 feet. On the rug, a glass coffee table with a concrete Hercules supporting the weight from beneath. Eight of the ten chairs were taken up by six men and two women. The two women were playing with their nails. Three of the men were reading the newspaper, two others were watching the women. There was one man, however, that was watching the door. Past all the chairs was another, narrow hallway, which led to an atrium and a pool where a statue of Poseidon stood over the doorway with his trident. The smaller room was also filled with plants, white and yellow orchids adorned the coffee table, and finally, the concierge desk.

"Alright men what d'ya think of the test?" Logan asked while he sat with his hands folded leaning forward with his elbows on the table causing his eyes to become almost hidden deep in their sockets. It had been 15 minutes, but all the men felt they retained nothing and answered few questions.

"Pretty damn frustrating, boss," Brian said as he rubbed his short curly hair.

"Well it looks like the hardest thing for you guys was observing the people. You nailed the details about the decorations, the exits, elevators, what color the flowers were but you didn't know how many chairs were occupied, what color hair the doorman had, how many men were reading the newspaper or which man was watching you. This is what we'll focus on. Being able to walk into a room and scan it is essential. I want you to start doing this wherever you go. In fact, I want you all to start changing one thing about yourself, your clothes, or the places you go in order to practice this. Make it hard. Everyone should be looking for things that are different. The more you practice the better and more normal this will become. Any questions?"

"You gonna play too?" Ryan asked as all the men looked at Logan.

"It sure wouldn't hurt," Logan replied after a short pause. "OK. I think that's enough for the morning. Grab some lunch and meet at the PT field." Logan stood up and walked to the window gathering a look. "The rain stopped. We can run but someone better check the sports hotline and make sure we're still on for our softball game tonight." Several of the men smiled. They loved playing softball. Logan's Heroes they called themselves.

The men met one hour later at the PT field and did their five-mile run where again Logan led from start to finish. When the run was over, Ryan called the Moral Welfare and Recreation office to see if their softball game was still on.

"We're a go for softball boys!" Ryan said excitedly flexing his biceps at the men. "I might just get to hit a few bombs tonight after all," he said as he kissed his flexed right arm.

"Keep dreamin'," Dubs said as he showed off his swing with an imaginary bat. "You just get on base and let big papa pump hit ya' home—boom!"

Logan just looked down and shook his head with a smirk on his face. "You guys are something else. If you were as bad in the classroom as you are on the field I would've left a long time ago."

It was a perfect summer night at Camp Lejeune, North Carolina. Logan's Heroes had the 2100 timeslot and were playing Marine Corps Team 3.

Everyone loved playing under the lights of a softball field. The crowd was rather large for an inter-mural game. Both sides of the field had three sets of bleachers that went six rows high and they were all full of Marines, their wives, and children. A few fans brought popcorn from home and the scent permeated the air. Occasionally a waft of beer came through from the small contingency of fans at the far end of the bleachers. They were being as respectful as they could be, given their current state of intoxication. The night air had everyone second-guessing whether they needed a coat. Thousands of mosquitos hovered around the lights high above, and took turns dive bombing the stands, welcomed by DEET and swatting of hands.

The game eventually began and Logan's Heroes couldn't buy an out. Logan was sitting in the stands next to the head of the softball league, a civilian named John. After watching the team make errors left and right, Logan finally asked if he could play for the team just for tonight. John said it wouldn't be a big deal if the other manager didn't care. John and Logan went over and asked Sergeant Wilson, the opposing team's manager, if it was OK.

"Once a Marine always a Marine!" the sergeant responded.

Logan slipped through the opening of the gate into the gravel filled dugout.

"Alright let's get three quick ones so 'big papa pump' can get us goin'," Dubs said talking in the third person. All the men laughed and took the field.

"Batter up!" the umpire yelled as Tom finished his warm-up pitches. Tom had an uncommon hobby of changing his facial hair monthly if not weekly. Today he had a goatee. He had green eyes and needed to wear glasses, but rarely wore them, forcing him to squint through life.

This, among other things, was a reason not to put him into a defensive position on the field.

The first batter for Marine Corps Team 3 stepped up to the plate. He was short, solid and presumably quick being the first man in the lineup. He watched the first two pitches go outside.

Ping! The bat screamed after making contact with the third pitch, the sound reverberated until the bat hit the ground. The speedster from MCT-3 was already rounding first as Logan was turned completely around running for the fence and not looking for the ball. Looking up would only slow him down and he knew where it was going. As Logan saw the warning track approach he decided it was time to find the ball. He looked up, saw it was falling to his right, and adjusted accordingly. He reached for the fence with his left hand and for the ball with his right. The ball bounced out of his glove and back toward the outfield where Ryan was struggling to get there in time. Ryan dove outstretched and caught the ball.

"One out," Logan said as he jumped down from the fence. Ryan threw the ball in and the second batter came up, a bit larger than the first. He hit the first pitch, a screamer, at Migs who quickly gathered it up and threw to Dubs at first.

"Two outs!" shouted Logan from the outfield and showed everyone with his hand. The third batter was a monster. Tom threw one inside and the 6'5" Marine took a step back and drove one into the parking lot 200 feet beyond the fence. Nobody said a word on that one.

The game went on for another hour before ending in the fifth due to time restraints. The score was 12 to 9 in favor of the home team; Logan's Heroes. They were now one and six on the season. They decided to celebrate.

The team all went out to the closest watering hole they could find. Dubs sang karaoke and Ryan and Brian sang back up to "Livin' La Vida Loca." Tom got drunk and started trying to repair a broken bar stool and was thrown out for not listening to the bartender's repeated requests for him to get off the floor and leave the chair alone. That happened at about 0100 and the other men decided to leave too. The fun was over.

chapter
EIGHT

Paris is beautiful at night, thought Amir Qasmi as he looked out the hotel room window. He was tall, but the window extended at least another foot allowing for an uninterrupted view. As he turned left toward the wall his eyes focused on his own reflection in the mirror. He studied his face, a chiseled jaw line, his dimples small and deep. His hair was dark and combed back matted to his head. He looked down at his robe, white, with a logo of the Four Seasons hotel.

It's a shame, he thought as he began to smirk at himself in the mirror. Tomorrow is July 14, Bastille Day, a day that symbolizes the uprising of the modern French nation. He turned to look back out of the large window. He fixed his eyes on the Eiffel Tower shining elegantly in the night. Who knows if anyone would ever see this beautiful sight from this window again. *It's nothing to be concerned with,* he thought to himself and closed the curtains. He picked up the phone and dialed a number.

"Code word please," a voice responded after two rings.

"Christmas 27," Amir said. A series of several beeps, a click, and three rings followed.

"We're on. Meet at location A tomorrow at time schedule one." *Beep.* The phone hung up on both ends. This was the hotline all members of the group called to receive updates for scheduled events.

Amir went to bed, and within a few minutes, was fast asleep.

It was 0730 on July 14 and Amir was again staring at his face in the mirror. He wasn't smirking this time. He was stern as he inspected his face, taking in every detail. His dark brown eyebrows demarked his thin, wrinkled forehead. The slight wave that had been absent in his hair last night had now returned. The pores on his nose were large and open and the shadow of his beard was thicker than the night before. The phone rang.

"Hello Mr. Qasmi, this is your wake-up call."

"Thank you," he responded and hung the phone up. He then picked the phone up, called the front desk, and asked for a taxi.

The air was thick, but comfortable for Amir as he walked outside of the hotel, waiting for his ride.

"To the Musée du Louvre please," Amir said as he entered the taxi.

They arrived 20 minutes later. Amir paid the man 30 euros and went back to the trunk to retrieve his backpack. He waved to the cabbie through the back window and the driver left Amir standing in front of the Louvre. It was still ten minutes until the museum would open at 0900. There was a large group of people waiting to enter and many more walking the streets and courtyard around the giant glass pyramid. Amir was to meet his group inside the museum by the Masterpieces of Islamic Art from the Aga Khan Museum exhibit at 0930, and a second meeting at the Mona Lisa at 1030. He stood in line and waited for his ticket.

"What ticket would you like?" asked the woman at the register.

"The combined," responded Amir. It was the most expensive but allowed you into the entire museum, which would be necessary for the several meetings.

"Thirteen euros please." He was inside the museum at 0915 with map in hand finding the temporary exhibit on Islamic art.

Upon reaching the exhibit he saw one of his men, Sharif. They greeted subtly and waited together for three more individuals. Moments later, the five team members were all together. Each one took turns commenting to each other on a different work of art to help remain inconspicuous. After a crowd passed they immediately got to business.

"Yes, I'm ready. I'll go to the northeast side on the second deck."

"I'll go to the northwest side of the second deck."

"I, the southeast side on the first deck."

"I'll be on the southwest side of the first deck."

"I'll check all positions when I see you leave," Amir said as he adjusted his heavy backpack. Everyone watch for me to leave. I want you to stay for one minute then leave your bag where you stood. I will set off the charges five minutes after I leave. The mission starts at 1400 hours." The team dispersed.

Amir was admiring much of the artwork as he made his way to the Mona Lisa. It was not the first time he had walked the halls of the Louvre and he had a couple favorites that he wanted to see. He liked the sculptures and found it amazing that someone could create a perfect three-dimensional piece of art. He admired art in all its forms. It was incredible when artists could move people emotionally. He was envious. He knew how to lead, how to kill, but very little of other things. He could have stayed in the museum all day but he needed to quickly get to the Mona Lisa. It was already 1015.

He was the last to arrive at the Mona Lisa and felt even her eyes staring coldly at him due to his tardiness. The famous painting seemed darker, colder than he remembered. The smirk she adorned appeared as a dismissive smile of annoyance, or worse, disapproval. Amir swallowed hard. His eyes narrowed and he was brought back to the realization this was not a pleasure trip. He was following orders.

"You're late Amir," one man said softly.

"I'm sorry it was five minutes. I didn't want to walk fast. Someone might notice an Arab walking fast through a famous museum with a backpack on."

"Anyways, we have done surveillance and everything looks good. The last few days they have had tons of visitors and it's been pretty demanding on them to search everyone's bags."

"Good," Amir said as his stress level decreased. "1400 hours is confirmed."

The team excused themselves from the mob and walked their separate ways.

The clock was moving slowly as Amir checked his watch and entered a taxi. "Eiffel Tower please," he said to the driver and they were off.

It was 1147 and the sun warmed the city as if Paris was an incubator. Amir rolled down the window and got some air. He could smell sewage down one street, fresh bread on another, and coffee on a third. *It was hard not to love Paris,* he thought to himself. They came to a red light and Amir caught his reflection in the rearview mirror. It caught him off guard. Such careful insight earlier into the details of his face was now smoothed out and he almost didn't recognize himself. It was like stepping back from *A Sunday on La Grande Jatte* by Georges Seurat and seeing a clear, different picture.

Amir arrived at 1215 and strolled around the grounds surrounding the Eiffel Tower. There were a lot of people out celebrating the day with family and friends. Several groups were having a picnic; other young children were kicking soccer balls or throwing Frisbees. A few artists were scattered about the landscape all taking advantage of the afternoon sunlight as it silhouetted the tower with an aura of intense golden light. Amir saw more children running and playing tag throughout the crowd and he wondered how many of the faces he saw today would not be seen again tomorrow. He saw lovers embracing, kissing, walking hand in hand and flirting, but it all meant nothing to him. Amir had no family, no true friends and few acquaintances. He was a "working man" and he had a job to do. He was a leader and wanted to show that now more than ever.

It was now 1330 and time to execute the job. He had received no phone call to cancel the mission so he proceeded as planned.

He found himself in the back of a short ten-person line at 1345. It was moving fast due to the security officer's ability to scan through bags at break-neck speed. Amir was happy to see how meaningless the searches were. The officer seemed to be more interested in the ladies than what was inside their bags, or anyone else's bag for that manner. Amir took note of the officer's weakness and allowed a group of young American girls to go ahead of him in line. All the girls smiled at him and adjusted their large bags on their small shoulders. He smiled and looked up at the tower. It was his turn now.

"Place your bag on the table, sir," the officer said as his eyes stayed locked on the group of American girls. They returned the officer's gaze. Amir gently placed his bag onto the table and zipped it open. The officer haphazardly looked into the bag, then reached in with a small metal wand. He moved a few things around, a European tourist magazine, a camera, Amir's passport, a pack of gum, some trail mix, and a bottle of water.

"Alright take your bag," said the officer finally looking up at Amir for the first time.

"Thank you," Amir replied with a humble grin, a nod, and removed his bag from the table placing it onto his back. The security guard moved onto the next unlucky young lady in line.

Amir walked toward the tower. From there on out there was little in the way of security monitoring; maybe a few cameras from local ATMs or banks that could possibly see what was about to unfold, but the quality of recording in these devices left something to be desired. Amir thought maybe someone's cellphone would catch one of the team member's faces but he wasn't nervous about that either. He knew the men all had flights out that night to different parts of the world. He himself was going to America. By the time any agency received the video they would be long gone.

Amir reached the staircase at 1401. He looked around and saw two men, one on the northwest leg and one on the northeast leg of the tower with their backpacks. He quickly climbed the stairs and saw a third bag on the southwest corner of the second floor and one of his men with his bag on the southeast. He nodded respectfully at the last man and he returned the favor. Amir thought he would put the icing on the cake.

It was not part of the plan but Amir had bought the more expensive ticket to the top of the tower. He had stared out his window for three nights looking out onto this magnificent structure and he had to go to the top. He got into the elevator with 20 other people for the thrill of seeing the views from above. It was a slow ride, uneventful. Few people talked because everyone was a stranger. Amir was excited.

He walked out of the elevator and was greeted with a rush of warm air hitting him in the face and blowing his hair back. It was gusty in the higher altitude, but no less warm. There was little shade on the top of the tower and the metal was hot to the touch. He was amazed at how far he could see with this panoramic view. His hotel was easy to find and looked rather small from where he now stood. The people far below looked like multi-colored sprinkles on a green frosted cake. He stood on the northeast section looking straight down the edge of the building. Another gust of wind blew him forward almost knocking him into the railing and caused him to refocus on his mission. He snuck in one last look.

He checked his cellphone, no calls, 1415. He took off the backpack and opened it, removing a small knife with an unorthodox serrated pattern to resemble a key. He took the knife and cut along the seam in the bottom of the bag and pulled the bottom out, along with his bottle of water. Underneath lay 20 pounds of high-grade explosives. There was a detonation cord already implanted into the soft grey material so he just hooked his phone into the detonator and it was ready to go. Amir took one look around taking careful note of all the people on the deck with him.

He saw two families, all busy looking at the scenery and another set of people hugging and talking to each other. A group of tourists were on the southeast corner all taking pictures of each other. All together there were 30 people up there with him. He looked down toward the elevator chute and saw that it was still descending.

Quickly, Amir unhooked one of the backpack straps. He walked to the northeast corner and pretended to tie his shoes. Then, making sure nobody was watching him, he slid the pack around the ledge letting it slide down the length of the pole that marked the corner. He held onto the loose strap and reattached it to the backpack when it reached the bottom of the pole. It dangled in free air and all you could see was a small, inch wide strap along the base of the pole; if you knew where to look.

Five minutes later the elevator was back to the top floor. Amir, with water in hand, allowed the 23 people off the elevator and got on with the tour group of 15. The entire way down Amir listened to the heavy German accents of a group of women who, from what Amir could understand, were high school friends from 15 years ago.

He was excited now. The month of planning have paid off. He reached into his pocket and pulled out a second cellphone. This phone was not turned on. It still had the plastic protective slips covering the glass parts. He turned the prepaid phone on and waited for the opening chime to finish, finally seeing he had a solid signal. All five of their phones had been produced by an independent company hired by Amir. The programmer allowed for all five phones to ring if a certain number was called. Having this feature allowed Amir the luxury of simultaneously detonating five bombs.

The elevator doors opened and Amir looked at his watch: 1435. He turned to his left and saw his two men making quick eye contact. As he came down the stairs his eyes met those of the man on the northeast corner. The time had started. The man on the northeast corner looked to the man on the northwest.

Five minutes can feel so long at times like these. Amir's pupils dilated. Fight or flight kicked in and he had a hard time feeling the ground beneath his feet. Amir had passed the police officer and, once again, the officer was looking at women and not the Middle Eastern man who was now short one backpack. Amir took another sip of his water and kept walking away not looking back.

Finally, his phone indicated the time was up and the team began to walk away. First the two on the second floor came down the stairs after leaving their bags by their respective legs of the tower. One went to the north, one the south. Five seconds later the two men on the lower level had dumped their bags into the trashcans that were conveniently located next to the support legs. One man went east, the other west.

Amir found himself struggling to make the call. In total, ten minutes had elapsed since he initiated their drop. He was far enough away to be safe but he just stared at his phone, at the number, his finger floating microns away from the call button.

"Do it," he said softly to himself. "Do it," he said again more aggressively as he flexed his body. His heart felt as though it would burst from his chest, the hair on his arms stood on end and he was sweating profusely through his shirt. His water was long gone but he still held the bottle, squeezing it repeatedly, the crackling noise of the plastic was keeping him grounded in the moment.

A twitch, a momentary spasm sent a digital signal to five phones at the speed of light. Before Amir realized his thumb truly touched the screen, the ground shook with grief. The evening lightshow which dazzled millions of visitors paled significantly to the horror Amir unleashed on the metal structure. Flames, molten metal, shrapnel whizzed through the air. For the moment, the entire city just stared as life paused in the seconds before panic set in.

One scream turned to dozens, expanding exponentially as reality began to set in. Everyone began to run, but some were unable to escape the towers death spasms. Amir hadn't thought the explosives possessed the power to take down the Eiffel Tower, but as he watched the events unfold, he became entranced in the beauty of the twisting metal. The top fell first, toppling sideways away from the initial blast. It fell hundreds of feet before smashing into the lower structure. The impact was so great the east-most leg buckled, causing the entire tower to bend in half, a sinister curtsy for her final show.

Amir watched as people jumped from the observation deck. He saw dozens more disappear as the tower fell to its final resting place as a tangled web of metal and death. The wave of fleeing Parisians and travelers was quickly approaching him. Amir threw the phone to the ground, smashing it underfoot, and kicked at the pieces, scattering them on the ground. He stood for several minutes longer watching the metal glow in the intense fire as terror set in, taking everyone hostage.

NINE

0500 couldn't come soon enough for Logan. He had been suffering night terrors yet again. They happened less and less, but seemed as though they carried more intensity. Logan was already staring at the ceiling thinking about how today was supposed to be "hotter than average" for this time of year according to the local Fox affiliates. He turned on the five o'clock news and the ticker at the bottom of the screen was more than enough to intrigue him.

"Terrorists strike Paris's Eiffel Tower killing at least 150 people." He sat staring at the television intently, willing the anchors to give him more information.

"Details are scarce at this time, but sources close to the investigation are not saying much more than they believe it to be a well-known terrorist cell out of Iran."

"Not much to go on," Logan said as he pulled his t-shirt over his head and turned off the TV.

Logan was always critical of the news media. He hated listening to reporters beating a dead horse, constantly talking in circles about the same information just until they could add another detail.

"Hey Logan," Dubs said as he walked out to the PT field. Migs said he's gonna be logging some hours in the Blackhawk today. He said if you can make it a learning experience he'd be happy having everyone come down for a ride."

The rest of the men showed up within the next five minutes all saying "hey" to one another before going on their run. Along the way, the sun began to intensify and Logan began to brainstorm ideas about the incident in Paris. He was already surprised that none of the guys had brought it up. *When would the video from the terrorists be released to the media with demands? Which group was responsible? Would he have any old contacts affiliated with the investigation? Could he use all of this as a training tool?* By the end of the run Logan had made up his mind.

"Alright everyone, hit the showers, we're gonna meet Migs at 0900 for some flight time in the Blackhawk. I want everyone to watch the news broadcast at 0700. We'll discuss later."

"Is he losin' it?" asked Ryan to Aaron being discreet as possible. "Watch the news?"

"I don't know, but usually when he tells us to pay attention to something it ends up being pretty damn important later so you just better watch it and shut up."

Whap, whap, whap! sounded the rotor blades as Logan walked toward the Blackhawk at 0830. He could see Migs inside making final checks of his hydraulic systems and digital displays. He and his co-pilot, Lieutenant Dave Henderson, were working the fuel and passenger weight figures when Logan ducked down and approached Migs.

"Hey Migs, got your message from Dubs. We're gonna take you up on your offer. Think you'll be ready to go at 0900?"

"Damn it Logan, I can't do math and talk at the same time!" Migs said jokingly and winked, although it was hard to see the gesture due to the pilot's helmet. "Yeah we should be ready about then. I can take everyone. With this bird, I can take a whole squad."

"I don't need to be reminded of that," Logan said as he quickly dismissed the memory of the bloody helo ride with Sherman that tried to creep into his mind.

"We gonna be takin' off soon Migs?" Brian hollered as he walked up behind Logan.

"Yeah if I can get a chance to finish my preflight with Dave here!" Dave looked out at what was now the entire group of men.

"No tickets needed here guys, get in the back."

"Everyone ready?" Migs asked and tried his best to look back where the men where all seated and waiting.

"Tower, this is HE-1 awaiting clearance, over."

"Roger, HE-1 you're clear, watch the wind out of the east, it's gonna be gusting all afternoon, over."

"Will do tower, thanks," said Migs as he quickly started turning the rotors up and focusing on an even takeoff.

"You're clear," announced Dave as their altitude topped the nearby power lines and trees. Migs then pulled a hard-right turn and cleared the airport's airspace.

Logan sat with his eyes closed in the back of the Blackhawk listening to his body as he often did on the helo rides. He loved how the chopper could just about put him to sleep with its undulating turns, constant background noise, and how Newton's law was always obeyed, no matter the consequence. As for the rest of the men, they were all the window seat types. They enjoyed seeing the sights and feeling the turns. It was a joyride for all, one that Logan somewhat greedily decided to have. Since the run this morning he'd thought of how this could be educational or purposeful, but he gave up trying and decided to make it an easy afternoon. Logan's eyes opened as he felt the familiar sensation of hovering to touchdown.

Three . . . two . . . one, Logan thought to himself as they touched down one second later. He grinned at his precision.

"Ya' can't stay here," Dave said looking back and pointing his thumb at the door.

"Listen up," Logan said after all the men had cleared the helipad by about 50 yards. "We're going to the room now for class. Grab a lunch. We're gonna be there for a while today."

Logan stood at the cherry table and waited for all his men to sit down. The harsh sunlight that beat them down on their run just hours before was still burning bright outside scorching the earth. But, in this room, it was pleasant.

"I'm guessing everyone now knows why I wanted you to watch the news," Logan said matter-of-factly. "I think I can use it as a teaching tool. We'll brainstorm possible scenarios, who's responsible, reasons why, how they did it. We may even shed some light on how the media, and/

or government, can spin information for the public." A bead of sweat rolled down Logan's face and slapped itself onto the table. "So, to start with, who are likely to be key players here?"

Logan had quickly developed his own theories from his experiences. His mind was in another place, with a much different, older, more experienced set of people. He had drifted back into a CIA quiet room where, along with several intelligence officers, he would systematically determine where he would deploy to in order to further investigate, or, more often than not, kill.

"Come on guys! Let's start talking in here!" Logan sternly said, slapping the table with an open hand smashing the sweat that had just landed.

All the men looked at Logan as if he were possessed. They were used to seeing a different side of Logan: one who was laid back, neutral if not happy in his demeanor at any occasion. Even the men joked about how they couldn't believe Logan was as good as his legendary status would lead them to believe because he didn't seem to be "crazy enough." At that point, all the men in the room understood that anything was possible.

"Well, I heard this morning on CBS that they believe it was suicide bombers but they are unsure where from," said Tom shyly, not keeping eye contact with Logan.

"Well there's a start," Logan stated as he released his hand from the surface of the table and settled down into a chair with his hands behind his head. "Where are suicide bombers most prevalent?"

"Middle Eastern."

"Muslim . . . Muslim-extremist."

"OK, those aren't bad answers but let's expand our scope here. What does history tell us? Asians are just as likely to kill themselves for a cause. Samurai would kill themselves for dishonor. Kamikazes are another example, more specific to dying for a cause. Recently, Americans have begun killing for their causes such as school shootings, mass suicides for religious reasons, et cetera. No matter how crazy these reasons are, it's happening."

"Logan this is all new and I have no problem brainstormin', but I think I'm speaking for everyone when I say I have no clue what to say," Ryan was visibly confused waiting for Logan's response.

Logan removed his hands from behind his head and placed them interlocked on the table leaning forward as if he was trying to get closer to the men so he could whisper.

"I apologize for being a little on edge. You know my background and things happen fast and ideas are flying everywhere during meetings after one of these bullshit terrorist attacks. To tell you the truth, this is the first time I've been teaching a course while an incident occurred. So, let's take it one step at a time and we'll get through everything we know up to this point."

Slowly the Marines worked through the very rough details they had from several news sources and put together a few hypotheses. The men soaked in the knowledge as Logan spoke for a few hours. It was fun and encouraging for Logan to see the men understanding ideas and expanding on them without many questions. Logan was impressed.

"Alright guys, it's 1700 hours, later than usual but I think we have talked enough circles. Go on home and see if any of your possibilities pan out. My guess is we will be getting bits and pieces for the next month, with the majority of it coming by the end of this week or early next. See you all tomorrow."

chapter
TEN

"First, I will say that I am very disappointed in the liberties you took with the placement of the explosives. You compromised the mission. They've analyzed the explosives and found it to be U.S. C4. Your carelessness has now compromised the mission and you need to rectify this. I'll bury the information on my end but the leak needs to be addressed. His name is Antonin Mercier and he needs to disappear. He told the press and I can't control that. I want at least five possible sites for the next attack. All of them must be in the U.S. But first, handle this Antonin, understood?"

"Yes," Amir said from his prepaid phone as he sat in the Olive Garden in familiar Vernon Hills, Illinois. "Do you want me to send it encrypted through your email or call you?" Amir waited for the answer as the waitress brought out his soup and salad. He politely nodded and the slender, dark haired beauty floated away effortlessly.

"Email's fine, just make sure you update the software before you send it. I don't need to get caught because your encryption codes are outdated."

"Understood sir. You'll hear from me soon."

Amir was sitting at the bar in the Olive Garden. It was the same spot the men who assaulted his father sat that fateful night.

As Amir sat there, eating, he recalled his youthful self. He was eager, full of life, motivated to lead and prove his worth to his country. The only dream he ever had was to be respected, to be a leader worth following. He had that, for a time. Then some ignorant fools destroyed his life. He realized it had been years since he thought of his father. He felt distant, like an outside observer of what used to be his life. He had neither emotion, nor empathy for what felt like someone else's life. He felt caged under Jenkins' thumb. He wanted to lead his own men, accountable to nobody. He planned his own missions, had his own contacts. Amir felt he worked off his debts to Jenkins long ago. He owed him nothing.

Amir finished his meal and drove to the closest Starbucks. He needed a Wi-Fi hot spot. Upon arriving, he ordered a caramel mocha.

"Would you like whip cream and caramel drizzle with that, sir?" asked the chubby young girl, barely 18.

"Uhhhh, sure," said Amir barely looking up from his iPhone.

"That will be $5.26 sir."

Amir looked again at the menu, then at the register and noticed that he had been charged extra for the caramel drizzle and whip cream. Annoyed, he paid for the coffee and vowed to himself never to return. He went to a chair in the front corner by the large windows. He quickly made a VOIP phone call using Starbucks' free Wi-Fi.

"Shifty," Amir heard after three rings.

"This is A. I'm gonna need another gift. You want to make some money?"

"Ummm . . . well, you know me. I guess I can help you out again but it's gonna take a few weeks. How long can you give me?"

"I can wait two to three weeks. But I'll call you back in one to find out a date for pickup."

"Well, I can't promise you anything, but I'll do my best."

Amir hung up the phone, sat, and relaxed as he drank his overpriced drink.

Chicago

"Well someone talked," Dominic mumbled through his BLT in a briefing room in Chicago's FBI office. "No big deal though, just happened a little sooner than I thought it would be. Ever since we went into Iraq the French are a little quick to release information that makes the U.S. look worse. Anyway, the press will go nuts over the fact that it was American C4 that blew up the Eiffel Tower.

"Alright let's make it airtight. Find the person who talked and make it quick. If they weren't American then we'll contact their government, give them the disappointment speech, and let them know that our intelligence, well, we just won't have any to pass along to them for a while until they seal the leak." Dominic had now finished his sandwich and took a long drink of water. "Samantha, you're gonna be in charge of this."

"Yes, sir," Samantha nodded as she jotted some notes on a pad or later. She was a quick worker and a good one. She was in the DHS for a few years before Dominic met her three years ago on a Joint Terrorism Task Force assignment. He enjoyed how she meticulously went through details at a quicker pace than average. The test scores he obtained from her file showed she had potential well below her pay grade. One phone call to her boss at DHS gave Dominic the OK, and a "funny to see you here" moment between Samantha and Dom was all it took.

"OK, everyone back to work. Samantha, call me when something comes up. Washington wants anything we get. They have a whole team working on this one."

A whole team? Samantha thought. She had been on countless "leak" cases before but they were almost always solo missions at this level of intel, and definitely not teams. Samantha approached Dom at the head of the table. She did it methodically, acting as if she was searching through her purse, looking for a specific object from its infinite bounty. The charade ended as the room finally cleared.

"Who put this team together, Dom? Do they not trust me anymore?"

"Nothing like that Sam, they're just a little worried about the press on this one. American C4 in Paris of all places. You should only worry about whether or not I trust you. I am the branch chief and I'll back you up on anything."

"Alright Dom, but you have to admit this is a little strange. If there is more information I should know please tell me now."

"Everyone in this room knows as much as I do. If there's more information I'm obviously not in the position of 'need to know.'" Dominic added hand quotation for comic effect, at which Samantha had to smile. "Alright, if I hear anything, I'll let you know. Make sure you do the same."

"Always do."

"I know."

Camp Lejeune

0645 Brian and Tom were in the gym doing their strength workouts and keeping the chatter to a minimum. Enlisted as well as officers filled the gym without prejudice or ranks being thrown around; all were on equal footing here. On every wall surrounding the weights were pull-up bars worn smooth from years of use. A few men preferred using chalk to get a better grip, which left a slight, but noticeable, haziness to the air. Two TVs were mounted in the far corners of the gym, both broadcasting different news channels as every waited anxiously for more information of the attacks in Paris.

"Hey boss, do you mind if I jump in?" Brian asked Tom who was finishing a set.

"No man, have at it," Tom said standing up and shaking out his long, lean arms. "Did you catch the news today? Logan was right. Late this week, early next."

"Yeah, we'll see how much of it is right, remember the spin factor."

"You've been watching Bill O'Reilly too much man. Hurry up and get your set done."

"How's your kids, Brian?"

"Brian, Jr.? He's been trying to walk already, Bella is a terror, I'm just glad her mom is so tough."

"I remember those days, just wait till junior high man. Chelsea just hides in her room and listens to music. I even caught her sending pictures to some fucking kid in her class man."

"Well I won't hold my breath. Come on let's get outta' here and grab some chow."

"One more set. I'll meet you in the locker room."

Nobody went to the locker room after that last set. The news network aired a teaser for information regarding the Paris attacks after the commercial break. Most men stood by their machines watching intently, hands on hips, eyes focused. The volume was turned all the way up but was still difficult to hear due to noise from large fans circulating the otherwise stagnant air.

"Everybody shut up!" an anonymous Marine yelled from the back.

"The latest details to come in regarding the Eiffel Tower lead investigators to believe it was Middle Eastern. They used backpacks placed in strategic locations, which caused structural instabilities that subsequently led to the collapse. Details involving the type of explosion are sketchy, but some reports state that it was American made C4 explosives leaving investigators confused at this time. There are very few witnesses coming forward, however, those who have remember seeing at least three men, fitting Middle Eastern profiles with backpacks. The descriptions have been used to develop these three sketches. If anyone has any information regarding these men, please contact your local authorities and they will assist you in bringing your information forward. A group has yet to come forward and claim the incident. When we come back from the break, our seven-day forecast."

BB-5 was dark and the monitors were on, giving it an eerie glow as the men came in. Logan was waiting at the front of the room watching what sounded like a news feed when he noticed the men coming in.

"Well, I think I was pretty close with the timeline, huh boys?" Logan sighed as he leaned back in the chair with his arms folded behind his head. All the guys smirked as they grabbed their seats, allowing the blue light from the computer screen to envelop them like an aura.

"Did everyone see the news this morning?" Logan asked the men as he hit a button on the control panel located on a platform next to his chair. They all nodded. "Well, I won't waste time telling you how well you did on your brainstorming session Monday. One thing I want to touch on is that a lot of the media is saying that some sources say this, some sources say that. Often times these so-called sources are within the investigation and don't want to be mentioned because they may get in trouble for passing on intel. Which means this information is sometimes extremely crucial. On the other hand, it could be misinformation given by anyone from the guilty organization, to some bum on the street trying to get their 15 minutes of fame. Either way, do not dismiss anything until you yourself have ruled it out."

"What's the next step?" asked Lonnie.

"Well, we have a lot of field agents within Europe and the Mideast so we just try and gather intel through them. Typically, some things come in immediately from those agents who aren't a high commodity or deeply rooted individuals. There is a hierarchy to the agents used. Some are expendable in their location, if their cover was blown, getting them out would be no great loss. However, the other extreme is that it often takes years to get inside government systems or terrorist organizations. Those individuals are only called upon or expended to deliver information of the highest priority. We wouldn't risk trying to contact them unless it was critically important. Understand? We let the analysts take in all the information and put it together using the intel, as well as all their intuition, to make logical conclusions about an incident. Of course, we can help with that from time to time, but typically we are the next step."

"What would that be?" Lonnie asked.

"The counter strike, the silent kill, the interrogation of terrorists, whatever they tell us to do," Logan responded calmly as he looked Lonnie in his eyes, then subsequently gazed around the room attempting to read the minds of all the men. Some met his gaze where others, like Tom, did not.

Tom was never the killing type, even when he was young growing up in northern Iowa. All his friends would shoot at squirrels and birds with their pellet guns but he would just watch. He had joined the Marine Corps to get money to continue schooling with the G.I. Bill.

Logan then told the men a few of his mission stories, leaving out some of the highly-classified details and none of the anecdotal, humorous accounts that showed the men he did have a greenhorn status once upon a time. Most of the humor wasn't comical in the moment, for example when his MP-5 jammed shortly after breaching a door of an apartment building in the northern Syria. It required quick thinking and innovative maneuvering to dive-roll past the point man and kick over an end table. The apartment ended up being empty and his CO at the time was never going to let him live it down.

"Improvise!" Migs exclaimed cutting Logan off.

"Adapt! Overcome!" All the men joined in the Marine motto and this made Logan laugh.

"Yes, exactly," he said pointing at Migs.

Logan went on to tell his men of his first spec ops in Iraq with the digital camera. He even told the men about the wig-wearing supplier.

It was the first time he revealed such details to anyone outside of the mission debrief, but he trusted these men more than any other group he worked with in the past. It could have been the fact that a terrorist attack had just happened and he was feeling sentimental, but then again, Logan was rarely sentimental. He realized for the first time since starting his black ops lifestyle, he was allowing himself to bond with individuals again. He would not, however, allow himself to talk about Sherman.

Dubs sat and listened to every word Logan said. He was so curious about who Logan was and how he became that way. Dubs had no siblings to look up to, no older role models back home in Milwaukee. He looked at Logan as his role model, his older brother, his friend. He wanted to be closer to Logan in order to understand him. Dubs was afraid of life. He had no goals, no interests outside of the Marines. He desperately wanted someone to take him under their wing and Logan fit his ideal description.

"Alright guys that's enough with the stories," Logan said as he stood up turning off his computer.

"We got softball tonight, 1800 hours. You gonna play again Logan?" Migs asked.

"I'm in."

Chicago

The FBI in Chicago was all hands-on deck. They were using every angle they could, every connection they had throughout Europe to try and figure out where the explosives came from. A few bridges were burned, and mended, but very little information was coming through. Nobody was eager to give the FBI any information that wasn't absolutely verified. It was a terribly serious international situation.

Samantha sat in her office all afternoon making calls. She had a list that Dominic wanted her to get through as fast as she could. After that, she was to cold call people from news agencies that have been connected to people close to the events of Bastille Day. If none of this panned out she had to begin calling military families who were connected to demolitions teams and have access to C4.

"Thanks again and I really appreciate this Mike. I owe you one," Samantha said to the American asset inside French borders with the cover of working for CNN.

"I think you owe me a couple," he responded in French and then abruptly hung up the phone dispensing with the pleasantries. Samantha didn't care. She got what she needed.

She hustled to Dom's office and knocked while entering.

"Dom. It was a French policeman who was present when testing the explosive material. He insisted on being there and since he found the residue. The French government let him."

"What's his name?"

"Antonin Mercier. He leaked the info."

"Thanks Sam I'll get back to you as soon I hear something."

"Call me on the cell, I'm going home for a bit."

Samantha had just pulled into her garage in her west suburban home when her phone rang. Checking the caller ID, she was surprised to see Dominic calling her from his cell.

"Please hold while the line is secured," the all too familiar sound of the recorded woman spoke in both Dom's and Samantha's ears. It took approximately five seconds before Dom could speak two words that froze Samantha in her place.

"He's dead," Dom said and waited for a response. Dom was an easygoing guy, but when pushed he could really get some work done. With this news, Dom was ready.

"Samantha, did you hear me?"

"Yes . . . I'm just trying to gather my thoughts. How long ago?"

"Apparently, several hours. What else did your source say? I want to know everything."

"Dom, I don't believe this is an accident at all."

"Tell me what you know," he said in a hollow voice.

"OK, my source said I was the third American to call for the information. He was kind enough to tell me that one was CIA, and another was NSA. He said they called about a day before I did."

"That's it?"

"Yes. Very short call. I have a feeling it was a hit Dom. I don't know why. I think it was a really bad idea, and this whole thing is just plain weird to me. Ever since you said there was a team of men on this . . ."

"OK, stop there. Do you really think the U.S. government killed this guy? Sam, you and I both know that we aren't that sloppy. I'm gonna call Washington tonight, see what's going on. I'll talk to you when I get something."

"OK," Samantha said as they walked to the front door.

Camp Lejeune

The bar was always cheerful, especially on a Friday night. Penny pitchers and special shots every 15 minutes leads to an environment perfect for both memorable situations and forgotten nights. Logan's Heroes were celebrating yet another win, they had a streak going now.

"At least we found a use for pennies," Dubs said as he drank straight out of his own pitcher. Dubs was sitting at the head of the dark, heavily lacquered table, which was designed to fit six, however, ten were seated in close proximity. Each of the men scouted out different locations around the bar so nobody would miss a funny moment or a lovely lady. The lighting was good and the ceiling was high, which made people watching easy. Logan liked practicing his skills and tried to watch people doing ordinary things, such as taking items from their pockets. He watched what people seemed interested in as well. He kept himself sharp that way, and nine out of ten times he was right about who was going home with whom that specific night.

"Alright guys. This is a training op," Logan said with a smirk.

"Oh shit!" Dubs bellowed from across the table and everyone laughed. Even a few of the Marines at the next table had a hard time not smiling at the way he said it.

"Everyone has to get information, or an object, from anyone in the bar. You have till 2300 hours and right now it's . . . 2150. Better get after it." Logan smiled as he laid back in his round back bar chair taking a drink of his Bud Light.

"This is too easy," Lonnie said as he walked away from the table straight for the light-skinned African American girl standing by the bar. All the men had discussed how beautiful she was just moments ago. Lonnie was often compared to Tyrese Gibson in appearance, so it was no rare occurrence for him to have women swooning over his smooth smile and flawless skin. It was his plan to elicit a handful of information, most likely a few of her likes, dislikes, a few quirks and, more likely than not, her phone number.

Migs and Tom chose to lumber around the bar at different intervals and steal people's drinks. They focused on the most inebriated, followed closely by those who placed their drinks down to dance on the small 12 by 20-foot hardwood dance floor.

It was about 2230 and Lonnie came back to the table. "She is from Louisiana, visiting her brother for the first time. She is single, going to Drake University, and is studying pre-pharmacy. I also have her number, but that's not information you need."

As this was happening, Logan was giving Lonnie his undivided attention. He had even placed his cellphone on the bar table.

"Look at that," Dubs whispered as he leaned into Ryan. "I bet we can take his phone. How awesome would that be?"

"I don't know man," Ryan said nervously, but smiling.

"Here's what we'll do. When the other guys start coming back he'll be distracted. I'll move to the seat next to him. After I get there, walk around behind him and get his attention. Once he turns around I'll swipe the phone. We gotta do it as close to 2300 hours as we can because he keeps checking it for the official time."

"It's worth a shot," said Ryan. "It's 2249. We can't wait that much longer."

"You're right," Dubs said as he finished off his pitcher, waited a second, then moved to the first seat. One minute later Ryan walked behind Logan.

"Logan!" Ryan said loud enough to catch even Dubs off guard. Logan snapped around.

"Yes?" Logan said as his eyes met Ryan's. The Marine stood frozen. He didn't think far enough ahead to have a reason to yell for Logan's attention.

"Ryan, if you decide to distract someone and make a grab, make sure two things occur. First, have a good distraction, and second, don't have a grab man who stands out in a crowd." With that Ryan shrugged and took a drink of beer.

"Samantha who?" Logan heard Dubs say in a flirtatious voice. Immediately Logan's blood froze. He turned to see Dubs was talking on his phone.

"Give me that damn phone Dubs." Dubs handed Logan the phone with a laugh.

"She sounds hot! Whoa!" Dubs yelled so loud the whole bar heard.

"I didn't know there was a Mrs. Falcone," said Ryan as he took his seat.

"Hang on I have to find a quieter place," said Logan as he stood up and headed for the door. He was confused, irritated at his men, and concerned about why she was calling—especially at that hour. It had been three years.

"Have you been drinking?" Samantha asked. She could always tell.

"Yes, Samantha a few. Is everything OK?" Her voice made his heart rate increase and immediately all traces of the alcohol in his system was negated by the adrenaline flowing through his veins.

"I'm in Chicago and yes, everything is fine with me. I just needed to talk to you about something that's been getting to me."

"Talk to me Samantha, I've always been here for you."

"I think it'd be best to talk to you with a clear head. No offense, but I remember you weren't exactly on your toes after a few drinks and I need you to be. Just promise you'll call me back at this number whenever you get up tomorrow. Deal?"

"Deal."

"We'll talk to you then. Bye Logan."

"Wait," he said not knowing why.

"What's up?"

"I'm glad you called. It was good to hear your voice."

"We'll see about that tomorrow."

Logan walked slowly back into the bar staring blankly down at the floor, and the screen on his phone still lit up as his arms hung low at his sides. He remembered how three years ago he left her car at 0400 after several hours of emotional conversation left them split for the final time. He remembered his anger, his fear of her new job opportunity with FBI. She was supposed to be a field officer and the thought of losing her became too much to bear. She wasn't going to change her mind. It was best they parted ways. During the first several months leading up to the job they fought intensely. He thought the tracks from her tears would permanently be etched into her skin.

He loved her thick, brown hair and that small speck of black that seemed to float in her brown eyes. *How did she look now? Was she still single?* With the avalanche of emotion cascading through his brain he reached the table where his Marines sat. He was separated from his conscious. Several verbal jabs were thrown at Logan with no reaction.

He was like a boxer out on his feet.

"Guys, it's been a good night. I'm tappin' out. I'll see you on Monday," Logan said in a hollow voice after ordering one last shot.

chapter
ELEVEN

Saturday was as good a day as any to check your email. When you're a man in a prestigious position such as military advisor to the secretary of state you don't really get days off. Especially when you are working off the books, or more accurately, working on your own. That is precisely what General Jenkins was doing that particular morning at his home in Washington, D.C. He plugged in a portable hard drive with encryption software and turned the computer on. One new message left in his Yahoo account draft box. Opening it, he saw that it was from Amir, and encrypted. With a smile, he clicked the file and the encryption software went to work. As Jenkins waited he walked to the kitchen to grab a snack.

Five minutes later he returned to see five pictures, all of U.S. targets. There was also a message explaining Antonin was taken care of, but he merely skimmed through the text. He already knew the details. Jenkins himself had received the report on the death of the Frenchman. Jenkins had a contingency plan in place which would have guaranteed Antonin's death if Amir hadn't come through. It was too important not to.

The first image file was the Hoover Dam, which would be absolutely devastating if destroyed. The water supply to Las Vegas, Los Angeles, as well as a multitude of other cities would flow down river out of Lake

Mead. It would also destroy the power grid in the southwest. The second was the Saint Louis Arch. He immediately deleted that one from the possibilities because the collateral and direct damage wasn't enough. It was just another symbol. The third was the Water Tower Place in Chicago. Jenkins liked this one not only because the copious amount of lives it would take, but also because of the immense collateral damage to the economy. The fourth was the subway system in New York, but Jenkins simply rolled his eyes, cliché. The last photo was in Washington, D.C. itself. It was a picture of the White House, which Jenkins knew was a joke and dismissed that one as well. General Jenkins had his mind made up; Chicago.

Camp Lejeune

It was around 0800 when Logan opened his eyes and adjusted his pillow as he slowly came to. Samantha was quickly on his mind. He remembered dreaming about her, but none of the details. Logan decided not to lay in bed and try to doze off for another few hours. He turned on the TV and went into the galley kitchen to grab some breakfast.

The TV proved mind numbing. He walked back into the kitchen to put his bowl in the sink. Logan smiled. Samantha had always tried to get him to put dishes right into the dishwasher rather than the sink. He hadn't thought of things like that for a while.

Everything this morning reminded him of Samantha. It was frustrating him. It took more than a year to work her out of his thoughts; two more years to stop fighting the urge to call her. He looked at his call history and saw her number. He had deleted her contact three years ago but never forgot the number. It was unfair how deep those digits were etched into his mind. That's what dialing it hundreds of times will do, even if you never hit the call button. This time he did.

"Hello," Samantha said after the second ring sending Logan's heart racing again.

"Hey Sam, it's Logan," managing his best not to sound shaky. Last night he had both liquid and peer courage, but at this moment he was shieldless and alone.

"I know, I have you in my phone. Never took you out. I can't believe you have the same number. Either way, I would have found you," Samantha said with a chuckle.

"Yeah, changing numbers makes it hard on everyone." He knew she was strong but she sounded completely separated from the fact that they had been so entwined. He again flashed back to the last time they talked in the car. She was so heartbroken.

"Logan, I need to talk to you. Can I meet you somewhere?"

"Ummm, yeah you tell me where and I will do the best I can. How serious is this Sam?" Logan finally asked a question with substance.

"You know who I work for, you know what I do, and right now, you're the only one I can trust," Samantha said being somewhat evasive. "I know it's been a while. Maybe after we can talk, unprofessionally, and catch up. But right now, I need you."

Those words lit an unquenchable flame inside Logan. Immediately all signs of a hangover vanished as if a heavy fog lifted to reveal the sun. He was thinking extremely clearly.

"Where, and when?" Logan said as he turned off the TV.

"Well, where are you? Can you catch a plane to Chicago? I think if I travel too much right now they might know. Wait, I'll drive to Milwaukee. I have some college friends up there I can visit. I'll meet you on Water Street tonight. I'll bring some of my girlfriends, bring some of your boys. At the least they might have some fun."

"OK Samantha, I'll see what I can do. I'll call you in an hour."

"OK Logan. Bye."

Logan quickly called the base's Executive Officer, General Mitchell Anderson, whom he established a close bond with since saving his nephew's life in 2003.

Logan had just been rerolled into Second Battalion after refusing to continue covert ops with Colonel Jenkins. When they first met, Anderson was a Lieutenant Colonel and the commanding officer of Marines Second Reconnaissance Battalion. Logan and his recon platoon had just gotten back from a two-day "bang and clear," securing a city block that the 2/2 Light Infantry Battalion was supposed to spread out and occupy. However, when the recon team got back to the forward operating base, they saw Colonel Anderson asking for volunteers. Thirty or more Iraqis moved into the furthest buildings that the recon team had just secured. It left part of the 2/2 vulnerable, having not anticipated the Iraqi presence.

Colonel Andersons's nephew was part of the 2/2 Light Infantry Battalion and his platoon was isolated in one of cleared buildings, being held down by two snipers. In addition to that, the Iraqi soldiers were moving in on their building.

Colonel Anderson didn't want Logan to go on the operation because he'd been up for 60 straight hours, but Logan wasn't taking no for an answer. Plus, Anderson had already witnessed how capable Logan was and knew his presence would be welcomed. Logan was still a lone wolf, having been back in his Recon platoon for less than two weeks; he hadn't even learned most of their names. His platoon brothers had been just as dry with him, but such was the way of a Recon Marine, focused on the job and their brothers, less on what they called themselves.

Logan grabbed an MP-5, several magazines, and dropped all his unnecessary equipment from the previous days. He filled a canteen and drank half of it quickly, and poured the rest over his head and neck, rubbing it through his hair and across his face. He threw the canteen on the folding table and walked out of the tent and into the hot, bright day.

He hadn't even waited for the rest of the team to assemble. He enjoyed being alone, and knew the streets from the previous assignment. He ran down the street on the east side of the buildings, staying in the shadows of the late afternoon sunlight.

"Marine!" he said loudly into a doorway of a concrete building riddled with bullet holes.

"Marine!" he heard several men say inside.

Logan entered and quickly counted all sixteen of the men. "Where's the sniper?" he asked the second lieutenant.

"We think he's down that north–south street about five stories up. Can't get a good look because of the second sniper."

"Where?"

"No eyes on that one. We're guessing east, but not sure."

"Who's got a scope?" Logan asked, looking for a long-range weapon. A private came forward with an M39 and ACOG scope. "This the longest we got?" Logan asked, scanning the room.

"Afraid so," the lieutenant said.

Logan took the M39 from the young Private First Class. "Private Anderson?" Logan asked, looking at the private's smooth face, figuring he was barely twenty.

"Yes, sir," he responded.

Logan gave him a once over, noting his thin, but wide, frame, seeing the family resemblance to his uncle, but said nothing to the young man.

Logan left the doorway he entered on the south side of the building and went around toward the north, staying against the east side of the building, shielding himself from the possible second sniper.

Finally, he hit the intersection that traveled east to west in front of the building that housed the marine platoon. He squatted down low and peered through the scope, the triangular reticle pointing toward unknown targets. He scanned each window, each crack in the building, and every car that stood abandoned on the street. Logan solely focused on the structures that gave the possible shooter a sightline of the Marines.

He saw the sniper. He was eight stories up and focused on the west side of the building. The man was covered, deep within a dark hide, but Logan had been trained well and spotted him as easily as a man would spot a white ball on the golf course. Logan took a moment to lay prone on the concrete and secure himself behind the rifle. He took a deep breath in and gauged the wind, then let it out. Again, he breathed in deeply and allowed the air to leave his lungs as he melted down into the ground, becoming one with the concrete.

Pop, pop, pop, Logan heard shots being fired from inside the building. He saw the sniper come to life and turn slightly, clearly acquiring a target. *Pop, pop, pop,* he heard again. Quickly the bursts turned into several men yelling and an uncountable barrage of ammunition seemed to let lose, a myriad of different pops distinguishable as a variety of automatic firearms. Quickly, Logan steadied himself and took a shot—*boom!*

The head of the sniper in the eighth floor quickly snapped back in a red blur and his rifle laid down flat. Logan leapt to his feet and sprinted back toward the south end of the building. He slung the M39 over his left shoulder and readied his MP5. He charged into the building and immediately saw ten Iraqi soldiers trying to stay in cover as the Marines from within laid down fire toward the door. Logan unloaded his MP5 in their backs, and with a vengeful sweep of the barrel, he slayed the men. He thought of Sherman in that moment, wishing closure would come from the bloodbath, but it hadn't. Logan just felt the familiar loneliness.

"Marine!" he yelled up the stairs as he stared at the bloodied bodies.

"Marine!" they yelled back to Logan. He walked back into the room to see a dozen more Iraqi dead, and Private Anderson laying on the ground with the lieutenant pressing into his chest, a large wound hemorrhaging blood out of his leg.

Logan lunged forward and grabbed the lieutenant and threw him off Anderson. He took his own shirt off and tied it tightly around Private Anderson's leg. "Marine! Get over here and tighten that dressing!" he yelled to one of the men standing and watching. Logan then began doing CPR. The radioman was talking to the forward operating base. A medic would be there in less than five minutes.

In those five minutes Logan had already gotten Private Anderson breathing and he had a weak, but present pulse. The tourniquet was tight and the bleeding had stopped as well. The medic arrived and further stabilized the private, administering morphine and an intraosseous line into his sternum.

Logan grabbed the M39 and walked out into the street on the west end of the building, knelt down, and quickly located the sniper on the fifth floor. Logan felt his adrenaline start to bottom out and his head became dizzy and his eyes blurred as he knelt, uncovered, in the middle of the street. The marines from inside the building watched in horror as Logan stayed exposed against the Iraqi sharpshooter.

A moment later, Logan rolled out of his kneeling position and behind a parked car. *Boom!* A high-caliber round shattered the ground where he had just been kneeling. Logan breathing was hard, he was scared, and angry with his complete lack of concern for his own safety. He had, for a moment, wanted to die, to allow himself a chance to be free of the loneliness, but then he thought of Samantha. She had been the reason he decided to go back to Recon, to be surrounded by his brothers.

He took a deep breath, calmed himself, and turned to face the sniper. By now, the marines of the 2/2 platoon had come out and began taking shots at the sniper. They realized Logan had already taken out the sniper to the east and they were safe to engage the primary sniper. Logan steadied the M39 and took two slow and deliberate breaths.

Pop! One shot, one kill. Logan dropped the M39 behind the car, and walked back into the building, helping the medic place Private Anderson on a gurney and carry him back to the base.

Private Anderson was medically discharged from the corps, having lost his right leg, but not his life. Mitchell Anderson had a soft spot for Logan ever since.

"General Anderson, sir," Logan said through the phone trying to sound as serious and sincere as possible. It had been five years since they last spoke. "I need to take five or six men on a training mission. I feel they're at an accelerated rate and they're the only ones worth passing this course. I want to make the most of this class."

"Well Logan you sure get straight to the point don't ya'? I like that, so I'll tell you what. Whatever it is, go for it. I'll sign off on any costs but not on any injuries you understand? Don't be reckless and do not make me regret this." The last words echoed in his head. Logan had a few regrets in life and they were impossible to get over.

"I won't let you down, sir. I can tell you all the details when we get back."

"No need to. I trust ya' son."

"Thank you, sir," Logan quickly hung the phone up and called his best men.

"Migs, are you busy?" Logan asked in a neutral tone.

"No, did I miss something?"

"I have a job for you. It's of a highly sensitive nature and I cannot discuss it over the phone." Logan thought if he was going to make it a training mission he might as well make it realistic.

"What do I need to do?" The idea piqued Migs' interest.

"I need you to call Dubs and Lonnie. I am going to call Ryan, Brian, and Tom. The seven of us are leaving tonight, that's if everyone is willing and committed to helping the country. Have everyone meet me at the BB-5 in one hour."

"You got it Logan."

"What do I tell my wife?" Migs asked Logan as he discussed the proposition.

"This is the beginning of what you signed up for Migs, if you weren't serious about this line of work then you should back out now. My advice, tell her as little as possible. Tell her the country needs you and leave it at that. Logan was being very stern in letting him know it was one way or the other.

"OK, boss, BB-5 in 45 minutes. See you there."

"Sounds good."

"Dubs!" Migs was screaming and banging at his apartment door. "Wake up man. Damn, I gotta talk to you. Come on man get up!" Migs was frustrated as he checked his watch. Only 15 minutes till they were supposed to meet Logan.

Dubs was notorious for turning his phone off or silencing it at night, especially a night where he brought a lady home. Migs knew where his bedroom window was, and getting to it on the fourth floor wasn't going to be easy. He quickly ran to the end of the hall and climbed over the steel guardrail. From there, he grabbed with his fingers in between the bricks and slowly gathered himself for the leap to the small, concrete window ledge of Dubs' room. He noticed that the curtain was blowing out of the window, which meant one thing; it was open.

Three, two, one jump! Migs told himself, grasping the ledge with his hands. He quickly pulled himself up into the window to see Dubs, standing shocked in front of the window, naked. The next thing he heard was screaming from the young blonde girl, no more than 21, as she lay frozen in terror at the stranger climbing through the window.

"You could have knocked man," Dubs said as he laughed finally unfolding his arms and helping Migs into the window. Migs turned quickly to his left to see the young girl spring from the bed into the bathroom.

"Not bad, huh?" Dubs asked as he grabbed some briefs from the drawer.

"Yeah, whatever Private Shmuckatelli. You need to leave your phone on. I don't have time for this. We need to meet Logan in 10 minutes at BB-5. Important shit so let's pull it together. Yut?"

"A little more notice would have been nice."

"I've been trying to get ahold of you for 30 minutes! Look man," Migs said finally smiling at the situation. "Get the chick outta' here. We need to beat feet."

"My name is Shannon asshole!" the mystery woman said from the bathroom as she exploded out, not forgetting to slap Dubs, then kiss him, on the way out.

"Thank God she introduced herself because I didn't even remember her name. Last night was fun though, right?"

"Yeah. Now let's get the hell outta' here man!" They laughed for a few minutes as they ran.

"I can't believe you came through my window!" Dubs said through heavy breathing. Migs just rolled his eyes as they came to a stop at the entrance to the building.

"Logan was not playing games this morning when he called me. Put your game face on. Rah?"

"Ooh Rah!" Dubs exclaimed in response as both men walked into the building.

Chicago

Samantha hung up the phone with Logan and decided to call her best friend first. It was something she had been meaning to do for quite a while, but, as always, her career had gotten in the way. She dialed Jen, and walked into her room to pack.

"Hey Jen!"

"Samantha! It's been a little while, you must be pretty busy. Is it a man?" Jen loved to make Samantha feel uneasy.

"No, it's definitely been work. How have you been? You see the girls much?"

"Oh yeah! It's ironic you called. We are actually getting together tonight at Buck Bradley's."

Samantha was as close to shock as one could come. She thought she would have to work hard to get the girls together, especially on short notice.

"I'll be there. What time?" Samantha said with such excitement that she even surprised herself.

"Shut up! Really? The girls are gonna be so excited."

"You know what? We should hit up Water Street too, just like the old days. See how many of your fellow Cheeseheads try to pick us up."

"That sounds fun. We're meeting at eight at Buck Bradley's. If you want to stay tonight at my place, then meet me here at six or seven. That way we don't leave any cars downtown. You remember my address, right?"

"Not the number, but I remember you're on the east side and I remember all the turns. No need for directions."

"I don't know how you do it but I could have used that type of brain in grad school. We'll see you tonight!"

"See ya' then," Samantha said excitedly. She almost forgot the real reason why she was going to Milwaukee. Her phone began to ring.

"Hi Logan."

"I'll be landing at 1745 with six of my friends. Show us a good time would ya'?" Logan joked trying his best to bury the past and match her demeanor as he hung the phone up. No need for long conversations now. He had men walking in the door.

Camp Lejeune

The mood was tense and nervous as Logan stood, arms folded, in the front of the room. He still felt a fire burning inside as Samantha's voice reverberated in his head, I need your help.

"OK, this is serious shit. I can't tell you anything except this. You six are the best I've trained to date and that's why you're here. Enough mushy shit. We have a plane to catch at 1430 hours. That gives us about two hours to get your shit and hightail it out to the airport. We are flying civilian so dress accordingly. We will be back by Monday. Any questions?" All the men were silent and all had been in positions where questions were not supposed to be asked.

None of the men checked bags at the airport and to the surprise of Logan, all the men were dressed to impress. They each sat in random seats several rows apart. For them this would be fun, but for him it was all business. *I wonder what she looks like now?* He closed his eyes as he leaned the coach seat back, a little earlier than the flight attendant would have liked, but he didn't care. He thought of Samantha's long dark hair, how he enjoyed it most when she straightened it, but the natural curls were also very attractive. *Would she wear her glasses?* She hated wearing them but she couldn't see a thing without them, always squinting. *Would she smell the same? Would he get close enough to tell?*

"Ladies and gentlemen this is your captain speaking. We are beginning our final descent. Milwaukee weather is nice, 77 with a five mile per hour wind off the lake. Local time when we land will be 5:47. Thanks for flying with us and have a pleasant trip."

"Milwaukee!" Dubs exclaimed. This is my hometown man! Logan what are we doing here?" Dubs yelled several rows back toward Logan.

"We're visiting your parents," Logan said giving him a very stern look.

Dubs really needed to control his outbursts or this would never work out for him. Logan had forgotten Dubs was from Milwaukee. How could I forget that? *I need to be less distracted, I'm slippin'*, Logan thought as the wheels touched down and the men remained silent as they got off the plane.

"Let's find a hotel, then I'll tell you the next move," Logan looked at the men just before they got into the cab van. "Keep your damn mouth shut, I do all the talking. Everyone okay with that?" Logan looked directly at Dubs.

"Yut," the men responded quietly.

It was 1800 when the wheels of the large van started moving toward the city. Dubs sat in front with the driver. He was so large it made no sense for him to squeeze into the back. He stayed silent the whole ride into the city, as taking in all the views from his hometown. He barely missed it. He had very little to come back to.

"Welcome Mr. Falcone. You need two connecting rooms?" the stocky man working for Hyatt Regency asked Logan.

"Yes. Each with two occupants," Logan thought it was obscene to charge more for additional people in the room. He would never pay for four people in a room when he could get away with two. *Some of these guys might not be returning to the hotel tonight anyways*, Logan joked to himself.

"OK your room numbers are 623 and 625, they have a door in between."

"Thanks."

Logan walked back to the sitting area of the lobby where the men were waiting for him to return. "623 and 625. I get my own bed guys, the rest of you can share, or floor it, chair it whatever, I don't care, SITFU," Logan said still attempting to maintain his stoic demeanor. "Let's get up to the rooms and you'll be briefed."

"Rah," a couple men said and they walked to the elevator.

The vertical ride was silent. Logan stood in front of them, on purpose, to allow them to give each other looks. The elevator doors opened to a brightly lit, wallpapered hallway. It was an elegant hotel, elaborate light fixtures, very good detail work in the crown molding and matching décor. Logan took the key for number 625, then gave the other key to Migs, who took aboard Dubs, Lonnie, and Ryan. Tom and Brian roomed with Logan. It was the more mature room.

Logan entered his room and noticed similar décor in the room, very subtle colors but the paintings on the wall were more intricate and impressionistic, which he hated. The room was standard, two queen beds, a bathroom with a shower/tub combo. Logan unlocked the connecting door and knocked on Migs' door. They knocked back and opened the door. Logan noticed the same details and even the same pictures in the neighboring room, except they were mirror images of those found in 625.

"Alright everyone in my room," Migs, Dubs, Lonnie, and Ryan all followed Logan into the room excited about finally getting briefed. "I appreciate, for the most part, you guys were pretty discreet. Dubs, I think it goes without saying the outburst on the plane was childish and hopefully it was the last time."

"It is, I felt really stupid after that one."

"OK, as I said, you wouldn't be here if I didn't believe in your potential. So, Dubs answered my phone last night and luckily, she didn't hang up. The woman's name is Samantha and she works for the FBI."

"FBI," Lonnie said. "I have a cousin who works in the L.A. office. He loves his job."

"Good to know that I'm not the only one with friends in different sectors of the government," Logan said sitting at the hotel room desk. "I called Samantha back this morning and she said she needs help. She's very independent and never asks for help, especially from someone outside of her agency. Your job tonight is to have fun. We are going to Water Street and bar hop with the locals. At some point, we'll be meeting up with Samantha and a group of her friends, which I can personally vouch for are biscuits. I'm gonna talk to Samantha. She's worried that someone might tail her and she doesn't want to travel a lot. Pretty easy first gig huh?"

"Hell yeah," said Lonnie as he high fived Dubs, then Ryan. "It looks like we have a couple wingmen too. Don't start talking to the hottest ones 'cause that's not your role."

"Got it," Migs said with a smile as he rubbed his hands together. "Being a wingman is a good time, no pressure. Haha."

"I don't know if I can stay out two nights in a row," Tom said, half joking.

"Well, we'll head out about 2100 and start walking around. I have a feeling I know which bar they will be at. You guys have to be impressive tonight. However, as this is an operation, we need to make one thing clear. Do not talk about being in the service or what you're doing here. You are just some guys at a bar. That being said, you can get plowed, do some plowing, I don't care. Just make sure it's consensual. And, keep your damn phone on Dubs!"

Seeing Milwaukee again was therapeutic for Samantha. She was immediately sent back to her college years as she walked and smelled the air. It was a mild afternoon. She got in her car and headed north on I94 toward the city. As she watched out of the window she saw how much things had changed in the seven years she had been absent. The highway had been redone, mostly, every bridge overpass was beautiful, the exits were somehow different but she couldn't put a finger on it, and the road was smooth. She came into the city and saw Miller Park from her window as she looked west; she had so many memories from tailgating. She let herself get excited. She has deserved to let her hair down for some time now.

Knock, knock, knock! Samantha stood outside Jen's condo door and waited for an answer. She could hear Rascal Flatts blaring through the door. *Knock, knock, knock!* Again, Samantha pounded as she heard the song end and the volume die down.

"Samantha!" Jen screamed as she opened the door with a towel on her head. "You're always early," Jen said as she took the towel off shaking her light brown hair around. "And you're ready! Got your overnight bag?"

"Right here Jen, and I'm not that early. You said six or seven, I chose six."

"Well that just means you can help me get ready."

I don't wanna' spend another lonely night ooohhhhhh! Rascal Flatts began to harmonize and totally drown out their conversation. Jen ran to turn it down.

"That was a fun concert."

"The best. I'll never make it up to you." Samantha had gotten backstage passes for Jen and herself seven years ago.

"So why did you decide to come up here Sam?"

"Well, I was going to see if you wanted to get together next weekend, but once you told me everyone was together tonight I couldn't pass it up."

"I haven't told anyone you are coming tonight. It'll be a surprise."

"Sounds good to me. By the way you look great. What have you been doin'?"

"Well, I started doing triathlons! God, we really haven't talked in a while have we? I'm doing a couple this year. I just needed something besides work."

"I understand," Samantha said with veiled annoyance.

When Samantha and Jen arrived at the bar it was dead. Very few tables were being used so it was easy to spot a group of old college friends laughing loudly.

"Samantha!" all the girls exclaimed at Sam and Jen.

"Oh my God! I can't believe you're here!" said Christine as she put her Amaretto sour down and hugged her.

"Hey girl," Ashley said and followed with a hug of her own. Followed by three more—one from Casey, Amanda, and Amy.

"You look good," Amy said as they all sat around a small table with a view of the long bar counter.

"Thanks, I missed you guys. It's been way too long. Anybody dating?" Sam figured she'd ask. After all, she knew there would be a group of Marines in their near future. Hopefully good looking, if not, at least they would be in good shape.

"I'm engaged," said Amy and Ashley, both showing off their rings to yet another person.

"Both of your rings are beautiful," Samantha said with a twinge of jealousy. She quickly thought, and dismissed the idea that if she were still with Logan they may have been engaged or even married by now. "So, are we going to get some food or not?"

"Let's just get a bunch of appetizers and talk for a while," Christine said as she set the menu down.

"Sounds good to me," said Jen. "But, Sam and I were thinking we should get down to Water Street tonight too. Just like old times." They all let out a group squeal as only a group of women could, and ordered their drinks and appetizers. Samantha decided to get a glass of cabernet and nursed it trying to maintain a clear head. Maybe after she talked to Logan she would completely let go, but only after.

"Do you remember when Amy turned 21?" Jen said and all the girls erupted. Amy was the youngest one so it was a wild night in Milwaukee for the ladies.

"I don't think Amy does, or should I say I don't think she wants to?" Casey joked as she waved the waitress back over to the table. "Alright ladies, Jagerbombs. It's tradition!"

"Good point," Ashley said.

"What can I get you ladies?" the waitress asked.

"Seven Jagerbombs and we'll pay the tab now too, thanks," Casey said as she pulled her hair back into a ponytail. The drinks came and they all split the tab. Surprisingly, Samantha only drank half of her wine and decided to save face by taking the shot.

It had taken a few bars but Samantha and company finally decided on Fitzgibbon's Pub, their usual place. At least seven years ago it was. They found a table to settle in at about 2230.

"Oh my God, Samantha," Ashley said with all trace of laughter fleeting from her already pale complexion. "Is that Logan?" All the women looked toward the entrance. A group of seven very fit, very clean-cut men were walking in.

"It is him!" said Jen as she turned toward Samantha trying to read her expression. It was too late. Samantha was already gone.

"Logan!" Samantha hollered and waved as she walked toward the entrance that was crammed with people trying to get into the door at 2300 hours. "Logan!" she yelled again. This time he heard. Logan turned to his left and saw her. His head went numb, his world slowed, and he was at a loss for words.

"You're Samantha?" asked Dubs and extended his hand. "I was the guy who answered Logan's phone last night. I just wanted to say sorry for that. We were playing a joke on him. It just happened to ring while it was in my hand. My name's Aaron, but everyone calls me Dubs."

"Hi Dubs," Samantha shook his hand and then turned to Logan who was just staring at her long, straight hair.

"Hey Samantha," Logan softly said as they awkwardly shook hands. Samantha loved his rough touch and nothing changed.

"Did you bring friends?"

"Yeah, there all over at that table," Samantha said turning to point in their direction. "You'll remember them. Let's go over and everyone can do introductions there."

Logan, Samantha, and the boys all walked the 50 feet over to the corner table where the women, especially Casey, sat in wide-eyed anticipation.

"They sure are good lookin' from across the bar," Amanda said.

"No shit. I like that big one. I bet he's a handful. He looks young, too," said Casey as she eyeballed Dubs.

They exchanged pleasantries and engaged in group conversation for a good hour. Logan and Samantha constantly eyed each other, both visually assessing their respective conditions, as well as determining the right time to step away. It was 0045 when Logan leaned in toward Migs.

"I'll be back. Sam and I are gonna talk. Keep everyone together, nobody leaves yet, OK?"

"Yeah, I can't see anyone leaving. We're all having a good time, plus, you weren't wrong about Sam's friends. They are pretty cool, and damn hot, too."

Logan stepped toward Samantha who was just listening in on Casey and Dubs. The conversation was full of sexual innuendos. "Let's go," Logan said in her ear as he caught the smell of her skin. Again, he was knocked back, however, he was getting used to the feeling. The two of them walked around to the other side of the bar for privacy. It was a little noisier, but they could deal with it.

"OK, Samantha you're up."

"Logan, I really appreciate this. I don't think I have to tell you, but I don't ask for help. Period."

"I know. That's why I came. I thought it had to be pretty serious. So, come on. Lay it on me."

"Well, I know you saw the news about Paris." He always broke down news reports when they lived together in the one-bedroom apartment in Chicago. "And I know you most likely heard it was American C4, right?"

"Yeah. That's not why I'm here though. Is it?"

"Right. It's more than that. First, can I ask you a very straightforward question with no bullshit?" Logan was shocked at her choice of words.

"Shoot," he said in a quizzical voice.

"Were you ever asked to kill a person who leaked a story?" Logan stone faced.

"Samantha, I can't answer one way or another on that. It's classified, and if you had clearance, you would have looked it up and not dragged me all the way here to ask that question. You can't ask me questions like that."

"I'm sorry. I didn't ask you to come here for that. I called a contact in Paris to find out who told them about the C4. It ended up being a French policeman. His name was Antonin Mercier. Now comes the really strange part. I've worked a good amount of these 'leaked information' cases, and usually I am the only one assigned to find out who it was. The consequence of the leak is usually a reprimand from their government, and that's it. Logan, this time Dominic, said there was a whole team of men looking for the leak. When I talked to my source he said that I was the third American calling asking the same questions. He said that the other two called the day before and he already told them the same information. One was CIA, and the other was NSA. Now the man is dead because his house burned down. The press in Paris said that it was a cigarette that started the fire, but this is too much Logan."

"What does your boss think?"

"He thinks I'm overreacting and the government was not involved in his death. We both agree if it was a murder and the government was involved, it was very sloppy with extremely poor execution. I mean really, the guy told his one secret. It's not like he had any more!"

"Yeah that's strange, Sam. What are you gonna do?"

"Dom said he was going to call Washington and get back to me tomorrow. I'm sure with nothing." Sam slouched. Logan placed his finger under her chin and gently lifted her head so her eyes met his. Lightning struck them in that moment. The thoughts of the murder and intel all went away and for the briefest of moments they were frozen in space, in a time that had passed between them years ago.

"You keep me in the loop on this you understand?" Logan said trying to get himself disconnected. "If things get really hairy then I'm gonna get involved. I still know people but I'm not owed a lot of favors. They need to count."

"Thanks again, Logan," Samantha moved into Logan and hugged him. It was something quite unexpected but nice, like a cool rain on a hot, sunny day.

"Let's go let loose a little now," Logan said pulling away, trying his very best not to get caught up in the moment but the scent of her hair nearly brought him to his knees. He still wanted to protect her after all this time. Maybe the alcohol will keep him from saying it out loud. He was once again scared for her safety; possibly now more than ever.

"Sounds good to me. By the way, what do you think about Dubs?"

"Loyal and a prankster, overall a good guy. Why?"

"Cause I think he's gonna go home with Casey tonight," Sam gestured back over to the table where Casey was standing with her back to Dubs front and they were dancing like it was a high school prom.

"No shocker there Sam. Saw that one coming." Logan walked behind Samantha on the way back to the table. He led her from behind, placing his hand on the small of her back. He liked seeing her and she enjoyed the familiar touch. It was a shame the walk back to the table was so short.

The night went on until closing time, 0200, where they all went back to their respective homes or rooms for the night, except two. One was Samantha who was staying at Jen's condo. She knew trying to drive to the west suburbs of Chicago would be a mistake between the alcohol and her exhaustion. The second one was Dubs, who took a taxi to Casey's house. She promised to have him back at the hotel in the morning, and vowed to drive them all to the airport for their 1400 hours flight. Logan hoped she would remember, and Migs made sure Dubs did not turn his phone off.

chapter
TWELVE

"It's been a week Shifty. Any timeline?" Amir asked through a payphone.

"Hey A," Shifty barked back with a hint of disgust. He would have appreciated a little small talk or at least a friendly hello. "Five days. This Friday pick it up behind the recycling trash bin in the back of Walmart. It gets picked up on Wednesday so nobody should be messin' around back there. I'll have it there by 0600. When can I expect the cash?"

"Your daughter's birthday is the next weekend correct?"

"Yeah?" Shifty said, not shocked that Amir knew facts about his life, but scared that Amir brought up his daughter. "You'll receive a package in the mail from your mother-in-law in Oregon. It will contain two gifts. The one that she meant to send, and another from us, with a special gift inside for you."

"Sounds good enough," said Shifty and hung up the phone, "asshole."

Amir wasn't done. He had one phone call to make. He called a 1-800 number and after three clicks he heard another dial tone.

"Yes," was the response Amir heard.

"Maverick 1986."

"When's a good time to travel to Chicago?" Jenkins asked through the receiver giving Amir his target choice.

"This is the time of year. The weather for this weekend looks great. Friday is the best, but it definitely leads into a good weekend," Amir responded without missing a beat and steady in his delivery. It sounded like a benign conversation to anyone who may be listening, however, its true meaning held deadly consequences.

"Well, this weekend sounds good. I have no plans and will call if something changes. Thanks." Jenkins had okayed the mission and hung up the phone. Amir did the same and looked at his watch. A total of 15 seconds had elapsed.

Chicago

Dominic sat on his deck drinking coffee. The air was dead and the birds were loud. He had been up all night practicing his "lines" and making sure it was worth calling. Dominic was nervous calling Washington on a Sunday. Weekends off were in high demand in the intelligence business, so calling to see how Antonin Mercier died, and if America was involved, may annoy a lot of people. Dominic dialed.

"Ernie Hayes' office," the operator said through the receiver.

"Hi Cheryl, this is Dominic Costa, Chief of Intelligence Operations in Chicago. I was hoping to talk to Ernie about some recent events brought to my attention. Would he be taking any calls today?" Dom asked in a very polite manner.

"I'm sure he will," said the sweet-sounding woman on the other end. "I can patch you directly to his cellphone if that's OK."

"Sounds good to me."

"Please hold."

"Ernie here," he said with a gnarly voice from years of smoking cigars.

"Hi Ernie, this is Dom Costa in Chicago. I hope I'm not bothering you."

"Nope, just getting ready to watch your Cubbies play the Senators. Pretty good team your boys are fielding this year."

"Yeah, they'll choke in the end," Dom said playing on the lightness of the mood.

"OK, Dom what you got for me?"

Directly to the point, gotta like that, Dom thought. "You know Antonin Mercier died?"

"Yeah, fire accident. Why do you ask?"

"I was talking with one of my team members, Samantha Baker, and we found some alterations from the norm—"

"Samantha Baker," Ernie interrupted Dom before he could start the next sentence, making a mental note for himself. "I've heard her name in a couple meetings. She's a good agent from what I recall."

"Yes, she's good, she's my ace. In fact, this is one of the discrepancies. In the past, with a low-level breach like leaking the American C4 we would have assigned one agent like Samantha on the case. For this French leak we had a team. Why?"

"Dom, American C4 used in a large terrorism attack on an irreplaceable landmark is far from a small leak. We needed to get to the bottom of it as fast as we could. We used a Joint Terrorism Task Force to search their sources in France and piece this together ASAP."

"That's true Ernie, but apparently, they all use the same guy at CNN Paris, because Sam was the third American calling with the same questions. Where was the interagency communication on that one?"

"Well, Doyle Smith wanted everyone working independent to make sure the intel gathered would all match up to the same guy." Doyle Smith was the Secretary of State.

"I guess that also makes some sense, but it's a pretty awful coincidence that Antonin ended up dying the day after we found out it was him, you know?"

"I agree Dom; it would be lazy. Not a well thought out plan. I know you're probing me for more information on this bud, but all I can give you is shit you already know. If it was a hit, then it was made at pay grades even above me. I'm an intelligence operator, not a black ops mission coordinator. Two separate divisions my man, and they are pretty strict on what gets out. Even more so in the last year since General Jenkins became the military advisor to the Secretary. That guy really knows his shit and makes sure Doyle is listening. Anyways, you wanna' put a friendly wager on this game? We'll settle up at the budget and analysis meetings next month."

"Alright, dinner and a beer."

"Sounds good to me, and listen. You've been smart enough to make it this far at your age. Don't let this one get to you. It was one French cop who smoked too much anyways. At least that's what his landlord said to the papers. Have a good one."

"You too, Ernie. Thanks."

"And one more thing. The ladies can get emotional on these things. Make sure Samantha Baker doesn't try and dig too deep. She's got a good career going too. Gut feelings and snooping behind closed doors can bring severe penalties. That's not a threat. I don't have skin in this game. Just good old-fashioned advice."

"You got it Ernie. I'll talk to her tomorrow," Dominic hung the phone up feeling mostly better. He had some residual doubts, similar to those people who wonder whether or not they closed their garage door. Cognitively they reasoned that it was OK, but deep inside a small flame of denial still burned. *I'm not stoking that flame,* Dominic thought as he turned on the Cubs game in his spacious sports room in his basement.

Monday usually feels a little better after a weekend catching up with old friends. Samantha walked into her office with two things on her mind: How good Logan looked, and whether Dom came through and talked to Washington. She wore her lucky outfit, Navy blue pants, a coat, cognac heels, and a matching gold necklace and watch. Her hair was straight and pulled back into a tight ponytail. She was so awake this morning she bought an orange juice before work rather than coffee. Samantha decided not to wait for Dom. Looking at the clock, she noted it was 0830. She knew Dom usually got to work by 0700 so she left her office, making sure the door locked behind her, and went through the noisy, cubicle-filled room full of intelligence agents and computers.

Dom was sitting at his large, oak desk as she walked into the doorway. She did like the décor in his office, a few quality paintings—one was of a large sixteenth century naval vessel battling choppy seas. She loved the colors and how it seemed so lifelike. On a couple of occasions, it looked as if the waves were moving. The majority of the time Dom worked without the fluorescent lights on because the south facing six-foot windows allowed in a lot of natural light.

"Hey Samantha," Dom said as he closed a manila envelope on his desk, placing it face down onto another dozen or so. "Come on in and grab a seat. Close the door behind you." Samantha moved into the bright room and took a seat in the tan leather chair. "I spoke with Ernie Hayes in Washington about France. He told me the orders came directly from Secretary of State Smith. They wanted several verified sources that's all he said . . . about that."

Dom hesitated to finish his thought while he played out two scenarios in his head. Samantha was the type that took constructive criticism well, but, when a threat or consequence is thrown in she tends to feel as if it's a challenge.

"What is it Dom? What else did he say?" Dominic's body language was speaking to Samantha.

"To sum it up he asked that you not try to dig into the situation," he sat slumped in the chair, worried eyes meeting Sam's.

"OK," Sam said somewhat frustrated with the comment. "Is that what he said or is there more?"

"Yeah, that's it," Dom decided to leave the threat part out.

"Alright Dom, but for the record, I still think it smells funny. That's all I'm saying."

"I know Sam, but I think it's for the best. Look, if I get any intel on this you're the first to know. I highly doubt anything else will come of it, but I promise."

"Thanks Dom."

"Alright Samantha, I gotta get back to the weekend material. I'll brief you after the 1000 meeting."

Samantha was surprisingly feeling some closure on the situation. She trusted Dom, he was a pretty straight shooter. They respected each other enough to be honest and she expected nothing less of him at this moment. As she walked back into her office she felt the weight of the weekend slip away. She stretched her arms overhead and yawned as she sat down in her black swivel chair, unbuttoning her jacket. She was feeling a little tired as the adrenaline wore off. She looked down at her desk and noticed she had three of her own manila envelopes in the drop box on the door. She walked over to the steel box and used her magnetic ID badge as a lock release and opened the door. One was from Afghanistan, one from Germany, and the last one from France. They were all three recently decoded by Rachel Trim, a second-year decoder who, before the government job pay increase, was working for Norton Antivirus as an encryption engineer. Samantha liked Rachel's work. She liked how Rachel would prioritize her decryptions based on Samantha's interests. Or at least it seemed that way.

Sitting down at her desk she opened the one from France.

OPERATION CANCER
SUCCESS WAS ACHIEVED. NO

COLLATERAL DAMAGE NOTED. PUBLICITY
AS PLANNED, FUNERAL IN 3 DAYS.

What the hell is this about? Samantha asked herself, immediately getting the familiar anxiety from this morning.

"Rachel, can you please come into my office?" Sam requested through the receiver.

"When did you receive this message?" Sam asked as she held up the folder from France. Rachel had barely managed to close the door behind her before the confrontation.

"I believe it came in late Saturday night. Look at the back cover, it'll tell you." Samantha took a second and noted that Rachel was correct: 2145 local Chicago time.

"Rachel, I need all the information to the U.S. from this source within the last two weeks." Samantha was on to something, which most likely meant that she would not be eating lunch. She annoyed they had a briefing meeting in ten minutes. "Keep this between you and me. It's probably nothing and I don't want to bring Dom into this, giving him one more thing to worry about."

"OK Sam," Rachel said without hesitation.

Camp Lejeune

Monday was a little awkward at Camp Lejeune. Logan decided to make it official and let the other Marines in his course know that they would not be passing. He called in Tristan, Ethan, and Calvin into BB-5 before anyone else.

"Alright guys, I hate doing this but I like to be straightforward. You three aren't going to continue in the course. It's nothing personal but I talked to General Anderson and he feels as though the class should be, in his words, 'streamlined.' I appreciate the effort. We'll be seeing you around." The three men headed out of the room, all taking turns shaking Logan's hand on the way out.

"Logan!" Dubs exclaimed as he walked into BB-5 after about 20 minutes. "Thanks for the trip to Milwaukee. I had a good time, and thanks for the wake-up call for my stupid shit on the plane. I'm gonna be a lot more professional now. I love this shit."

"Glad to hear it Dubs." The two men sat in silence, taking in the light from the windows. It was 0900 hours.

"Logan," Dubs said hesitating.

Logan looked over toward Dubs. "What is it big man?" Logan gently replied.

"It's tough to say . . . I mean, when we went back home, Milwaukee, I had nobody I was excited to tell. I only have the Marine Corps," he sighed deeply and looked at the table.

Logan sat for a moment looking at Dubs. He felt empathy. Dubs had somehow struck a chord in Logan and it terrified him. Logan had confidence in Dubs' abilities as a soldier, and he was very impressed at who he was as a person. He made Logan laugh more than anyone has in quite a while. He was selfless and wore his emotions on his sleeve. Logan loved that, was almost jealous of it.

"Dubs, we're the only family you need," Logan said surprising himself.

"We?"

"Yeah ya' bitch. We. If you need anything let me know. Now, do you need a straw Marine?" Logan said smiling.

"Aw man, fuck off," Dubs said laughing at the reminder to "suck it up."

Lonnie, Migs, Ryan, Brian, and Tom all entered five minutes later.

"Alright guys, quick point of interest before I debrief you on what Samantha told me. I called Tristan, Calvin and Ethan in this morning and told them they are out of the program. You in this room have passed. I know the program isn't quite over, we still have three weeks, but I am going to focus on teaching you as much as I can. Now, Samantha told me the person who leaked the story to the media was found dead. She seemed to be under the impression that it was our government that did it. I'll admit to you guys that it's a bit of a stretch, and a damn sloppy job, but Sam is amazingly accurate with her hunches. She also said that her superior, a man named Dominic Costa, was going to be calling Washington about the issue this weekend. Once I hear more, I'll let all of you know. You are my think tank on this one. Any questions?"

Logan trusted these men. They were HIS Marines even if it was only for a couple more weeks. He had watched them for the last five weeks. He knew them inside and out, and now he had started to care for them. Maybe it was the situation, the terrorism they were all experiencing together. Maybe it was seeing Samantha again. It didn't matter either way. He had a mission and wouldn't allow himself to fail.

"Is this all for real?" Lonnie asked as he looked at Logan with a smirk.

"See for yourself," Logan hit the switch that brought the screens down in the front of the room as the projector hummed and warmed up. Thirty seconds later an internet news article from France was visible on the 120-inch screen.

"I can't read that boss," said Brian as he searched through the article for any sign of recognizable text.

"This article was written two days ago. To sum it up, a French policeman was killed in a fire. His name was Antonin Mercier. He was the man who found the explosive residue, and was allowed to be present when the explosives experts revealed the compound and source."

"What's your take on all this Logan?" asked Migs.

"I think that anything is possible. I don't try and formulate any conclusions without intel. Remember, I was more an operative, not an analyst. I did what I was told, and read people in real-time scenarios. If this was a situation that involved the U.S., then it was a call that could have been made by only a few people. The head of the CIA, secretary of state, or the president. Which goes without saying this would be a very serious accusation, and this is why Sam contacted me. She has a good career going and snooping into her superior's records wouldn't help her climb the ladder. We're gonna sit tight here with business as usual, no mention of anything to anyone outside this room. If you're going to talk about it, not over a phone, and make sure nobody else is around. If it ends up being nothing, then at the least it was a good training opportunity."

Chicago

Samantha walked straight as if she was in a tunnel and the light was Dominic's office. She was conscious of only two things: the envelope from France and his doorknob. The next few seconds were a blur as she walked through his open door and began reading aloud the report from France.

"Sam, I know nothing about Operation Cancer. You're starting to make me nervous about the entire situation. Look, you're level three clearance, which means you're two steps down from the really good stuff. If it were that big of a secret then that envelope would never have hit your desk," Dom responded in a defensive manner pointing at the envelope Samantha brought along with her.

"Unless they wanted it to be that way!" Samantha said in a yell that was more of a whisper through her teeth. Her eyes were bloodshot. "It's been on world news that this guy is dead, what would be the need to send a message with level five clearance? This was just to cross all the t's and dot all the i's, and you know it."

"Don't put words in my mouth. You're becoming irrational Samantha. This is not a conspiracy. I'll make another phone call, but only because it's protocol when an operational status report comes in. We're not even supposed to get those. Ernie has the clearance, I just don't think he's gonna give me everything you want to know, especially because he told you to keep out. Shit Samantha. Don't bring this up anymore. I'll bring it up to you."

"Fine!" Samantha stormed out of the room frustrated. She saw Rachel as she walked back toward her room. Rachel's eyes met Samantha's with a hint of concern and inquisition, but Sam just keyed into her room and quickly shut the door.

Northern suburbs, Chicago

Amir sat in a hotel room. It was dingy, the air was stale, and the desk he sat at was poorly lit. The hotel had always been smoke-free but a light scent of cigarettes still wafted into his nose. From time to time he took a deep breath to convince himself he was smelling it. The air conditioner rattled without rhythm but it kept him comfortable. He absolutely refused to leave his room. The hotel was full of families and their children running to and from the pool. It drove him crazy seeing the children running through the hotel screaming and hollering like nobody else heard them. He found it selfish, uncivil, a lack of poor parenting; one of the problems with modern America.

The stage is set. I will pick up on Friday. We will go forward as planned Saturday. The weather will be fair, so enough people should be going downtown, and more likely than not, a lot will

end up at our location. Activate your phones Friday morning. You will receive a text with a definitive operational time as well as meeting location. Any questions should have already been asked. We've scouted for a week now.

Amir hit the "save as draft" button in the Yahoo account and logged off. All the members of the terror cell had access to the internet and subsequently the account. The wheels were again in motion on the terror machine. Amir stared into the mirror at his Key Lime Cove hotel room in Gurnee not thinking about why he originally chose this hotel. He was a sucker for new things, and the indoor waterpark was especially new to the area so he thought he'd try it for a couple days as he waited for Shifty. But, right now, he was thinking about how amazing it was that a group of highly trained individuals from across the globe could work together for evil. He knew in five short days, they would again shake the world, this time, on familiar soil. It was bittersweet for Amir, but Chicago was next.

THIRTEEN

They all read the email at roughly the same time. It was standard procedure for most of them. Breakfast, email, then whatever else the day may bring. All of them had been in America before, just not the Midwest. Vladimir and Basil worked in New York, Raul Garcia and Sharif Itani worked in Los Angeles, and Nikita had always been a close associate to Amir, just not close enough to visit him in his birthplace, Lake County, Illinois.

Vladimir sat in his rental house located just five minutes from Lake Michigan, in Zion, a small town just south of the Wisconsin border. He opened his backpack to charge his phone. It had been a few days since they bought their prepaid phones, and Vladimir was meticulous in his affairs. He would, most likely, turn the phone off and on several times, as well as charge it daily until Saturday.

Basil closed his laptop and stretched his arms grabbing his English tea and walking to the nightstand in his downtown Chicago studio rental. He loved the sliver of blue he saw between the adjacent buildings as Lake Michigan teased him, leaving him wanting more. Before leaving MI-5 as an operative, he often fooled around with various women, which is what led to his demise. He never got to live his life in her majesty's service, so he left the organization. Basil loved the feeling of flirting with disaster and the life of espionage, so he quickly dove into the underground scene, working his way up several organizations including the IRA where he used his former training as a demolitions expert to the fullest. Eventually he outgrew the IRA when he met Amir by "chance." Basil never knew, but that meeting was organized by a higher power, an individual who had worked with both Basil and Amir on different government projects—someone who still oversaw their work.

Basil grabbed the modified MP3 player from the nightstand that he had been working on for the last several days. The cheap Chinese MP3 was easy to program. It was redesigned to be a detonator for all the explosives when a certain sequence of buttons was pressed. He then turned his attention to the thirty-something woman that still lay in his bed asleep. He tried hard to remember her name but he had completely forgotten. He laughed to himself as he scratched his head. This was nothing new, he was awful with names. She would remember his though, *American women love the accent,* he thought as he began to make breakfast. It really didn't matter if she remembered his face. It wouldn't make the news.

Chicago

Tuesday morning Samantha was up and leaving for work earlier than normal. Monday night was uneventful and Sam was eager to find out if Dominic had talked to Ernie. She wasn't tired, but knew herself well and grabbed a coffee on the way. Depending on the news, she may finally let herself relax and hit a wall.

"Samantha. In my office now," Dom said sternly as Sam exited the elevator. Sam was caught off guard. The two of them quickly, and quietly, went into his office. He gently touched her back leading her into the room as he closed the door behind them. The light was pouring in the windows as she sat down in the familiar chair.

"I didn't call Ernie yesterday Sam. Would you like to know why?"

"Absolutely," Sam said, attempting to be stern with Dom, but failing miserably allowing her facial expressions to scream concern.

"He called me. He said that the Chicago office was trying to access level five intel and operational reports. More specifically, those originating in France, or going to France from the U.S.," Dominic paused and crossed his arms allowing Sam to take in the information. "I spoke with Rachel last night and asked her not to come back for a few weeks till this is all figured out," Dom said looking at Samantha with great concern. "I tried to reason with you on all of this. I was on your side, but when someone in Ernie's position tells you to drop something, you do it."

"What did he say about Operation Cancer?" Sam asked without an ounce of concern. She was on to something now and she knew it. "Why would they be monitoring those access attempts so closely? It usually takes a day or two before you hear about things like that. I just did that yesterday afternoon."

"Damn it, Sam!" Dom exclaimed slamming his hand on the desk and cutting her off mid-thought. Sam had never seen Dom like this. He was completely overwhelmed by a stew of anger, disappointment, and regret boiling his insides. "You're under observation," Dom said as he slumped in his chair and did not make eye contact. "They're performing an investigation and that's all I can tell you. You're aware of the protocols. I suggest you stay low, don't try anything strange because they'll be watching. Grab your personal effects. I will escort you out myself."

"Dom," Sam said as her eyes welled up with tears, overcome by the situation.

"Samantha, if it's any consolation, I'm not on their side. I think you just got a little overboard. It was Ernie Hayes and who knows who else above him. I don't think it's permanent. Just go lay low, keep your phone on."

"OK, Dom."

Samantha quickly gathered a few things from her office and took a quick glance over to Rachel's workstation just to make sure this was all truly happening. She left with Dom holding onto her arm just above the elbow. The touch was meant to comfort and console, but she felt numb.

"OK, like I said, leave your phone on. Take a vacation, travel and see some friends. Just remember, they're watching you," he said softly opening her car door for her.

"I got the hint. Thanks Dom," Samantha said and quickly rolled up the window of her car. She showed the parking officer her ID and sped away, waiting till she hit the highway before grabbing her phone.

Washington, D.C.

Doyle Smith was more than annoyed to have to make a call like this. He was being overwhelmed with calls and emails regarding the incident in Paris. All of them were people fishing for answers involving a "conspiracy" to cover up evidence. None of these "fisher people" were government officials except Sam. He dialed Ernie.

"Ernie, how's the situation?" Doyle bellowed into the receiver after two rings.

"Handled sir, she's not going to be accessing anything for a week. We put her on a temporary watch. Dominic's a smart guy."

"Excellent. The state of U.S. intelligence already has a black mark thanks to the media. If an internal investigation story about a hit on a French policeman got to the media, we would all be putting together resumes."

"I hear ya' Doyle. Listen, General Jenkins has a lot of good ideas, right?"

"Yeah, he's the one who's helped me with a lot of this French situation. He's done more black ops and off-the-book work than anyone I've heard of. Trust him much further than I can throw him."

"Good. I thought you said that last time."

"Why do you ask Ernie?" Doyle said with a hint of concern. After all, he was talking with the Chief of Intel in D.C. Any question of Ernie's wasn't empty.

"I just wanted to know if it was you or him that came up with the idea to shut Samantha out."

"It was a joint decision."

The answer was bullshit and Ernie knew it. It was like a high school break-up. Doyle didn't make that call or he would have said so. Ernie never thought the new secretary was very strong, and this proved the point.

Camp Lejeune

Logan had finished his PT with the guys. He took a long shower letting the cleansing water run over his body hoping to clear his mind. He was processing emotions he hadn't felt in years. Empathy, worry, love? He was being torn apart from the inside out. Anxiety was affecting him more than he realized.

Logan walked over to the counter, towel around his thinning waist, and rubbed at the dark circles under his eyes. His phone was blinking blue. Waking the screen of his phone he noticed a voicemail from Samantha.

"Logan, I have something for you. Our place, tomorrow, I won't be there but something else will be. Thanks."

He knew the spot: an old tree in the middle of a field near Camp Lejeune. It was their first real date. He had taken her around the base, followed by going out to a bar, dancing, and, subsequently, trying to walk home. They wandered far off course and rested for the night under a large oak tree. It became their spot when they wanted to get away from everything and everyone. It was one of the only places Logan felt truly at peace anymore. He had already visited it twice since being back on the base.

It was early the next morning when Logan found himself walking toward the gnarled oak tree. The morning air was thick and fog had amplified the sun's rays, creating a golden backdrop for the large, billowing tree. He couldn't help but think about Samantha every time he came here. He was concerned for her, wondering why she would dead drop items at their special spot. As he reached the tree he saw the spot they slept, the west side of the tree near a large root. Nestled under the root he found a manila envelope. He had seen these envelopes before, and, as it always did, the butterflies began to take laps around his stomach.

What is Operation Cancer? Logan thought as he looked at the intel report. He remembered writing several of these once missions had been completed. He was instructed to be as short and vague as possible, conveying only the necessary information. He folded the paper and put it in his back pocket. He walked away from the tree without a ripple of emotion on his exterior, but inside he was battling back class five rapids on the Colorado.

"OK guys, we have some new information," Logan said in BB-5. "I told you we'd start late today. The reason is because Sam contacted me yesterday and told me she needed to give me something; a dead drop."

Logan held up the envelope and placed it on the table. He paced back and forth as he talked, burning nervous energy which was slowly taking over his body.

"I need to know that everyone in this room is in for the long run. If this turns bad, that oath you took a long time ago to protect the United States against all enemies, foreign and domestic, is going to get a whole lot more domestic real fast. I think Sam is onto something and it's NOT small."

> OPERATION CANCER
> SUCCESS WAS ACHIEVED. NO
> COLLATERAL DAMAGE NOTED. PUBLICITY
> AS PLANNED, FUNERAL IN 3 DAYS.

"This was received in Chicago late Saturday. I think if we did some investigating we may find that the timeline correlates to our French friend Antonin Mercier's funeral yesterday."

"Whoa," was all that Dubs said as he leaned back in his chair. It was an expression all the men in the room felt.

"What's next?" Lonnie asked, with an abnormally flat affect.

"We wait. If this thing gets legs and starts to move, I'll talk to General Anderson again, tell him we are going to do some real intense training. He's all about this stuff guys. We'll get the OK. I don't want to push buttons I don't have to yet. I'm gonna call Sam this weekend and figure out what's up. If I hear from her sooner, I'll fill you in. Now, I think this goes without saying, but keep your mouths shut. Go home, watch the news, and think about your training. We may be using it sooner than you thought."

Chicago

Often anticipated events come faster than hoped for; other times, slower. In the case of Amir, this day came rather quickly. He had spent most of the week enjoying his former hometown. He visited all the familiar restaurants, drove past his old high school, and thought about how emotional he had been back then. He found himself driving all over Lake County, disgusted with himself and how he used to care about what these people thought about him. He was better than them; beyond them now.

"Nikita, we need to meet. Everyone will go to Basil's place downtown this afternoon. You call Sharif and I'll call the rest."

"Good," was all Nikita said. She was a straightforward, lean, blonde-haired woman who rarely smiled. Most women her age would have had kids, and possibly grandchildren now, but she was perfectly happy pushing her body and mind to the limits. She loved Pilates and it loved her right back. Her waistline laughed at size 00 jeans, but loved a bathing suit. Nikita, however, did not.

Washington, D.C.

General Jenkins sat in Secretary Smith's office as they always did on Friday mornings sharply at 0800. He met with Doyle to sum up the weeks' activities and go over threat analysis for the weekend and, on occasion, the next week.

Smith sat in his beige, leather chair and his fingers danced across the light brown accents on each of the arms. Jenkins, in stark contrast to Smith, felt much more comfortable with matters of national security while sitting on the opposite side of the modern, clutter-free, glass desk. His choice of color on the walls was questionable, with one mahogany accent wall and sharp, high gloss white for the other three. Several plants broke up the space and the bookshelf was somewhat abstract, with several overlapping borders and acute angles supposedly acting as bookends.

"Secretary Smith, in light of the recent attack in Paris, and based on information from several analysts, I think it would be wise to increase the threat level for travel this weekend."

"We can't cry wolf you know," said Smith. "If every weekend we increase the threat then nobody will pay attention."

"You're right Mr. Secretary," Jenkins said. He already thought through the entire conversation. Jenkins had only worked with Doyle Smith for eight months, but had been able to read him for the last six.

"OK, so I'm thinking not to raise the threat. Unless, you have some absolute dirt from a highly reliable source for this weekend in a major city. I'm guessing that's not the case or I would have heard it first thing. Now, as for your recommendation on watching Samantha Baker. Ernie Hayes in Washington tells me she's being watched and is on a temporary suspension for a week."

Good, Jenkins thought, his plan was coming together brilliantly. "No watertight leads on anything this weekend. I'll let you know if anything solidifies. I think we're done here, that's all I had Doyle," sighed Jenkins as he stood up extending his hand.

"We'll see you next week then Jenkins," Doyle returned the favor, standing, and shaking the general's hand. Jenkins smiled.

chapter
FOURTEEN

The terrorists got together in the early evening at Basil's place just as
they had for the last three weeks. All the players were hardened with
experience and trained by the best. Vladimir and Nikita were both
KGB, however, they had never worked together before joining the ranks
of Jenkins' crew. Raul Garcia was part of the Bandera de operaciones,
or the BOE, a select branch of the Spanish Legion, which made him
highly trained and cold enough for any task. Sharif Itani, a Lebanese
informant of Jenkins for many years, had proved his worth many times.
The loyalty between the two of them was unmatched by any in this
group. Amir was the last to show up to the condo, and he brought in
an army duffel bag. After setting it onto the floor, he shook everyone's
hand in the room.

"Do you have our faces?" Vladimir asked.

"I do," said Sharif as he walked toward his suitcase. He dragged
it over and opened it, revealing several plastic bags. Within each was
their identity for the following day. "As we discussed, the faces are all
different from last time, but are all Middle Eastern."

"This is what I want," said Amir bringing the attention back to
himself. "We must maintain the stereotypical look, that way we continue
to get the prototypical response."

"What time should we plan on securing our charges, and what time is detonation?" Nikita asked, once again getting straight to the point.

"Between 1000 and 1100 hours bags need to be placed. 1300 is go. Basil has the detonator, and it will work up to two miles away. A quick review. The food court is in the basement and is our primary target. If we place the charges next to support columns, we can take out all six levels in the core of the building. A secondary location would be near the escalators, again on the lower floors. They are stacked on top of one another all the way to the top, so if we take out the bottom, then we have a good chance of destabilizing all levels. There are usually trashcans at every level near the escalator so no worries. Lastly, we're staggering in and placing the charges. Once a charge is placed mark the can. We can't afford to put multiple charges in one location."

Chicago

As typical of most mid-August weekends in Chicago the streets were busy with visitors. Union Station was operating at full tilt. The stores on Michigan Avenue were beginning to unlock their doors allowing the thick, hot air to roll in. The early sun seemed amplified along the east–west streets as the sun was funneled through the tall buildings, and the lake shimmered like a field of tiny mirrors.

The sky was full of seagulls and the ground was full of doves, all fighting an unseen battle over discarded food. Breakfast was in the air making everyone hungry for pancakes, eggs, coffee. Tourists, who drove themselves into the city slowed traffic as they took in the sights. A few kids were sitting down next to five gallon buckets, warming up their drum sets, pounding out improvised beats before the rush of people came into the city.

Amir took note of all the city offered as he stood in Millennium Park with a blue backpack strapped over both shoulders. He had a Nikon D80 digital camera around his neck, which he used a moment ago to take a self-portrait of his reflection in the giant steel bean sculpture near the center of the park. Having been to Chicago many times, he knew approximately how long it would take to get to Water Tower Place. He took his time meandering down several streets. He walked past the Chicago Theater, over the Chicago River, and then past

Garrett's Popcorn, which already had a long line forming. The smell of popping corn lured people in as if it were the Pied Piper.

Amir made his way back east down Monroe Street and decided to walk down to the Yacht Club and take in the flat blue lake, as well as some beautiful boats. The sidewalks became more densely populated and it gave Amir a flutter in his stomach. As he came within a few blocks of the club the smell was becoming more and more intense. It wasn't terrible, just a familiar, fishy scent. He stayed for a while watching the yachts glide silently over the smooth water.

Vladimir had kept to himself by listening to music the entire train ride from the Waukegan Metra station to Union station downtown. Ironically, he sat near several dozen naval enlisted men from Great Lakes Naval Base on the way; none of them thought twice about what Vladimir had in the seat immediately to his left the entire trip. Nor did they seem to notice that he was wearing a mask when he smiled back at them.

His train arrived at 0936 and Vladimir went straight to work. He walked at a fair pace down toward Michigan Avenue, over the Chicago River, and under the Amtrak. He walked into the lobby at Macy's on the ground level of Water Tower Place. He smiled at the tellers and went up the escalators, the smell of fresh flowers in the lobby filled his nose, but it had no effect on his mood. Upon walking into the central portion of the mall he immediately went to the food court and located six cement pillars in the center. Quickly, he ruled out three options: one, because it was already marked, another because a family was sitting near the pillar; and a third because there was no way he could leave a bag unattended in the open space around the pillar.

He quickly chose the next pillar to the right of one that had already been marked. He quickly grabbed some food from the nearest vendor and took a seat next to the pillar, a trash receptacle to his immediate right.

Vladimir was angry. He couldn't get over how consumer-driven the American society was. Advertisements for every possible thing from food to underwear were attacking him. It annoyed him and he sneered as he looked at a young couple tumbling through the grass in order to advertise a pair of shoes that were barely in the picture.

After fifteen minutes, he gathered that nobody was paying any attention to him so he lifted his backpack onto his lap and extracted a lunchbox. He placed it onto the table for another two minutes waiting for the right time. He saw a large group of kids approaching from the left and used it to his advantage. His back was covered by the wall, and as the group of approximately ten teenagers loudly passed he pulled the handle on the lunch box, activating the bomb. He placed it into the trash bin while standing up. Vladimir then went around the can, marked it with spray paint. Five minutes later he was outside and headed toward Grant Park, his exit strategy.

Basil, Raul, Nikita, and Sharif had all taken turns placing their respective charges in the food court near one of the six pillars. They all used their backpacks placing them into the trashcans while nobody was looking. The crowds were getting larger, which made it easier to scan the immediate area for witnesses.

Amir finally arrived at the mall at 1045 and walked immediately to the food court. Combing his thick beard with his hand and after adjusting his heavy glasses, he noticed that five of the trashcans had the markings on them. Pleased as he was to see this, he noticed that one of the trashcans was receiving some special attention from the maintenance staff. The worker, dressed all in blue, was looking at one of the trashcans, and then he lifted the lid. Amir stood in anticipation. He calculated how to handle the situation before their operation was discovered. Amir walked briskly the 50 feet toward the worker as he was beginning to talk on his radio.

"Yeah Rob, we're gonna need someone to come get rid of this bag, I don't have time to take out the trash. I got a whole grid of lights out in the display case at Jared's and they're telling me they can't sell a thing if the guests can't see the merchandise," said the maintenance man in a dry, monotone affect.

"Alright we're gonna send someone out there shortly. How many are getting bad already," said the voice on the radio.

"It's not emergent. I'd say we could still go an hour, but that may be pushing it for some of these cans. I just wanted to let you know so it's officially on the to do list."

"You got it."

Amir continued to walk past the maintenance man as he placed the lid back on the can. Both men then approached the escalators where Amir exited on the first floor, while the worker continued upward toward Jared's Jewelers. Amir knew that time was extremely limited and that the potential was great that the C4 may all end up being taken out to the dumpster within the hour so they couldn't wait till 1300. He also wanted a guarantee that at least his bomb would not leave. He knew that the second-floor escalator would be the best floor for his bomb.

It was 1052 when he got off the escalator on the second floor. It was the busiest floor of the mall as most department store entrances were located there. After ten minutes of sitting on a bench people watching, he dispatched his pack in the trash can, immediately walked out of the Macy's, and across the street to the Loyola Museum of Art.

Amir searched systematically through the floors of the museum, making sure to smile at all the workers and wave off any attempts to assist his needs in finding exactly what he needed. It took 15 minutes but he finally found Basil, or, the Middle Eastern man whom Amir knew was Basil in disguise. He was reading a book on tourism in Chicago.

Amir sat three tables away from Basil within plain sight and pretended to read a pamphlet on exhibits coming to the museum. After an additional five minutes the men made eye contact. It was all Basil needed. He understood that if Amir was not following his own exit strategy. It could only mean one thing: the execution time had changed.

Quickly, Basil rose from his chair, stretched and placed his reading under his arm. He walked directly to the main floor where the bathrooms were located. He took the closest open stall, sat, and pulled out the detonation device from his pocket. No matter how many times he made detonators it always made him excited to finally put it to the test.

The entire museum shook and the lights browned out for a few seconds, then returned to their full strength. Basil heard screams from all around him as he walked out of the bathroom. It was 1143, and another terrorism attack had been completed. This time, on U.S. soil.

Basil walked out of the museum and saw very little. His views were obstructed by thousands of people running in every direction. Cars were stopped in random positions all over the roads and sidewalks; drivers and passengers were getting out of their cars. For the moment, they were in shock, not responding to the horror that was before their eyes. Hundreds of people spilled out of Water Tower Place stopping the very few cars that were still trying to drive down Michigan Avenue. Larger people stampeded the small and the frail. Parents screamed for their children; children cried so loudly they couldn't hear anything over their own voices. Those observers who stood far away were pointing their phones or cameras at the carnage and terror that was happening. Very few took steps to help. Those that did were immediately busy triaging the wounded, escorting people to safety, and helping children look for their parents.

Ambulances, firefighters, and police responded to the sudden destruction of a perfect day. They came from every angle. By the dozen, firefighters stormed into the building. Police officers helped move bystanders out of the way and helped triage for the medical staff. The scene was slowly coming into control and despite the massive number of injuries, the stress level was decreasing. The emergency response was flawless. However, nobody knew that structurally the building was ruined. No responder knew how many people were still stuck in the lower food court. Nobody knew that the escalator shaft, as well as the stairwell, was blown out at the second floor leaving thousands stranded on several floors above.

Thirty minutes after the explosions the west side of the building collapsed. The casualties were immeasurable. Along with civilians, several dozen Firefighters were inside. Police officers and EMTs stood frozen, looking at the only cloud in the beautiful blue sky. It was a dark—smoke and debris—filled cloud that continued to expand and consume the entire skyline. The birds were gone—having either been incinerated by the blast or flown away to safer areas. The only smell in the air was burning. Not the type of smell associated with nights around a campfire, but the noxious, lung-burning smell of plastic, clothing, and rubber.

Even people driving into the city noticed the stark contrast in the skyline toward the east. A gentle easterly breeze which just an hour before was giving gentle relief to the warm humid air, now spread an ominous cloud of smoke and debris though the city. The cloud made a larger, more defined streak with each passing moment. The commuters turned off their Pandora Radio, iTunes, and MP3s, and turned on the radio stations searching for news about what was happening in the city. No station was yet broadcasting, but everyone knew the worst had occurred.

Camp Lejeune

"We apologize for the interruption from your regular broadcast to bring you this breaking news. There has been an explosion in Chicago. The details are scarce at this time, but we know that it occurred along Michigan Avenue. We will be back throughout the afternoon to bring you further details as they emerge. Thank you and we will now return to your regular program."

Before the news anchor had spoken his last sentence, Dubs had already picked up the phone.

"Logan!" Dubs exclaimed as soon as he heard the phone connect. "There was an explosion in Chicago. I just saw it on TV. I was watching the Alabama game and they cut in with the news feed."

"What did they say?" asked Logan in a calm, smooth voice.

"There was an explosion. They had no details but would come back throughout the day with more as they get them. Do you think Sam might have any more details?"

"No. Typically the media is really good for the first 12 hours. They really dig into a story. After 12 hours, we need contacts. Keep watching the news, call everyone and let them know what's going on. . . . Don't worry about Lonnie he's calling me right now. I'll call you if we need to get together sooner than Monday morning."

"Sounds good. Later."

"Lonnie. I already know, Dubs just called me. Keep watching the news; I'll let you know if we need to meet sooner than Monday. Odds are 50/50 right now so have your phone ready."

"OK Logan, sounds good. This is some crazy shit though, isn't it?"

"Yeah, but at the same time it could be a gas explosion."

"I guess that's true. OK Logan."

"OK."

Chicago

Samantha had just walked into the door from a quick, hot run through the neighborhood when she noticed her phone was blinking. She took off her headphones and kicked off her shoes as she walked to the entertainment stand in the living room. *Two messages and five missed calls?* I've only been gone 25 minutes. Two calls were from her parents, the other was from Dominic. She immediately felt queasy looking at Dominic's name, remembering how upset she had been ever since the Operation Cancer and the "they are watching you" speech. She decided to quickly call her mom back instead of listening to messages. After all, Dom occasionally tended to call too much. Sam walked to the kitchen to grab a snack.

"Samantha, are you OK?" said a winded voice on the receiver. Taken back slightly at the trepidation in her mother's voice she became distracted from her hunger. She focused on her mother's voice, it wasn't often she showed these emotions.

"Yes, Mom I'm fine. What's going on?"

"Oh thank God," she exclaimed cutting Samantha off in mid-sentence. "Your father was sure you didn't travel downtown that often anyway and that I shouldn't worry."

"Worry about what mom?" Samantha asked as she quickly walked back across the mahogany floors to her living room and turned on the TV. Before her mother could answer, she saw the devastation. Water Tower Place had been reduced to half its size. A helicopter was flying over the site and it was easy to see the debris that had cascaded onto Michigan Avenue closing the street. There was a large divot in the center of the building where an obvious explosion had occurred. People were being forced out of the area by police officers, while others were pushing their way through the crowds running as far as possible, as quickly as they could.

It was gut wrenching for Samantha. She heard the faint noise of a familiar voice as her hand slowly lowered the phone from her ear. She sat for several seconds, feeling her pulse pound in her temples, chest, and hands. The hair on her arms began to stand up on end. She gathered herself and lifted the phone up to her ear. "Mom, I'll have to call you back later. I need to call into work."

"OK sweetie, as long as you're OK. Love ya' talk to you later."

"Love you too. And Dad."

Samantha quickly hung up the phone and dialed Dominic.

"Samantha, we need you here ASAP," Dominic said skipping the pleasantries.

"Do we know anything?"

"We know it's bad. Lots of people in the city today Sam, that means lots of people were shopping. We are looking at a really fucked up situation. Excuse my French. We need all hands-on deck. I don't care about the probation either before you bring that up right now. I'll handle any heat that comes up for you accessing the files. Right now, I need you."

"I'll be there within the hour. Send me updates while I'm comin' in if you got 'em."

"Will do, but right now we got nothing. I'm pulling up all threats made for this weekend, you can help me get through them when you get here. I gotta call Ernie and see if he knew of anything too. Talk to ya' soon."

When Samantha got into the office people were running everywhere and it seemed as if the employees had multiplied. There were people from the FBI, CIA, and JTTF. There were three times as many people as there were seats, although nobody was using them. It seemed disorganized at first, but she quickly gathered her thoughts, looked for the appropriate people, Dom, Rachel her assistant, and finally, Cheryl, Dom's assistant.

"Samantha," Rachel said as she grabbed her shoulder from behind slightly stunning Samantha in the process. "Here is a preliminary list of all threats made against Chicago for the last week. Mr. Costa said get started following up on these while he finishes up his meeting with the CIA and NSA."

"Thanks Rachel. If anything comes through rush it right to me. OK?"

"You got it."

"And don't worry about anything. Dom already told me I'm back 100 percent."

"I wasn't," Rachel said as she handed over the envelope, smiled, and walked back toward the chaos of the room. Samantha turned and scanned into her office. She sat down and skimmed over the two-page printout of possible terrorist threats for the week, and their probability statistics, which were in the second column. The location of the attack was the first, and the source of the information was the third.

The list was in descending order from most likely threat, to least, and included 30 places. It was heavy into the baseball season and both the Sox and the Cubs were doing well. The Sox were at home that weekend which made the threat possibility high, and so that was near the top of the list. The Cubs were away, so that was a highly unlikely spot. O'Hare Airport is always threatened, usually making the top five on a weekly basis. This week, it sat in third place behind U.S. Cellular Field, and the Shedd Aquarium where there was a grand reopening of the dolphin exhibit. Samantha scanned further down the list and finally saw Michigan Avenue, number 26, possibility extremely unlikely by an analyst, Winters.

This is a pretty broad threat, Samantha thought to herself. *The entire Michigan Avenue?* She saw a contact number after the name and reached over to her desk phone and dialed.

"Winters' office, this is PFC Sean Diggery."

"My name is Samantha Baker and I work for the FBI. It's regarding the Chicago attacks today. I need to speak to Winters please."

"Sure ma'am, give me one minute and I'll try and reach him. He's not in today but I can have him call you if that works?"

"Actually, I would rather just call him now; can I have his number?"

"No problem ma'am."

"Thank you PFC Diggery," Samantha said after copying the number down on a Post-it and verifying it verbally before ending the conversation. She reached over and hit a second line on her phone and rapidly put in the analyst's number.

"Winters," a rough voice answered the phone.

"Winters. I am Samantha Baker from the FBI. I am calling about you registering a possible terrorist attack on Michigan Avenue in Chicago. Are you aware that there was an incident there today?"

"I am. What do you need to know?"

"Anything you can tell me. We need more details if you have them. How you came upon this as a target, how long ago, who might be involved."

"Well I had an Army captain send me the message from Afghanistan. He was interrogating a couple suspected extremists and they mentioned a couple key words for us, basically Chicago, and shopping district. There were no more details other than we received it early last weekend, and that it was a very small, unorganized cell and to be honest, I really felt as though these terrorists were trying to use scare tactics. I don't believe they had any ties to U.S. cells, nor did they have the funding to get their people or supplies into the U.S. I only sent the message along because it's protocol."

"Thanks. So, it's your opinion, based on this report you received, that you really don't think it was this particular group? Why?"

'Well we looked into it. We considered bank statements, known associates, and a variety of other things. We tailed their known associates and it was reported back to me that they were extremely unorganized, did not seem to be serious in any way. More often than not they skipped their prayer times. We were actually considering taking them off our watch list, but we will keep an eye on them because of this attack threat."

"Sounds good. Can we have the document sent to us that you gathered this intel from? I think it will just close the loop on the scenario. We can interpret it here for ourselves as well."

"No problem Ms. Baker. I'll have them send it over right away. You should have everything within the hour."

"Thank you. If you hear anything at all, please call me."

"Will do. Good luck."

"Thank you," Samantha immediately hung the phone up and walked to Dom's office where he was meeting with various other agency officials. She knocked on the thick, cherry door without reservation.

"Come in," Dominic said without delay, no doubt knowing the reason for the interruption must have been important.

Samantha charged into the office. Dom quickly rose from his chair to greet her and pointed to an open spot on the couch next to Bill Whiteside of the CIA and Chuck Renfro from NSA, both highly respected men in their branches. Samantha sat down, crossed her legs, then began to speak.

"I just got off the phone with an analyst, Winters, from D.C. He filed a threat possibility for Michigan Avenue."

"We're well aware of this," barked Chuck cutting Samantha off. "We know of that terrorist cell and we are documenting their activities. They seem to be a pretty tactful bunch and it's been hard to get good intel on this close group."

"Do we know anything about them?" asked Dom. Intrigue was the expression on his face as he leaned forward from his chair toward Chuck.

"Well, we know it's possible they did this in Chicago. We didn't have enough time to set up a surveillance team once we got word of a threat. They are a new player in the terrorism world and they most likely already had their man, or men, here in the states following through with the plan by the time the intel leaked."

"We got the info from one of our spooks in Afghanistan," said Bill, causing Dom and Samantha to quickly avert their transfixed eyes from Chuck. "Just this week I was contacted by Washington, someone from Secretary Smith's office notified me of the possible attack in Chicago, but they also said that the Secretary was not going to increase the threat level, and, in fact, he had lowered it. So obviously, they may know more than us, but this time, they were wrong."

"No shit," said Dom as he sat back into the chair. "What's the plan moving forward?"

"It should be an inter-agency situation. Obviously, cooperation is crucial. Between myself, Bill, and Dom, we should be able to run this investigation. We all already have people on the scene, if you hear anything, inform the rest of us."

"We should be the filters here," interrupted Bill. "The intelligence community has not been getting the best reputation the last decade so nothing can get released about the investigation unless we say so. Make sure your people aren't talking to the press, their co-workers, or their families. All we need is evidence to support someone's conspiracy theory about the government and we'll have another Hollywood movie portraying us as monsters."

Dominic looked over to Samantha as everyone stood up. "I can agree with that," he said, not taking his eyes off Samantha as everyone shook hands and walked toward the door. "We'll be in touch," Dom said as he closed the door behind them leaving only himself and Samantha.

"OK Samantha tell me what Winters said," Dom sighed as he walked back behind his desk gulping down a tall glass of water.

"Well, he said something a little different than what Bill and Chuck did."

"I assumed that by the way you looked as they told about the Afghani terrorist group. I want to know your side of things."

"Well, Winters was under the impression that this specific group was very unorganized, and not funded well. He didn't think they had the ability to get their people and supplies into the U.S. It's strange how there are two different ideas about the same small group."

"Yeah, but we have to remember these men were debriefed from

Secretary Smith's office. There's one more thing Samantha . . . they knew about your probation."

"So what?"

"You're not worried about that? Well, I am. You have a history of doing things off the book and not following the rules. Case and point is Operation Cancer. I'm not getting into that again, but we really need you to be on top of the regulations and being a team player on this one. I can't afford losing you, or causing this office to be investigated. It already seems as though they don't want to include us in the investigation."

"I know Dom. What's the plan?"

"We keep digging for intel. I gotta call Ernie again, see if he's heard anything. I'll get back to you."

Samantha walked toward the door with an anxious stomach. She often got that way when things didn't end with closure. The entire country was still shocked and looking for answers that were unable to be given. She walked back to her office, sat down, and began looking through notes and intel reports that had come in while she was in Dom's office. Not much to go on, but a start.

FIFTEEN

The weekend was a blur for everyone. In fact, it appears there was no weekend at all. Everyone was working overtime and checking on various intel reports, brainstorming sessions, drawing up profiles on every terrorist known to the intelligence community. They had even begun drawing up hypothetical profiles for possible terrorists, yet to be named. However, despite what Winters said, the prime focus was on a small, ill-defined, and poorly funded group out of Afghanistan.

The Chicago office of the FBI learned a lot about the Afghan group, numbering between 30 and 45 individuals, ten to15 of which were actual players, the rest were more the equivalent of obsessed fans. The FBI was getting a lot of their information through Bill Whiteside, who, in turn, was getting it from Washington and presumably the Secretary of State. The group was funded by a variety of private Middle Eastern, Saudi, Iranian, and Pakistani sources, but the paper trail was a mile long. It would take a team of officials months to track down just a fraction of the laundering that was taking place, according to Bill and seconded by Chuck.

Knock, knock.
"Come in," Dominic said as he continued to read through the stacks

of reports on his desk just sent by Bill this dreary Monday morning.

"Did you go home at all?" Samantha asked as she noticed his loosely knotted blue tie that he had worn on Sunday in the office. His top button was also undone and his usual clean shave and neat hair were a mess.

"No, been here working things out. Getting a lot of intel from the Washington group. Why did we never see any of these threats? All Chicago threats are supposed to go to us. We're the local group. Bill and Chuck keep telling me it was because the threat level work up was too low of a chance, but I'm not sure I buy it."

Samantha walked closer toward his desk and looked at him in disbelief. "What are you saying Dom?"

"Nothing . . . I'm just getting worked up over nothing. I just keep allowing these thoughts into my mind."

"What thoughts?"

"Feelings, hunches, I have all kinds of scenarios playing out in my head but there is no way they can be possible."

"Dom, if there's anyone in the world that understands, it's me. Do you want to know why I came in this morning?"

"Ummm. Yeah what is it?"

"I have a feeling . . ."

"Oh, Samantha not now," Dom said as he stood up from his chair, rubbed his face in his hands and walked to the window. "We need more than feelings on this Samantha. Find me some evidence and we can start to give this thing legs. Until then, don't confuse me with hypotheticals. OK?"

Noting the amount of stress he was under, Samantha simply nodded, bit her tongue for one of the few times in her life, and left the office. It would be tough to find any evidence, especially if the reports coming in were driving Dom to think something was wrong.

Camp Lejeune

The weekend had been uneventful for Logan and his students. Mainly they just stuck to watching the news and looking over the internet for the latest info on the Chicago terrorist attack. Logan, on the other hand, was being somewhat closed off. He knew that the men would bring him all the news from the weekend and he wanted the information to be fresh, instead of boring. His thoughts were crisper that way. Instead, he decided to read for the majority of the weekend, and, on several occasions, daydream of Samantha.

"Close the door please," Logan said to Lonnie as he entered the room. He was the last to arrive, still finishing the egg sandwich he had for breakfast. The men opted to start their afternoon session one hour earlier than typical because they wanted to discuss the Chicago situation. "What do we know?"

"Not much more than what we knew on Friday," Migs said in frustration as he leaned into the table with his elbows.

"Yeah, it seems like all the media knows is that backpacks were used to carry the explosives and that it happened in the lower level of the building."

"Not much more than that," Lonnie said swallowing his last bite of breakfast, leaning back into his chair, his bald head shining as a mirror reflecting the fluorescent lights above.

Tom, who was sick of wondering what was going on, finally asked, "Logan what do you think?"

"I didn't listen to much this weekend, but from what it sounds like the government put a lid on this pretty quick. The media has little to no access, which doesn't surprise me for two reasons. One, when 9/11 happened there was a media blitz, too much misinformation going out created an aura of confusion and disorganization. The second is that it's embarrassing. The intelligence community is already looked at under the microscope. With the government likely knowing about the incident and the event still happening, this could really cause distrust. So, I'm not surprised we know very little."

"Did Sam call you?" interrupted Dubs who seemed to be expecting details about the Chicago incident.

"No. So what would the investigators be gathering?"

"Type of explosive."

"Yeah Brian, what else?" Logan redirected quickly getting back on track.

"How much or how many backpacks were used?"

"OK Migs. Anything else?"

"How about the surveillance tapes?" Dubs exclaimed as if having made a huge discovery.

"Good idea Dubs. They're probably studying them in great deal determining if they can see the individuals who left the packs."

Dubs, with a large smile on his face, sat back into his chair with his hands behind his head. "Do you want those tapes Mr. Falcone?" Dubs said teasingly, having a rather large secret.

"What the hell is that supposed to mean Dubs?" Lonnie asked confused as looked at Dubs, an awkward look on his face.

"Just what I asked. Let's just say a guy in Chicago owes me a favor."

"How many lives have you saved Dubs?" asked Tom jokingly as all the men laughed.

"This one's different. I grew up with this guy. I set him up with his wife. He works with a large security firm in Chicago, and I'm 99 percent positive he has access to those videos. All I need to do is tell him we're doing a special training course on terrorism and we're in."

"Go make that phone call Dubs. I'll be honest, you do that, and we'll really have something to go on. While you're at it, we should get all the security tapes from nearby cameras. ATM machines, traffic cameras, everything. Ask for it all, get what you can."

"You got it Logan. I'll be back."

Chicago

Tony was driving to a call on Michigan Avenue for a consult with a firm on the latest audio/video surveillance equipment. The air was light so he had his convertible top down. It made it hard to talk on the phone when going between business calls, but it was a welcome relief.

Business had picked up dramatically since the attack, their call volume had doubled over the weekend so Tony's schedule was full. It didn't matter to him; he was happy when he was working. He loved his job, and his wife, Katie, very much.

Tony and Katie had been high school sweethearts and last year they were married. It was hard for Tony to work up the courage to talk to Katie, but with the help of a mutual friend, Dubs, he had gained the confidence to ask her out. As Tony parked his 350Z in the parking garage his phone buzzed. Looking down, he noticed it was an old friend.

"Dubs, what can I do for ya'?"

"Hey Tony, how's Katie?"

"Good man, things are going good. I've been getting tons of calls since this Chicago thing. You back in the states now?" This was the first time since just after the wedding they had spoken.

"Yeah been back here about eight months now. In fact, I'm in a special course on terrorism. That's why I'm callin' you."

"Callin' me? How can I help Dubs?"

"You're still working for that security firm?"

"Yeah."

"I need a huge favor."

"Anything, you know that."

"I need copies of all the security tapes from Saturday. The Water Tower Place, and as many other ones you can get from around the city. I know it's a lot to ask but I wouldn't ask if it wasn't important."

"I know Dubs. I know we have the tapes, I'll have to talk to a co-worker who made the master tapes for the FBI. It should be easy to get those to you. Just tell me where you're at."

"Camp Lejeune."

"OK Dubs, count on it being there within the week."

"Sweet. Tony really appreciate it."

"Anything for you. I can get in real trouble for this so make sure you don't do anything stupid. Take it easy."

"You know me too well. But I'll be good. You too."

The Chicago's FBI office was abuzz as the evening drew near. They had received the audio/visual surveillance from Water Tower Place on Saturday morning and a dozen individuals had been looking over the tapes. The focus was primarily on the lower level, including the food court.

The team in charge of reviewing the surveillance was in the basement of the FBI building, in a plain white room. There were large LED computer screens lining the room, and in the front, a massive projector screen for group viewings. Over and over the group exchanged videos around the boring, dimly lit room. The team was focused on abnormalities, which included individuals with backpacks, people who were by themselves, and, because of the intel provided about the Afghani group, people of Middle Eastern heritage.

"I've seen nothing on these tapes. Maybe we should look for

something else?" a young, curly haired technician said as he ate his fries from McDonalds.

"Just keep looking Brent, and lay off the McDonalds! You get all the equipment greasy when you touch it, and look what it's doing to your body!"

Brent looked down at himself, frustrated at his lack of self-control.

"I'm just saying we've been looking for hours and there's nothing on these tapes. Maybe we should look at a different day or time?"

"No Brent, any other day or time would mean that a cleanup crew could have taken out the trash and noticed it, or the bomb would have been in a dumpster. Occasionally it takes time to find evidence Brent."

Brent turned his back to the screen, stared at the small amount of food that rested in the bottom of his bag, and threw it out. He smiled to himself.

Bill Whiteside was surrounded by unfamiliar things in his Chicago hotel room. The hotel was nice, but uncomfortable. He liked being home in his own bed, with his own kitchen, and his own bathroom. At least he had his regular alarm clock, the iPhone he just hung up.

"Son of a bitch," he said quietly to himself. He looked back down at his phone and deciding there was no time like the present, he called Dominic Costa.

"Dom this is Bill. How are things on your end?"

"Stagnant. We haven't seen anything yet on those tapes. I'm hoping something turns up soon."

"Well, I've got something for ya' and you're not going to like it," a short pause ensued as Bill sighed and grabbed his intelligence report. "The explosives were American C4, Dom."

Dom remained on the line but his mind went two different places. The first was disbelief, wondering how this could be possible. The second place was France, and Antonin Mercier.

"Bill who else knows about this?" Dom asked recalling how Antonin died shortly after the press got wind of the C4 explosives used in the Eiffel Tower attack.

"Very few people. I'm callin' Chuck after this, then it's Doyle and his man Jenkins, Ernie Hayes, and a couple other key players. We're trying to keep a lid on this because if this leaks to the press we've got a serious situation on our hands. There were only two people working on the composition of the explosive material and they were senior bomb experts who've worked on several high-profile cases. Believe me, they understand the closed lipped situation we're in now. Anyways, thought I'd tell ya' as soon as I heard. Let me know if you get anything on those tapes."

"I'll let you know. We'll talk to you soon Bill."

"Take it easy Dom. Oh, and one more thing . . . I like that Samantha Baker. Got a good feeling about her. Why don't you tell her what I told you and see what she can sniff out? Might want to put her on the videos too."

"Oh. Ummm. Alright then Bill I'll let her know, but as far as her looking into the tapes, she's not that type of woman. Easily distracted and needs to be constantly moving. Sitting her in front of a screen would get us nowhere."

"You'd know best Dom. We'll be in touch."

Samantha sat at her desk pouring over intelligence reports as the sun began to slip behind the buildings outside of her smoky, tinted window. The fluorescent lights hummed in constant chorus without taking a breath. The pile of reports was six inches thick and she had already gone through half of them, all the while realizing that it was a futile attempt. Every report she had read was a threat on Chicago within the last six months and 99 percent of them were so unrealistic that she chuckled at a few.

She was in the middle of a report on derailing an Amtrak train when she heard a loud knock on the door. She quickly shot her gaze to the door and shouted, "come in." She was as tight as a spring from reading all afternoon and had been looking for a reason to communicate to the outside world.

"Oh. Hey Dom. What's up?"

"I know I don't ever come to your office, but I thought it would be best to tell you here. I just got a call from Bill Whiteside," Dom said as he closed the door and sat in the black leather and chrome chair opposite Samantha. "Do you remember Antonin Mercier?"

"Of course. Does he have something to do with Chicago?"

"Not directly, but do you remember your theory on how he died?"

"Yeah because he was the one who insisted on being there for the chemical tests on the explosives, then leaked the evidence to the press."

"Well, Bill told me what was used in Chicago. It was American C4. I don't want to know anything about your methods on how to find out where the C4 is coming from, but you can go or do whatever you need to. This is priority number one as far as I'm concerned. We stop the supply; we stop the terrorists."

"OK Dom. I'll do what I can. But do you believe me now?"

"I'm getting there," he said with a hint of fear in his eye as he stood up, fixed his clothes, and left the room. Samantha had a call to make.

chapter
SIXTEEN

It was the kind of day that made the asphalt sticky when you walked on it. Logan was sitting on his loveseat having just finished dinner when he finally decided it was time to turn on the small window air conditioner in his apartment. Logan rarely used the air conditioner, but tonight he just wanted to be comfortable. He closed the windows in his apartment and then tinkered with the cooling unit until it finally blew out smooth, chilling air. The initial shock of cold made the hair on his arm stand at attention and a small shudder went through his body. It was like jumping into a cold lake on a hot summer day. Logan stood at the air conditioner taking it in.

Bzzzz . . . bzzzz . . . bzzzz, his phone vibrated on the kitchen counter. He didn't want to walk across the humid apartment, but duty called.

"Logan!" Samantha exclaimed through the phone. "I need your help. You won't believe this but Dom told me I have free reign to do whatever it takes to figure out the Chicago attack. Logan the explosives were American C4 just like in Paris."

"When did you find this out?"

"Five minutes ago. Dominic just got the information from the CIA or FBI and he immediately told me. I think Dom is starting to believe me about the conspiracy in Paris."

"I am, too," scoffed Logan. "Wait, are you on a secure line?"

"Yes, don't worry."

"Good. Do you have any leads on who's responsible?"

"They keep saying this group out of Afghanistan, but I talked to an intel agent who gathered the info from an Army captain on the ground there. He filed the report on the Chicago threat and he said this particular cell is completely unorganized and unfunded. Things just don't seem to be adding up Logan."

"Sounds like it. So, what do you need me to do?"

"Find where the C4 is coming from. My guess, there's someone in the military selling it. There aren't many guys that have access to the amount that was used."

"I have a couple ideas. I'll call you in a couple days. If anything else comes up, then let me know."

"Sounds good. My phone is always on."

"Ditto. It always has been," Logan said squeezing the phone in frustration. *Why say that now? Why say that ever?* he thought to himself.

"I know," Samantha said after taking a moment to catch her breath.

She blinked hard and controlled herself. It was something she'd always wondered. Did he ever think of her during these last few years? The answer came in a most awkward time but she felt warm, excited, loved.

"Thanks Logan."

"Anytime."

Logan, now more thankful than ever for the air conditioner, laid in bed thinking about how the terrorist could have gotten their hands on the C4. It could be that they stole it, but even to steal it you had to have access and that doesn't come easy. He thought about who has the most access to the explosive and a long list went through his head. He knew at any point in the chain of command the C4 could have been ordered for training ops and it would be nearly impossible to find the exact source of C4, let alone the exact person. It's documented, in and out. Whatever materials leave should be on a master list. A cross reference of these people with ops, training or otherwise, would be needed to see if things don't add up. Frustration set in. There would literally be hundreds of ops and materials being used. How far back would they need to go to find an anomaly? This explosive could have been taken out years ago and held for just the right occasion. Logan remembered an uncountable number of occasions his recon group would practice both demo and live fire drills. Multiplying that by thousands made the task seem impossible, but it was the only possible lead. Now, how could he get all this information?

He laid in the bed staring at the off-white ceiling in the room dimly lit by both the moon and the street lights, casting a confusing glow of yellow, amber, and gray. Logan thought back to his Marine days, his recon days, and his CIA days trying to remember all the instances when he ran into C4 and who was involved. Everyone seemed to have access to it. He finally passed out around 0100, completely frustrated.

Logan's alarm beat him to the punch and woke him from his slumber at 0600. The sun shone faintly through the windows and immediately Logan began trying once again to work out how the terrorists got their hands on the C4. He walked to the air conditioner, turned it off, and opened the window allowing thick, warm air to bleed into his apartment like thick molasses. He leaned forward onto the windowsill and took a deep breath enjoying a slight salty touch to the air. Feeling revived despite his lack of sleep, he walked to BB-5 to meet the men.

"Hey Logan," said Lonnie as they shook hands.

"Lonnie, you've trained with explosives, right?"

"Hell yeah that's what I do man, you know that. Why?"

"I'll get to it. Just gonna wait for everyone so I don't repeat myself."

While they waited, Logan continued to work the situation over and over in his mind as the sun's rays pierced the glass in their room. It was going to be a wickedly hot day.

"Alright listen up. Samantha called me last night and asked for my help. I stayed up late trying to figure it out and I couldn't." He paused, kicking uncomfortably at the dirt. "So, we're gonna work on it all damn day if we have too. She told me that the explosives used in Chicago were American C4. It's the same stuff the terrorists used in Paris. Now, my question is, how are they getting it? All I could come up with is that a lot of people have access to the explosives and I have no idea how to narrow the search."

Lonnie looked at Logan now realizing the need was great for his expertise. "Logan!" Lonnie exclaimed causing everyone to snap their gaze to him. "When we were in our explosives school, the instructor was in charge of getting the C4. I remember he had to notify in advance for the training session and then had to sign it out."

"Is it easy to get large amounts for a training class?" asked Logan excited about having a plan of action forming.

"Oh God yeah. We had bricks of the stuff. We needed to practice setting the charges, disabling them, using them. We could have breached a hundred doors with the amount we were using."

"Is there any way to get it without checking it out?" asked Migs intensely.

"No, that's why you need to give notice."

"Is there any way we can see who's been conducting training classes and using the C4?" Tom asked while stroking his goatee.

"Yes," said Logan determined to find the person responsible for supplying the C4. "I'll talk to General Mitchell. He already told me he would help me in any way he could. Hopefully Dubs' guy in Chicago came through and you start watching video. I'm gonna go talk to the General."

General Anderson sat in his chair, his reading glasses on looking at the latest training schedules for Second Battalion. It was tedious work below his pay grade, but he insisted on being active in even the small day-to-day decisions.

Knock, knock, knock. Knuckles rapped soundly on General Anderson's door.

"Come in. What do you need Bobby?" the general asked in a jovial tone. The sergeant's name was Roberts, but everyone called him Bobby for short in boot camp. It stuck, and he liked it better than Sergeant Dick, which had also been used by his drill instructor.

"Logan Falcone says he needs to speak to you, sir."

General Anderson looked toward his left at the wooden clock hanging on the wall, noting the time was 1045; 15 minutes before a telephone conference with Secretary of State Doyle Smith and the Joint Chiefs to discuss the deployment of Second Battalion overseas.

"Send him in Bobby."

Bobby left and Logan walked into the rather spacious office of General Anderson. On previous occasions, Logan had taken note of General Anderson's collection of war relics. The walls were adorned with black and white pictures of a dozen different American monuments surrounding a framed, 30 by 20-inch remnant of a flag which was destroyed during the Pearl Harbor invasion. Directly behind General Anderson's desk hung several rifles, one representing each major war the U.S. has been in since, and including, the Civil War. It was all typically impressive to Logan, but this time, he was distracted.

"Logan, you don't look yourself. I'd have to guess that you're worried about something and I'll tell you that doesn't make me feel good. What's on your mind?"

"We need to keep this conversation between us," said Logan as he closed the door and approached the leather chair in front of the general's desk.

"Of course. If you need it to be that way, then it is."

"For now, yes. I got a call last night from an old friend who's working for the FBI. This person is right in the thick of this Chicago investigation and called me asking me for help."

"Help with what? Logan just spit it out I'm a grown man!"

"Sorry Mitchell. They said that the explosives used in Chicago came back as American C4. If you remember the press in France leaked it was C4 at the Eiffel Tower."

"Why come to me? I'm certainly interested in some bastard using our explosives on civilians, but I'm not sure what you're asking me. Especially if I'm not supposed to talk about this to anyone," General Anderson sat back into his chair, crossing his hairy arms.

"I used the guys in my class and we did some brainstorming. We know all C4 must be signed when taken from the inventory. I want to know if there is any way we can get our hands on all orders placed, location of the orders, and the signature of who was checking it out. We need to cross reference that with training dates, training operational needs, timeframe in relation to terror attack, and anything else we can think of."

"I can get that for you. It's going to take a day but it will be delivered to your apartment by 0600 tomorrow morning."

"Soon as you get it sir. We need it."

"Well I'll get it to you whenever it comes in, whether it's five minutes or 24 hours."

"Thanks Mitchell." The two men shook hands and locked eyes.

"If you find this son of a bitch I want him in my office before anyone else gets to talk to him. That's all I want for helping you."

"Deal."

General Anderson released his grip and Logan left taking a quick peek at the flag on the wall.

Dubs was alone in his apartment, sitting on the corner of his head, eyes locked onto the floor, but seeing nothing. His mind was racing, unable to process the sensory input. He was struggling with the realization someone inside the armed forces could do something against America. He joined out of respect, out of duty, to find a way to prove himself. He remembered the oath he took, the blood he shed, the work that continued to go into representing your country. His phone lit up on the bed next to him, and he was snapped back into reality.

"Hey Dubs, it's me. When you get this give me a call. Ironically, we had a guy going down to North Carolina for vacation. He owed me a favor and took the video down there for you. He'll be there this afternoon and wants to meet up ASAP. Talk to you later."

Dubs immediately called Tony back.

"Tony!" Dubs said smiling. "Got your message."

"Hey Dubs I gotta make it quick. The guy's name is Mike, and he's in the area. He said he'll meet you by the main gate and you can just pick them up."

"Easy enough. This guy must owe you something big huh?"

"You could say that. I got him his job."

"That's a good reason. How soon can he meet me?"

"Right now. Ten minutes good for you?"

"Yeah, I can get there. Thanks again Tony."

"Not a problem. Let me know if there's anything else. By the way, we got you just about everything within a two-mile radius so you have more footage than you asked for. It will take a long time to get through it all so good luck and I hope you realize what you're getting into."

"Haha, yeah Tony we know. Call your guy I'll meet him in ten."

"OK Dubs. Talk to ya' later. Oh, and before I forget, the missus says hi."

"Well hi back. Take it easy Tony."

BB-5's technology was being used to its full potential. Logan and

Dubs had just reviewed the size of the video files and realized the enormity of digital information they had in their hands. There were hundreds of hours of video from Water Tower Place covering the 12 hours of activity leading up to the explosion, covering every possible angle, entryway, store, bathroom and escalator. It included various other cameras across the city from traffic cameras to ATM machine cameras.

Each of the men were sitting at their monitors watching different closed circuit videos of the events from Saturday in Chicago, focusing on the Water Tower Place. Logan had reminded them of all the clues to look for: solitary, benign personality, forgettable, lingering, avoidance, and to look for backpacks. He reminded them how to scan the frame, locating individuals at the extremes of the image captured and not just what was directly in front of them. It was going to be tedious and boring, but the men were determined to find the terrorists.

Several hours of film went by without a peep. Everyone in the room was starting to fatigue as their eyes grew heavier and their minds began to wander. There had only been two instances where Logan put a video up on the large screen for all of them to evaluate, but both were false alarms.

"Alright guys let's call it an evening," said Logan as he looked at his phone, which read 2200. "We're all getting tired and the videos will be here in the morning. No workouts or training tomorrow. I think this is our priority for now. I should also be getting that list to cross-reference tomorrow for the C4. I'm expecting us to get on that."

"What time tomorrow?" asked Migs as he stretched his arms high overhead.

"I'll be here at 0700. You can all come at any time after that. Any other questions? Alright. Give me the disks. I'm not leaving them in here." All the men handed Logan their disks as they left the room.

PFC Charlie Gray was nervous as he held the envelope under his right arm. He received it only ten minutes ago. General Anderson was firm and intimidating when he told Charlie not to let anyone else see the envelope. Charlie nervously walked toward Logan's apartment, making sure to avoid taking shortcuts that would cause him to walk across the grass and draw attention. Looking down at his watch he noted it to be 0615. He then double-checked the address on the door, 27, and knocked.

Logan had been up since 0500 waiting for the package.

"Hi sir," said Charlie to the stranger standing before him. Logan simply nodded and took the envelope from Charlie. Logan barely remembered being where the young private now stood. Logan closed the door and left him standing in solitude, taking his first deep and relaxed breath of the day.

Logan took the envelope and immediately tore into it. He placed it on the table and began to page through the information. The sign-out logs were single spaced and included everything Logan requested. The date, requested and signed out, what it was to be used for and how much. Also, for the active events, where the C4 was actually detonated, there was a verification date of when the drill occurred. As he continued to scan the pages, now totaling 15, he quickly realized this was much more exhaustive and time consuming than he ever thought. He thought to call Samantha, but figured if she wanted more people to know she would've already asked them for help. He decided that the video surveillance would have to wait to find the source of the explosives.

Logan arrived at BB-5 at 0700 and saw Dubs, Migs, and Lonnie were already waiting to get into the room with their breakfasts in hand.

"How's it going Logan?" Dubs asked with a nod.

"Watcha' got there Logan?" Lonnie asked as curiosity took hold of him.

"It's our priority," Logan stated as he held it up in the air and walked toward the door.

The men were eager to get to work watching the videos even though the previous night it had been boring and tedious. Each man went home last night and tried to think like a terrorist and plan his own attack, and each man had their own agenda for the day.

"New priorities guys. I got the information from General Anderson about the C4. We have all the information here needed to legitimately consider who was taking the C4. I'll be honest, we're going to have to work a lot of hours. I already made copies so we all can look over it." He slapped the papers down onto the large table. "First off, let's go through and make sure anyone who made one order is taken off. We'll get started with that. Any questions?"

The men were going to perform what was asked of them no matter what their agendas had been. Plans change and they need to adapt, that had been ingrained in them for some time now. The Marines sat in silence, each with a highlighter looking for names that came up more than once. It was tedious, looking through 15 pages of single line text, like a large matching game. As the hours went by the sun shined brighter and brighter through the window as if encouraging the men to press forward. Some had begun to write out on a separate sheet so that they had a running tally. Ryan, who was meticulous with every detail, was also writing down the dates of the orders and pickups.

"Hey Logan, I'm done," Ryan said shortly before they were going to break for lunch around 1130.

"What do ya' got for me?" Logan asked as he walked over to Ryan and stood behind him eyeballing the handwritten notes.

"These are names of everyone who logged out C4 two or more times over the last few months. I think we should narrow the dates down to within a week or two of the attacks. That would shorten up the list some."

"That sounds good. Everyone else check his work." The rest of the men all took turns glancing over what Ryan had written down.

"Looks good to me boss," said Migs as he nodded his head in approval.

"Yeah me too," said Dubs, and then the rest of them nodded in turn with agreement.

"Alright let's all go get lunch. Take a break, clear your head. I'm pleased to see we're making headway in some area."

Chicago

Brent was determined to earn respect. He was sick of being the pitiful employee, the punch line in everyone's jokes. He had come into the office earlier than anyone else this mild Wednesday morning, to look at the Chicago tapes. He went through their secure entrance, greeting the regular officer with a smile and a relaxed salute quickly waddling down the wide corridor toward his desk. He swiped his ID, pushed through the heavy metal door, and took an immediate left toward the viewing room.

Brent tried to tell people last evening, it seemed as though they were getting nowhere by watching the tapes from the Water Tower Place but it fell on deaf ears. So, this morning, he decided to watch closed circuit video from shortly after the incident. Brent began watching a video from a security camera directly across the street from Water

Tower Place. His main focus was on individuals who seemed unaware that there was an explosion. Typically, people will flock to see what happened, or they run away in absolute horror. He was looking for someone who is indifferent. He focused one.

The man Brent followed on the tape was of Middle Eastern appearance. This particular individual was walking outside of the mall, approximately 30 minutes before the explosion. He noticed the man turned southbound on Michigan Avenue and continued to walk that way out of frame. Taking careful notation of the time, Brent then found a tape which would continue to monitor the man's as he walked. This second video was a little sharper than the video he was initially watching. It was a traffic camera from Michigan and Chicago avenues facing south, making it easy for Brent to follow the man for a while.

Brent was ultimately able to determine that the man strolling down Michigan Avenue was fairly stocky in his build; he also had a bit of a five o'clock shadow. The mystery man was not going into any stores, nor was he even considering them. Brent's interest grew more as the man continued to walk south without showing any interest in his surroundings. Brent followed the man as he continued over the Chicago River and into Millennium Park.

The moment the explosion happened was easy to see. Everyone began to panic and run in every direction, but this solitary man remained calm. Brent noticed the man approach the fountain. He sat down on the edge and grasped at his face several times. It was strange to see this man so calm as he observed the chaos around him. He then unbuttoned the top two buttons on his black polo shirt and it appears he was itching his chest frantically. Seconds later the man pulled off a mask and set it into the water. He then got up, took his shirt off revealing a blue tank top, and began to walk away. Brent had found something and nobody could take this away from him.

Brent made several phone calls to his superior, but no answer. He decided the next best thing to do was wait for Dominic at the main entrance and talk directly to the boss. Brent tried leaning against the wall in the hallway, but he was too anxious, and paced the halls periodically instead. Brent checked his watch for what seemed like the fifth time in the last minute and noted it was still 0645.

"Dominic!" Brent ran toward the head of the Chicago FBI office, words spilling from his lips like starch in boiling water.

"Can I help you?" Dominic asked stopping to fully take in Brent's disheveled appearance.

"I've been reviewing the tapes from Chicago and I know I found something. You need to look at this." Dominic reached up to grab the thumb drive from Brent's large, stubby hand.

"Well, let's go take a look at this in my office. Don't say another word until we get there. You understand?"

"Yes sir." The men walked purposefully toward Dom's office where they immediately stood in front of the computer screen as Dominic placed the thumb drive into the computer. He logged into his secure network and then handed the controls over to Brent to cue up the video.

"What are we looking for here?" asked Dom finally breaking the silence.

"Do you see that Middle Eastern man in the black polo shirt?"

"Yes," Dom said as he moved in toward the monitor for a closer look.

"He's what we've been looking for. Just watch. I tracked him all the way from the outside of Water Tower Place just 30 minutes before the explosion. I just had a feeling about the guy so I wanted to watch him."

"Well holy shit," Dom stood erect and smacked Brent on the back. "Well big boy this is huge. You get me the video of him traveling from the mall to this location. Put it all on one drive. I need to send this to a few people. This is great. What did you say your name was again?"

I don't know that I ever did, Brent thought to himself, annoyed at how flustered he had been. "It's Brent."

It was now 0715 and Brent made his way back down to the viewing room anxious to do his part. For the first time in his new job he may get respect, and maybe, even a smile or congratulations.

He scanned into the viewing room again and noticed two co-workers beginning the tedious task of running through gigs of digital media. He thought about getting up and grabbing coffee, heavy cream, and four sugars, but he stopped himself. He had an important role for the first time and he couldn't screw that up—not selfishly for himself.

As Brent scanned through the videos, cutting portions of tape and pasting them into a new file, he quickly became overwhelmed by the fact that this was more than interoffice politics. He had spent only five minutes completing the short rough cut digital file on the terrorist and decided to show his coworker, Ashley, who was as close a friend as he had. Just the day before she had grabbed some of his fries, which was the friendliest gesture he had in weeks.

He quietly called over to Ashley who was seated just a couple stations to his right. Her peppy curls bounced as she turned toward Brent, her eyes veiled annoyance. He smiled and waved her over. She looked at her screen rolling her eyes ever so slightly, and paused the video.

"What is it Brent?" Ashley asked from behind impatiently with hands on hips.

"Morning Ashley. I want you to watch this," Brent said as he cued up the tape to the beginning. "I came in early this morning and found this. I won't show you the entire thing but we'll go through quickly." Brent hit play and the Middle Eastern man with the black polo was on the screen. He fast-forwarded it through the boring parts of tracking him down Michigan Avenue. "Just stick with me Ashley. It gets good," Brent said as he heard Ashley shift her weight and sigh. "Here, let's go to the end," Brent fast-forwarded to the fountain. "Do you see the Middle Eastern guy in the black polo?"

"Yes."

"Well, focus on him." As they both looked, Brent began to smile and tap his foot on the floor to keep from talking. He was excited to have a colleague see what he had done. The moment came when the Middle Eastern man took off his mask revealing dark hair, and white skin.

"Oh my God Brent, what did you find?" Ashley pulled up a chair next to him to examine the video closer. Brent rewound the clip and they watched again. "You know, I can enhance the image of his face if we can get a good square shot."

"I think we can do that," a voice said from behind.

They both turned around and saw Adam Wanewright, the department head, sipping his coffee.

"So, when did you find this Brent?" Adam asked.

"This morning sir. I notified Dominic already and he watched it. I'm making him a copy of it so he can distribute it."

"Very good, very good," Adam said as he took another sip of coffee. "Everyone listen up," the unfazed supervisor belted to the media room now running at full capacity. "We have a new priority. Let's put this on the big screen."

Adam reached down and hit a button on Brent's computer that had never been touched. Seconds later, what was being viewed by Ashley and Brent, was now being watched by the whole office.

"I want everyone to take a good look at this son of a bitch because he's the key to Chicago. I need a full-frontal photo, and we're gonna find out who this guy is. Any questions? Didn't think so. Let's get moving."

"Morning, Chuck and Bill. I decided to conference you and fill you in on what we found. One of our tech people observed a suspect walking away from the incident in Chicago. They tracked him and found him taking off a mask and his shirt, throwing them into a fountain a couple miles away from the attack."

"Well I think we need to see this video," Chuck responded in a grumble.

"I agree," seconded Bill, a bit more optimistic in his tone.

"As do I gentlemen," said Dominic who was now taking note of the time. "I think we can get it to you well before lunch through the servers, but if you come down here we can do it ASAP."

"I'm on my way," said Chuck.

"I am, too. What's your team working on now? Did the video get a good look at him? Are we able to identify him?" asked Bill.

"It's pretty hazy, and to tell you the truth I only had a quick look at the video. Our people have several angles of the places in question so we're going to track this guy until we get a good image."

"Sounds like you're on it Dom. Be there within the hour." Chuck hung up the phone.

"Dom, you should call over to Ernie and let him know what you've got."

"That's my next call. See ya' soon." Bill hung up and Dominic accessed his second line and dialed Ernie Hayes in Washington.

"Ernie," the director growled as he picked up the receiver.

"Hey Ernie, it's Dominic Costa. I got something for ya'."

"OK Dom, lay it on me. Hope it's good."

"Me too sir. Our tech people found a suspect leaving the scene in Chicago."

"I'm listening."

"They tracked a Middle Eastern man leaving the scene for a couple miles. The explosion occurred and he's seen taking off a mask and throwing it into a fountain."

"I need to see the tape," Ernie said as he sat forward into his chair as if trying to dive through the phone. The mask made Ernie nervous because he knew that the government had once used masks that were quick and easy to get on and get rid of in the intelligence field. You needed something to get on and off within seconds but still be of high quality. Ernie remembered the later stages. It bothered him to hear terrorists possibly using it.

"I already have a man working on it. We should have it in the hour, then sent to you digitally immediately after. We're also trying to get a good frontal shot to see if we can get an ID on the perp."

"Well that's a good start Dom. Let me know as soon as you get it."

"Will do sir."

The tech department of the Bureau worked hard throughout the afternoon. By noon they had found several frontal shots and were now trying to decipher the true identity of the terrorist. He had short dark hair, a very wide jawline, and thin eyes. He was clean-shaven and had a very hard, worn look on his face. Nobody in the room recognized him immediately so they were putting him through all the known databases trying to get a hit. The image was also passed up the chain of command and everyone was looking into who the perpetrator was.

"Alright everyone, I'm proud of ya'. Got to love technology. Let's start looking for other leads. I think we have more than enough to work with. As you know, the ID process can take some time so let's not waste any. While we wait, we work. The CIA and FBI are accessing world databases as we speak. DMVs, military, medical, et cetera. Brent, good work," said Adam as he addressed the tech department. Brent felt an immediate rush of satisfaction and stuck his large chest out slightly, with pride.

Washington, D.C.

Washington was abuzz with the latest news from Chicago. The information had trickled up the chain of command and the image found itself in the hands of the Secretary of State Doyle Smith, whose heart was filled with even more hatred for the terrorists now that he had a face.

"I need Jenkins in here," Doyle said sternly as he keyed the phone to his assistant. Doyle was still bitter over the fact that Jenkins was so nonchalant over the intel regarding Chicago the Friday before the bombing. From now on he was going to be watching closely.

"Morning Mr. Secretary," Jenkins entered the office.

"I know your background Jenkins. Is this guy someone we need to worry about?" Doyle slammed the photo on the desk and pointed at the image of the strong-jawed man.

Jenkins stood motionless staring at the picture before him. Jenkins quickly ran through his overseas operations to make sure he never worked "on the record" with Vladimir before answering the question. Of course he wanted to say no, but if he had worked with him it would obviously look bad lying at a time like this.

"I'm not sure," Jenkins said expressionless. "I've worked with a lot of guys Mr. Secretary. I'm gonna have to look hard into this, but nothing strikes home with this guy immediately," Jenkins said as he diverted his gaze to meet Doyle's.

"Well let's find this guy. I want you to look in all databases, special forces, KGB, MI-5, everything. We need this guy now." Doyle was steaming and passionate about his role in the U.S. government. For the first time, Jenkins was seeing the full onslaught of a man lead by emotions.

"I'll get right on it, sir."

"Good. Let me know the second you find anything."

"Yes sir," Jenkins said with a small, but present lump in his stomach.

Jenkins walked into his office and locked the door. He logged into his computer and accessed his email.

We need to talk immediately.

He placed the message in his draft box and then logged off. The message should reach Amir within the day. Jenkins then called in a few favors accessing covert databases to find the identity of the terrorist. Jenkins knew that it would only be a few days before the government would score a hit on Vladimir Novikov, he just wanted to make sure Amir handled the situation before the intelligence community did. The screw-up seemed to increase in severity as Jenkins pondered the possibilities. For the first time in his twenty plus years of black ops and infidelities toward his own country, he was starting to sweat.

As Jenkins sat alone in his office, he began reflecting on a time long ago. He only thought of one thing in times of high stress. The only time in his life he was truly terrified. It helped him stay grounded in the truth of his everyday life now. Nothing compared to that moment, before or since, that fateful month in Afghanistan decades ago. He used to relive the moment daily, but he has since come to terms with the fact that it will never truly go away despite how many times he tried to make himself numb to it. Jenkins closed his eyes and gave into the flashback.

It was a late evening patrol through the mountains. Jenkins was a lieutenant and leading his platoon. Gunfire in the distance made him pause, and he told his men to get low and shut up. Jenkins went up onto a ridgeline approximately 50 yards ahead of the waiting platoon.

As he approached the crest he heard more gunfire, but this time, it was from behind. He dropped to his buttock and turned downhill toward his men. They were all screaming, shooting wildly into the trees at unseen targets. Something was shooting back at them, and they weren't missing. One by one his men were falling. Jenkins hurdled down the hill and into the woods toward the south attempting to find the shooters. It was difficult to see through the trees and the shadows as the sun was setting below the crest of the hill. Everything was an eerie color of gold and green. He never saw it coming. He was struck from behind and carried away.

He was drugged. He was forced to kill American solders with his own sidearm. He was told to take his own life and multiple times he tried, but the gun was always full of blanks when he put the gun to his tear-filled face. It took five days of torture until he broke. He broke so bad that he told them about how he stole baseball cards from a local store when he was eight. He told them of the time that he used to sneak into his friend's older sister's room and look at her panties. They laughed at him—all of them except one man. He sat in the corner, never saying a word, but watching every moment of every day. It haunted Jenkins. This man was always there. He never slept, he never ate, he never even drank as far as Jenkins knew. For the next several days after he broke, the silent man protected Jenkins, gave him food, water, talked. Jenkins told the man about his family, all his dislikes, his likes, where he came from. Jenkins told him locations of anti-air, ammo depots and where weak spots were at their forward operating base. But, Jenkins still got nothing of interest from this man, not even his name.

After two more weeks of torture, this silent man came to Jenkins, untied him, and told him two simple things. First, and most important, he would be in contact with Jenkins in the future. He said that anything Jenkins needed he would provide for, monetary or otherwise. The second thing was that Jenkins must do as he says, no matter what is asked of him.

Jenkins had heard of Stockholm syndrome, but he felt it was not appropriate for his own inner terror. The man he followed was a friend. He released Jenkins and he owed his life to the man. Jenkins was terrified of being imprisoned again and he knew that this secret man could, at any point, reveal what really happened during those four weeks. He had killed Marines with his own service weapon. He had told the enemy where their forward operating base was, which made Jenkins accessory to killing dozens more Marines when cars crashed through the security gates and blew up. He didn't want that publicized. He had worked for decades to rectify that wrong. Who cared if civilians on any continent had to die? Soldiers die every day.

chapter
SEVENTEEN

The sun was hot and the breeze cool as Amir strolled along the beach in Barcelona, Spain. He decided to take a walk before his dinner and enjoy the sand in his toes. He'd been watching the news for much of the last few days, staying up to date with any news from Chicago. He wasn't worried, but if something leaked through the press he would have a head start.

He enjoyed looking at beautiful women as they packed up their belongings and headed home after a day at the beach. He smiled at a few and they smiled back, one even stopped to say hello to the tall, clean-cut Amir. They conversed shortly in Spanish. Amir invited her for drinks later that evening and she politely accepted. Amir then walked to his apartment two kilometers from the beach.

The apartment was simple and furnished. It was part of a timeshare that he had purchased. It allowed him to visit twelve different condos in different countries around the world, which suited him nicely. In fact, the four other terrorists were partaking in this luxury. Nikita was in Mexico, Basil was in China, Vladimir was in Italy, and Sharif was in Chile. Amir liked the separation from work and "home," never having to go to the office.

He walked across the living room toward the window and sat down at his rather simple bamboo desk. He pulled his laptop out of his satchel bag and opened his email. Secretly from the rest of the team, there was a second email account in which Amir and Jenkins spoke in private. The purpose of this email address was in case the inevitable occurred and one of them was found out. Amir had checked this email dozens of times over the years and it was just going through the motions, but it was part of the protocol.

He checked the draft box and for the first time there was a message.

We need to talk immediately.

Amir didn't hesitate. He picked up his cellphone, took careful note of the 1945 Barcelona time, knowing that Washington, D.C. was six hours behind. Jenkins would still be in his office so he needed to get in touch with him discreetly. He placed the cellphone down on the desk, and instead emailed him back. He was confident Jenkins would check the email before the end of the day.

Received. Contact me through my cellphone I will be available.

Tonight was going to be a working night, regardless of who he met on the beach. He contemplated what the bronzed beauty might wear to the bar. The venue was probably one of her favorites since it was she who recommended they go there. Amir assumed she'd know a few people there and she felt safe. He sat back folding his arms behind his head, and daydreamed about what could have been a fun night.

Chicago

The office slowly emptied after 1900, until only Dominic and Samantha remained. The present silence contrasted with the roaring that occurred just hours earlier. It was the same lightheaded, ears-ringing feeling that occurs after listening to a concert.

"So, what are your thoughts?" Dom yelled to Samantha from across the office. Sam got up slowly from her chair and walked toward him. She'd rather not yell across the office, even if it was empty.

"No opinion yet. I just really hope we find out who this guy is Dom. I'm a little nervous about the other thing we have going," she said cross-armed, leaning onto the doorway.

"I want nothing to do with it but I do trust you completely. Having said that, I'm a little nervous because YOU'RE nervous," he smirked.

"Well, don't be. I know what I'm doing, I just want it done faster, you know?"

"Absolutely."

They strolled through the lobby remaining silent for the first time that day. It was nice to have thoughts that weren't immediately spewing out of ones' mouth during brainstorming sessions. They both waved and smiled briskly as they walked past the security desk. The parking lot was nearly empty and they both had a visual on their cars that were unmoved the past 12 hours.

"Goodnight Dom. Call me if you hear anything."

"Ditto," said Dom with a smile. "You know if Logan finds something I might have to get him a job." Dominic gave a slight, accepting smile.

Samantha returned the smile while saying, "You couldn't pay him nearly enough."

Washington, D.C.

General Jenkins had checked his email hours earlier, but he waited till 2100 hours to call Amir. He knew the call volume at NSA would dramatically increase at this time, helping the conversation slip under the radar. Jenkins had been tempted to use his private secure line, however, if suspicions grew toward him, his phone records would be evidence enough for a conviction. Jenkins took this into account and decided to make the call from a payphone some 20 miles from his house.

"Yes," Amir said as he still sat in the same spot he settled into hours before.

"Vladimir was seen. He was lazy and revealed himself in public."

"What's my role here? His mistake. He dies, not on me," Amir said confidently, defiantly.

"Make it look accidental or natural. The government's going to find out who he is within a couple of days and then they'll hunt for him. It would be best if they never found him."

"OK. It will take at least two days."

"I'm aware, but you have a two-day head start so don't waste any time. Do you know where he is?"

"Exactly where he is."

"Good. I want you to do this yourself. No help. The fewer the better."

"Couldn't agree more."

"Notify me when it's done. Do your fucking job. Remember I can destroy you in one sentence. I own you."

"Will do, adiós."

Amir hung up the phone and immediately headed for the door. He had a plane to catch. As he locked the door behind him he began going through his mental cache of techniques he could use to subdue Vladimir. He exited the building and got into a cab.

"El Prat," Amir said to the driver who quickly set off. He glanced down at his phone, 0345, and began working out the possible flights he could take to end up in Florence, Italy where Vladimir was currently staying. Amir was starting to feel energized and exhilarated at the opportunity for a challenge again. He sat back in the seat and smiled, listening to the classical guitar sing through the speakers in the cab. Amir allowed himself to daydream about the day when he could finally take Jenkins out of the equation and have his own life back.

chapter
EIGHTEEN

The week was flying by and everyone was working as fast as they could, trying to beat some unseen countdown. The longer the terrorist had since the incident, the more likely they were to escape. But now, with a couple of leads, the intelligence community was starting to get some traction. There were a few other possible hits, but none of them panned out like the one Brent had found on Wednesday. The JTTF had tracked another suspicious individual out of the mall but they lost him as he walked into a building on Wabash. The DHS and FBI were pulling hotel registries, running all the names through their databases trying to generate a hit for any wanted, watched, or known aliases of special operations technicians from anywhere in the world. No hits had come up so far, and it was already Friday morning, six days after the attack.

"The mask used in the crime was a lead in itself and meant that well-funded and knowledgeable individuals were at this particular attack," Ernie said through the receiver frustrated with the fact that he had repeated this for the third time.

"I understand what you're saying Ernie, but Jenkins still feels like it's that group in Afghanistan we should be targeting," said the Secretary of State. "I'll tell you what. If we don't hear anything related to this

Afghan group by the end of the day, I'll put my priorities elsewhere. We have a team headed by analyst Winters' contact over there, and they're watching them like hawks."

"Alright sir. I just want you to be informed. Trust me, the mask that's being used by at least one terrorist is something I know a lot about. Several years ago, I was part of a development team that brought these to life, so forgive me for being a little emotional about the work of colleagues, as well as myself being used against the U.S. For Christ sakes Doyle, the mask was designed to prevent this from happening!" He raised his voice for the last point.

"I understand Ernie. Keep me in the loop."

"Obviously!" Ernie hung up. He placed his hands on his head and pushed his wavy salt and pepper hair back causing his eyebrows to rise. Again, he was disappointed with Secretary Doyle's reliance on Jenkins for what should be his call.

Ring. Ring. Ring. Ring. Ernie picked up the phone with one hand still grasping his hair in the other.

"We got him sir," the voice on the other end said with an eerie calmness to his voice.

"Who is he," Ernie said as he slowly released the tension to his scalp.

"You're gonna love this. Vladimir Novikov—ring a bell, sir?" Ernie let the name sink in for several seconds. The name was obviously Eastern Bloc, but he couldn't recall the name. "He's former KGB."

"Are you certain?" Ernie asked hard into the receiver.

"Ninety-eight percent match using facial recognition sir. We then found a picture of him on file and used an aging program and it's a dead-on match sir. I'm sending the image to you on the server." Ernie quickly accessed the secure folder and began the quick download of the side-by-side comparison picture.

"Yeah, that looks good alright. Great work. We need known associates and pull up everything we got on this guy. Where he sleeps, what his favorite food is, how he puts the toilet paper on the holder, everything. We need to find this guy ASAP."

"You can count on it sir."

Ernie hung the phone up and immediately called Secretary Smith back to tell him the news.

"This is Ernie Hayes I need to speak with the secretary, it's urgent."

"Hi Ernie, one-second, he's with General Jenkins," a sweet, even voice said on the other line almost calming Ernie down.

"Thanks."

"Ernie I've got Jenkins here. I'm going to put you on the speaker phone and he can explain the theory about the Afghan group."

"Hi Ernie. Here's the—"

"The terrorist's name is Vladimir Novikov!" Ernie interrupted Jenkins impatiently, causing all conversation to stop.

"Please repeat that," Secretary Smith asked as he turned the volume up on the phone.

"Vladimir Novikov. He's a former KGB officer. We don't know much about him yet, but we're getting the info from NSA as we speak."

"That name rings a bell," Jenkins said as he began to plan his next few sentences carefully. "I believe we had a few conversations with him during the cold war. He was trying to buy his freedom by giving some of my black ops guys information. I personally never saw him but the name, I definitely remember the name."

"Do you think he would have bombed Chicago as a type of revenge for not trading intel for safe haven in the U.S.?" Secretary Smith asked as he folded his eyebrows into an intense scowl.

"There's no telling what men are capable of," Jenkins said as he turned away from Doyle Smith, looked down, and began pacing the room. Doyle had just given him his biggest out. Vladimir is the leader of his own rogue team. "I wouldn't put it past him," Jenkins said looking up at the art on Doyle's wall. "He could just be one bitter asshole out for revenge. Who knows? A guy like him could have found several others who hate America too. That might be your team. Make sure you look for known associates with your background check."

"Ahead of you on that one General," Ernie said on the other end of the line. "I'm gonna get going. I gotta call Chicago. We'll be in touch."

"Alright Ernie good work. You were right about the profile of the terrorist."

"Thank you, sir."

Jenkins stood with hands on hips, face stern, eyes focused on the table. He estimated it would be at least a week before they had a fix on any of Vladimir's known contacts, and possibly longer to find him. He was confident in Amir's ability to handle the situation within the next few days. Jenkins' face relaxed and his hands slipped down off his hips and he sat down relaxing back into a chair. His hands were clean, and he was still safe.

Chicago

Dominic and Samantha were talking in his office as they both drank their coffee on Friday morning. Dominic had bags under his eyes. Samantha decided that putting her hair up ran a distant second to getting a few more minutes of sleep this morning.

"I slept like crap last night," Dom said to Samantha as he plopped down into his chair. "I kept thinking my phone was going to ring so I woke up every 15 minutes."

"Yeah, same here. I guess in this case, no news is just no news."

"Guess so. Have you heard anything about the C4?"

"Not yet. I figured it would take a while, but I'm pretty confident we'll hear something within the next few days," Samantha said as she blew on the top of her coffee.

"Dominic, line two for you. It's Ernie from Washington, says it's important," Cheryl's voice said through the intercom.

"Thank you," Dom said as his eyes inquisitively met Samantha's.

"Hi Ernie I got you on speaker. Samantha Baker is here with me if that's OK."

"Absolutely. Get right to the chase then. NSA notified me a few minutes ago that the terrorist seen in Millennium Park is Vladimir Novikov. He's former KGB and that's all we know right now. Jenkins in Washington says he knew the name and that he tried buying asylum in the states for intel, but we didn't help him. Possibly a grudge thing."

"What do you think Ernie?" asked Dom reaching for more intel.

"I got nothing more than that Dom. Off the record, that Jenkins is a snake. I'm watching him 'cause something just seems off about the guy." Ernie was going to say more about the relationship between Jenkins and Secretary Smith regarding who really runs the office, but he didn't feel as though Dom needed to know all his opinions.

"Yeah, I don't really know him."

"Alright Dom keep working hard out there. Eyes always open for another attack, however unlikely it may seem at this point."

"Absolutely sir, take care."

"Well Sam what ya' think of that?" Dom asked hanging up the phone.

"I think Winters and his guys deserve a few days R&R for having to watch those Afghanis. What a waste of time."

"I agree. Things are starting to snowball now Samantha. Hopefully, we get our hands on this guy and question him. Maybe we can offer him asylum now if he tells us how the operation worked."

"What if he is the operation Dom?"

"Let's just work one detail at a time. NSA is going to run his known associates and get all the info they can, so I think we need to just stay on the tapes and the C4."

"Sounds good."

"Alright, let's go tell everyone what we heard, maybe we can backtrack Vladimir from the mall to his hotel now that we know what we're looking for. We may be able to see other terrorists if they're staying in the same hotel."

"Good idea Dom, I'll go tell them what to look for."

Camp Lejeune

The base had evaporated away and was replaced by one room full of paperwork for the men in Logan's select group. For the last several days they had done nothing except go through videos and paper trying to solve the source of the explosives. The first day was quick, they narrowed down the search significantly, but there was no way of differentiating the last three possibilities. One individual was in the U.S. Army as an explosives instructor, a second was an anti-terrorism agent working for a JTTF as a special operations officer, and a third was a Marine captain who also worked with demolitions training. All three of these men had checked out explosives within the two weeks leading up to both attacks, and all three took enough to cause the damage in Paris and Chicago. It was frustrating for all the men in the room, except Logan. He had the answer.

"OK guys, I've had enough of this. We're going to talk to all these guys. I'm gonna go talk to Mitchell and he can have someone question the Marine out in San Diego. I'll call Samantha and get her people on the JTTF officer, which leaves us with the Army guy out of Fort Jackson,

South Carolina." Logan looked down at the table picking up the final list. "Maybe now I can teach you some of the hardest techniques. Interrogation."

"Fine with me," Lonnie said with intent and fire in his eyes.

"Yeah, I think everyone's ready to get out of this room," Dubs said groaning and leaning back in his chair.

"Migs, you got enough training in that bird of yours?" Logan asked Captain Martinez.

"I could use a few more," Migs responded, crossing his meaty forearms and smiling through his bright, white teeth.

"Alright, call Lieutenant Henderson. We're not gonna leave him behind."

"You got it boss."

"OK everyone we'll get lunch there. Meet me at 1030 that's . . . 45 minutes from now, on the pad. I gotta let the general know."

"Yeah baby!" Dubs yelled with the excitement of a boy who was suddenly allowed to play with a toy he'd been eyeballing for hours.

"Haha, take it easy man," Tom said laughing and shaking his head.

The men filed out of the room eager to meet the EOD instructor Sergeant Heath Grainger. Logan went toward the main building straight for General Anderson's office.

Logan reached the general's office and was immediately allowed to enter.

"Morning sir," Logan said as the men shook hands.

"Well, to what do I owe the honor Mr. Falcone. Sir? Don't know if I've ever heard you address me like that before." Both the men shared a brief smile. "What's on your mind Logan. Did you find our man?"

"Not exactly, sir, but we got it down to three. One's a Marine, a second in the Army, and both are explosives instructors. A third is an operative for a JTTF team. I think we need to get all three of these guys ASAP so I'm taking my guys to Fort Jackson, South Carolina immediately on a Blackhawk. Of course, if that's OK with you. I thought you could have someone talk to the Marine in San Diego, and the FBI would handle the JTTF operative."

"Not bad Logan. Let me make one phone call then I'm comin' with you."

"Sir?"

"I thought you understood our agreement. I want to be the first to talk to this guy. I may be biased, but no Marine would do this. I'm gonna have someone pick this guy up out in San Diego, but in the meantime, I'm going with you to Fort Jackson. Sound good soldier?" General Anderson asked causing a rush of memories and emotions back into Logan. He was so green once; so confident in his abilities, invincible. It reminded him of how vulnerable and terrified he now was in comparison.

General Anderson and Logan burst through the doors of the main building and strode toward his Humvee, which had pulled up as they reached the street. "Perks of the position," General Anderson nudged Logan as he saluted the driver and slid into the back seat.

"The airfield, sir?"

"You got it."

Logan and the general both got into the back seat for the short ten-minute drive. Logan enjoyed the familiarity of the large back seat.

"Logan what do you think about this whole situation?" General Anderson interrupted Logan's daydreaming.

"I think I don't know enough to make an appropriate evaluation. Although, I know my friend told me there have been more breaks in the case, but she couldn't reveal them at the time. I'm sure I can give you a more accurate picture later, but the one thing that bothers me about it all is that it's our explosives."

"Yeah, no shit. You keep me in the loop on everything you hear."

"Will do, sir." Logan's mind rushed with thoughts about Paris and some of the questionable things that happened there. "General do you know anything about what happened in Paris?"

"Not much."

"Well, it was our C4. The guy who leaked that information mysteriously died. On top of that, I know messages were sent to the U.S. regarding an Operation Cancer and that it was a success with no outside casualties. Could you find me an Operation Cancer?"

"I'll see what I can do Logan. I'm guessing you think it was a black op to kill that Frenchie?"

"Not sure. But I do know in order to make an informed decision, you need to be informed," Logan said looking at General Anderson for the first time since entering the Humvee.

"I agree. That's why I'm comin' with you. We're here."

The men climbed out of the car to see the Blackhawk that was just finishing its preflight check.

"How much do you weigh sir?" Logan asked the general nonchalantly.

"A buck eighty-five," the general said.

Logan ran past the men and straight to the helo where Migs and Lieutenant Dave Henderson were working the numbers.

"Migs!" Logan yelled over the noise of the rotors spinning.

"Hey, Logan, sorry we're about ten minutes late, it took a while to get a hold of Dave."

"No problem. The general is comin' with, work the numbers with an extra 185 pounds."

"You got it boss," Migs said and Logan waved to Dave who was less animated than last time.

Logan walked back to the men and ushered them over to the general who was standing 100 yards from the helo in silver rimmed aviator glasses and his hands on his hips. As they approached, the men saluted. "Alright the general is comin' too. He wants to question Sergeant Heath himself and I have no problem with that. Do any of you?" Logan said addressing his men. "Didn't think so."

The squeal from the turbine on the Blackhawk pierced the air and Logan looked up to see Lieutenant Henderson give the takeoff signal. "Let's move!" shouted Logan who then led the men to the chopper. They climbed in from both sides and decided to close the doors for this flight. With a quick vertical takeoff, they were off in a west, northwesterly direction toward Fort Jackson.

"Well General what angle are you gonna take with this guy?" asked Logan breaking the nervous silence of the chopper.

"I'm pretty sure he's gonna know something's up so I'm going to just lay it on him, see what he says," Anderson said with a shrug looking out the window.

"Do you want me in there with you?"

"Yeah Logan you can come in. You have more experience with this, so if he doesn't come clean then you can use some of your tricks. Teach these other guys something while you're at it," General Anderson said pointing nonchalantly around the chopper at the men.

"That's my plan. We're gonna need a closed-circuit camera 'cause I don't think it'll work out having all these guys in the room with us. Our guy will clam up."

"Good point. We'll get it all," General Anderson said while staring out the window at the world far below.

Fort Jackson

"Bye sweetheart, I'll see you in a few hours," Sergeant Grainger said to his wife before kissing his young daughter, Kristen, on the forehead and going back to work. He wasn't sure if Kristen even felt the kisses. She was suffering from a rare, and expensive, neurologic condition that left her immobile from the waist down. It was tough for Grainger to think about having to take care of Kristen for the rest of her life, but he loved her.

It was a short walk back to the demo school where Grainger instructed. As he entered his office he was surprised to see two men already sitting inside. One was dressed in civilian clothes, and the other, a one-star general from the Marine Corps.

"Excuse me," Grainger said as he took a step back and began to close the door he just opened.

"Sergeant you're in the right place," General Anderson said as he stood up and walked to the door, pushing it back open. "I'm General Mitchell Anderson and this is my associate," Anderson said nodding his head toward Logan.

"I'm confused," Grainger said as he took a few more cautious steps into the office while General Anderson closed the door behind him and locked it.

"Well to be honest Grainger, we are too. I'm a straightforward guy, and I'm about to get to the point. Why don't we all have a seat?" There were only two chairs in the office so General Anderson and Sergeant Grainger took them. Logan preferred to stand during interrogations anyway. "I need to know one thing Sergeant, where did you perform your last four training ops with C4?"

Heath "Shifty" Grainger was stunned. His mind was floating as thoughts of Kristen, his wife, his career, and Amir all wafted through his mind. Grainger was no longer standing still in his office, but frantically running in his mind. It took everything he had not to fall apart right at that moment.

"Well sir, I have my training logs in my file cabinet. I can grab them?" Grainger was buying time. He was afraid that if he opened his mouth the wrong thing might come out. He was honest when confronted with serious situations. The sergeant got his paperwork and handed it to Anderson who opened it and paged through the information.

"How long have you worked in the demo school?" Logan asked as he stepped away from the shelf he was leaning against and crossed his arms.

"Eight years," Grainger said calmly and with confidence.

"How much C4 is used during each training operation? I only ask because after eight years of training I would think you had it down."

"Well, yes, you're right. I typically use the same amount with every training operation," Grainger said becoming slightly more comfortable with the way the conversation was going.

"I just find it interesting that you took out more than usual on a couple key dates Sergeant. July second, and July nineteenth. Can you explain why this was the case?" Logan queried as he walked to the sergeant's desk and leaned his fists on it. "Here, look for yourself," Logan pulled from his pocket the list of names, dates, and amount of C4 checked out. "If you notice, your name is highlighted in blue. On those two specific dates, why was double the normal amount taken out? Wait, don't answer that. General sir, can you look up these dates in his training logs?"

"Sure can," General Anderson said breaking his stare at the sergeant. "Here ya' go." General Anderson slapped the binder on the desk pointing out the first date to Grainger.

"Explain," Logan said as he once again crossed his arms and waited. Grainger slumped in his chair. His head was blank and he felt pressure release from his soul. Looking up he began to speak.

"He contacted me a couple times . . . he needed the explosives but I had no idea why . . . I think he used the fact that I needed money for my daughter's medical bills. How did he know about her? He knew everything about me and I know absolutely nothing about him . . . the drops were secret and never the same . . . I feel ashamed for doing it . . . I know something bad must have happened because you guys are here, but I swear I didn't know why he wanted it! Just that he paid well."

Shifty paused for a moment and looked at his hands. "He knew so much about me . . . I thought maybe he was black ops. Someone not to question. Not a terrorist. It's hitting home how stupid I am . . . I'm ready for any punishment you have to give me. I can help find him if you want."

"I could rip your throat out right here right now you traitor," General Anderson said grabbing Sergeant Grainger, lifting him out of his chair, and slamming him against the wall. "What a fucking pussy. Using your daughter as an excuse. Buck up son you're not the only one struggling!"

"Hang on a minute General," Logan said walking around the desk and grabbing the general's hand from around Grainger's neck. Grainger sunk down to the floor and gasped for his next few breaths.

"Logan maybe you should leave," Anderson barked as he threw Logan's hand away. Anderson quickly bent down and grabbed Grainger by his shirt and lifted him back to his feet punching him in the stomach. Grainger doubled over in pain and General Anderson reached back for a right cross to send Grainger back to the floor.

"Do you know how many American families are suffering greater than you are?!" Logan grabbed Anderson's arm not allowing him to throw another punch. Anderson looked back at Logan with fire in his eyes, hardly recognizing Logan.

"Sir, I have an idea," Logan whispered with a calmness in his voice that began to quench the flames burning within Anderson.

"Better start talking fast 'cause right now, I's about to be judge and jury. Kill this bastard right here and now."

"Alright sit back down," Logan said as everyone took a minute to compose themselves. Grainger straightened up his shirt and leaned forward in his chair giving into the pain and spasms in his abdomen. "Grainger, how often are you contacted by the buyer?"

Grainger sat frozen, eyes fixed on General Anderson.

"It's only been two times," Grainger flinched seeing Anderson adjust himself in the chair.

"How does he contact you?" Logan asked gently.

"Who the fuck cares Logan! How much time are we gonna waste? He's a traitor. We're gonna take your daughter away you son of a bitch. How's that sound?"

"Answer the question Grainger," Logan insisted, never taking his eyes off the specialist.

"Telephone. Different number every time."

"Did he call your cellphone or house?" Logan asked, as his own heart began to race. This was like a puzzle with missing pieces and he had a feeling one piece was about to be discovered.

"Cellphone. Conversations are really short."

"Can you remember the dates that he called you?"

"No, nothing exact, within a week from when I got the C4," Grainger said while looking down at the desk. His eyes began to water and he was fighting back the tears. His chest was becoming tight and a lump was growing in his throat.

"Here's the deal Sergeant. We're the only one who knows what happened. We're keeping this conversation in this room. You're going to keep living your life. If the buyer contacts you, you contact us. That simple. Do you understand?" Logan said as he walked around the desk, placing a firm hand on Grainger's shoulder and glanced at General Anderson who nodded in approval.

"I will," Grainger said as tears began to slide down his face, the weight of his treason finally landing on his shoulders. Logan handed Grainger a business card and the two men walked out of the room closing the door, allowing Grainger a moment to collect himself.

The Blackhawk landed back at Camp Lejeune at 1630 and the excited men got off. Migs began their checklist. Logan was satisfied with what had occurred during the visit with Shifty just hours before. General Anderson, on the other hand, was very unsettled, and wished he was still asking Sergeant Heath Grainger the same question: "Why?"

"Well General, I appreciate you comin'," Logan said as the men were about 50 yards from the chopper.

"You really haven't lost your touch Logan, that's for sure," General Anderson said with a sigh. "I just hope he calls."

"I think he will Mitchell."

"Yeah, well good learning experience for your boys. They seemed impressed on the way home."

"Yeah, they get excited about a lot of things. Have a good evening General," Logan said as they shook hands and parted ways. Logan then turned around and noticed the rest of the men were still milling about talking. Logan wasn't in a hurry so he just stood and waited for one of them to look in his direction. When Lonnie finally looked his way, Logan gave him a gesture to come over to him.

"OK guys. General Mitchell lost his shit in there. I wasn't expecting that. I'm a bit disappointed in how he reacted but didn't want to say that in the helo. I would have hit him with harder questions, making him sweat more, try to bleed it out of him. I'm not certain we got everything out of him. I didn't have a chance to talk to him the way I wanted. But, at least he came to trust me following the general's abuse. I'm sure he'll call. Until then we need to focus on the tapes. Find another terrorist if we can. At the very least, you saw how to save an interrogation. I'm heading out guys. Gonna call Sam and let her know about Grainger."

Logan knew he had at least a ten-minute walk back to his room so he decided it was finally time to call Samantha and give her the news.

"Hi Logan," Samantha said as she sat back in her chair at work and rubbed her eyes. She had spent the last three hours reading reports on possible sightings of Vladimir, none of which had looked promising. "Let me call you back on a secure line." Several seconds passed as she picked up the LAN line in her office.

"I've got some news for you if you're ready to hear it," Logan said picking up on the first ring. He smiled knowing how happy the news would make Samantha.

"Thank God someone is making progress," Samantha sighed.

"We found the source of the C4 and he's an Army sergeant. He said he's gonna help us by letting us know when this terrorist calls him again. He's selling to the guy because he says he needed the money for his kid's medical bills. Whatever. I couldn't care less about why he has been doing it. We can handle the sergeant and I'll keep you in the loop. Any news on your end?"

"We've got nothing new. We know the guy in Chicago and his name is Vladimir Novikov but other than that we have nothing. Right now, we have people using facial recognition trying to find where he stayed, how he got into Chicago, his aliases and his known associates, but nothing so far. I'll let you know too Logan."

"Sounds good. Call me if you need me," Logan said as he reached his front door.

chapter
NINETEEN

Amir was enjoying the local food at a small Venetian eatery late in the afternoon. He was a sucker for local venues and found himself immersed in the Italian culture despite being there for less than 24 hours.

"Grazie," he said to the beautiful Venetian woman who brought his wine. Amir gave her a subtle smile and wink as she walked away, and her wavy brown hair seemed to bounce a little more. He was relaxed and patient. Of all the places he had a timeshare, this one was the most relaxing. He watched people walk down the old brick street and heard the loud discussions of a group of men fighting over whose ball was closest to the pallino as they played bocce.

Amir remained observant in position as the sun finally began to set behind some of the old brick buildings across the street, and cascaded beautiful orange hues toward the top of the rolling horizon. As he walked into the cafe to pay, Amir saw his waitress and she smiled at him, this time nervously pulling at her apron. He waved and quickly turned to avoid a conversation. He knew she was already intrigued, and girls that easily interested were of no interest to him. He was on serious business anyway, and that was the only reason he was in Florence: to kill one of his own.

Vladimir left the condo about 2100 hours and went down to the local bar he found two nights before. It was one of the few bars in

Florence that had a selection of Russian vodka and that pleased him greatly. Vladimir was a creature of habit and rarely tried new things so it was difficult for him to enjoy Italy. He found himself sitting in the corner just as he had two nights prior, and talked to no one. He rarely looked up from his glass. He tried to get a buzz quickly. At least that was something familiar for him to hang onto.

He hated the Italian character. Everyone was family-oriented, loud, and constantly trying to entice you to try everything from food and wine to games. He deeply hated the language, especially the inflection in the voice. He walked up to the bar asking for a bottle of vodka while several of the locals were yelling in the opposite corner over something mundane, he assumed. He returned to his corner and, gradually over the course of the next two hours, finished the bottle.

It always took a lot to get Vladimir a buzz, but he didn't just stop there tonight. He was stumbling as he left his spot in the corner, creating a bit of a scene as he exited the bar. A couple of the men tried to steady him but Vladimir would have none of it and quickly wrenched his arms from their hands, giving them a glazed over look of displeasure, and left the bar.

The walk home was uneventful. He tried looking up at the stars but that just made him dizzy. A couple of times he just about lost his balance crossing his legs back and forth over one another in a scissoring gait. He walked down the last winding side street and ultimately reached the condo, fumbling momentarily with the keys. He opened the door, turned on the light, and was immediately brought out of his drunkenness by a tall, dark man standing in the foyer.

"Amir, what are you doing here?" Vladimir asked as he quickly closed the door.

"You were seen Vladimir, you were lazy!" Amir said hitting him in the face with brass knuckles.

"That's not possible—I was careful." Vladimir was on the ground spitting out blood and teeth barely holding onto his consciousness.

"How careful could you have been? They have you on tape, they have you taking off the mask Vlad! They have a picture of your face and are looking for you in the databases. You're out Vlad." Amir made the last comment calmly as he knelt close to Vladimir's face.

Vladimir began to stumble around again but this time it was different. His thigh muscles were firing uncontrollably and his hands began to cramp. He felt nauseous and confused. His heart began to race and his pupils dilated.

"What did you do to me?" Vladimir said as he lay on the floor, writhing in pain as his intestines began to spasm. He then began to feel an invisible flame scorching his skin.

"You don't recognize this?" Amir said in a calm voice as he sat down slowly on the floor next to him. "You've used this before on several people. I know, because you're the one who introduced it to me."

Amir grabbed Vladimir's head and looked into his eyes that were now bloodshot, impossible to discern the iris from the pupil.

"Poison," Vladimir said through his fractured teeth as he slowly slipped away.

"Oh, well that's easy. I'll just tell you since you don't have long to live. You see Vlad, you're an easy read. For example, I knew that you wouldn't be out during the day, so I ate an early dinner just two blocks from this condo. I wanted to make sure you were still here before I came after you. I knew that you would probably have found a place that sold Russian vodka just a few blocks from here, because I mentioned it to the owner a few months ago. How ironic that something I had designed to be a nice perk for you, ended up making this job so much easier. I knew you would come home drunk and just come right into the house so that's why I put contact poison right on the doorknob when I saw you stumbling down the street."

Vladimir lay silent. He was breathing, but it was very rapid and shallow. Amir reached down for a pulse and found that it was very erratic. He knew it would only be moments before Vladimir died.

Amir began to clean the mess Vladimir created in his panic. He picked Vladimir up and took him out to his car. Amir knew just the spot to put his body. A place one hour from the condo that offered Vladimir a nice view of the ocean every day, or until a hiker found him. Amir looked around one last time and made sure to turn off the light and lock the door. It was his timeshare after all.

As he looked left he caught his reflection in the mirror. His eyes were dark, like hollow pits under his furrowed brow. The light from directly above was accentuating the dark contrasted features. His wrinkles appeared deeper, well defined. He had a thick, stubble beard that revealed little of his once soft, smooth skin. Amir smiled, turned out the lights, and left.

Washington, D.C.

Jenkins spent most the afternoon in his own office looking through files of black ops he was a part of over the years. He was looking for anything linking to Vladimir, and came up with nothing. Jenkins was in the clear even if the government found Vladimir. He leaned back in his black leather chair and took in a deep breath as he looked around his plain office.

The walls were void of any artwork or memorabilia, and were still only primed from when he first took the office over eight months ago. The windows were large, allowing light in, but Jenkins rarely opened the blinds. His desk was the only piece of furniture worth mentioning in his office and that was because it was from the previous resident. The dark cherry wood and fine handcrafted detailing stood out against the plain room.

Jenkins took note of the time, 1700 hours, and decided it was time to check his email. The most recent saved draft was new to his eyes.

It's done. I'm going back to Spain.

This put Jenkins even more at ease knowing Vladimir would never be found. He logged off his email, grabbed his suitcoat, and walked out of his plain office.

Chicago

The search had begun for Vladimir Novikov. The CIA and FBI were investigating the existence of aliases and known associates, while the NSA and FBI were figuring out if Vladimir had been traveling under any of his pseudonyms. It was easy work to look into the vast amount of data the government had collected on this attempted defector, it would just take a little time. So far there were eight known aliases, and a mountain of known associates that the agencies would have to comb through to determine the likelihood of each possibility. In the meantime, dozens of technicians were looking at videos and using the latest facial recognition software to determine where Vladimir had stayed in Chicago, and what airports or transportation he used while traveling. America was working on her biggest lead, the only lead.

Dominic was just walking into his brightly lit kitchen at 0600 hours when his cellphone rang. He walked quickly over the rough slate tile of the kitchen and on to the hollow sounding wood floor of his living room. Dom didn't even bother checking his caller ID these days; it was always "Private."

"This is Dom," he quickly answered looking back into the kitchen hearing the fresh coffee that was brewing. No matter how many times he heard that gurgling noise it always made him think something was wrong.

"Hey Dom, this is Bill Whiteside. We got Vladimir leaving on a flight to Italy the day of the bombing. Caught him on a camera using a new ID. We're contacting our people out there. We're gonna find where this guy's hiding within the next few days."

"Great news Bill. Anything we can do from our end?" Dom said squeezing the couch cushion in his hand as he anticipated the next move.

"Honestly Dom, I think our best bet would be for you to continue looking at the tapes. Work backwards, try and find where he dropped the explosive, and see if there are any shadier characters slipping in and out of the area."

"Will do Bill. Keep me posted. Oh Bill! Is this something I can tell Samantha?"

"I would say you could tell Samantha and that's it. Keep a lid on it till we find this prick. We'll talk soon."

"See ya' later Bill."

Dom quickly got dressed and ran out of the house with his phone to his ear. Dom closed the door with his free hand, having forgotten his coffee. The news had been enough to wake him up. Twenty minutes and two rings after talking to Bill, Samantha picked up her phone.

"Hey Dom," she said beating him to the punch.

"Hey, good news. When are you gonna be at the office?"

"Twenty minutes."

"OK, well I'll be in your office in 30, then we can talk. When you get there, make sure we've got people looking at those tapes. Have them work back to following our terrorist when he has the bomb, then when he doesn't. I know we've been doing that already but have them pay attention to how long between the two times, and try and find any more people with backpacks in the area and follow them too, one-by-one if we have to."

"Sounds good, Dom, see ya' then."

Samantha strode into the office showing her ID, and immediately went to the media room where Brent and Ashley were working on the surveillance tapes. Samantha located Adam Wanewright, the supervisor, and walked directly toward him.

"Hey Adam," Samantha said and held out her hand.

"Hi Sam," Adam said putting his clipboard down and shaking her hand, smiling wide as he admired her beauty up close.

"Adam, I talked to Dom this morning and he specifically said he wanted people watching the tapes from Water Tower Place again. He wants Vladimir tracked with his backpack till we lose him, then see how long it takes till we see him again without the backpack. You guys should look for suspicious people during that time who have backpacks, Middle Eastern, and track them from both before that time and after. See if we cannot find more terrorists. We know the bombs went off in the food court so I would say focus in that area for now, until we get the timeline."

"OK Sam sounds good, it's gonna take a good amount of time."

"I think we all understand, but let's hope sooner rather than later," Samantha said already walking out of the room as she waved behind her without looking back.

Samantha walked up the stairs to her floor. She waved hello to everyone, stopping at her assistant Rachel to pick up one message and a stack of new files, and went into her office.

She opened the door tossing the files on her desk and read the message. It was a useless, every day reminder that there is still the standard part of the job going on while they investigated the attack in Chicago. Samantha decided to wait till Dom came in before starting any other work. After all, it was only another couple minutes.

Knock, knock, knock.

"Come on in Dom," Samantha said from inside her office. The door swung halfway open allowing Dom to slip in and close it quickly behind. Dom sat down in the chair opposite Samantha at her desk with a slight smile on his face. "What is it Dom?" she asked smiling herself at this point, very interested in what he had to say.

"They found our friend Vladimir boarding a plane to Italy the day of the attack. Bill Whiteside told me they've already contacted people and are working in finding him."

"Well that's great news."

"Yeah, but I don't think Bill expects him to talk, and frankly neither do I. I expect that's why he's telling us to look at those tapes so hard. If we nail Vladimir, who knows if we will ever find the rest of them. It's possible they have communication protocols. If one doesn't call in then they cut off communication with each other and disappear," Dom said as his smile turned to a look of concern.

"Hadn't thought of that. I already talked to Adam and they've started watching the tapes from Water Tower looking for more suspicious people we can track. Hopefully, we end up with a few more now that we know what we're looking for."

"Yeah, I hope we find a couple more too or else this one lead might lead to a dead end," Dom said as he stood from the chair adjusting his pants.

"Dom, before you go, I have some information for you, too. I'd like it to remain between us for now."

Dom sat back down.

"Sure Sam."

"OK. I spoke with Logan. They found, and spoke to the source of the C4."

"Oh my God Samantha who all knows about this?" Dom said leaving his mouth slightly open in surprise.

"Logan didn't tell me, but if I still know him, very few. If he trusts them, so do I."

"Excellent. Who is he?"

Samantha sighed and looked at her hands clenched together. "He didn't tell me. But, he did say that the person was an Army sergeant, and that he's now working for us. He's supposed to call Logan when the next drop is supposed to be made."

"An Army sergeant? My God, one of us?" Dominic said slowly, taking the news in and digesting it. "I honestly have no idea what to say at this point Samantha . . . I guess I'm just glad Logan's on our side," Dom dropped his hand from his head and looked at Samantha with a small smile. "You really need to keep me posted on anything you hear from him."

"Will do Dom."

He slowly walked out of the office almost forgetting to shut the door on the way out.

Spain

Amir entered his condo and immediately remembered the girl that he stood up just a couple days earlier. For a moment he felt sorry, but that vanished by the time he locked the door and strode over to his computer. He checked his email, nothing, and decided it was the right time to post one of his own.

Vladimir is no longer with us. He may have compromised us and needed to be eliminated. Do not travel until you hear from me again.

Satisfied with the message, Amir saved it as a draft and logged off. He walked over to his French doors and opened them, gazing out into the sunny afternoon. He strained, looking through the slivers of open air that were pinched between the buildings to catch a glimpse of the beach. On some days, it was as if the buildings had swollen in the salty, thick air, and this was one of those days. He could barely see the sand and surf and decided it would be best just to go there. Maybe he would run into the girl again and apologize. It would be more of a challenge that way, and the task appealed to him.

TWENTY

The case was starting to cool. No new information had come in for several days. August was marching on and football was being played all over the country, which was something Samantha looked forward to. Friday nights were the best. She loved driving home and seeing all the lights at the local high schools. It reminded her of brisk, fun-filled nights screaming for her high school team, of her high school crush, James, who played running back, and sneaking alcohol from the parents of her friends. Samantha knew her drive home this evening would most likely be fighting traffic. She hopped into her car and drove to work knowing that Friday was not the end of her workweek. Reminiscing, she left the house.

Samantha arrived at the office early and noticed that Dominic's car was already there. She went to their department and found it was only the two of them. Neglecting to go into her office first, she walked right up to Dominic's door and knocked. It took a few moments but she heard a muffled "come in" from the other side of the door.

Dominic looked a wreck. He was not shaven, nor was his hair treated with the care and precision it usually was. His shirt was wrinkled and his red and white striped tie was poorly knotted.

Five days passed before everyone heard the news. It trickled down from Italy, to Ernie Hayes, to Doyle Smith and Jenkins, down to Bill

Whiteside, who called Dominic to say that Vladimir Novikov had been found killed at a scenic overlook near Florence. It was as if the gears in a well-oiled machine exploded, destroying the device beyond all recognition. The worse-case scenario had come true. They couldn't even interrogate him, and no leads had yet panned out through the security tapes.

"What's wrong?" Samantha asked taking in the scene as bright light raced through the open slits of the blinds to the left.

"We found Vladimir . . . dead," he said while staring down at the desk in front of him. *Wham!* He slapped his desk forcefully, causing some of the other papers on his desk to lift into the air and settle, slightly out of place.

"How?" Samantha said quietly as she closed the door and approached the seat.

"Preliminary results say alcohol poisoning and possible heart attack," Dominic said as he picked up an envelope, waved it around flippantly, and threw it across the desk to Samantha. She opened the file and saw a picture of Vladimir and read what was below.

Known to consume large amounts of vodka, father died of heart disease and mother had a massive stroke leaving her dependent. Autopsy performed and revealed blood alcohol level 0.32 and the heart was enlarged and significant coronary blockage throughout. Liver also demonstrated cirrhosis to a significant degree.

"Well Dominic, what's the next step?"

"That's my problem, Sam. I don't know. Bill wanted me to find another lead on those tapes. We haven't found anything." Dominic stared at her. "I want you to listen to something I've been thinking, and I need your honest opinion."

"Sure," Samantha said inquisitively, crossing her legs and adjusting in the chair.

"I think this is just a little too coincidental. This guy had been a heavy drinker for decades and suddenly he dies?"

"You sound like me now Dom."

"I know. Do you think this is weird?" Dom asked leaning forward in the chair.

"No. But what are you getting at. Do you think someone inside FBI or CIA is in on it? I hate to say it Dom, but sounds like Antonin Mercier all over again. American C4 on both incidences too, Dom."

"Well, I say if an Army sergeant is, then anything is possible. Samantha, we have a former KGB and an Army sergeant as the two suspects we know of. Honestly Samantha, I feel so torn between telling Bill about this Army sergeant and Logan, but I don't know who to trust right now."

"Geez Dom you sound so paranoid," Samantha said concerned.

"I know," Dominic sighed deeply. "You know, you're about the only one I truly trust right now. If you trust Logan, then so do I. Tell him about Vladimir and let's hope that sergeant calls him soon."

"OK Dom," Samantha said bending forward trying to catch his eye as he once again stared at the desk. Dominic looked up feeling her stares.

"Don't look at me like that. I'll be fine. I don't need you to be concerned for me. I'm a big boy," Dominic said adjusting his tie and rubbing his hands through his hair realizing how much of a mess he appeared, both outside and in.

Washington, D.C.

Washington, D.C. was relatively calm on Saturday morning. The weather was poor, 65 degrees and drizzling since the evening before. The grass was puddling water but the steady sound of rain on leaves was an ideal change from the normal traffic and street noise of the week. Jenkins walked with his Rhodesian Ridgeback letting the week's events run off his back with the water. It seemed as though every step he took was a little lighter and stronger, and he held his head a little higher as the rain slid down his smooth cheeks. Even the dog trotted along a little more quickly following the lead of his master.

Jenkins was happy with the way the week had gone. It was two weeks since the attack in Chicago and no new leads since Vladimir. He knew that the investigation was well on its way to going cold. Jenkins rounded the corner for the final stretch home and even waved at a couple strangers in their cars. He walked in the front door and took the dog's leash off, giving the dog a quick slap on the hindquarters. The Ridgeback shook the water off and took a playful trot into the living room to lie on his blanket.

Jenkins took note of the time, 0930, and went into his home office.

He logged into his computer.

It's time to plan for the next move. Choose three targets and get back to me.

He walked into the living room and sat next to his wife, put his arm around her kissing her on the cheek, and watched TV.

Spain

Amir was getting dressed for a "second" date with the same girl from the beach. It had taken some convincing, which he thoroughly enjoyed, but they were now going out. She was upset that he missed the first date. It was her favorite bar, but she was absolutely against setting it up at the same place for the second time. She was worried that he would stand her up again in front of her friends. They were going to dinner. His goal for tonight was to get her to that bar, and ultimately into bed. He was relaxed, carefree, in charge.

He threw on a purple button up shirt and white linen pants. The night was warm, but he wore the light pants to cover his scar. He hated feeling vulnerable and nothing made him feel weak like someone asking him about his scar. It reminded him of his first mission. His only mistake; the one time he wasn't in control of his own mission. He vowed he would always be in charge from then on, and he had been. Amir had time to kill before leaving so he decided to check his email. He smiled as he read the draft from Jenkins. He responded quickly.

Los Angeles, Saint Louis, or Boston.

He then notified the rest of the team that another operation was going to take place.

We're moving again in two weeks. It will be Los Angeles, Saint Louis, or Boston. Details to follow within two days.

Amir grabbed his sandals, walked out of the condo, and strolled down the street. It was a cool evening and the moon shone brightly even though it was still dusk. The clouds to the west were a variety of pinks and purples all morphing into darker shades in the east. He took a deep breath of salty air and began his walk toward the restaurant. Amir was relaxed as ever, especially after the email he received from Jenkins. It was a sign that the heat from the attack had not found its way toward him and they were, at least for now, in the clear.

Amir saw lots of beautiful people as he meandered slowly through the streets. He had called ahead and made a reservation at one of the top seafood restaurants in the area.

"Do you have a reservation for tonight?" the host asked as he entered the restaurant.

"Vladimir," he had a fun little chuckle to himself as he said the name.

"For two?"

"Yes."

"It will be about ten minutes. You can wait here or at the bar if you would like," said the man at the counter.

"Here is fine," Amir said as he smiled and turned around to see his date walking down the street in a tight red dress and black heels. He also noticed she didn't have a purse or even a handbag.

"Well, you made it this time," she said jokingly as they kissed on the cheek.

"Of course. I see I'm going to have to pay for this all by myself. I didn't know that was part of the deal," he said with a playful grin and held her hand above her head so that she could do a full spin allowing him a look at her from all angles.

"If the night is worth it, maybe I'll pay you back later," she said and bit her bottom lip as they walked into the restaurant.

Camp Lejeune

Logan was again sitting in his room trying to work out who else could be involved in the terror attack. The news had long since exhausted all the facts and scenarios, but the networks continued to bring in their experts to discuss the possible culprits. Occasionally, Logan would listen in to hear an abstract opinion but he rarely got ideas from the experts on TV. Logan found out a long time ago that the experts on TV are rarely the best analysts. The best are hidden from the public eye.

Logan's phone began to rattle the small wooden desk.

"Hey Dubs what's going on?" Logan said as he slumped down in his chair.

"Hey Logan, the guys were wondering if you wanted to come down to Tom's tonight. He decided last minute to have people over."

"Yeah, what time is everyone goin'?"

"Oh, like 1800 hours. I know it's short notice but you've got nothing to do, right?" Dubs said jokingly and laughed into the phone.

"Well yeah you've got a point Dubs. I'll be there."

It was 1825 when Logan decided it was time to leave. He didn't want to be the first one at Tom's house, making small talk with Tom's wife, Angela, didn't appeal to him tonight. As he walked outside into Saturday evening he paused for a moment feeling the temperature was quite a bit cooler now than a few hours before. He decided he would need the jacket and jumped into his green Jeep and headed off the base.

As he drove west out of the base he put his aviator sunglasses on cutting the glare from the sun so he could see down the street. The car absorbed the heat from the sun and Logan began to sweat into his clothes a little. He opened all the windows and hung his arm outside. Immediately the air began to mix, causing a whirlwind of warm and cool air circulating around his body as the temperature began to neutralize. A few miles down the road he made the last turn, and pulled up to Tom's two-story home.

"Hey!" the men erupted. They had all been standing in a circle each holding a beer, and all wearing civilian clothing. As Logan approached, the circle opened and the men all took turns shaking hands. Tom walked over last with a bottle in his hand and held it out for Logan.

"Here ya' go Logan, thanks for comin," Tom said as Logan grasped the beer and took a good long drink.

"No problem," Logan said smacking Tom quickly between the shoulder blades.

"Alright Logan, settle a bet for us," Lonnie said and all the other men groaned and laughed. "Shut the fuck up," Lonnie said with a smile and his hand in the air. "Are you and Samantha gonna get together or what?"

"Oh, man Lonnie what's your problem!" Migs said and pushed him into a lawn chair. A couple of the other guys punched him too once he was seated.

"Don't answer that shit Logan, he's drunk already," Migs said.

"I don't mind the question, just the intent. I don't know if we'll get back together. Between you and me I hope so." Logan then looked at Lonnie sitting in the chair and pointed his beer hand directly at him. "But if you were asking for permission to slide in and try to get her you better watch yourself. I've taught you a lot but not enough that I can't still whip your ass."

"Ohhh!" the men screamed and laughed at Lonnie as they pushed him around the yard while he sat in the chair.

"Well since Lonnie brought her up, have you heard from her?" Ryan asked as the mood became a little more serious.

"Not a thing," Logan paused to think and was immediately taken back to just a few hours ago. "It's probably not a good thing that we haven't. I think she would have called me if there was any good news." Logan took a drink from his beer.

"Do you think Grainger will call?" Dubs asked in nervous monotone.

"Well I sure as hell hope so. It may be all we have at this point. I don't think he'll run. If he loves his girl enough to turn on his country, he loves her too much to leave."

"Good point boss," Migs said and stared at the ground that was slowly becoming monochromatic as the sun began setting far behind the trees. The green grass was darkening and the details of the stamped pavement were fading into a flat surface. Tom's wife Angela walked outside a few minutes later and lit a few citronella candles and the guys began working on starting a fire. It was gonna be a long, fun night.

Throughout the night, the men swapped war stories, joked, and drank. Everyone participated at varying levels. Logan sat back and just took it in for the most part. Most his stories were classified, but the men worked on him and he told a couple stories from when he was a Marine. Lonnie shared the most, but they were related to his relationships with women, and often in poor taste, but everyone still laughed. Migs told a long story about when he was in flight school and how he almost crashed the helicopter when he was messing around trying to fly low altitude through a valley in the Tennessee mountains.

The beer eventually ran out, and those who could drive, Logan and Migs, gave the rest rides home. It was 0030 when everyone finally got home safely. Logan opened the door to his apartment and was immediately reminded of the work that still needed to be done. He was grateful for a fun evening off. He walked over to the bed, plopped himself down face first into the pillow. For the first time in two weeks, he had no problem sleeping.

Washington, D.C.

Jenkins awoke early on Monday morning beating his alarm clock. He was excited to check his email knowing Amir would have written him back by now. The anticipation of picking another site to bomb was giving him butterflies. He fed on the ability to make his "friend" happy. Jenkins still felt as though he owed his life to the man.

Logging onto his computer he hit each keystroke methodically, taking each key and smashing it to the bottom of the plastic housing making a sharp, hollow click. He checked the inbox, which he knew would be entirely spam, just to drive up a little more anticipation. Finally, he checked the draft box and found the three suggestions.

Jenkins sat back in his chair and thought about the three cities. He closed his eyes and contemplated each one in detail.

The first one he thought about was Boston. The positives were large population, highly detrimental to morale. The negatives were a lot of police, even more patriots, and Jenkins liked the Red Sox.

The second city was Los Angeles. The same positives were present as in Boston, plus there would be more of an economic effect, and a wide variety of ethnic diversity. However, the negatives were that Los Angeles had become extremely well protected. Jenkins knew that there was a large influx of agents from FBI, CIA, and JTTF teams into L.A. so that was not a good spot to attack.

This left Saint Louis. It was another Midwest town with adequate population. Security was relatively minimal and due to the small town feel it has never been a hotspot for terrorist threats. The two biggest positives for Jenkins were that the Rams were going to have their season opener in just three weeks, and it just may cause more of a morale downfall than the bigger cities. Jenkins felt as though attacking a minor city would create fear because it would show that any size city was vulnerable. Jenkins smiled as he gave his short reply.

Saint Louis. Season opener Rams at Edward Jones Dome.

Chicago

Monday morning at the FBI office in Chicago was running like sludge. It was like a team down ten runs in the bottom of the ninth. The only reason they were playing was to save face. The entire division had now heard about Vladimir being found dead and there were no other leads to work with. The media room was still frustratingly watching video from the Water Tower Place, but it was with menial effort. At this point every technician had watched the tapes dozens of times with no hard follows. It had been a frustrating week already.

Dominic was in his office reading over threat reports for Chicago when his phone rang. He looked up from his manila envelope and watched the little red light on his desk phone blink as his phone rang two more times.

"Dominic," he said as the light on his phone turned from red to green.

"This is Ernie. I want a status update on what you've got with the Chicago incident," he said impatiently in a hollow voice.

Dominic sighed deeply and regretfully said, "Nothing new Ernie and I'm frustrated as hell. You heard anything?"

"We've given up on watching the tapes from the incident. We're focusing our search on the hotel lobbies in Chicago using facial recognition and the closed-circuit feeds. We've narrowed it down initially to a five-mile radius. We found Vladimir walk there and I'm assuming the rest did too."

"Well Ernie, I think a new direction is definitely warranted," Dom said releasing some of the pent-up frustration he had building since Vladimir was found dead. For a moment, Dominic had the urge to tell him everything that was frustrating him. American C4, Antonin Mercier's death in Paris, now Vladimir's death in Italy. How were all the leads dying mysteriously? The entire room felt as though it began to darken and all he could focus on was the wide, dark, wood grain on the desk in front of him. His heart rate increased and his mouth became dry. Quickly Dominic began realizing that if this was a conspiracy he didn't know if he could trust Ernie. Maybe Ernie was calling to get intel in order to kill another potential lead? Dominic's head began to clear and his moment of weakness began to turn into steel resolve. "What would you like us to do here?" Dominic said after what seemed like him an eternity, but in reality, it had been only a breath.

"I think we have that covered. I want your team to watch the streets thirty minutes before the event. Look for anyone Middle Eastern, follow them wherever they go."

"You've got it Ernie. Tell you if we hear anything," Dom said.

"Sounds good. Talk to you soon."

Ernie hung up the phone as he bit the end off a Cuban cigar. Smoking cigars was both a relaxation technique and a pleasure. Ernie rarely stressed about anything but an attack on U.S. soil got his blood boiling. Ernie had also been stewing on the possibility that someone inside the U.S. government had a hand in the attacks, but he was a true patriot and still thought that no American could be a terrorist.

Ernie had been a Marine, his father was a Marine, his grandfather had fought with honor and distinction during WWII as an Army Airborne and his great grandfather fought in trenches during WWI. None of these men were strangers to valor, love of country, and loyalty to their brotherhood of soldiers. Neither had any of them shied away from talking about their experiences and those of their peers. It's what helped them become such likable leaders, political advisors, heads of state.

Ernie relied on this rich history to find encouragement in the worst times. America has always found a way to win, to adapt, and to overcome. America has been loved and adored, respected and idolized for decades. *Why would a citizen ever want to take their country from the top of the food chain? Why bite the hand that feeds you?* Ernie thought.

New York City

"Welcome back to America Mr. Smith," the female customs agent said to Amir as he passed through security at JFK airport in New York. "Do you have a connecting flight?" she asked trying to pass the time as the other agent quickly looked over his baggage.

"Yes, I do," Amir said with a grin as he stared through the agent with his dark, brown eyes until she finally averted hers. Amir then glanced up at the departures, and noticed that his connecting flight to Saint Louis was departing in 90 minutes.

"Thank you, Mr. Smith," the woman said and handed him his belongings. Have safe travels!" she said smiling at him, parting her chubby cheeks forming deep creases that hid the corners of her mouth. Amir nodded and leisurely walked away carrying his bag in his left hand.

Amir eventually saw a gate in Terminal C where he noted the next flight was 54 minutes away. Amir took out his laptop, turned it on, and grabbed a headset plugging it in to the audio and microphone ports. He took full advantage of the free Wi-Fi and made a call from the internet to his favorite supplier, Shifty.

"Hello," Shifty said on his end of the receiver, slightly distracted because he was just getting home and hugging his daughter.

"I'm in need of your services," Amir said coolly in the phone. Immediately Sergeant Grainger knew who was on the other end. Grainger put his daughter down, walked into the bedroom, and closed the door.

"I'm listening," Grainger said as he looked into the mirror above the dark stained dresser and bit down hard on his molars.

"I'll set up a pickup for one week from today. I'll call you two days before that to tell you where the drop will be."

"That works," Grainger said. Both men then hung up.

Shifty sighed deeply at the thought of another attack on his home soil. When he first said yes to Amir he had no idea of the ramifications. He never thought it would be used against America. Shifty sat on his queen-size bed staring at his hands shaking even as he interlocked his fingers and squeezed as hard as he could. He was so angry at Amir and had wanted to scream at him. Shifty remembered the conversation with Logan and General Anderson. He looked into his phone contacts and found Logan's name. Amir getting caught would be the ultimate payback. Shifty immediately called Logan knowing that once Amir was caught, he himself was going to prison. Shifty almost didn't care as he stared at his daughter's picture on his bedside table.

Camp Lejeune

Logan was with his men in BB-5, discussing other avenues to track the terrorist. The same conversation had taken place just days before, but it was hard to find another topic with the attack still being so fresh.

"Guys, I think that the best thing we have are the recordings. I haven't heard anything from Samantha in a while so I'm assuming they are still following the one lead they had: Vladimir. We need to find something here to push things forward. We all know he's dead, but he still may be able to tell us some things on these tapes. Follow where he went, see if he met with anyone." Everyone sighed in frustration and adjusted in their seats.

Logan felt his pocket start to vibrate and was quickly distracted from the somber mood in the room. He looked at the caller ID and saw a number he didn't recognize. Typically, he would ignore the call, but with everything going on he decided to answer.

"Hello," Logan said in a neutral voice.

"Is this Logan?" the nervous voice asked on the other end of the phone.

Logan's mind moved quickly through thousands of voices he had heard over the years and matching them with faces. In a matter of seconds, he put Shifty's face to the voice and was awakened with a burst of adrenaline.

"Did he contact you?" Logan's words leapt from his lungs instinctively, caring little of pleasantries.

"Yes. He's going to schedule a drop for one week from today. He'll call me two days before to tell me where."

"OK Grainger here's what you do. Make sure you do everything as usual. You need to get the explosives, and you make the drop. I don't want to catch him, I want everyone."

"I'll call you when he calls me back."

"Absolutely. Keep me in the loop no matter what."

"OK Logan."

Logan looked up at his men. They each donned a grin. Logan walked forward toward the dark, smooth table. The fluorescent light was reflecting off the surface causing a glare. The glare made it difficult for Logan to see Dubs who was sitting directly across from him with his hands behind his head. Logan placed his hands on the table, leaned forward onto his hands reducing the glare, and brought everyone into focus.

"Alright guys here's the deal. Grainger was contacted by his buyer. He says the drop will be one week. I'm gonna go and talk to the general. He wanted to know everything. Plus, I'm gonna get us out there. We can scout out the areas, then we can watch the drop. We'll get a chance to use all the things we've gone over in this class. Now, this is the most critical part and I want you to think about this all week. This guy we're tracking is a professional. He will be better than all of us so we cannot be cautious enough about what we're doing."

Logan left the room and checked his phone noting the time was 1350. He knew the general would be in his office, having returned from eating lunch around 1300 hours. Once Logan was outside he decided to run to General Anderson's office.

It was only three miles, and walking would have taken way too long. The anticipation drove him nuts. It was mild, 72 with a slight westerly breeze. The air was salty and the sky was overcast. Logan ran on the sidewalks and would occasionally veer in to the street when too many Marines crowded the walkway and slowed him down. He enjoyed the run as it burned off some of his nervous energy.

Logan stopped running at the front of the building that held General Anderson's office, noting the time was 1423 hours. He rushed into the building squeezing past two Marine first lieutenants, took the stairs to the third floor, then down the long east hallway to the large corner office. As he walked into the office he saw Sergeant Bobby.

"Hi Logan," Bobby said as he looked away from the paperwork on his desk.

"Hey Bobby, is the general available?" Logan asked with his hands at ease behind his back.

"Yes. Just give me a second to make sure he's not in the middle of something." Bobby then picked up the phone and called the general.

"General Anderson do you have a second to speak with Logan Falcone?" A short pause ensued and Bobby hung up the phone. "He says he'll be right . . ."

Boom! The door shot open and General Anderson was striding through it, his hand outstretched to Logan as Bobby finished his final word "out."

"How the hell are ya' Logan?" the general asked shaking Logan's hand and giving it a very firm squeeze.

"Can we go in your office?" Logan said with a stern, demanding look of someone who was in authority.

"Absolutely, let's go." The general placed his hand on Logan's shoulder and guided him into the office first. General Anderson quickly closed the door and walked around his desk passing in front of the window disturbing the hot rays of sunlight that were cascading onto the desk. General Anderson took his seat and Logan sat directly across. The two men locked eyes and immediately knew, without exchanging words, that the conversation was going to be productive.

"Grainger called me," Logan said with an I-told-you-so grin.

"Well?" General Anderson said dismissing the grin and maintaining his professional edge. It wasn't hard for the general to remain serious; he was, after all, extremely aggravated with the knowledge that a U.S. Army sergeant was responsible for supplying the explosives.

"He said a drop will be made in a week, and he won't know where until two days beforehand."

"I suppose he's going to call you once he knows the locations?"

"Absolutely, General," Logan said moving toward the end of his seat to ask the question that he had come to ask. "I'd like to take the men back to Grainger's location. That way we can look into the area and be on site for the drop."

"Logan this is serious business," General Anderson said crossing his arms and sitting back into his chair displaying the dominant posture that he so often used.

Logan, still optimistic, said, "I trust my men General. I wouldn't have brought it up otherwise. They are just as eager to catch this asshole as we are. I will be leading the surveillance, nobody'll step off the path I set for them. I can promise you that."

"Well, Logan, it's just one of those things you know . . . you want to just do it yourself and make sure it's done the right way." General Anderson uncrossed his arms and placed both hands on the desk, tapping his fingers as if playing a keyboard. "Alright, I want to know your travel plans, when you're leaving, when you arrive, and most importantly, any further information on this guy."

"You've got it General," Logan said standing up and reaching out his hand. "I promise." General Anderson shook Logan's hand but stayed seated as the weight of the decision still fell heavily on his broad shoulders.

Logan left quickly so the general had no chance to change his mind. Logan had no room for an unpredictable General Anderson on this one.

Logan sighed deeply as he slowly walked back to his temporary apartment deciding whether he was going to call the men now or later.

He began to review everything the men went through. They covered tailing, evasion, gait analysis, how to break down the environment and assess the scene. The guys learned about bugs, GPS tracking devices, communication options, dead drops, and disguises. He wondered if they'd absorbed it all, or if they just knew what he wanted to hear during the classes. Either way, they would need to be prepared, or, they could die.

Logan continued to ponder the idea as he felt the sun begin to wrestle its way through the slivers in the clouds. The sun seemed to inspire Logan's mind. One idea began to drown out all others until Logan realized it was the only option. He took out his phone and called Dubs.

"Hey Logan, what's the word?"

"Call all the guys, we're gonna meet. We need to talk everything out. General Anderson is gonna let us go to Fort Jackson and begin to stalk possible drop spots," Logan said, feeling a flutter in his stomach.

"OK Logan where and when?"

"Now. My place. Hope to see you within the hour."

"Sounds good. You gonna cook dinner too?"

"Yeah, we'll get some damn pizzas, now hurry up," Logan said.

"OK."

The darkness of the evening set in earlier this night than usual. The clouds had thickened up over the course of the last two hours and created a curtain, blocking the sunlight. It was mild, and Logan had the windows in his apartment open allowing the cool breeze to circulate through. The men sat around the apartment on whatever they could find.

"Alright guys, here's what you're here for," Logan said swallowing the last bite of his pizza and wiping his hands against one another cleaning away the crumbs. "This is a final exam. I need to know that everyone here is ready to go on this mission. We're going to Fort Jackson and its vicinity. We need to scout potential drop points, review evasion tactics, disguise ourselves, and tail our objective. The buyer that Sergeant Grainger is working with is going to be watching his back and performing evasion techniques. We cannot be seen or sensed, because if we are, I can assure you, we'll lose our lead, the other terrorists, and someone in this room may even be dead." Logan paused after this for effect.

The men became somber, as if just realizing the depth of the situation they stood in.

"The only people in the world who know what's going on are the ones sitting in this room, and General Anderson. I need us all to grasp the fact that if we fail, we fail the country. So," Logan said grabbing the sheet of paper, "what should we talk about first?"

For the first time since the course began not a single sound was made. Not even Dubs had a sly remark or a quick joke. The men sat still as if they were rebooting their brains, reprogramming for the task at hand. As Marines, they were taken through many physical and mental challenges requiring them to adapt and improvise. The men in the room were also recon, so they were specialists in being unseen while watching others. Slowly, Logan's men began to settle in with their new task. One by one they began to look up from their plates.

The evening ran late, wrapping up about 0200 and the pizza was long gone. Logan was a good host and allowed them to snack on anything they wanted, which ended up nearly cleaning out his apartment.

"I know it's been a long night guys, but I'm proud of you. I'm confident you know what you're doing and I'll still call the ball at Fort Jackson."

"Migs!" Logan barked, which caught everyone a little off guard. Logan's voice had generally been mild and even.

"Yeah Logan," Migs said brightening up a bit. Migs had nodded off.

"Call Lieutenant Henderson tomorrow morning. We need to accompany us on a training op taking us back to Fort Jackson."

"Yut!" Migs responded.

"Alright guys head home. Plan on being gone for at the least a week. Make plans accordingly." Logan stood up as did all the others. Dubs stretched his large arms up overhead and let out an awkward noise. Each of the men filed out and Logan closed the door. He took the several steps to his bed while taking quick note of the chaos that was left in his apartment. It would only take a few minutes to clean, but he was going to bed at this point. Cleaning would happen in the morning.

Morning came quickly, but Logan was wide awake. The anticipation of the upcoming days boosted his adrenaline leaving his mind flying through scenarios. An hour later he had cleaned the apartment from the night before. He finished the job by taking out the trash. As he walked toward the dumpster, he began to feel anxious, as if he forgot something.

Logan and his men had worked out how to scout, tail, counter survey, analyze body mechanics, and gather details, but never discussed the possible drop. Logan realized that Shifty really needed to notify him ASAP in order to get access to the drop. Logan also concluded that the buyer, whoever it may be, would have already scouted the area and may have co-conspirators keeping an eye on it. The trip may get even more difficult than originally thought.

The thought process continued to evolve in Logan's mind after throwing his garbage in the bin. Logan remembered that when serving the CIA, they used satellite imaging to track and follow certain individuals if they knew where the culprit was at a given time. It would be the best shot at finding and tracking the buyer without getting caught. Logan jogged back into his apartment and grabbed his cellphone. He quickly dialed Samantha from memory.

Chicago

Samantha was preparing to leave the house when her phone started ringing on the entertainment table in her living room. Her heels clunked unevenly on the hardwood floors as she walked to the phone. She turned it over to see that it was Logan.

"Hello," she said with a hint of "who is this" in her voice despite the caller ID.

"Hey Samantha. I've got some big news," Logan said getting straight to the point.

"Thank God!" Samantha exhaled and plopped down on to the couch, pausing her daily routine.

"Yeah, I heard from the sergeant. He said the buyer contacted him and is ready to buy within the next week."

"Well that's good Logan, what's the next step? Where's the drop?" Samantha said as she quickly grabbed a magazine to write on; it was the only thing she had.

"That's the reason I'm calling you. We don't know anything at this point. Sergeant Grainger will call whenever the buyer schedules the drop location and day. We know that it will take place in the proximity of Fort Jackson, but that's it. We're expecting a call two days prior to the drop. This is where I need your help. I think the best idea for this mission is to get satellite surveillance on the drop. We can follow the buyer and possibly catch some of the other men he's working with."

"Logan that's a great idea!" Samantha exclaimed. "I'm just nervous. I'm not sure who to trust."

"I understand, maybe Dominic would know. Fill him in on what I told you and see if he has any ideas. Let him know if he wants to talk to me he can call me at this number."

"I will Logan, but Dom already told me that he would rather remain in the blind when it came to you. I think he will gladly take the intel though."

"I'm sure he will."

"I'll call you if we figure something out. Be careful Logan. Have a backup plan."

"I know. I'm just trying to figure out what to do if we don't get that satellite. Call me."

Samantha took a deep breath, calming herself and recapping the conversation. After two-minutes, she grabbed her purse, banana, and water, as she left the house.

The ride into the office was hazy, the kind of morning that preceded a warm humid day. It was in stark contrast to how clear Samantha's mind was. It was as if someone came in and reorganized her mind, throwing away all the useless information and scattered theories until only Logan's new intel remained. It was the first time since Vladimir that they had anything to go on, and it was a huge step forward. Having this new information made Samantha feel as though everything they were working on, the security tape reviews, the known list of associates, and the terrorist cell in Afghanistan, were all a monumental waste of time. But, there was one more thing that trickled back into Samantha's mind. Her thoughts of conspiracy.

Samantha's heels clicked rapidly onto the tiles as she walked straight for Dom's office upon arrival. She knocked once, walked in without waiting for permission, and immediately started talking.

"Dom, I know you told me to keep you out of Logan's business, but something has come up."

Dom sat back into his chair, gently placing the file he was reading down on the desk without a sound. He crossed his arms. "Continue," he said, then made a gesture for her to close the door and sit down.

"Logan called me this morning. The supplier called Logan and told him a drop was going to be made this week. We know the general area is around Fort Jackson in South Carolina because that's where the supplier is currently stationed. Logan suggested we get a satellite up over the area and we can track the guy from the drop to wherever he goes."

"Yes," Dominic said as he stared blankly at his desk. The information seemed to overload his mind. He closed the meaningless file on his desk and sat in silence for about 30 seconds. "What about your theory that someone inside is helping?" Dom asked, finally looking up.

"That's what I need to know from you. Who can we trust? Who can we ask to divert a satellite over Fort Jackson?"

"Bill Whiteside from CIA. I guarantee we can trust him. Ernie Hayes, too, I bet they would be able to get that satellite over Fort Jackson, no questions asked. I'm gonna call them and tell them it's just between us for now. The fewer the better."

"I agree, and you would know best Dom," Samantha said sighing as though fully letting her guard down now that she had passed the information along. She sank deep into the chair and relaxed while Dom dialed both Bill Whiteside and Ernie Hayes.

"Hello gentlemen," Dom said having completed the conference call. "I have Samantha Baker with me and she's come across some rather good intel," Dom winked at Samantha signaling her to keep Logan a secret for now.

"Well, what is it?" Ernie said through his teeth as he bit down on his cigar.

Samantha began telling Dom, Ernie, and Bill, Logan's conversation in detail. She covered who the supplier was, when the drop may be made, and how the buyer would call again two days prior to the drop. Samantha let them know she would be notified of the drop time, and then she asked her own question.

"I need to know if we can get a satellite over that area so we can ID and follow the buyer. He may lead us to his associates and get them all in one big hit."

There was silence for only a few seconds, but Samantha felt as though she was holding her breath for an hour as she stared at Dom.

"I think we can make that happen, right Bill?" Ernie said to his CIA counterpart.

"Absolutely," Bill said nonchalantly.

"One more thing," Dom rudely burst into the conversation before it went any further. "We want it to stay with only us few in the know. There is also a reason to believe someone inside is helping these terrorists. We already know there is an Army sergeant who is supplying the explosives."

"Good point Dom," said Ernie who spit out a piece of tobacco from his cigar. "Bill tell your people it's a training exercise, put your rookies on it, your best ones, and tell them I'll be watching. That should make it easy. You can look over their shoulders the whole time and they won't suspect a thing. We need it done right."

"I agree," Bill said. "I have two guys in mind already."

"Well, if that's it then, let's get this thing going," Ernie said.

"Yes, that's it," Dom responded. "We'll let you know as soon as Samantha hears anything. Goodbye."

"Well, that went smooth," Samantha said with a smile from ear to ear.

"That it did," Dom responded and sat forward in the chair. "I just hope this breaks the case."

"Me too," Samantha said softly. She hadn't realized it, but her breathing was heavy, and her plain blue button up shirt was rising and falling with each breath. Her hair was down and wavy because she hadn't been concerned with the way it looked in recent days, letting nature take its course.

Samantha walked out of Dom's office and called Logan.

"Hey, you're gonna get that satellite. Everything went over very smooth and only three more people know, Dom, Bill Whiteside CIA, and Ernie Hayes Chief of Intel D.C."

"Great news Sam," Logan said sighing. "We're going to Fort Jackson soon. I'll let you know as soon as I hear from Grainger where the drop will be."

"OK Logan. Talk to you soon."

"Bye."

chapter
TWENTY-ONE

"The temperature in Myrtle Beach is currently 82 degrees under partly sunny skies. The local time is 10:30 a.m. Thank you for flying U.S. Airways."

Amir left his window seat, squatted down to avoid hitting his head, and grabbed his carry-on from the overhead bin. This was the worst part of traveling by plane, getting out of the cramped seat, then waiting for all the slow people to grab their items. However, he waited patiently to exit the plane despite his annoyance. He nodded his head at several strangers, and smiled sweetly at the young flight attendant who smiled back, turned away, and walked toward the front of the plane. Amir followed shortly behind her and left the plane.

Amir strode through the airport, head held high taking in everyone he walked past. He was heading toward Enterprise to pick up a rental car. The exchange went well. He used a fake ID and credit card, going by the name Mark Delaney. He rented the car for a week. Amir had an easy drive to Fort Jackson ahead of him.

Amir rolled the windows down and turned the radio up. He was having fun driving down the highway with the wind trying to drown out the songs on the radio. The highways were wide open and he could seemingly go as fast as we wanted. He didn't, however. He hit the cruise control going just above the posted speed limit and let the sun bathe his skin.

He had wanted to show everyone he was a true American, not a first-generation immigrant. Full of motivation, he had once climbed the ranks of an enlisted man about as fast as anyone could go. It would have been easy for him to go to college and become an officer, but, that wouldn't have changed his ultimate downfall following the tragedy with his father. It also would have made him wait four years to prove his worth.

Amir exited off 120 west as he neared the end of his route. It was much hotter now, close to 90 with 75 percent humidity; the radio had told him 20 minutes ago. He turned on the air conditioner but kept the windows down while decreasing to residential speed. As he approached the first traffic light, he saw a sign for Sesquicentennial State Park. Amir immediately decided the drop would be there. Now it was a matter of the specific location. He was going to scout it for the next two days and determine the best location within the park.

Camp Lejeune

It was an exciting morning. Logan and the men were about to go back to Fort Jackson and be put to the test. The guys all met at the airfield where Lieutenant Dave Henderson was already performing the preflight checks inside the Blackhawk, while Migs was walking around the outside checking the helo over.

"Hey Logan," Migs said as he came around the front of the helo.

"We ready to go?" Logan asked as the two men shook hands.

"Yeah, just about ready to spin 'em."

"We got the satellite," Logan said to Migs as the men began to pile into the Blackhawk.

"Well that's great," Migs said with a look of concern.

Logan sensed something was bothering Migs. Logan raised his eyebrow and crossed his arms as if to say out with it.

"Logan, do we know when the drop is? and where?"

"No, but Shifty will call. We covered this," Logan said disappointed.

"I know, but have you seen any weather reports lately?" Migs said as he reached into his pocket pulling out the weather report for the next five days. Logan grabbed it from Mig's hands staring at him for a moment before finally looking down.

"It's hurricane season Logan. The flight coordinator debriefed me this morning because he wanted us to be aware of the weather for our return trip."

"Shit," Logan said as he read the reports, seventy percent chance of coming inland by Thursday or Friday. "It's Tuesday!" Logan said, crumpling the paper in his hand. Logan noticed the sudden silence amongst the men and walked over to them. He nodded for Migs to follow.

As Logan walked toward them, he held the weather report up. "This could be a huge problem. We got the satellite surveillance, however, we can't see a damn thing through a hurricane. So, we have to make a backup plan. The hurricane may come this far inland. Everyone go home and grab your fatigues, face paint, NVGs and everything else just in case we can use it while we are there. I'm not sure what the backup will be. I won't begin to work on it till we find out where the drop is. We'll meet back here in a half hour."

Fort Jackson

Amir woke up early and went to Sesquicentennial State Park after grabbing a coffee from the gas station. He approached the park entrance and paid four dollars to enter. He asked the male retiree in the booth for a map of the park, placing it on the passenger seat and took a drive, making careful mental note of the layout and areas of interest. He noticed the roads didn't access the entirety of the park. It was time to park the silver Ford Focus and take advantage of the hiking trail.

He walked toward the trailhead where a detailed map was displayed. Amir looked over the map and saw that it was 1.9 miles in total. There were possibly three bridges over small tributaries that could be good drop points. It was something Amir was going to scout this afternoon. He needed to determine how much foot traffic came through the area, if it was close to picnic areas, if there was a small or a large viewing area. Amir scanned the map one last time and tentatively settled on the second bridge. There was no campground or picnic area around it, and it was also the furthest from the parking lot.

Amir headed off in the midday heat. The crushed gravel cracked underfoot with each step he took. He kept his head up, looking around periodically as the trees or underbrush opened to small, green fields, picnic areas, or campgrounds. So *far not so good*, he thought as he passed over the first bridge and saw even more picnic areas, a restroom, and camping areas. Amir didn't get disappointed, however, and marched on toward his original choice; the second bridge.

About 500 yards after the first bridge the trail tightened up. It became more undulating and the underbrush and trees thickened up so much that it was impossible to see into the woods. It was warmer in this part of the trail because the air was thick and stagnant due to the dense vegetation. Amir smiled slightly as it seemed that once more he was right. Several turns later he came across the next bridge.

The second bridge was smaller than the first, but it was still at least ten feet wide. The bridge was shaped as a shallow arch, which created a lot of clearance under the steel and wood structure. Amir walked onto the middle of the bridge and leaned onto the rail. It was the first shade that he'd been under in the last hour. He looked out toward what some would call a lake, but in reality, it was just a large swelling of the river where three or four tributaries merged before they all flowed further downstream. Amir looked down past the slate blue rail down at the water running out underneath him. He realized he was standing over the only water feeding out of the lake. He slowly turned a full 360 degrees taking in the elements. He noted the continuance of the thick trees and dense underbrush. The path from both sides of the bridge had a bend in the trail within 50 yards. It was a perfect location for a drop.

Amir then walked the rest of the way across the bridge to check for an exact drop position. He walked down to the water level right next to the bridge and was easily able to see underneath. It was dark and damp, smelling of mild mildew from the cedar wood planks that were used for the tread on the bridge. Amir checked the trail behind him making sure nobody was there, and went under the bridge. The first step caused his foot to stick in the thick mud briefly, straining an old calf wound. *Footprints*, he thought as he sat down right next to the base of the bridge higher than the mud line on hard packed earth. He would have to consider that a negative.

Several hours later, and having witnessed minimal foot traffic, Amir came out from under the bridge. The closest he got to being found under the bridge were two nosy Labradors who were sniffing around, while their owner walked slightly ahead. It was now solidified in Amir's mind; this would be the drop location.

Amir got back to the hotel and immediately called Shifty. He used a scrambled SIM card in his prepaid phone he purchased before leaving the airport.

"Hello," Shifty said sternly as he answered the phone.

"Shifty, we have a drop location. Sesquicentennial State Park. You're to leave it under the second bridge. Once I receive it, you will receive your payment, as always."

"When do I drop?" Shifty asked while gathering his belongings from his desk.

"Tomorrow morning." Then Amir hung up.

Shifty sighed deeply, knowing that his next move was to call Logan and get the plan to capture the terrorists in motion. Shifty was, however, very nervous because if things went bad, if Amir found out what Shifty had done, Amir would kill his family. Shifty quickly shook the negative thoughts and called Logan.

Fort Jackson had turned out to be a lot of waiting. Logan and his men were sitting in the empty barracks that General Anderson had organized for them. It was typical, tight, concrete; all the beds were bare mattresses leaning on the walls. None of the men, except for Logan, had even bothered setting up their bunks.

A phone began to ring and everyone grabbed for their own.

"Hello," Logan said looking up at the men.

"Logan, this is Shifty. I have the drop spot."

"Great, where?"

"It's a place called Sesquicentennial State Park. There's a path that goes through the park, he says under the second bridge. Apparently, there are three bridges, so no matter which way you go around the park it's still the second."

"That's great Shifty now do your part. This is almost over. I'll do my best to make sure you can see your daughter again," Logan lied, a white lie, ensuring Shifty's allegiance to the cause.

"Yeah . . ." Shifty said with a hesitation. He felt a weight lift off his shoulders, only to feel a jab into his stomach over what could happen to his family if things went wrong. "Logan, don't let them know it was me. I know I'm already fucked, but my family is alive and I'd like it to stay that way."

"We'll take it from here Shifty. When's the pickup?"

"He told me to drop it tomorrow morning. I'm not sure when he will pick up."

"OK Shifty. Call me with any additional information, if you get any."

"I won't get any, but I'll call if I do." Both men hung up.

Everyone sat silent in the barracks waiting for Logan to speak. It was quiet enough to hear the air going in and out of Dubs' huge chest.

"The drop is tomorrow morning at the second bridge in Sesquicentennial State Park. There's a path through the park that the bridges are a part of. We need to gather the gear, get ready for an overnight, through a hurricane. We need to prepare for the worst to catch this asshole. Latest weather report says it's still a 70 percent chance the hurricane's path makes it this far. That means no satellite. It won't be able to see though the cloud cover. I'm still gonna call the general and get it overhead for tomorrow just in case."

"We need to bring NVGs, camos, face paint, jungle warfare scenarios. Sidearms with silencer just in case this guy has stalkers out there, but ideally, we're not using them. Understood? We're to be unseen and unheard. We're going in tonight, staying overnight, and maybe more if we need to, so grab some rations, water, whatever. My guess is he will be picking up tomorrow no matter the weather."

"Logan," Migs interrupted. "We're ready." This calmed Logan down a little. He realized he was rambling.

"Good point. We'll use Henderson," Logan said responding to Tom's earlier comment and looking around.

"Dress in street clothes with a backpack full of our gear, change in the woods. Henderson leaves. We would only need one van," Lonnie said.

"OK. Good plan."

"General Mitchell, this is Logan. I wanted to let you know that we have the drop and time. It's tomorrow at Sesquicentennial State Park."

"Excellent. You're going to scout the place, watch the drop?"

"Yes sir."

"Alright, well fill me in when you can. I'm sure your team is going dark. Let me know when you come back up."

"Ooh Rah sir."

About an hour later the men were at Sesquicentennial State Park and were approaching the second bridge from both sides. It was late evening, the park was closing, and there was a bright red sky. The trees were still and the air was mild. The forecast said rain would begin early morning, and, depending on how far the hurricane came inland, it could strike Fort Jackson some time mid-afternoon. The men all congregated at the bridge at about 1945.

"OK guys, looks like behind the bridge in the tree line you see someone coming toward the bridge you let us know. He could be anybody, or sending anybody. Remember, the drop is under the bridge, so it should be obvious. Let's move. Fifty meter spread in each direction. Go into the tree line by water so that you don't leave any sort of tracks. This guy is a professional, he'll see everything."

Overnight was uneventful. The men kept each other up by talking through the radios, telling stories, and looking around for possible holes along their line of sight. The men slept in two-hour shifts alternating until the park opened at sunrise.

Dubs had the clearest line of sight to the eastern sky and radioed the men that the sun had begun to come up. The sun crested over the tree line poking through the dark purple slits of storm clouds that marched westward across the sky at a rapid rate. It was the leading edge of the storm. Logan looked upward analyzing the sky, knowing that the satellite was perched high overhead. Only time would tell how useful the technology would be. More likely than not, as always, they would need the men on the ground. They knew that shortly they should see Shifty.

"I've got movement," Lonnie said into the VOX radio. All the men immediately dug in and waited to hear more. "One male, carrying a backpack and a camera. . . . It's Shifty," Lonnie said with a little excitement in his voice. Lonnie had the position nearest the parking lot where he could determine the make, model, license plate, and color of the cars. He could also see some of the path after the first bridge.

"Roger," Logan said as he remained in position nearest the second bridge behind dense trees and underbrush. He pulled out his binoculars and waited for Shifty to come into frame.

Shifty meandered down the path taking in the park, and often looking up at the clouds. It was easy to see a storm was coming quickly. He crossed over the first bridge and paused for a moment. Shifty didn't know why it was so beautiful. He didn't know it was due to the morning sun squeaking its way through the clouds creating long shadows and rich, diverse colors that are typically washed out under the afternoon sun.

"I got him in sight," Tom said from near the first bridge. "He's stopped just after the bridge. He's taking a few pictures it looks like."

"Copy," Logan said and reviewed the path in his mind noting Shifty's exact position.

Shifty brought the camera down from his eye and reviewed a couple of pictures. He smiled, slightly, as he turned the camera off and began moving down the trail. He stopped several more times taking pictures as he grew nearer to the second bridge.

"Got him," Logan said as Shifty finally rounded the apex of the turn and entered his field of view. He took note of Shifty's backpack and camera, as well as how he was dressed—jeans and a t-shirt with sunglasses resting on the top of his head.

Shifty reached the second bridge and climbed the arched walkway to the middle. He stood there for a while looking over the water. He was thinking about his family again; mostly his wife, who would have to carry the weight both financially and emotionally of his daughter's illness. Shifty began to get emotional and took a deep breath looking down at the rail he was leaning on. A small flicker of anger and a large stomach pang of regret enveloped him as he watched the water rush under the bridge. *How many free moments do I have left?* A few minutes later he gathered himself, adjusted the strap on his backpack, and looked toward each side of the walkway. There was no evidence that anyone was coming from either direction and he decided it was time to make the drop.

Shifty walked down the far side of the bridge, then down to the waterline. He looked under the bridge and saw the large clearance between the water and the bridge. There was also a steady, steep slope to the bank that allowed for little to no chance of water ever reaching the bottom of the bridge. Shifty proceeded under the bridge, guiding each step of the way with a hand along the bank. Once situated beneath the bridge his eyes took a moment to adjust to the darkness. He looked around for the best location to place the bag, and soon noted that the metal beams supporting the bridge made a nice ledge. He took his backpack off, reached as far back toward the landing of the bridge as he could, and placed the bag. Shifty let out a long, deep sigh, and turned back toward the water running under the bridge. He sat there momentarily thinking one last time about his family. The anger he started to feel earlier returned as a fire, a hatred raised up inside of him that he couldn't recall ever feeling before. Shifty couldn't figure out if the anger was at Amir or at himself. He punched the bridge over and over again until his shoulder burned and he could no longer lift his hand. Blood dripping from his knuckles and dissolved into the water flowing beneath him, as he stayed under the bridge for a few more minutes of freedom.

A flash lit up the sky. Logan looked up noting a change in the hues above. There was now a steady flat gray and purple color to the sky. Over the course of the last hour watching Shifty none of Logan's men had noticed the warm hues of the early morning turn to the bland, purple hues of an approaching storm.

"He's on the move minus the package," Logan said to the men.

Shifty kept walking the trail, finishing the loop instead of just turning back around. He felt it was probably one of the last times he would enjoy a walk.

"I've got him," said Migs. "No backpack, still taking some pictures."

"I got him too," Dubs said deeply into the VOX.

"OK guys, copy," Logan said. "I'm getting a lot of wind noise now; we need to switch off VOX before the wind gets blowing too much. The men all switched over to PTT and geared up for the storm and the wait. "Ryan and Brian, you guys haven't seen Shifty?"

"No boss," said Brian.

"No," said Ryan.

"Lonnie, is he back to his car?"

"Sure is, getting in right now," Lonnie said as he watched Shifty drive away.

"Well, that means Ryan and Brian, we need to get you to adjust your position. Ryan, move to a higher position opposite Lonnie to get a second set of eyes on the parking lot. Brian, just try to get a better angle on the path. Move down from Dubs and the bridge. We had no eyes between Dubs and Lonnie and that's a lot of missed coverage."

It had already been three hours since Shifty pulled out of the parking lot. The rain steadily increased, as did the wind, creating a dull roar as the rain slapped the leaves. The occasional thunder and lightning added depth to the noise creating a full percussion section. For Logan, the steady drone was soothing, and had put him to sleep many nights over the years. The sound, as well as the amount of rain, would drown out any small mistakes the men might make.

Logan reached around into his bag, grabbing his favorite snack, beef jerky. He had already taken all the pieces out of the package and placed them into the waterproof pocket to avoid making noise when reaching in. He placed a piece into his mouth, chewed it till it was soft, and left it between his teeth and cheek to soak. Logan keyed his mic, "Check in."

"Nothing sir," said Lonnie.

"Me neither," Tom quickly stated.

"Nope," Migs said taking a small drink from his canteen.

"Nothing," Dubs said.

"In position down the path from Dubs sir, and I've seen nothing," Brian said.

"I'm in position, too. I found good elevation, I can see the entrance, the entire parking lot, and about the last quarter mile of the loop in either direction," Ryan said.

"Sounds good guys. Great position Ryan. Thought a sniper like you would have eyeballed that position from the beginning," Logan joked and all the men smiled slightly at the attempt to relieve some tension. "Stay on your toes. We may be here for a while. Get some calories in you."

The time continued to pass slowly for the men. The rain began to fall in sheets and the wind was swirling, often blowing the rain into their faces. The ground had become saturated and Logan's position on the back of the stream threatened to become compromised. The water level was rising every minute and the wind was bending the trees as if they were tall reeds in a pond. All the men knew by this point that any chance of the satellite helping track the terrorist was out of the question.

Amir looked out of his hotel window and smiled. He knew nobody was going to be at the state park, and in fact, it would probably be closed. But that wouldn't stop him. He thought, for a moment, that the need for a disguise was unnecessary. However, the moment was fleeting and he placed the mask over his head, and used a blonde wig to cover his black hair. He walked to the mirror and put in his blue contacts. He didn't mind the face he put on today. He slid his hand down his smooth cheek and could sense the muffled touch through the mask. He smiled, and the mask responded with a natural, smooth movement.

"How, cheese, tickle, open, witness," Amir said as a quick way to work through several other facial movements to check the quality of the mask's movement. It was still perfect. He looked at his watch, it was 1420. Looking at the television he saw that it was now Category 2 winds, and decided he wouldn't wait any longer.

Lonnie was straining to see through the rain that was pummeling him in the face as he watched the parking lot. "The rain is fucking with me. I've got almost no vision. The wind's right in my face."

"No worries guys, I have eyes on a car pulling in," Ryan said from his new position. He had much better luck with the wind at his back.

"I've got it too. It's a silver Ford Focus. Can't make out the license plate number though," Lonnie said.

"Copy. Let's get a good look at him guys," Logan said as his heart began to race. His vision was improving now as if his brain had a program that eliminated distortion from the rain. He fixed his eyes on the bridge and waited for word of which direction the terrorist would be traveling down the path.

"Contact is on the move, heading toward me," Ryan said.

"Copy," Logan said. "Alright Brian, Dubs, Migs, he's heading your way first. Keep an eye out, intel on what you're seeing."

"Got it boss," Brian said.

"Copy," said Dubs and Migs.

"Lonnie!" Logan said with intent.

"Yeah," Lonnie said squinting through the rain trying to get a look at the man leaving the rental car.

"As soon as you hear Brian key in on the contact, can you get close enough to the car to get a read on the license plate?"

"Yeah I can."

"Perfect. Read it out, we'll all remember it. You cannot leave any trace. No path through the vegetation, no footprints, no mud out of place. If you can't do it, don't even try," Logan sternly said into the mic.

"Copy."

Amir started to jog down the trail. He didn't want to be in the rain for a half an hour, he wanted to get the package and get out as fast as possible. He got onto the path, and despite the fact he was on crushed gravel, he heard sloshing of water underfoot as opposed to the crunching sound of the gravel.

"I've got him. He's jogging," Brian said. "He's moving at a pretty good pace."

"Lonnie get moving," Logan said. "Dubs, Migs, get some details when he passes, what he looks like, how he moves, height, weight, age."

Lonnie squatted down and moved forward through the underbrush. He was about 30 yards from the parking lot, and 40 yards from the car. He felt that if he could get halfway there he could make out the plates. Lonnie glanced back and saw that he wasn't leaving a trace of evidence and kept moving forward.

"Eyes on," Dubs said.

Lonnie was now 25 yards away and still couldn't read the plates.

"He's coming up on the bridge now, Logan," Migs said. "Couldn't make anything out specifically. Just blonde hair, runs pretty smooth, looks to be somewhere in the 30s maybe 6 foot 3."

"Good enough Migs. Lonnie where are we on the plate?" Logan asked watching for the contact to get to the bridge.

"Twenty yards away. Still can see him," Lonnie said calmly as he had almost reached a clearing where he would surely leave a path through the smaller brush and tall grass.

"You've got five minutes to get it the way this guy is moving," Logan said. "I've got eyes on," Logan said loudly into the mic. "He's gone under the bridge already."

Logan was reading everything about the man, making calculations and observations without even thinking, just placing them into memory for analysis later.

"He's exiting from under the bridge. Lonnie, you've only got three," Logan barked.

As Amir came out from under the bridge he grimaced and grabbed his right leg for a moment. Amir developed a limp, and began to run in an awkward manner. As Amir ran back toward the car, he reached a clearing and the wind nearly brought him to the ground, pressing into him with extreme, steady force. Logan absorbed it all. It was strangely familiar, the way the man moved. He ignored that feeling for the moment and just took everything in.

"Tom, he's on the move, and Lonnie, we need that damn plate number."

Lonnie had moved in closer. "RW9 2709, Illinois plates, Enterprise license plate cover." Lightning lit up the entire sky as it struck a tree nearby. The thunder roared for several seconds and the radios crackled.

"Say again Lonnie!" Logan said through the wind.

"Romeo. Whiskey. 9.2.7.0.9. Illinois plates."

"Everyone remember that, now get the hell out of there!" Logan demanded. "Ryan, watch the car leave. Once it's gone, we need to get ourselves out of here and contact the general."

"I've got him Logan, he's limping, but still running. He's got the backpack," Tom said.

"Copy, I saw the limp, too."

"Back in position, Logan," Lonnie said breathing heavily and looking down at his shaking hands.

"I've got him running to the car now," Ryan said. This caused Lonnie to look up again into the rain that was now pummeling them. Several minutes passed as Lonnie searched through the rain, the drops fell like daggers into his eyes.

"He's gone," Ryan said. Lonnie never saw him leave. The rain was too thick, and his adrenaline was still driving his thoughts.

Logan reached into his backpack once again, pulled out a cellphone, and called Fort Jackson. "We need a pickup," he said loudly while cupping his hand over the receiver. Then he hung up.

"Alright guys, meet on Lonnie's position, we're still on high alert. Ryan, you stay put with eyes on the parking lot till we are all there. I'll call you then."

"Copy, Logan."

The rest of the men simply began walking out of their hides and through the vegetation to Lonnie. It took a little over 20 minutes before they had all assembled. The group of men hunkered down to await the van that should arrive shortly.

"Ryan, time to come down, we're watching the parking lot."

"Copy Logan, on my way. Give me five."

"Will do bud," Logan said and slapped Lonnie on the back squeezing his shoulder. "Romeo, Whiskey 9.2.7.0.9. Illinois plates?" Logan asked Lonnie.

"Ooh Rah!" Lonnie exclaimed through the wind and rain.

The van showed up 30 minutes later. The men, completely soaking wet, were beginning to feel the chill. None of the men discussed a thing during the hour-long trip back. The wind had blown the van onto the shoulder of the road on several occasions, and Henderson took it upon himself to drive through red lights because there wasn't another soul on the road. At best, the van could only drive 20 miles per hour or the rain would make visibility zero. Tree limbs were crawled across the roadway like a scene from a horror film but Henderson pressed on, dodging them and never lifting his foot from the accelerator. A voice on the radio cut into the music and stated that the hurricane was still a Category 2, and the worst was yet to come in the area of Fort Jackson.

They came to the entrance at the base, stopping briefly at the guard station. The soldier came quickly to the driver's door, looked over his ID and car stickers, and waved him through with a salute. Henderson navigated the base very well. He was taking one-way streets, alleyways, an even went off road twice to get them to the barracks quickly.

"Thank you," Logan said extending a hand as they exited the van.

"Not a problem, sir."

Logan opened the door to the barracks and was greeted by a semi-circle of men standing in front of a familiar face, General Mitchell Anderson.

"Logan," the general said, nodding and walking toward him extending his hand.

"Well, I would ask what you're doing here, but I'm sure I know," Logan said wiping his face to get a better look at the general.

"Well that damn satellite wasn't gonna work and I wanted to talk to you face-to-face, just in case this storm wanted to crap all our means of communication. Can't trust the tech, can't go wrong with face-to-face."

"I agree with you, General," Logan said with a smile. He loved the general's ability to shed his ranks and come down and talk to the grunts instead of shuffling paperwork and shaking hands.

"What do you got for me Logan?"

"We've got a license plate number on a rental car. I say we track this guy's ID, watch where he's traveling. My team will follow him, watch for who he's working with. Once we get the entire party, we'll take them out," Logan said matter-of-factly.

"I'm not so sure I want them dead Logan. These guys may have answers; they may work for someone in this government. I need to know," General Anderson said pointing his finger down at the ground repeatedly throughout the statement.

"I'm in," was all Logan said.

"Alright men, good work, get changed up, dry, and get some chow. We need to debrief and get moving on this ASAP," General Anderson said turning around to address the rest of the men.

The men broke down the events of the day to the general. Each spoke in turn about the drop location, about Shifty, they gave a description of Amir and how he moved. It was a lively discussion with good input. Logan had trained them well, and they had caught everything Logan did regarding the suspect.

"Tom. Describe the limp he had," Logan said as he placed his hands into his eyes and closed them trying to watch the events over in his head as if watching a movie clip. He slowed it down as Tom began to talk.

"Uh . . . Well, no question he was favoring his right leg. It was easiest to see that side based on my point of view."

Logan looked up and took a deep breath. Sighing, he said, "Yeah that's exactly what I saw. I'm not sure what happened under the bridge to get him to change his gait like that." Logan sounded frustrated. He understood gait, he never forgot the way someone moved, and Logan knew he'd seen that limp before.

A couple of hours passed and General Anderson made a "training mission" for some young first lieutenants who were looking to impress their superiors. He gave them the license plate for the car and had them track the renter. They were to determine how the individual arrived at the airport, from where, when, and then when the individual was leaving and where they were going. That was the entire mission.

The storm began to die down and so did the men. The prior 24-hour adrenaline rush had now bottomed out and the men were drained.

The conversation was ending, they had circled around the topic several times already and exhausted every angle. They knew the man may have been wearing a mask, based on previous intel from Chicago, so the entire description could be useless aside from the height and the gait. Even the weight could have been altered with wraps to make him appear skinnier, or other objects to make him look heavier. Everyone decided it was time to call it a night. The general stood, and the men saluted. General Anderson gave a quick salute in return and he walked outside into the steady drizzle of the waning storm.

The men hit the rack hard that night. Everyone was sleeping within five minutes of lights out and nobody was stirring. Logan rarely slept, but this night was an exception. Whenever he was intensely focused on something during the day, it often found its way into a dream. Repeatedly he watched the suspect run in slow motion, both before and after the bridge. The advantage of dreams was the free camera feature in which, somehow by magic, he could change his perspective and watch the terrorist run from different angles.

Instantly, a change in the dream occurred. It was a whole different time and location. Logan was back in Iraq watching a weapons drop. The transition was seamless and easily understood, as it often is in dreams. Logan recognized the scene and looked down at the road. He saw a man running, limping. Repeatedly he watched. It was the man's right leg.

Instantly Logan awoke. He looked at his phone, 0200. He was wide awake and had made the connection. Logan knew he had seen it before, that limp, and now he knew from where. It was the job he took, the only one he took, under Jenkins. Logan looked at his phone again, 0204. He figured it didn't matter, she would want him to call. He got up slowly and silently, taking his phone outside. He dialed Samantha and waited for her to pick up. Three rings went by.

"Hello?" Samantha said quietly into the receiver.

"I know it's late but I need to tell you. We saw him."

"Can you ID him?"

"Actually . . . I think I've seen him before. The way he moved. I know I've seen this before. I'm going to need to figure this part out on my own. Reach out to a few friends. I just wanted to tell you the mission was successful."

"Thanks Logan."

chapter
TWENTY-TWO

It was Friday morning; the weather was mild in the Chicagoland area as Samantha went out the door to go to work. She opened the garage and put her sunglasses on. A moment later she was on the street and turning on the radio.

"It's Friiiiiday morning everyone. Start to the weekend," the morning radio guy exclaimed through the speakers. Samantha quickly dismissed the wishful thought of actually working a typical nine-to-five and getting a full weekend off. She didn't call Dom about her discussion with Logan, she would rather discuss that topic in person in his office behind closed doors. She was going to put Dom on his heels. But, for the first time she knew he would be understanding.

Samantha walked straight to her office. She quickly looked over the documents on her desk, but was too distracted. She needed to talk to Dom so she wasn't comprehending anything she was reading. She placed her brown leather purse in the drawer of her desk and walked out toward Dom's office. She decided to say exactly what Logan told her and see where the chips fell. Her relationship with Dom seemed to be at an all-time high.

"Enter," Dom said after the three knocks Samantha placed onto the door. Dom looked up from his desk to see Samantha once again standing in his doorway. He smiled, stood, and made a gesture for her to sit.

"What's up Samantha?" he said reading her body language.

"I heard from Logan," she said pausing.

"And?" Dom said leaning forward in his chair.

"They saw one of the terrorists."

"Well that's great!" Dom said slapping his hands together, leaning back into his chair, and relaxing through the shoulders a bit. He had a wide grin and his eyes sparkled.

"Yeah . . . it is . . . except he said something else that bothers me," Samantha said, which quickly dulled the gleam in Dom's eye and evaporated his smile.

"Out with it Samantha," Dom's frustration was noted in his voice.

"He recognized the terrorist—not his face, but the way he moved. Dom, I trust Logan. He's a freak at how well he can remember little nuances in the way people move."

"Jesus Sam really?" Dom asked and pushed back from his desk. "That's a bit of a stretch, isn't it?"

"I get it Dom. Let's just trust him. He's gotta talk to a few people then he'll get back to me."

"Hopefully with better intel."

South Carolina

Amir began his Friday morning at the computer.

Package received.

He wrote in an email and saved it as a draft. Amir then thought he would trade in his rental car for a sportier model to use for his drive to Saint Louis. He called Enterprise and extended his rental period as well as exchanged the Focus for a new black Camaro. Amir then got ready for the day, put on another face that matched his ID photo, and checked out of the hotel, grabbing a muffin from the free continental breakfast on the way out.

It was barely 1000 hours and Amir was already on the road in his shiny new black Camaro. The windows were rolled down and he was breathing in the clean air following the hurricane. It seemed a good storm always cleaned the air, making it smell fresh and new. The sun was out, and damage was everywhere, but the highways were clear. There was a beauty to it, however morbid that thought may be. The damp scenery added depth to the color making the greens greener and the browns exhibited a gradient of hues. He enjoyed seeing what kind of power mother nature could display. It was much more than anything he could ever accomplish with his limited, man-made explosives.

After three hours on the road he had driven far enough to escape all the disaster left in the path of the hurricane. It was as if nothing even happened. He was mildly disappointed knowing he wasn't seeing any more devastation. The air became heavy and thick as the sun continued to climb. He rolled the windows up and turned the radio on. He didn't care what was playing, he just wanted background noise. It helped his mind stay focused instead of wandering off.

He began focusing on the Saint Louis job. They were down one person. He knew the Edward Jones Dome was a large venue, which meant it would be easy to get in undetected. They would again use the false bottom packs in case security wanted to use the useless metal wands to dig through the pocket of the bag. The best time to go would be when the gates opened. Saint Louis fans are fanatics about their teams and line up early to go in. He would just have everyone find a spot in the middle of the line, possibly behind or in front of families with small children so security would be slightly distracted. The location of the C4 would be the only curveball. He would have to see the facility first, which meant getting into a preseason game. He pulled the car into a gas station to fill up. As he did so, he used his phone to purchase one preseason ticket, and four random single seat tickets for opening day. He used his credit card, Mark Delaney.

Camp Lejeune

Logan, General Anderson, and the men had an uneventful ride home on the helo. Migs and Dave Henderson gave them a nice, smooth ride, with an occasional joke from Dave. After landing and letting the helo spin down, Logan told all the men to head home, get a good meal, say hi to their families, and they would get together the next morning at 0700 in BB-5. Everyone dispersed, exchanging quick goodbyes. Logan was left with General Anderson.

"Well Logan, gotta say great op. You got a usable lead on this asshole," General Anderson said.

"Yeah." Logan hesitated, trying to decide whether or not to tell General Anderson about his revelation. "I've seen that guy before."

"The terrorist?" Anderson said placing his hands on his hips, slightly confused.

"Yeah, it sounds weird, but when I was in Iraq, I was doing a black op surveillance mission. I was supposed to take pictures of a weapons drop for the militia. RPGs. The seller was a man who was wearing a wig. I know, because I saw dark hair underneath a blonde wig as he ran away to the car at the end of the sale. The more important part is that I remember his limp. He'd been shot. It was the same limp as the guy in the park."

"Well, what does it mean?" General Anderson asked raising an eyebrow.

"It means this guy's been doing it for a while. You know who General Jenkins is?" Logan asked.

"Yes, of course, he's the advisory to the Secretary. Never liked the guy. Slimy."

"Well, he was the XO on that mission. Nothing felt right about it and I barely made it out alive," Logan said quickly reliving the events.

"Where are we going with this Logan?"

"I just want to look at Jenkins' missions. See how many failures and successes he had. I just got a feeling about him and it's growing stronger."

"I can, but this is a serious step you're taking. I never liked the guy, but I don't want to go head hunting on that basis. The only problem is keeping this kind of searching a secret."

"I understand," Logan said sighing.

"I'll look into it. Give me a few days to get everything together. After all, I have stars on my shoulders. I can get the info," General Anderson said tapping his left shoulder and smiling.

Saint Louis

Sunday morning Amir woke up early, 0700, and went down to the lobby at the Renaissance Saint Louis Grand Hotel where he was staying for the next two weeks. It was quiet as he strolled, nodding at the middle-aged woman behind the check-in desk who was standing at attention. He smiled when she did, and went to the free breakfast. The preseason game was going to start at noon, and he planned on walking the streets a while beforehand. He knew that he would have plenty of time inside the stadium to figure out the best locations for the explosives, he just wanted to work out the different exits and possible escape routes.

Amir made quick work of some eggs and sausage, and walked out into the sticky, late summer air with some orange juice in hand. The buildings provided ample shade while he walked east down Washington past the metro station, then north on Broadway toward the stadium. The area was already buzzing with people due to the proximity of the America's Center Convention Complex.

Amir finished his orange juice and threw the cup away as he passed a trash can on the corner. He took out his cellphone and noted the time was now 0815. The sun was steadily rising, growing stronger by the minute as it began its ancient arc across the sky. The buildings were becoming useless as the sun climbed higher and higher. As Amir walked down Broadway he felt the sun begin to touch the back of his neck. The warmth was intense, but felt good on his own skin, because, for a change, he wasn't wearing any disguise.

Amir walked a few laps around the stadium and along several streets crisscrossing the area. He understood the layout, he noticed the high traffic streets versus the low traffic by the way the intersections and crosswalks were laid out. He knew there would be people everywhere before, during, and after the game. He wanted the busiest intersections for his co-conspirators to meander through after they left the game.

The gates opened at 1100 for the 1215 game and Amir stood in line for less than five minutes. The security was slow and deliberate, due to the low volume of people coming into the gate. Amir realized that going into the main gate on game day would be the best idea, because security would be hurried and quick with their inspections. Being opening day, they would be a little rusty and scattered too, probably having a few rookies.

Over the next four hours Amir took full advantage of the time he had in the stadium. He didn't watch a single play, just inspected the entire facility from the top down. He took careful note of how each level was supported by the one below. He noticed that some of the main supports were located under the upper deck just above the lower section. Amir thought that the best idea would be to damage the upper levels, and have them cascade down onto the lower ones. He knew the sections near the 50-yard line are the most desirable, and therefore hold the most fans. The main concessions were under the upper deck as well, so if the collapse was great enough, it would kill anyone on the walkways, too. It was obviously the place to set the explosives.

Amir began to focus on the supports, where they were located, and how he could destroy them in the most inconspicuous ways. Again, he noted several trash bins next to the pillars, just as in Water Tower Place in Chicago, but he thought it may pose too high a risk. There was a lot more foot traffic in these halls, and someone was bound to see them throwing bags in the trash. He also realized that the amount of garbage was astronomical, and more likely than not, the trash would be taken away before they had a chance to detonate.

Amir took a trip into the bathroom, where he noticed it was surprisingly empty. He also noticed that the stall closest to the wall had a metal beam in the corner. It was part of the structural support for the upper deck. He knew placing explosives there, between the beam and the wall, would work. He washed his hands and left the bathroom, having found one spot.

Amir then had another thought. The location was ideal, of course, but they only had a limited amount of explosives, and the magnitude of what he was trying to do by taking down the upper deck began to seem ridiculous. He switched his thought process to which could create the most paranoia. In the craziness, hopefully people would end up trampling each other. The plan changed at that moment. He would have the team plant the C4 in the bathroom, but then also near the main entrance, so people wouldn't be able to leave. He continued to walk through the section beneath the 50-yard line. He found two additional, inconspicuous, low traffic places. He had his locations chosen, now he would notify the team.

Camp Lejeune

It was early Monday morning, when General Anderson's phone rang. He was shaving and let it ring three times while he dried his hands. General Anderson looked down at the phone recognizing the number. It was

Sergeant Bobby.

"Mitchell," the General said picking up the receiver.

"Good morning, sir," Bobby said formally. "I've got some news I'm sure you wanted to hear right away."

"Let's hear it then," the general said in a calm voice as he turned the speakerphone function on and finished shaving his upper lip.

"We've got some action from that special project you gave those Marines, regarding a Mark Delaney. They want to talk to you directly. That's all they said."

"Sounds good Bobby, see you shortly."

General Anderson hung the phone up, dried his face, and put his shirt on. As he walked out of the bathroom, he called Logan.

"General Mitchell," Logan said as he picked up.

"Logan," the general responded sternly. "Apparently, we've got a hit on a Mark Delaney. I don't know what yet, I have to call them when I get to my office, but I thought you should be there while I do. Get this ball moving forward right away."

"Good plan. I'll meet you there," Logan said grabbing his keys. He waited for the general to say goodbye, more as a technicality than an obligation. Logan walked out of the apartment and jogged over to General Anderson's office.

"You got here fast," General Anderson said. Logan grinned and they shook hands. "Let's go make this phone call."

"Morning General, Logan," Sergeant Bobby said as they walked into the office.

"Morning," both men responded in unison and entered the general's office as Logan closed the door behind them. The number for the general to call was sitting on his desk on a green Post-it. Both the general and Logan remained standing as he dialed the number and then hit the speaker button. General Anderson looked up at Logan, placed his hands on his hips, and waited as the phone rang, shifting his body impatiently.

"Task force Tango," someone said through the speaker after several rings.

"This is General Anderson."

"Hello, sir. We have had some action on that name you gave us. Actually, some significant information," the anonymous voice said through the phone.

"Well get on with it," General Anderson said placing his hands on the table and leaning in.

"OK, we have a hit on a rental car, the silver Focus, but also, Mark Delaney returned it, and rented another one. He has a different location for the return of the vehicle, and it's Saint Louis."

"Excellent job," General Anderson said through the receiver and smiled at Logan.

"Excuse me, sir," the voice said hesitantly.

"Yes, go ahead son," the general responded still smiling.

"He also has a hotel reservation. It's at the Renaissance Hotel."

The general paused for a moment, allowing the voice to continue talking if there was more to be said before asking, "Is that it?"

"No sir."

"Let's spit it out soldier God damn it! What's with the piece-by-piece bullshit?"

"He bought several tickets to the Rams game, opening day, and a preseason game that took place yesterday."

"This is all good information. You did great work, son. Keep me posted on any more traffic on this guy's credit card."

"Will do, sir."

General Anderson picked up the receiver, and then hung it up, ending the call. He then raised his eyes to meet Logan's. "I guess you're going to Saint Louis."

"It appears that way, sir," Logan said placing his hands on his hips and looking down for a moment. "You realize what this means right, sir?" Logan rarely called General Anderson sir, he reverted to his days as a soldier during pivotal moments like this. It was what Logan was most comfortable and familiar with. "It means they're going to attack the Edward Jones Dome."

"And now we know the date too. Opening day is when?" General Anderson punched the intercom to Sergeant Bobby. "Bobby, find out when the home opener is for the Saint Louis Rams."

"Yes sir, give me two minutes," Bobby responded and accessed the computer.

"Logan, we need them all," the general said somberly. "We can't just take this guy down."

"I know sir, we will. My men and I will take care of this."

The intercom beeped, "General Anderson sir," Bobby said.

"Go ahead Bobby."

"Sir, it's 9/11."

"Thanks Bobby," General Anderson turned off the intercom. He stood for a moment looking down at his large, wooden desk as he digested the last few minutes. He had a slight chuckle as it came to him. "Define irony Logan," he said looking up and meeting Logan's gaze. "How about kicking these guys in the ass on 9/11?"

"Feels pretty good sir," Logan replied as goosebumps cascaded down his arms. "Let me brief the men on what we're about to do, and then we can plan on getting us out there and take these assholes down."

"Sure thing Logan. Call me when you're ready."

"I know one thing. We're gonna need tickets to that game."

"Consider it done."

Logan left the office, and immediately got on the phone with Migs, and then Dubs. They would contact everyone else, and meet in BB-5 within the hour.

Logan's men sat patiently waiting for him to deliver the news. Each one of them knew it was big, and had a feeling it was a lead on the terrorist they had stalked just a few days ago. Logan strode into BB-5. He was smirking, though it was more indirectly, with his eyes not his mouth. Logan was excited, but guarded. After years of special ops and working for the government he knew that getting excited about anything was a stupid idea. However, his excitement, no matter how guarded, was contagious. The men started shifting in their chairs, their heart rates were increasing. They saw an unfamiliar expression on Logan's face but they knew it was positive and they were growing sick with anticipation.

"Where we goin', Logan?" Dubs finally said breaking the tension. For the first time, none of the men laughed at Dubs' outburst.

"What I've got, are home opener tickets for the Saint Louis Rams."

"Hey boss, what does that mean?" Migs said softly.

"It means we're going to Saint Louis, and right now. The terrorist rented a car, a hotel room, and bought tickets to a preseason and the home opening game. That's where things are gonna go down. We've already got our tickets; we're getting travel set up. We know the terrorist is at the Renaissance so we're probably going to stay there. It's close to the venue anyways. Notify your families. We're going to be there for a while. No details, just going on a training op. Yut?"

"Yut!" they responded.

The men sat back, serious, somber. It had been interesting, the course they were taking with Logan, but all their training from the last few weeks was about to come into practice. The men dispersed and awaited further contact before they left for Saint Louis, and their biggest mission yet. At that moment, Logan's phone began to vibrate in his pocket.

"Hello," Logan said not recognizing the number.

"Logan this is Sergeant Bobby. General Anderson wanted me to tell you that you have tickets booked for tomorrow morning 1100 hours flight to Saint Louis. It's on a civilian flight. I will email you the details if that's OK with you."

"I'd rather just come and grab them from you right now."

"Fine with me sir. See you shortly."

Logan stood staring at his phone as he began to talk. "Well guys better get home and hug your families," he said looking up at the men and sliding his phone back into his pocket. We leave tomorrow, civilian flight, 1100 hours. Civilian clothes only, bring your sunglasses. It's time we put this training into practice. We'll worry about accommodations and transport when we get there. Now everyone get outta here."

Dubs had nowhere to go, no family to talk to, and found himself thinking hard as he sat alone in his apartment. He needed a distraction, a way to stop his mind from driving him crazy. The thoughts of Saint Louis, the anticipation, the possibility of failure dominated his mind. He decided to go out, but didn't want to be alone.

"Hey Cap," Dubs said when Migs walked into the bar.

"How many you had already you crazy piece of shit?" Migs shook hands with Dubs and took a seat at the bar. It was 1700 hours and Dubs had already been there alone for an hour.

"Just one. I'm not trying to get hammered tonight man. I appreciate you coming down."

"What the hell else do I have going on?"

"Yeah that's the truth. I never even see you with a woman man. Sometimes I wonder about you Cap."

"Yeah, yeah shithead keep talking. I just can't do what you do. I'm too afraid of STDs man. One day you're gonna get it bad."

"So, you ever had a girl like Logan had Sam?"

"I don't know Dubs. I mean I've had a few girls, longest one about a year. We haven't talked in a while though. You? Wait, are you baiting me? You gonna get me talking serious and sappy and call me out in front of the guys? Fuck this game."

"No, no, man," Dubs said coolly, looking down at his glass and swirling his drink.

"What's goin' on Dubs? No bullshit."

"It's gonna sound gay as fuck."

"Hey man, right up my alley, right?" Migs had a laugh.

"Awww man, I was being a dick. I can't turn that part of me off."

"Fair enough. But I asked you a question soldier."

"Recon has always been a brotherhood to me, but this feels like a family. I haven't ever been this close to people before. I've never had a girl. I mean, I've HAD girls, but never been exclusive. I'm not sure where I'm going with this, just to say I enjoy being around the guys, being Logan's guys. I don't want to do anything else." The two men sat for a few moments. Each reflecting on Dubs' transparency and vulnerability he hadn't shown anyone before.

"Why you telling me this? I mean why me?"

"Everyone else is married, married with kids, and then there's Logan. You're the one guy I can relate to, kinda."

"This shit's outta my wheelhouse man. You wanna' call Logan?" Migs asked knowing how most things Logan said Dubs held as gold.

"Fuckin' might as well!" Dubs said brightening up. He had wanted to call Logan but thought it would be weird. Now that Migs brought it up, he was off the hook.

Logan paused in his car before entering the bar. The lot was empty compared to the last time he'd been there. He recalled the moment when he and Sherman wrestled in the gravel, just fifty yards from where he was parked. How far he'd come since that moment. It was the last night Sherman was stateside; alive. Logan knew how Dubs felt. It was the same reason he and Sherman went out that night. To keep their head clear before shipping out, any way they could. Logan sighed, put his game face on, and went onside.

"So how deep in the shit are you two?" Logan said slapping them both firmly on the back.

"Shitfaced. We need a ride home," Migs said with slurred speech.

"Yeah, it took you over an hour to get here man, we drank a

shitload," Dubs said struggling to stand.

Logan stood examining them for a few moments. "You assholes can't trick me. You guys are both buying me a drink now." They all had a laugh and sat down at the table.

Another hour passed, and so did a few more drinks. The three men opened-up about love, life, and fears.

"OK guys I'm gonna let you in," Logan said gathering their attention. "Samantha and I broke up a few years back because I was terrified about something happening to her. I hated her for putting herself in a position that could get her hurt. We decided, after many fights, to break it off. Thought we'd be better apart. It worked, but it took a few years. Then she called."

"Shit makes sense I think," Dubs said. "I mean, if anything happened to any of our guys I'd be furious."

"Logan, you ever lost anyone close in combat?" Migs asked hoping to get Dubs a bit less worried.

Logan wished the question hadn't been asked. A month ago, it would have been easy to lie. A few less drinks, two men other than Dubs and Migs, and he could have veiled the truth.

"Sherman. His name was Sherman. He was my sniper; I was the spotter. He took a round in the liver. I carried him for ten klicks out of Mosul. He was alive when I checked him about an hour out from the exfil. When the helo got there, he was gone."

The men sat silenced. Logan's shoulders slumped over slightly and exhaled. "He saved my life more than once."

It felt good to talk about it. He hadn't even said Sherman's name in years. Logan looked up and saw Dubs and Migs staring at the table. He realized he was looking at two versions of himself from a long time ago. Both alone, both dedicated to the Corps, and both green in love. He knew how Sherman must have felt around him years ago.

"Listen guys, we need to keep our shit together in Saint Louis. We have the jump on them. It's an environment they can't control, full of people they don't know. We all need to make sure these emotions don't make the decisions for us. We'll be alright," Logan said, mostly for himself. He was terrified of losing another man on his watch.

"Yeah, let's get the fuck outta here," Dubs said chugging the last half of his beer. They shook hands and parted.

chapter
TWENTY-THREE

Saint Louis

"We have landed in Saint Louis, the local time is 1:13 p.m., temperature is a humid 93 degrees," the flight attendant announced with a few chuckles from the cabin. "We ask that you remain seated with your seatbelts securely fastened until we arrive at our gate. If you are taking a connecting flight, please check the board when you arrive in the terminal as some of the gates have changed. Thank you for flying with us and hope you travel with us again soon."

"Alright boys let's grab a ride downtown. We'll check in at the Renaissance and then head straight to the stadium. As you know, we have just under two weeks before the Rams' season opener. We have work to do."

The Marines exited the plane and walked down the corridor in silence toward the street. Each man was thinking about the task at hand, remembering the training Logan had worked into their heads over the last several weeks. As they reached the arrival terminal they began to feel the temperature gradient between the warm humid outside, and the dry, cool air from the airport. The doors opened and closed as people exited the building, allowing belches of warm humid air into the halls. It was almost an act of God that the cooling system could keep the heat at bay.

As Logan exited the airport he saw a taxi van and flagged it down. The driver swooped in quickly and hammered the brakes, stopping just next to where Logan and his men were standing.

"How we doing today fellas?" the African American taxi driver asked as Logan slid the door open.

"Renaissance Hotel downtown," Logan stated as he then opened the passenger door and sat down next to the driver. The rest of the men piled into the back still not saying a word.

The drive was an uneventful 30 minutes. They arrived at the hotel and checked into their rooms for the two-week stay.

"Ryan, Dubs, Migs, you guys share a room, Brian, Lonnie, Tom, you are sharing another, and I've got my own," Logan said to the men handing them all their keys. "Your rooms are joined so it can be like one big camping trip." The men all broke their stagnant stares and cracked a smile at the lighthearted comment. "It's important you guys stay loose and relaxed. You know these terrorists are good, and they'll run or fight at the slightest indication they're being watched. We need to tail this guy to find the others. Remember, he is in this hotel, last we knew. Let's go drop off our shit and get to the stadium."

Logan and his men walked the streets in downtown Saint Louis. As they headed north toward the stadium they felt the searing sun at every crosswalk. The buildings were casting longer and longer shadows, which provided some reprieve. The men all took note of the buildings, the streets, and the foot traffic at each intersection.

As they neared the stadium it was about 1700. Foot traffic began to slow down considerably. Most people were done with work and were heading home before the evening. A small minority of people were heading into bars for an after-work drink or two, and even fewer were heading downtown for dinner.

"Gets dead down here," Dubs said as they walked past the main entrance to the gate.

"Mhm," Logan said as he took in the scene. "We should probably go into one of these restaurants. If someone was watching the stadium they might notice a group of men just walking around looking and never stopping."

Migs kicked a rock that was perched perfectly at the end of a sidewalk and it headed across the street. "How about that pizza place?"

Dubs decided to break into a run across the street yelling, "I'm in!" Even a few strangers laughed watching the large man sprint across the street.

Dubs entered the restaurant and walked up to hostess. "How you doing this afternoon little lady?" he asked leaning into the counter and smiling at the young college coed. She smirked back and rolled her eyes. "I'm gonna need a table for seven," he said and held up the number five. Both laughed as the rest of the men walked in.

"Is he giving you the number seven bit?" Ryan asked seeing Dubs bring his hand down from overhead.

"Oh, and please sit us inside miss. That guy will sunburn outside," Dubs said, much louder than necessary as he turned toward Tom and the rest of the men who were laughing even harder now. The hostess grabbed a few paper menus and escorted them to their table, inside.

As they walked through the restaurant they noted it wasn't typical. It lacked the exposed brick, faux Italian street scenes, or greasy pub feel. Instead, it was very fresh, modern, well-lit with tall wooded panel walls wrapping all the way up and continuing on to part of the ceiling. There were also grey slate tiles on the floor and a long bar with stools.

"Here you are. Austin is your waiter. He'll be with you shortly," the hostess walked away; no doubt she was about to text her friends about this group of guys.

The restaurant was trendy, but empty. There was only one other group in the whole restaurant and they were off to the corner away from the action. Whether it was serendipitous, ironic, or purposeful, they were seated right next to the bar. Before Dubs even looked at the menu, he had already gathered the bartender's attention.

"Hey guy, before we go any further, what's your name?" Dubs said very kindly.

"It's Dan," he responded with a small playful bow. "What can I get for ya' sir?"

"Well, first thing, call me sir all night, that'll get you a bigger tip, and second, let's get two pitchers floatin' around the table. We'll go Budweiser because that's got the smallest carbon footprint around here," Dubs said smiling and pointing at the text on the menu. He really didn't care either way.

"Quit being a dick," Lonnie said laughing and threw a menu across the table at Dubs.

"I'm just trying to do my part," Dubs responded holding his arms out to the side as if he was being crucified. Dan finished pouring the pitchers and brought them to the bar counter. "Just put it on the bill for the table buddy, thanks."

"Will do, sir."

The men stayed for a few hours slowly eating pizza and drinking. Lonnie told a couple stories about his ladies, Migs told a few about missions he flew, Ryan ran off at the mouth about how he got sunburned on a recon mission, which he would most likely regret later on. Everyone prodded Logan for a story or two, but he just shrugged it off. Logan knew one thing for sure, nobody was assuming these guys were anything more than a group of crazy old friends. They tipped the waitress and the bartender well, and made the walk back to the hotel.

The evening was hot, but comfortable. The streets were quiet and the men were careful not to make themselves known. Logan had warned them before they left not to be memorable. As they made quick work of the walk back to the hotel, Logan gave them some instructions.

"Tomorrow everyone wakes at 0700. We'll take turns in twos and threes going down to breakfast. Remember, we have no idea if this guy will be wearing a disguise. I'm glad we did this tonight. It'll help us relax during the next few weeks. We'll save lives or watch people die in our arms. Make no mistakes about it. There's more at stake than anything you have ever done. These are civilians."

The last minute was silent. Everyone had sobered up after hearing Logan's statement. Every Marine understands their duty and Logan had reminded them of that very plainly. This was not an adventure, not a training mission, not a war-zone. It was civilian lives they were working around. It's an unpredictable and high stakes mission.

Two days passed. Logan's men were performing the surveillance of the lobby and generating possible suspects. One man was middle-aged, dark complexion, possibly Middle Eastern, but there was nothing impressive about him. He had a nervous and anxious behavior and that didn't fit the profile of their mark. A second man would always stare into the lobby at Logan's men as he ate his breakfast, but, when Logan was asked to check the man out he was quickly eliminated. Logan thought he was just an aggressive man who was sticking his chest out and told everyone, especially Dubs, not to engage. No slips ups at this critical time. Their favorite person was an older woman. She walked through the lobby back and forth everyday muttering to herself "I'm fantastic, I'm fantastic!" motivating herself over and over again.

The third day was different. Tom was sitting in the expansive lobby. He was enjoying taking in the atmosphere, watching families and businessmen, trying to guess exactly why they were in Saint Louis. He nodded to many, smiled at a few, but then he saw it, a limp. The man was tall, well-built, dark complexion and favored his right leg. Tom recognized the gait immediately. He waited for the man to leave the lobby and walked out after. He took a deep breath of warm humid air that dissolved all trace of the comfortable air-conditioned lobby he had exited. It focused him. It sharpened his mind, demanded that he focus on what was at hand. He leaned against the streetlight and watched the limp go down the street. He was sure he had their mark.

Tom followed the man for several minutes. At the first intersection, the man turned left. The next, left again. At the third intersection, it appeared as though the man would once again turn left so Tom turned right. Tom walked several more blocks then circled back toward the hotel.

"Logan," Tom said after the second ring. "I'm coming up. We're gonna need everyone. I found him."

Slowly the men filed into Logan's room. It was a bit cramped. "Well, Tom you have the floor," Logan said as Tom finally entered the room, smiling.

"I've got him. That asshole walked right out of here and I followed him through two intersections. He was about to make his third left in a row. I stopped, turned right instead, walked another mile or so then called Logan and circled back to the hotel."

"What's he look like?" Dubs said rubbing his hands together as he leaned forward sitting at the edge of the bed.

"Tall, athletic build, dark complexion. He had that limp. The same limp I saw when he was taking the C4 drop from Shifty," Tom said as he demonstrated the limp in the limited space between the bed and the dresser. The men sat in silence replaying the day in the storm watching their mark take the drop and walk back to the car.

"Here's what happens next," Logan said breaking the silence. "We'll keep taking shifts in the lobby, but now we will take shifts on the street too. We have to make overlapping surveillance. We can't allow ourselves to be seen. Remember we already have this guy, we are looking for his team."

Amir sat in his hotel room in front of the laptop. He had just gotten back from a very long walk around the city. Something felt different. He was nervous, suspicious. For the last two days, he felt as though he was being watched. He was taking extra steps to avoid people watching him. He took the stairs instead of the elevator, left the hotel from the service entrance whenever possible, took more and more illogical routes when walking. He had finally found a good spot for a meet. It had a high volume of traffic, always fresh faces.

Meet: Saint Louis, Mo. Saint Louis Art Museum.

Amir placed the email in the draft bin. Everyone should be getting the email that day. It would allow three days of travel. Amir enjoyed the peace and loneliness of an art museum. No small talking strangers, no loud obnoxious kids.

chapter
TWENTY-FOUR

Logan's men had their terrorist marked. It took three days, but they had his time out, 0845–0900. They had his route, typically five miles in duration; however, he would always cross into Forest Park at the same intersection. Logan had his men rotate at this intersection, Lindell and Kingshighway, as well as two guys in the park. They still left one man in the lobby and the rest were rovers between the park and the hotel.

"He's on his way," Tom said to Dubs. "He left 15 minutes ago with a satchel across his chest. It looks heavy. I'm walking to the park."

"Gotcha'. I'll watch for him," Dubs hung up the phone and began to walk south down Kingshighway, away from Lindell. He would walk for 30 minutes south, then head back north. Hopefully, the timing would be just right to spot their mark entering the park. As Dubs began his walk, he looked westward into the park and nodded a head toward Migs who was walking down a trail heading east. This was the cue to start the same 30-minute walk. Migs would walk west for 30 and then head back east.

"Logan, we're starting the walk."

"OK," Logan texted back. He then called Lonnie. "Lonnie time to tighten up. Come toward the park."

"You got it Logan." He was one of the rovers on this day. Lonnie was on Market Street heading west. Eventually, he would get onto Laclede and head through the Saint Louis University campus on his way to the park. He would enter the park approximately one half mile from the Lindell–Kingshighway intersection.

Logan texted Tom and Brian telling them to tighten up as well. All the men were closing in on the park. Logan was sitting near the zoo inside of Forest Park, two miles from the intersection.

Ninety minutes passed and there the terrorist stood at the intersection of Lindell and Kingshighway. Dubs was the first to see him. They stood across the street from one another. Dubs did all he could not to stare a hole through him. Dubs heart began to pound. His instinct was to attack the man, rip his throat out, dismember him, beat his teeth in.

Amir stood opposite, cool and collected, enjoying the walk without a care in the world. He looked north down the street, then south reading the traffic. He looked up to the streetlights and noticed that the traffic signal on Kingshighway was yielding, then the light turned red. Amir turned and faced across the intersection noting a rather large man. The walk signal turned on, and Amir began walking across the street. He made eye contact with the large man. The large man locked onto Amir and hesitated, not responding to the walk signal. Amir immediately took note of every feature of the man. His stature, his haircut, eye color, body language. He looked at how he postured, how the clothes fit him, and eventually, a moment later when the large man moved, he took note of his gait and cadence. He would watch for this man again. Amir continued walking into the park. He had to meet his team in just over an hour at the art museum.

Migs saw the terrorist as he entered the park. Migs turned right and headed south on Kingshighway and watched him walk westward deep into the park. Migs texted "heading westbound into park."

Logan received the text and began walking east, slowly. It took 20 minutes but he finally spotted the mark. He was about a quarter mile away and was not sporting the classic limp. Logan watched him. He was moving with a purpose. It was the only time he wasn't limping in the last four days. Logan knew today was different. He sent out a text: "converge on the zoo."

Logan wanted everyone close. The mark turned right onto Fine Arts

Drive. Logan looked at the time: 1215. Logan moved north toward the Grand Basin, a large pool with water shooting skyward in several different areas. Logan never looked back, never turned to see where their man was going. Logan was patient. There was only one standing structure the terrorist could duck into and that was the art museum. Logan texted Lonnie. "Walk to art museum, tell us what you see."

Lonnie made quick work of the two-mile walk arriving at the art museum at 1240. He saw no sign of the terrorist outside the building so he entered. It was much darker inside so it took Lonnie several moments to scan the main atrium. He spotted the mark walking toward two other people. Lonnie then entered the rightmost art room and looked at the artwork. He had no idea what he was looking at, but he tried. Lonnie left the room ten minutes later without a sign of Amir. Lonnie walked through the main lobby scanning both right and left, slowing every now and again as he saw a group. Finally, in the furthest room on the left stood five individuals. One of them was their man. Lonnie walked into the room immediately to the left of the him.

He took his phone out and texted the men. "Total of five people including our mark. They all got something from his bag."

Lonnie walked past the room again and snapped five images in quick succession with his phone. He sent all the images to the men. Lonnie locked his phone and looked back toward the group. One of them was staring. She was slight of build, blonde, and her eyes were cold. They locked eyes for a couple of seconds before Lonnie quickly recovered. He smiled and mouthed the word "hi," and winked. The woman rolled her eyes and rejoined her conversation. Lonnie finished the play by smiling and shrugging before moving on.

Logan reviewed the images. They were great. The five wore very distinct clothing, easy to observe. Logan sent a text to all the men. Each was to follow a specific individual. Migs and Tom would follow the woman. Brian and Dubs the shorter, darker man in the blue shirt. Lonnie and Ryan follow the older white man in red, and Logan would follow the Hispanic, muscular man.

The men waited outside as one-by-one the terrorists filed out. Logan's men did exactly as they were trained. They watched the terrorists all the way back to the hotel. Each suspect was studied in the way they moved and less in the way they looked. Logan's men remembered that they wore masks in Chicago, so likely they would do the same in Saint Louis.

"OK men what did you see?" Logan asked as the group finally came back together four hours after the art museum. They had all taken cabs back to the hotel in order to avoid being tailed themselves.

"Our mark had small, quick steps. Kinda' waddled a bit," said Dubs about the short, dark man.

"Ours lumbered slowly and barely hit his heels when he walked," said Lonnie.

"The woman really had nothing special. She tended to look around a lot but that's about it. She was very short, small, so maybe she would stand out in a crowd," Migs said.

"Well mine was unremarkable except for one thing," Logan reached into his pocket and pulled out his phone. "This tattoo on his hand," Logan held up his phone revealing a brilliant blue tattoo on the back of his hand. "I'll send the pic to you guys. We have four days before the game. We'll watch them closely and switch which suspect we tail for the next four days. We know they received the explosives. Lonnie got pictures of our man handing off the packages. Let's keep our eyes open."

Logan closed the door behind the men as they left for the night, and walked back toward the bed. Sighing, he picked up his cellphone to bring one last person up to speed.

"Logan, how are we doing?" General Mitchell Anderson said after the third ring. His voice was raspy, as if he had just been resting.

"Hello sir. We've had a breakthrough. Five terrorists accounted for. We know their locations."

"Well that's great work Logan. What else can I do to help? I wanna' crush these bastards," the general said the last sentence through clenched teeth.

Logan sat in silence for a moment. He considered bringing Samantha up to speed and bringing FBI agents in to assist in taking the terrorist down. "Well sir, I think I need a few Marines. I want guys I can trust and right now I can only trust my brothers."

"You got it Logan, but I'm coming too. You can stay in control and I will move on your command. I'll make sure the Marines I bring know what to do. Just keep me posted."

"I will, sir. But you guys need to be here by tomorrow for briefing on locations and the game is in four days."

"I'm making my phone calls as soon as you let me go Logan."

"Goodbye then, sir. See you soon."

chapter
TWENTY-FIVE

It was warm at 0700 on 9/11. The streets downtown were shaded from the sun by the tall buildings on the eastern edge of the city; but the Arch was on fire. The uppermost sections were so bright it was impossible to look at, bathing the Mississippi River in the glow of two suns. The heat was going to be relentless. Any rain cloud that thought of coming into the city that day was going to become a whisper. The one solace was the flags blowing lazily in the wind—a familiar but gentle breeze that hinted at a reprieve as the sun continued its trek across the sky.

Logan and his men had their assignments. Logan decided it was best to stick with the man who contacted Shifty, "Delaney." Lonnie was on the woman. Dubs was on the small, waddling man, Ryan was on the older man who didn't use his heels. Tom was on the dark man with the very small, quick steps, Migs was to follow the muscular, Latino man. Brian followed the man with the blue tattoo. Each man sat in the lobby of five different hotels eating breakfast and reading.

General Anderson and the Marines were waiting in three hotel rooms, seven Marines in each room. They wore plain clothes and were located within ten minutes walking distance to each of the hotels the terrorists were staying. The plan was on Logan's signal, take down the terrorists as they came out of the game and went back to the hotel.

Logan and his men would take pictures of the individuals and send them to each other, and the Marines, so that they would know exactly who to grab.

Two hours passed and Brian was the first to see his mark. The tattoo gave him away. His skin color was different and he was wearing a mask, but the make-up didn't completely cover the tattoo. Brian sent a photo to everyone. "Eyes on blue tattoo. He is wearing mask and skin is much lighter." The man in the blue tattoo also had a backpack. Brian followed him, but not closely.

"I've got mine too," Lonnie texted the group. "She's in disguise, but you can't fake petite." Lonnie followed her out.

"My guy is leaving, walks the same, looks pretty young, it's a mask. Definitely the old man," Ryan said.

"I've got the duck in sight. Still waddling away," Dubs wrote.

"Muscular, dark skin, long hair now, but this is my mark," Migs wrote.

Logan found himself pacing around the hotel lobby. It was already 1100 hours and no sign of the mark. Doubts began to creep in. He realized assumptions had been made about how the terrorist would handle game day. He took a few, deep calming breaths. He knew that all the other Marines were on their marks. He allowed himself to think of other possible scenarios, how his men could get hurt. Had they been made? Was the job called off? It couldn't be off, the terrorists had bags, they all had disguises. It was certainly a go.

Then Logan had a terrible revelation. Maybe his mark was providing overwatch. He wasn't going to the game at all. He would be somewhere with a good view and assessing possible targets, just as Logan had done years before. Logan knew he couldn't possibly find the terrorist with all the windows and buildings in the area, but he knew he could try to keep his men safe.

"I'm moving on the game. No sign of him. Maybe missed him so keep eyes open," Logan texted the men. By now Logan knew all the other terrorists, as well as his men, had entered the Edward Jones Dome. Each had likely found where the terrorist had left their bags and placed cell signal jammers appropriately.

Logan hailed a cab. "Meet me out front, I have on a black t-shirt and jeans," Logan texted his men as he rode in the cab. Seven minutes later, Logan arrived at the Edward Jones Dome. The first person he saw was Dubs. He threw money into the back seat as he fumbled out of the car. He ran toward Dubs who was wearing a Rams' shirt and khaki shorts.

"Get down!" he yelled to Dubs as they moved toward each other. Logan began throwing his arms into the air. "He's overwatch! Get the fuck outta' here!" he continued to yell through the streets, scaring everyone.

Suddenly Dubs froze with a confused look upon his face. A split second later Logan heard a shot. Logan snapped his head around toward the right and saw glass raining down from a hotel window directly south down the street.

Time froze, sound stopped, and Logan reacted on instinct. It felt as though five minutes passed by the time Logan ran to Dubs throwing him over his shoulder. Logan ran about a quarter mile east and set him softly on to the ground. By then, all of Logan's men were there to help.

"Migs on me!"

Migs followed Logan as he ran south down the street. They ran flat out for a half mile. "Get to the front of the hotel and watch for our mark!" Logan yelled through heavy breathing. "NOW!" Logan yelled pushing Migs quickly in the chest with one hand. Logan ran around to the rear service entrance to the hotel.

Logan waited at the back entrance against the wall. Logan wanted to cry. His emotions were out of control. He left Dubs on the street with a gunshot wound to the abdomen. It was all so familiar to him. He closed his eyes and Sherman was there. Not the happy, playful, big brother Sherman, but the one who laid dead on the Iraqi dirt while Logan pounded down onto his chest. He wanted desperately to go back to the Edward Jones Dome. He felt the need to be there for Dubs. The big man with a bigger heart. The "kid" who never once had been in love. *It should have been me this time!* Logan wrestled with the thought of himself being close to death for the third time in his life. Once with Sherman, once for Jenkins, and now here.

Two minutes passed and Amir came barreling out the back door. He had just run down several flights of stairs and his calf was terribly cramped. He was looking for relief, hobbling, and reaching down toward his leg, searching for comfort. As Amir stood up he looked left first. By the time he looked right, Logan was already barreling down on him.

Logan struck Amir in the face with everything he had causing both men to go to the ground. Amir wasn't unconscious, but dazed. Logan grabbed his radio and called to Migs. "I've got him, get back here!" Logan was reaching out to Migs. It was the only way Logan knew how to stop himself.

Logan reached behind his back and pulled out his 1911, placing it between Amir's teeth. For the first time the men looked into each other's eyes. Logan struggled hard not to pull the trigger. It was for Sherman he wanted to pull the trigger. It was for himself he wanted to pull the trigger. It was for Dubs he wanted to pull the trigger. Vengeance and rage enveloped him. He was floating above the ground, his gun felt like an extension of his hand. He almost pulled the trigger just to feel something.

"Logan the paramedics are here and are taking Dubs to Barnes-Jewish Hospital," Ryan said on the radio breaking the tension.

"One second," Logan said and he pulled the hammer back on his gun. His wits were returning, but he still felt like killing the man. Logan ground his teeth, he spat on the ground right next to Amir. He felt the breeze kick, up followed by a chill, but wasn't sure if it was the adrenaline or the wind blowing on his sweat covered shirt. He slowly started to pull the trigger. The men's eyes stayed locked on one another.

"NO!" Migs yelled running to Logan. "Don't pull the fucking trigger!" Migs said as he slowed and started walking slowly toward Logan. Logan blinked. He pulled the gun out of Amir's mouth, and released the hammer. He then tossed the gun to Migs and struck Amir one more time in the face knocking him out cold. Logan pulled out his phone. "General, we got 'em, and the bombs are neutralized. Go ahead and move in on the others."

Logan collapsed to the ground leaning against the wall. The weight of the moment finally pressing down on his fatigued shoulders. His blank gaze found Migs. "Thank you," Logan managed to say. His mouth was so dry he barely got the words out.

"No problem boss," Migs said while sitting on Amir's back. Migs had already tied the terrorist's hands and feet together.

chapter
TWENTY-SIX

Amir sat alone in a damp musty room. He looked around countless numbers of times trying to grasp any sense of where he was being held. Reaching up to touch his bloodied head he saw the ink still on his fingertips. Soon enough his real identity would be found out. But by whom? Who found him out?

"Samantha, Dominic," Logan said as they both entered the room. "I'm glad you came so fast." Logan handed them a piece of paper full of fingerprints.

"We're hoping we can get your assistance on this one. Off the books," General Anderson said walking across the room.

"Sir," both Samantha and Dominic said acknowledging the general's presence in the room. "I don't think that should be too hard. I brought my laptop," Dominic said reaching into his bag. Dominic took the computer out and set it on the one small plastic table they brought to the room. He scanned the prints and placed them into the database for analysis. "This may take a while. Maybe an hour or two?"

"Fine. We'll take our time. Let him bake down there for a few more hours. He's not going anywhere," General Anderson said through his teeth. "Logan, I can't go in that room. I'll likely kill him."

Logan sighed deeply. "Me too. Do we know the status on Dubs?"

"Nothing yet," Migs said as he looked at his phone.

Washington, D.C.

Jenkins sat in his home office. The clock ticking on the wall was the only noise, but Jenkins wasn't hearing it. He focused only on the day's events, or lack thereof. He had been refreshing his email every fifteen minutes for the previous several hours, but had given up at 2300. His desk lamp turned off and he blinked several times adjusting his eyes to the small glow of the light from his computer screen. He knew the timer for the lamp was set to turn off at 0100, but to be sure, he glanced at the clock on the computer; which confirmed the fact. Jenkins refreshed his email one last time. The refresh took him to the sign-in page. In frustration, he hammered in his password. The screen loaded; still nothing.

Something was wrong. Jenkins began wiping the computer completely down to factory settings. He opened his desk drawer and pulled out a small puck shaped magnet. He turned off the laptop and opened the bottom, pulled the hard drive and wiped the puck all around it. Jenkins then went to the garage and used a hammer to finish the job. He broke the hard drive into several smaller pieces. Jenkins decided it was time for a late-night walk.

He used the front door of his home rather than the garage. It was more inconspicuous. Jenkins walked. He walked the same route he would run every now and again when he felt the need to release some tension. It was a short route all things considered, a two-mile loop. On this night, it was crisp with a light fog and very quiet. The wind barely made a noise through the trees. He walked past a storm drain, reached into his pocket, and dropped a piece of the hard drive kicking it in to the drain. A few blocks later and around a curve he threw in another piece. He continued the same thing four more times along the remaining mile.

Jenkins walked inside, locked the door, and went into his office. He grabbed what remained of his computer and walked it to the garage, placing it in his trunk. Tomorrow he would go to a computer center and buy a replacement hard drive with cash.

Saint Louis

"We've got a hit," Dominic said at his computer. "He disappeared several years ago. He was arrested for a homicide and then was suddenly gone. Let's see . . ." Dominic looked deeper into the database. He typed "SUMEET PATEL" into the search field. "He was active duty Army. Served in Pakistan, was decorated. He's Pakistani descent. Seems the altercation involved an ethnic attack on his father," Dominic hesitated, pulled back from the computer and looked around the room.

"What is it? What's the hesitation?" General Anderson said placing both hands down on the table next to Dominic. Dominic looked at the general and turned the computer toward him pointing at the last paragraph.

"Sumeet Patel was last located at Great Lakes Naval base under the care of Naval MP. He was taken by someone from Intelligence Division."

"Jesus," General Anderson said and then read the words aloud to the room. "He's dark after that. No driver's license, no taxes, nothing."

"I would sure like to know if that person was Jenkins. I got a feeling it might have been," Logan said looking at the floor.

"Well, to be frank, I don't give a shit about hunches. We need proof. If we are gonna go after Jenkins, then we need a hell of a lot more than he met with this guy one time several years ago," Dominic said sharply, pushing himself back from the table and running his hand across his forehead.

"I agree," said General Anderson. He walked over to Dominic and set one more file on the table. "Now run these. It's the fingerprints from the other terrorists. Maybe it'll help."

Dominic sighed heavily and opened the folder. "Couldn't have washed their hands first?"

"A little blood gonna ruin the prints?" General Anderson said condescendingly.

"No. Should work just fine," Dominic responded.

"Good thing. We can't exactly get any more from them," General Anderson said looking around the room. "Don't worry. Nobody else will find them either. My Marines took care of everything," he said to Dominic who looked concerned.

"Comforting thought," said Lonnie standing up. "I wasn't excited about that plan. What happens if this guy doesn't talk?" The room was quiet. Everyone was thinking it but nobody said it.

"Well, he's the only one who can tell us anything. He's the ringleader, it was clear to see. He was the only one all along that could lead us to answers. The others were just pawns we needed to keep an eye on," Samantha said sternly. Everyone nodded in agreement. It was easy to accept that answer. "As soon as we know who these other terrorists are, I'm going in with him. Logan, you're too emotional and so are you General. Dominic, you always show your emotions and this guy will probably eat you alive. No offense, but the rest of you have no idea where to start. A woman in there might throw him off his defense. He's expecting a man."

"If he's not forthcoming with information we won't be waiting long to start using . . . incentives to motivate him," General Anderson said coldly. "We don't have time to waste. Whoever is controlling this guy already knows something went south. We need this to happen."

"Well alright. First hit on a fingerprint. Name is Sharif Itani. He's Lebanese. Expert in espionage, disguises. Known for his elaborate transformations. Missing for 12 years. Fell off the grid. Last assignment was Iraq," Dominic said reading the screen. He grabbed another set of prints and started the scan.

"Lot of help that is," said General Anderson in frustration.

"Where was the Iraq assignment?" asked Samantha.

"Looks to be Baghdad," Dominic said.

General Anderson walked over to his bag and grabbed a computer. "We have Jenkins' mission logs. Maybe there will be a correlation."

Samantha reached her hand out toward General Anderson who handed her the computer.

"Is there any way we can search by date?" Logan asked.

"Unfortunately, no. But it's chronological." Samantha sat on the floor with the computer on her knees and Logan sat right next to her. The two of them paged down quickly through dates. It began in 1995 and finished in 2015 when he became advisor to the Secretary of State. "Looks like he had several missions in the mid-2000s in Iraq." She looked further down the page pointing to one in Baghdad.

"The last one was mine," Logan said cutting her off before she spoke. Logan looked at Samantha, deeply into her eyes. "Move on," he mouthed to her. He didn't want her to read the op report. He knew how close he was to dying that day. It was the one mission he did with

Jenkins, but it wasn't worth the distraction from the objectives at hand.

"We've got another hit!" Dominic said. "Raul Garcia. Spec ops guy. We know relatively little about him. He was last heard from in 1999. He was stationed in South Vietnam."

"Looks like Jenkins was there in 1999. One mission. Failure. Two operatives killed on a recon mission at the border of North Korea. Incident was never public."

"OK so we are two for two. Seems coincidental. Let's see what the last two say," General Anderson said rubbing his chin, arms crossed on his chest.

"Basil Hall. Former MI-5, Great Britain. Last assignment was Ireland, 1990. Missing since. Explosives expert," Dominic said looking over his shoulder toward Samantha and Logan. He had already scanned the last set of prints.

"Jenkins had two missions in Ireland, dealings with the IRA. He led those ops doing a cooperative with Great Britain. There may have been more British ops but we don't have access to that."

Two hours passed. The room was full of silence. Nobody had spoken for an hour and they all waited for Dominic to reveal the last set of prints. Everyone had repeatedly looked at their cellphones, checking the time. Logan was still sitting next to Samantha but he had taken the computer. He was reading through his debrief. There was no mention of the camera, or its content. It was erased from history. He talked about it in every single debrief, yet it was not entered into the official reports. It was, after all, how he had gotten found. It bothered him. He closed the computer, shut his eyes, and waited, trying to clear his spinning head.

"Hmmm," Dominic said clicking the mousepad again. "Looks like this set isn't hitting any in the database. Wouldn't be the first time this happened."

Samantha stood up and walked several steps toward Dominic. "I need all the information we have on each of these people. We have three names, three histories. I can do without the fourth. I'm sick of waiting. This needs to happen soon. Right General?"

"Ooh Rah!" the general bellowed as he stared intensely at her.

"Alright Samantha," Dominic said paging back through the information. He quickly printed a photo, and an informational sheet on each terrorist they had, including Patel's.

"You are taking someone into the room with you Samantha. I don't like the idea of you being alone with him," General Anderson said uncrossing his arms in the corner of the room. He pointed at Logan. "You're going in with him, whether you like it or not."

"I can manage, as long as he can keep his hands-off Patel."

"I can manage," Logan stood up sliding his back against the wall. His knees were sore and stiff from sitting so long on the floor. "We're bringing this too." Logan said picking up a backpack they found in the terrorist's hotel room.

Logan and Samantha walked down the hallway together, silent, except for the hum of fluorescent lights hanging on the cold concrete walls. It was a maze of turns as they walked. Samantha grew more focused, more separate from the world around her with every turn. Their shoes scuffed the concrete underfoot, hers more than his. Logan looked at Samantha as he walked behind her. He took note of her posture, her stride, her demeanor. She was flawless, unfazed, and confident. He smirked to himself, realizing that maybe all his fears had been in vain so long ago.

"You think you can handle this?" Samantha said without looking back.

"I'll manage. What's your angle?"

"I'm just gonna let him know everything. Right from the beginning. I don't plan on wasting time with this guy Logan."

"Seems fair. What happens if you don't get anything from him? What's your out?"

Samantha stopped in the hallway. The humming from the lights was more noticeable now.

"Then you're up. Do what you gotta do," she grabbed his shirt collar and straightened it out.

He wanted to tell her what he was thinking. He was a bit weak in the knees and he wanted to kiss her. He gave up the thought of fearing for her life. He wanted to be back with her again.

Samantha and Logan turned down one last hallway and descended a staircase. One solitary light hanging above a lonely steel door lit the landing. Logan checked his watch, 0430.

Samantha reached up toward the door handle. Logan reached up quickly and pulled her hand away. "Are you ready?" Logan asked as she paused, reacting to his touch.

"I'm ready."

Bang! The hinges popped. The heavy metal door swung inside and echoes filled the long hallways. Inside, Amir sat calmly at the table with hands and feet secured in shackles to a steel plate anchored to the floor. Samantha entered the room first and she met Amir's eyes coldly. Logan entered the room and Amir's attention immediately shifted to him. Amir felt his head ache a little more. He sighed, clenched his teeth, and turned to face Samantha.

"We killed your friends," Samantha said slamming the folders down on the table. "We won't hesitate to do the same with you. We know you are the leader. We tracked you for a while. Clearly you make the calls, but, who tells you what to do? That's all we want to know. If you tell us nobody, then we'll take you down too, the snake, right here in this cold, dark room."

Amir stared at her for a moment, directly in her eyes. He then turned his gaze to Logan who stood in the left corner of the room holding the backpack. "So clearly you are a couple, or have been a couple. Because why else would this man be here? Who are you? FBI? CIA?" Amir directed the questions at Logan who stood unprovoked, unimpressed.

"I'm asking the fucking questions here," Samantha said opening the first folder. "You got a little wild Mr. Patel? Murdering for revenge? How'd you get back on the streets?"

"I'm sorry, but I don't know who Patel is."

"Sumeet Patel. We know who you are. Don't play dumb with us. I know you saw the ink on your fingers. No way you had the foresight to change your fingerprints. So, who helped you get out? The same person who tells you what to do?"

"Sumeet Patel . . . I barely recognize the name really. It's been a long time."

"Is there a more familiar name?" Samantha read into his suggestions.

"Amir Qasmi."

"OK Amir—"

"Ahhh! That's so much better!" Amir exclaimed cutting her off.

"Sharif Itani. How does that name sound? Known for elaborate disguises and counter intel. We know he fell off the grid about 12 years ago." Amir looked at the pictures. One was a shot taken at least 15 years ago. The other was a picture taken by the Marines who killed him. Two shots to the head with good precision.

"How about Raul Garcia?" Samantha questioned opening his folder, again with two images, one old, and one new, showing the precision headshots.

"And this one?" Samantha pointed at Basil Hall. "Explosives expert, British MI-5. Looks to me like you had a solid team. A counter espionage man, and explosives man and a few yes men with experience, maybe even a common goal."

Amir looked across the table. He pointed to the first folder, looked into Samantha's eyes, and said, "one." He then pointed to the next, "two," he said not looking away from her eyes. "Three," Amir stated with authority slamming his finger into the image of Basil with the precision headshots. He then lay back hard into his chair and brought his hands down into his lap. He shrugged his shoulders playfully. "Well, last time I checked, there was a fourth person I had with me," He shot a look over to Logan and said. "Guess you aren't as good as I thought?"

Logan stood, still unimpressed, but cautious. He was unsure how Samantha would be reading Amir and how she would react to his banter. Samantha made him more nervous than Amir. She had already played every card they had.

"Well I can help you out. HER name was Nikita Sokolov. She was a nobody ten years ago. You won't find her in any database. She was an orphan in Russia. She ran away, lived on the streets for years. I honestly don't know how old she is. Quite frankly, I don't think she even knew her own birthday. I made her an offer to help me. She enjoyed having a point to her life. She hated happiness. I allowed her to destroy that."

"Well, we'll check that out in our systems," Samantha warned without missing a beat. Logan was very impressed with her reaction. He felt more at ease.

"So! What else would you like to know? Who tells me what to do? Nobody. A better question, is who facilitates what I choose to do?" Amir said and waited.

"Who facilitates your actions?" Samantha played along.

"Well I thought you'd never ask. I will say, it's going to be a bit unbelievable and hard to prove. But, that's not my problem. My facilitator is a man named Jenkins."

Logan was lightheaded. The room spun but he stood still. It was all forming so fast and so easy. Amir was right. How would this be proven? This is circumstantial evidence coming from a terrorist.

"Well that's a bold statement. Are we just supposed to trust the word of a terrorist? A mass murderer?" Samantha said folding her arms.

"I can manage, but it will require my release, and it will have to be imminent. You see, we have fail safes built in. He knows that the attack in Saint Louis didn't happen. He just doesn't know why."

"What are the fail safes?" Samantha asked.

"What time is it?" Amir asked.

"You'll just need to tell me what the fail safes are," Samantha said checking her watch.

"Well, I haven't checked in and it's been more than 12 hours after a failed mission. He has already wiped and destroyed his computer's hard drive. So, you'll find nothing there I promise you. He will probably be looking into domestic operations located in the Saint Louis area over the past several days to weeks. He has access to that information, we both know that, but what will he find? You do realize that he has been at this for decades? He knows how to evade and how to tie up loose ends. He wants me dead. I'm sure of it," Amir said with a smirk.

"We aren't letting you go," Samantha shot back quickly.

"I said all that and all you have to say is no. Without thinking. Without looking at the bigger picture. I'm sure HE understands the bigger picture," Amir pointed his left middle finger at Logan still standing motionless in the corner. He then turned his hand so that he displayed his middle finger right in Logan's direction. "What do you say?" Amir questioned directly at Logan.

"You are talking to me!" Samantha spoke sternly and placed both fists knuckles down into the tabletop.

"Well, since we're talking, I would recommend you go and tell whoever it is that tells you what to do, what I'm saying before it's too late. I've given information freely and without holding back. I am done talking for now. Bring me someone who can make decisions. Oh, and did you really think that bringing my backpack down here would make me nervous? It seems amateur."

Washington, D.C.

Jenkins walked down the stairs and into his kitchen. Grabbing a cup of coffee, he sat down at the table. "You're late sweetheart!" his wife said and walked past him, kissing him on the head.

"Yes, I'm going in a bit later today. Gonna run out to the store. Computer broke, need some parts so I'm gonna stick around for a few hours and wait till they open," he smiled at her.

"Well let's go out and get breakfast," she said to him and smiled. Jenkins took a long sip of his coffee.

"Sure sweetheart."

Breakfast was good. He had an omelet with wheat toast and black coffee. He had no problem finishing his meal, however, he did have a hard time with conversation. Jenkins sat with his wife, but was distracted the entire time. He listened, responded, but wasn't actually present. It had been some time since he was present in body and mind when with his wife. Breakfast was the first time in nearly a month they had done anything outside of the home together.

"OK sweetheart, I will see you tonight," Jenkins said, dropping his wife off at home.

"I still don't see why you need to fix your own computer. Can't they just fix it at work?"

"I don't like to wait around for someone else. It's an easy fix." It was hard for him to lie to her. He was insulated at home. She would always be his alibi.

"Well, don't get me wrong, I loved having you home this morning. I love you." She kissed him softly on the cheek.

"Love you too, sweetheart. See you later."

Jenkins walked into his office at the Capital and closed the door. He reached into his bag and pulled out his computer and the hard drive he just bought. Making quick work of the job, he placed the hard drive back into the computer and booted it up. Walking over to his file cabinet he unlocked it and gathered up the reboot disks and began the tedious process of placing all his previous software on the computer.

While his personal computer was running software programs, he used his government computer for personal use. Jenkins began searching for operations that were taking place in Saint Louis. Only one came up: Training Op: General Mitchell Anderson.

Jenkins became uneasy. He knew General Anderson personally. They were both Marines, Anderson was slightly younger, but much more indebted to his country, and very motivated. Jenkins then looked for what the training op was, and found it unlisted. Jenkins closed the program and walked out of the office straight toward Secretary of State Doyle Smith's office.

Jenkins stood in the doorway and noticed the Secretary was reading a report. *Knock, knock, knock!* Jenkins knuckled the open door.

"Jenkins. How are we this afternoon?" Secretary Smith asked looking over his reading glasses toward the open doorway.

"A bit confused, sir, to be honest," Jenkins said entering the room and gestured back toward the door. "May I?"

"Go ahead," Secretary Smith said. Jenkins then closed the door. "What's on your mind Jenkins? I mean, I'm sitting here trying to figure out how this shooting incident adds up in Saint Louis. A precision shot with a military spec sniper rifle. We've locked everything down. It's all JTTF on the case. Wonder if local PD overlooked something or mismanaged evidence."

"Sir, I was just looking into things myself and may have found something," Jenkins was shocked at how easy the situation had become. Doyle was myopic and looking for an answer. "I saw that there was a training op. Marine Corps General Mitchell Anderson was lead. There was no description."

"Well what the hell we waiting for Jenkins? I'm gonna make a few calls and get back to you." Doyle said picking up the phone. "Jenkins, you know this guy?"

"Yes, sir I do. I'd rather keep a distance. If this ends up being related, I'd like to keep it from looking as if I am trying to help bury a problem for a fellow Marine."

"I guess that's fair enough. What's this guy like?"

"As far as I can remember, he's gung ho American sir, but it's been a while. Let me know what you find, sir."

"Will do Jenkins. Thanks for bringing this to my attention. Close the door on the way out."

Saint Louis

The walk back to General Anderson and the other Marines felt short. Logan and Samantha talked about what to do and finally concluded that Amir was right. They had limited time and resources. If Jenkins was truly involved, then he would absolutely be operating on a solution to his problem.

"General Anderson," Samantha said while she walked into the room. The men barely had time to look toward the door as she entered. "Amir, uh, Patel, just gave us Jenkins. It's circumstantial at best, but he says he can give Jenkins to us. It has to be quickly, and it has to be his way."

General Anderson stood and brought his hand to his chin and thought for a moment. "Logan. What the hell is she talking about? Who's Amir and what's with this Jenkins shit?" Samantha looked at Logan as well. They had discussed this very scenario happening. Logan knew General Anderson trusted him fully and would ask for his input.

"He's changed his name. Amir Qasmi. Says Jenkins gave him the name. I say we have one shot at Jenkins. Unfortunately, the shot includes letting Amir go and find us a bigger fish," Logan answered.

"Well I guess we'll see what this asshole has for an idea," General Anderson said and strode toward the door. Everyone else followed.

"What else did he say?" General Anderson asked as he followed Logan and Samantha down the hallway.

"He named the missing person. Nikita Sokolov. Said she was an orphan turned terrorist. She won't be found in any of our databases because she doesn't really exist. He says she doesn't even know her own birthday, or year, and for all we know this name may be made up as well."

"What the fuck," Lonnie said under his breath and shook his head. Logan glared back at Lonnie.

"From what you're saying about Amir and Jenkins, it really doesn't matter who she was. She's dead. She won't tell us anything anyway," General Anderson said.

Everyone went toward the room Amir was being held in. It was already 0930 and they were eager to try to move forward in some way. They all came around the last turn and saw the stairway. Logan paused and turned to address everyone. "I think it should just be us, General. This guy seems to want to put on a show. If we fill the room I think, he may take the time to put give us a monologue and stretch it out. Watch us sweat."

"Everyone else stay here. Logan, Samantha, and I will be going in. Quicker the better. OK, let's get this shit over with."

Once again, the large metal door released with a bang and in walked the team of three. Amir greeted them with a smirk. "Well, now we have a decision maker in the room. This must mean you are ready to listen to what I have to say."

"Start talkin' boy. We don't have all day," General Anderson belted cross-armed.

"Fair enough," Amir said with a pause. "As I told these two, after the bombs failed to detonate Jenkins would have continually checked communications. After 12 hours, he began a system of eliminating evidence. He is probably looking into operations that were going on in the area of Saint Louis, which no doubt after seeing you, must surely exist. So, I would say that he definitively knows of you being here. The question is, how will he handle it? He's done this for a while now. He knows how to bury evidence, how to eliminate loose ends. I am the loose end; you are the evidence. I can handle both." As he said the final sentence he lifted his hands forward and extended his shackled wrists toward the general.

"And how can you solve both? How can you deliver him to us?" General Anderson asked.

"I'll contact him. He'll come to me. He'll kill me. You'll have your evidence and I'll be dead."

"That's awfully convenient of you. You're now willing to be a martyr for the country you've committed countless and unknowable treasonous acts against? It's awfully hard to believe," General Anderson said as he walked toward Amir.

"Well, sir," Amir said condescendingly, "it's the only option you have." The two men froze glaring at each other. Amir's eyes were calm, patient, confident. General Anderson's eyes were filled with frustration and rage.

A phone rang, breaking the silence and the stare. General Anderson reached into his pocket and saw a restricted number. He looked at Logan who responded by nodding his head toward the door. General Anderson walked out and answered the phone. "Mitchell," he answered.

"General Anderson, this is Secretary Smith. How are you today sir?"

"I'm well, sir, honored to speak with you," General Anderson responded on edge.

"Before we start stroking egos, I need to have an answer to what the extent of your training mission is, or was, in Saint Louis. As you may have heard, we had a shooting involving a high caliber military spec rifle."

"Yes sir, I heard of the shooting. We were performing a track and shadow training op, urban warfare scenarios. We chose Saint Louis because it was a big city nobody has previous knowledge of in our group of men. We were not weapons live, and we weren't even carrying weapons for the trip. Simply tracking a high value target in urban setting," General Anderson said.

"Fair enough General. Can you get a debrief from the commanding officer and notify me of the details? We're trying to piece together all possible scenarios. For future reference, make sure they are detailing these training missions. I hate having to see these simple details missed on op reports."

"Will do sir. I appreciate the feedback. Would you like me to call and notify your staff when it is ready?"

"Sounds good General. Have a good day."

"You too, sir."

General Anderson walked back into the room and looked directly at Amir. Logan looked at General Anderson and knew something was wrong. He had never seen the look that currently rested on General Anderson's face. It wasn't fear, but it was damn close to it. "We need to clean this guy up Logan," the general said still looking at Amir. "You've got 24 hours to make contact. The clock has started." General Anderson took his eyes off Amir and looked to Logan, "We're all going to Washington."

chapter
TWENTY-SEVEN

It was just after 1700 when the plane touched down at Reagan National Airport. It was warm and sunny with a gentle breeze making the evening air desirable. It would have been an enjoyable afternoon under different circumstances. The group left the airport and got into two vans heading toward the Motel 6.

"OK, Amir here's the plan. We're going to be watching every move you make. There isn't an option," General Anderson said as the two men sat next to each other.

"I need two phones," Amir said. "It'll be the only way to contact me. He won't respond to emails. He won't even be checking at this point. Jenkins knows the risks involved in it."

"What's your plan?" Logan said, addressing the terrorist for the first time.

"I'll make contact. He'll come to me. You will be following me, so then you'll have him."

"How do you know for certain he will come? How do you know he won't just stay away assuming you've been caught? This all seems pretty fucking vague," General Anderson said clenching his hands.

"As I said, he wants to cut off loose ends. He's done it before, I've done it for him. Remember Vladimir? I'll entice him in my own way. He won't resist," Amir said confidently looking out the window, his chest prominent, head resting back into the seat.

The vans reached the hotel, a small four-story building. It was not much to look at and it could easily hide the rather large and conspicuous group. Samantha checked them all in. The rooms were adjoining with a door separating them. Those rooms would be the operation headquarters.

"Well, Amir, here we are. It's your show. I certainly hope this isn't a load of shit just to try and get loose. You'll never be out of our sight, no matter what the plans are," General Anderson said looking at Amir sternly.

"My plan's simple. I want to contact him. I'll leave a pre-paid phone for him, I'll require a phone too. You can watch me. If you get too close, then you screw the mission and miss your mark. No problem for me. I'm dead in the water either way," Amir said laying back onto one of the headboards with his arms behind his head.

"So what's the idea here Amir. You will just walk up to him on the street? Say hey we need to talk and slip him a phone? I seriously doubt you'll get close enough. Then what do we do? Jump him on the spot in front of potentially dozens of witnesses and then somehow bury that incident from the public eye?" Dominic shot back in frustration at Amir's arrogance.

Amir smirked and sat up at the edge of the bed. "I won't contact him in a public venue. I'll go to his house. I promise you he'll come to me. It's instinctual. He can't fight it."

"I'll go grab two phones," Samantha said and walked out.

"Dominic, can you get your hands on two tracking elements we can put in these two phones?" General Anderson asked.

"Not a problem."

It was 0600 and the sun was creating a golden orange flare in the entire sky. It was difficult to see anything when looking toward the east, which is why the van was parked about half a mile east of Jenkins' house. Logan, Amir, Migs, Lonnie, and General Anderson were sitting inside waiting for Jenkins to leave for the day.

Time went slowly and the van was silent. It began to get warmer inside as the sun rose higher. It was 0730 before they decided to open the windows. The warm breeze was far from a relief, they traded dry heat for humidity but no one complained; it was at least fresh air. Thirty minutes later Jenkins left. It was uneventful but it had happened.

"Here," Lonnie said handing Amir the phones.

"Do what you have to do. Everyone else is in a second van. If you don't text us updates every 30 minutes we will be moving in on you. We'll never be more than five minutes out," General Anderson said as Amir opened the door.

"I'm aware. I'll update you."

Amir walked down the street slowly. Logan watched Amir enter character. He began to walk fighting back his limp. He put a pair of sunglasses on. He was also wearing a Washington Senators hat to shade some of his face. Nobody driving by, walking their dog, or watching from inside of their homes would ever think twice about this man coming down the street.

Amir approached Jenkins' home, walked into the driveway, and around the side of the garage. He acted as though he had been there hundreds of times. There was a wooden door on the side of the garage. Amir checked the handle, it was locked. He stepped back and looked around the grounds. He noticed a few chicken wire fences around a vegetable garden just beyond the hedge line and into the neighbor's yard. He knelt and crawled the ten feet up to and under the hedge. It gave him access to the chicken wire. He made quick work of removing a few feet from one narrow section. Amir walked back to the door, folded the chicken wire into a straighter, sturdier piece. He jammed it hard into the lock and closed his eyes in concentration.

"One, two, three," Amir counted as he felt the tumblers contacting the wire. He pulled the chicken wire out several times to make small adjustments in the shape. Finally, after two minutes, he was in the garage.

Immediately inside the three-car garage was Jenkins' Camaro. It was bright blue with two white racing stripes. Amir smiled, took the chicken wire and dragged it all the way around the car. *Why does he get to have nice things?* Amir reached into the open driver's window and stabbed the chicken wire deep into the shiny black leather seats. Once he got to the passenger side, he saw a small SUV and an open space. Amir then walked around the SUV and opened the door to the home.

It smelled like bacon and toast. He heard a woman humming and the footsteps of her moving around the two-story home. He could tell she was just in the next room. He slowly walked through the house, silently, and turned the corner to see Jenkins' wife. Her back was turned to him. He took out one of the cellphones and took a picture of her. He then slipped behind a wall and hid in the kitchen. He spotted the bacon, toast, eggs and strawberries. He walked over and ate several strawberries and a piece of bacon. He walked back out of the kitchen and watched Jenkins' wife more. She was dusting things on the bookshelf. Books upon books were separated by many arbitrary items, a porcelain head of a dog, vacation pictures of their family, small statues of Greek gods. But one thing stood out more than any other. It was a shadow box that displayed a Purple Heart. It struck Amir as a joke. It infuriated him. *How can this traitor display an award in his home? How can he not feel guilty?*

Amir watched as she turned and exited the room. He heard the kitchen faucet turn on and he walked to the bookshelf, grabbing the shadow box taking another picture, this time of the purple heart. He then opened the shadow box and placed the purple heart in his pocket. *I deserve this more than you,* he thought.

The faucet turned off and he walked toward the kitchen, but this time, not quietly. Amir came around the corner and saw Jenkins' wife standing opposite him at the kitchen island. Again, her back was turned. He rolled his eyes, took out his phone, and snapped another picture of her. *Maybe I should just kill her. Put her out of her misery.* He stood there waiting. She wiped down the counter removing the last of the crumbs. The bacon, eggs, toast, strawberries all thrown out or placed into the refrigerator. Finally, she turned to throw the crumbs into the sink and saw Amir.

She fell backward into the counter and threw the rag into the air. She tried to scream, but nothing left her mouth. Trembling she began to cry out, "Please, please don't hurt me." A moment passed and Amir just stared at her. "Do you know who my husband is?" she said with authority.

"I'm not here to hurt you. If I were, it would have been over by now. I know who your husband is, and he knows who I am," Amir said coldly. "I have this phone," he held the phone into the air then placed in onto the counter, sliding it toward to her with one finger. He tapped the screen as he said, "I want him to contact me. It's fully charged. Feel free to call him from your personal phone and tell him about your visitor. I'll let myself out the front if you don't mind. Oh, and let him know he needs to paint that beautiful Camaro. It has a scratch."

"General Jenkins' office," Cathy said as she picked up the phone.

"Cathy, I need to speak with him immediately. It's very important."

"Well hello Mrs. Jenkins. Sure. Is everything OK?" Cathy was concerned.

After a very brief pause, Mrs. Jenkins said, "I just need to speak with him Cathy."

"Certainly. Please hold."

"Hi sweetheart everything OK?" Jenkins asked while looking over some paperwork.

As soon as she heard his voice she broke down. "A man was in our house today and he left a phone for you. He said you know him and that he wants you to call him. I'm so scared, are you in trouble?"

"I'm on my way don't worry. Could be an old soldier. PTSD. He won't harm you and he won't come back."

"But will you bring more people? How do you know he won't hurt you?" she said, her voice filled with panic.

"Sweetheart, it will be OK. This unfortunately happens to a lot of guys. This is your first experience. I've had many. I'll be home soon."

"I love you," she said calmly.

"Love you too."

Jenkins was furious. He walked out of the office, straight past Cathy, to the parking lot and roared away in his car. He knew it was Amir. Who else could it have been? Jenkins had no idea what to think, good thing it was only a fifteen-minute drive to get home.

Walking in the door he saw his wife sitting at the island staring at the phone. She looked up and saw Jenkins. She stopped biting her fingers for a moment to point at the phone. "It vibrated several minutes ago. I didn't look at it."

Jenkins picked up the phone and looked at the message. One showed three images: Two of them were of his wife, from behind, and the third was of his purple heart.

"I could have killed her if I wanted. More than once. I decided to take your other heart and then destroy something beautiful, your car."

Jenkins walked toward the bookshelf and saw the shadowbox, empty. "Where and when?" Jenkins texted back to Amir.

"Now. Abandoned streetcar tunnels under DuPont Circle. Enter at

20th Street NW. Turn left and walk till you see me," Amir responded.

"Sweetheart, I have to go," Jenkins said and kissed her on the cheek. He walked into his office on the way out. He unlocked his top desk drawer and reached inside grabbing his Beretta 9mm. He placed it in his waistline and walked out to his car.

"Mother fucker," Jenkins mumbled seeing his Camaro front seat out of the corner of his eye. He walked around to the driver side to get a closer look. "Son of a bitch!" he said much louder when he saw the gouges in his wet sanded paint job. It had been a 95-point car at shows. Jenkins went back into the house and grabbed his Camaro keys from the mudroom.

Vroom! The engine started up quickly and he slammed the gas pedal, threw it in reverse, and left melted rubber from in his garage, down the driveway, and into the street. It was 1230.

Amir had been walking through the underground tunnels for a couple of hours now, looking for alternate exits. The tunnels were foreign to him but he had heard of them years ago. He studied up on them a few years back as a possible exit strategy for a situation like this. Seeing them in person was a challenge however. He was sweaty, panting, grimacing from the pain in his calf, but he still searched on. He had to find a way out. He also found when he was more than 20 feet from an exit, he would lose cell signal. He made sure that every 25 to 30 minutes he would text Logan by exiting from the same place, 20th Street NW. Amir glanced at the phone. It had been almost 30 minutes since texting General Anderson and Logan.

He quickly ran up to the street level and sent a text to Logan. As he did so, he noticed Jenkins walking toward the entrance. Jenkins was looking around and Amir slipped back down the staircase undetected. He entered the tunnels and immediately turned left into the darkness.

Dominic began to walk north past the entrance to the tunnels. It was about 100 yards away and Dominic was walking in a mixed group of people. Several of them were in suits, all staring at their phones, while a few others were tourists easily discernible because they were looking up at everything and then pointing their cellphone at different signs and landmarks taking pictures. Dominic stood out like a sore thumb with his jeans and t-shirt, and he was fidgety. He quickly took his phone out and continued to walk at a slow pace toward the entrance. He stopped once and took pictures of a few historic buildings and a selfie next to a sign. He then returned to walking while staring at his phone as if critiquing his photo. Jenkins walked right by him and down the stairs into the dark abyss below.

"And now we wait," General Anderson said in a low slow voice. "We aren't giving this asshole extra time either Logan. Looks like he has 28 minutes. That'll make it 1350. He's got till then or we move in."

"We are moving into the tunnels in 28 minutes people, no matter what," Logan said into the receiver while staring at the entrance. "We have 25 left to find out anything else about these tunnels. Keep the comms quiet unless you have info. There has to be another exit we aren't seeing."

Several minutes passed and the communications were silent. Dominic continued to walk around outside the grounds. He had covered about a mile of walkway when he hit New Hampshire Avenue. "Dominic here. I've got a possible second entrance. New Hampshire Avenue. Lots of surface traffic here, but I could spot him if he comes out."

"We can get to your position in five. Let us know and we will move," Samantha responded quickly. Her voice was stressed. Everyone heard it.

Amir was waiting silently in the darkness, squeezing the purple heart that rested in his pocket. Several minutes passed before he started hearing footsteps. He also began to see a small light bounce off the wall, brightening with each second. Soon, he saw the outline of Jenkins. Amir turned his phone on and used the camera light as a flashlight. He pointed it in the direction of Jenkins, signaling him. Jenkins began to trot, trying to avoid several holes in the abandoned tunnels, making quick work of getting to Amir.

"What the fuck happened?" Jenkins said in the darkness through his clenched teeth. Even his whispers were echoing through the darkness. "Are we alone? What the fuck Amir? ARE WE ALONE!" he growled again.

"We're alone. We were made. There were men, I saw them for days. I shot one of them. They intercepted our explosives," Amir said.

"Where is everyone else? Were any of you captured?"

"I have no idea what happened with them. I shot and ran. Been in hiding since, but don't worry. There was a buffer between you and me. Nobody found me, nobody will find you."

"You're God damn right," Jenkins said pulling out his gun. "Where's my medal?" Jenkins said pointing the gun in Amir's face. "And why my car?"

Amir pulled the medal out. He lifted it slowly into the air. As it reached his eye level he noticed Jenkins glance over. Amir dropped the medal and grabbed Jenkins' gun from his hand. Amir then pointed the gun into Jenkins' face.

"If you only fucking knew how happy this moment makes me," Amir said with wide eyes and a sinister smirk. "I may have let myself get caught years ago! Could you imagine how much different my life would have been? I was a good son, a great soldier, a terrible ruler of my emotions. It was my only fault. Since birth really. . ."

Amir reflected briefly to a time when he was surrounded by bullying children on a playground, he was crying uncontrollably.

"Maybe working for you allowed me a chance to learn to control them. If that's the case, then I have no more weaknesses. I am a better leader. You, clearly, still have weaknesses. I knew you'd come for me. I told this to General Anderson and his mixed group of whatever the hell they call themselves."

Jenkins felt the sting. He knew he was done. He was not in control. Things made sense regarding Anderson's training op; he knew it wasn't normal and now he knew why. Jenkins felt guilty, sadness at the thought of failing his friend. *Would my friend ever know what really happened? Would he forgive me?* Jenkins heard water dripping. It distracted him. *Where was this water coming from? Where would it lead? Can I get out?* He grasped his right pocket where his phone was, the only way to contact his friend.

Amir saw Jenkins reaching for his pocket and shot the 9mm at Jenkins twice. The noise was incredible. Amir's ears were ringing, but could still hear the echoes of the shot as it cascaded through the underground tunnels. Amir looked at his watch. Twenty-five minutes till check in. Amir checked for a pulse, but knew the double tap to the general's head was probably enough. He searched Jenkins body for everything. He found his car keys, wallet, and three cellphones. He recognized the one he gave him and assumed another was a work phone, and the last was a personal cellphone. Amir left Jenkins' body and took the phones and gun, along with the medal.

Amir ran down the hall and placed his own cellphone at the bottom of the stairwell at the entrance. He made sure it was getting a signal. He then broke the screen and placed a few bloody fingerprints around the phone and wall. It wasn't his own blood, but it was his prints. It would have to do. He then ran quickly down the tunnels and up the stairs at New Hampshire Avenue, allowing the adrenaline to act as a narcotic for the searing pain in his calf.

He spotted a group of young kids and called them over. "Would you guys like a prepaid phone to have fun with? I only have one rule, and it's that you have to run far away from here before you play with it, OK?" The kids nodded, took the phone, and walked away.

Amir went back down the tunnels and began looking for a storm drain. He knew they still existed, they had to be used, otherwise the tunnels would have been flooded years ago. It took about ten minutes but he finally found one next to an abandoned trolley. It was plenty large enough to fit into as long as he got the iron grates off. He looked for anything with leverage. He jumped onto the trolley and began tearing at anything that was steel and long. Finally, at his third attempt at an overhead rail it broke free. He released the iron grating on the storm drain with the steel bar, climbed inside, and closed the grate. He brought the steel bar with him. He was free.

Logan, Lonnie, and General Anderson sat in the parking lot east of the tunnel entrance. It had been 25 minutes since Amir's last text. They continued tracking Amir and saw that he was still in the tunnel. It wasn't, however, the only phone they were tracking.

"Jenkins' phone is on the move," Lonnie said while watching his laptop screen.

"Eyes peeled," Logan said into his microphone. "It looks like Jenkins is on his way to the party."

"Understood," Dominic said as he walked down 20th Street.

"Copy," said Samantha from the other van. "You guys hear that?" she asked Migs, Ryan, Brian, and Dubs.

"Everyone remember that fucker is mine when this is over! Samantha remind everyone please!" Dubs demanded as he sat in the back of the van, his left arm in a sling.

"You're lucky to be here Dubs. Chill out, you'll get your piece," Migs said smirking. "I guess I shouldn't be surprised you'd get yourself outta' the hospital."

"I'm not even surprised he walked all the way to the mall for us to pick him up still wearing his hospital gown," joked Ryan.

"I'm not surprised that you somehow got someone to let you borrow their phone. But the fact that you could remember Logan's number? Damn. That's the shock."

"I'd whoop your ass but these pain meds are messin' with me," Dubs said while wiping his eyes aggressively.

Logan's phone vibrated.

"I'm still here. Waiting patiently. Don't worry about me."

"OK everyone, Amir checked in, reset the clock. Says he's still waiting so let's keep watching for Jenkins."

"I've got eyes on him Logan. Jenkins is approaching the 20th Street entrance," Dominic said softly a few minutes later. "I'm going to move toward the entrance and get a closer look."

The world seemed to be more chaotic than normal. So many people to look at, to study, to eliminate as a possible hit for Jenkins or Amir. They were spread out between two exits, and, if each man went their separate ways, Logan and General Anderson may have to decide who's most important.

"Where are the marks Lonnie?"

"I've got Amir standing down near the 20th Street entrance. Jenkins is still quiet. Not getting a trace. I'll let you know when it pops up," Lonnie said.

"I've got a group of kids entering New Hampshire entrance," Dominic said quickly.

Logan looked at General Anderson. The men shared a concerned look and waited.

"OK, they are leaving," Dominic said. "Nobody else with them. I counted them going in and out. There were eight.

"I've got a read on Jenkins phone," Lonnie said. "Shit! Logan, it says he's walking down New Hampshire!" Lonnie threw the laptop into Logan's hands.

"Dominic, follow those kids, something's happening. We're moving into the tunnels now!" Logan said loudly into the radio. He handed the computer to General Anderson. "Stay here sir. You have way too much to lose. Keep talking to us. Tell us where the signals are."

Logan and Lonnie sprinted from the car toward the 20th Street entrance. Migs, Brian, and Ryan sprinted toward New Hampshire Street.

Dominic closed in on the boys. He noticed that they were all looking down at what the tallest boy had in his hands.

"Hey!" Dominic shouted in their direction. The boys turned and they began to run. "Stop!" Dominic yelled and began to chase them. He focused on the tall boy with the object. "I'm gonna need some help here!" Dominic yelled.

"I'm on you," Samantha said and moved out in the van. She immediately saw Dominic and the boy.

"Jenkins' phone is moving fast now Dominic," General Anderson said into the comms.

"Yes, I'm chasing a boy. About 6'2", maybe 130 pounds. Approximately 14 years old, wearing green athletic shorts and a blue shirt. Heading west," Dominic said between several breaths.

"Yeah, you're on him. Stay with him. Jenkins' phone is heading west," General Anderson said.

The two of them ran in the street, then across a lawn, between buildings. The boy ran people over, pushed them down, and was almost hit by a car. Dominic was struggling to breathe; his lungs were on fire and sweat was burning his eyes. "Sam, do you still have us?" he barely got out between breaths.

"Yeah, I'm about a quarter mile east across the field. Keep going, I'll find a way to get over there." Samantha slammed on the brakes and laid on the horn.

The boy was fatiguing. His arms began to drop and his neck began to extend. Dominic saw it and it pushed him on. He knew the boy would quit soon, and he did. The boy brought the phone up, looked at it while running, then threw it into the grass. Dominic stopped running and picked it up. "I've got the phone. Come and get me damn it," Dominic said with his hands on the top of his head.

Logan and Lonnie had reached the bottom of the steps. It was total darkness except what little light made it down the stairwell reflecting off the white subway tiles lining all the walls in the tunnels.

"Lonnie light a torch."

"Yes sir," Lonnie said turning on his LED flashlight. "Shit Logan, check this out. Lonnie reached down and pointed at Amir's phone and some bloody fingerprints around it and near the stairwell.

"Find more blood. We need to trace it and see where it goes. I'll go left, you go right. Meet back here in five." They nodded and Lonnie ran off. "Mitchell, we are going out of comms range. I'll check back in five." After that, Logan went left down the tunnel.

The tunnel was dark but Logan moved quickly. It bent right and continued for several hundred feet. Then he saw it. A man lying on the ground face up. It was easy to see the man was dead, but not easily discernible who it was. Logan approached, cautiously. He wasn't sure if someone still hid in the shadows waiting to kill him as well. He got within 20 feet and saw it wasn't Amir, but Jenkins who laid dead on the tunnel floor.

Logan ran. He ran so fast the noise from his shoes hitting the concrete seemed odd and distorted. It was as if he was catching up to his echoes. He reached the stairwell in less than a minute. "Amir is armed and loose. He killed Jenkins and planted his phone here at the stairwell."

Lonnie came down the tunnel through the darkness. "Logan, there's no sign of him that way," he said pulling up to a stop.

"This tunnel has at least one more exit. Go back right and I'll go left. Look for any possible escape route." Lonnie went back down the tunnel into the darkness, his light reflecting off every surface like a moonlit lake.

Logan and Lonnie both inched their way down the tunnels. Step by silent step they cleared every corner, every archway, doorway, train car. Lonnie's heart was pounding as he searched around each obstacle. He was disadvantaged in the dark, exposed by his own light he used to search the shadows. Logan was angry—at himself mostly. He should have been in the tunnels, in the dark, with Amir. He was also scared. He dodged death three times now and felt his number might be up. He was finally letting people back in for the first time since Sherman died and Samantha left. Cautiously as he could, he watched for movement, for shadows, for a break in the guiding architectural lines throughout the tunnels.

Logan paused, thought for a moment, ran to the exit, and keyed the comms. "Mitchell, I think we should call in a murder. Get all the local PD down here. Getting people who know the area might be our only card. If D.C. police get him we can always have JTTF grab Amir saying he's a national security risk," Logan looked at his phone. "It's already 1440. We need to catch him soon or the search field expands exponentially."

"I'll make the call," Dominic said as he got into Samantha's van.

Logan and his men were all in the tunnels. They had upgraded to LED flashlights and the local PD was able to turn the lights on through the entire tunnel system. It revealed little. They had found several dead-end exits that had been filled in with concrete and bricks years ago. The tunnels were immaculate, aside from vandalism by way of unoriginal graffiti works. The local PD had brought in a historian and tour leader who knew the tunnels very well. Even the expert thought everything was in its place. The expert had to leave when he became sick after seeing Jenkins' dead body.

Jenkins laid in a pool of blood under a sheet. His wife had been informed and so had the State Department. Everyone wanted answers, especially Doyle Smith. He spoke with General Anderson directly who insisted he came down to the tunnels to hear the story in person.

General Anderson stood with Doyle for quite a while as the search for Amir continued. Doyle was brought up to speed on the entire case. From Paris to Chicago, from Shifty to Amir, and ultimately, Saint Louis, and now Jenkins.

"This is a tough swallow General, but, it does add up. I can't believe this guy was advising me on what to do day-to-day! I feel so ashamed I didn't see it. We need to get Jenkins' wife into protective custody and make sure she's not talking," Doyle picked up his phone. "Damn this place! I'll be back. Gotta go topside to get this call off." He stormed away staring at his phone, the time was 1945.

TWENTY-EIGHT

Two days had passed and there was absolutely no sign of Amir. The entire FBI the DHS, several JTTF teams as well as state and local police force was informed of the wanted man. Everyone had pictures, were briefed on former friends and associates, and the few aliases they knew of based on the information from Saint Louis. The FBI had also researched all purchases made with the credit card Amir was using and any other cards linked to that name. What they found was very limited. Aside from the hotels and car rental there were only a handful of random food purchases. The FBI had Amir's photo ID picture, as well as several taken throughout the Saint Louis area from closed circuit cameras. The FBI then ran it through their software, which allowed them to face match across all known ID images including driver's licenses, passports, FOID cards, and any other photographic ID. They received a few dozen hits that could have been Amir, but only two of them panned out. Those two were also dead ends with no credit cards.

Logan, his Marines, General Anderson, Samantha, Dominic, and Secretary Smith all sat quietly in the conference room. It had been more than 48 hours since everyone had last slept or even had a change of clothes. The entire mahogany table was covered in photos and documents. There were several dozen pictures of Amir walking into the streetcar station under DuPont Circle, however, there was not a single image of him leaving. There had not been a single photo anywhere in the country of him since exiting the tunnels. Nothing from airports, train stations, or traffic cameras.

"I think we all need to just get some sleep. The entire country is looking for this guy. I will get word immediately if we hear anything. It serves no purpose for us to all be fighting sleep for the sake of being here," Secretary Doyle said breaking the silence.

"Yeah alright. Sounds fair enough," General Anderson said standing while pushing down on his thighs. His body ached from sitting for countless hours. "Let's all get some shut eye. Mr. Secretary will let me know, then I'll call Logan and he can get us all back together." Everyone slowly stood and walked out of the room.

"Logan," Secretary Doyle said while staring at the table.

"Yes sir," Logan paused and looked toward Doyle.

"Stick around for a minute," Doyle said and pulled out the chair next to him. It took a few moments but the room eventually cleared. Doyle didn't look up until he heard the door latch shut.

"Logan you're either talented or you are an associate of these terrorists. Now, before you think I'm accusing you, I want you to listen. I wholeheartedly believe that you're on our side. You did amazing work, and without what you and your team uncovered I'd still have that traitorous bastard occupying that office right through there," Doyle said pointing through the doors. "I need you on our team if we are going to continue to have your input."

"I am on your team," Logan said, confused.

"No, I need you to collect a paycheck. To have a confidentiality agreement. To have full security clearance to help me track this asshole around the world if we have to. I'll be honest if nothing else with you, Logan. I don't see us finding Amir any time soon. It would be a whole lot easier with you being on the team, with the paperwork. You'll have all access to everything, I'll see to it. Financial incentive would be 25 percent more than you would make as a contractor plus governmental benefits," he paused. "And free travel." For the first time, his eyes met Logan's.

Logan sat for a moment contemplating the offer that stood before him. The money didn't matter, nothing had really mattered for years. He had been scared to commit to anything. A job, a woman, to himself, ever since Sherman's death. He bounced around from recon to CIA to contract work all to avoid the everyday commitment. But now he felt different. He felt connected to a group once again and it was a very welcome feeling. He didn't want this group to go away. Amir entered his mind. He wanted to find this man. More than anything, he needed to get the man who got away.

"I can do that, sir." They shook hands. "But on one condition," Logan said holding onto Doyle's hand. "I get a team, and I get to pick them. You can make it happen?"

"And who might this team be?"

"Dubs, Migs, Lonnie, Ryan, and Brian."

Doyle paused. He sighed. "I can give you three."

"C'mon Doyle," Logan said annoyed.

"I don't have a way to pay for more than you anyways."

Logan thought for a moment. He felt closest to Dubs, the young man who reminded him of himself from years ago. Migs was another man who reflected another time in Logan's life. He smiled. Lonnie always made him laugh with his stories, and he was a damn good soldier.

"Dubs, Migs, and Lonnie."

"OK son, go get some sleep. Nice to have you."

"And my men," Logan said releasing Doyle's hand. The men both stood up and walked out.

Virginia

It was a warm evening, the sun had set about an hour earlier, and there were thousands of stars in the sky. A bald man walked down a dirt road in Virginia. He was tall, tan, and broad shouldered. Handsome, some would say. He wore jeans and a white shirt with sweat stains all down his back and chest. He had a large CamelBak that was running low on water and a green messenger bag draped over his right shoulder.

"Hey, do you need a ride?" a young man in a pickup truck asked as he came to an abrupt stop with a cloud of dust surrounding the car.

The bald man continued to walk on without looking.

"Sorry, I didn't hear you," the young man said as he turned down his loud country music. "What'd ya' say man? I can let you hop in. I'm heading into town. It's about 20 miles. You can stay the night there or just grab some food. I won't ask too many questions. Don't be shy."

The bald man stopped, looked at the young man, and said, "Well, alright. Fair enough." The bald man climbed inside. "Thank you," he said and dug into his green bag pulling out a phone.

The bald man then began paging though the messages, reading through a few of the conversations and deleting the contacts one by one.

The country music returned, loudly, but the bald man didn't care. Once the messages were gone he decided to look through the email. Nothing of importance there, just a few spam emails that hadn't been cleared in three days. The last thing he did was look through the contacts themselves. He counted 30. He deleted them one at a time after looking at the names. Anything familial such as mom, sweetheart, or with first and last names he deleted. That left him only five numbers, which he reviewed one-by-one. One of the five was international. He recognized the country code: Saudi Arabia.

The bald man then reached into his messenger bag with his right hand and sat for a moment thinking. He reached his left hand up and rubbed the top of his head feeling the two-day stubble. No matter how often he had done it, having a shaved head felt a bit numb to the touch. It was as if his hair were the nerve endings on the top of his head. Without them he had little sensation.

"So how far to town?" the bald man asked.

"Oh, probably 45 minutes or so. Roads are rough out here. You wanna change the station? I love country but I'm a fan of everything," the young man said smiling, showing the fine cut tobacco that was stuck between his teeth. He had a straight white smile, a five-day beard, and a Miller Lite hat on. "Actually man, I gotta take a piss. I'm gonna pull over. Feel free to change the station."

The young man jumped out of the truck and walked to the side of the road. The bald man pulled a black Glock out of his bag. He slid over to the driver seat and pointed the weapon in the direction of the young man. Two shots echoed through the rolling countryside. The bald man climbed out and rolled the dead man's body off the road and into the ditch. He kicked the dirt around to remove any obvious trace of blood spatter. He climbed back into the truck, turned the radio off, and texted the Saudi number.

"This is Amir Qasmi. I killed Jenkins. I want help." It was a shot in the dark but Amir was desperate. He drove on toward the next small town.

Several minutes passed and he felt the phone vibrate. Picking up the phone he saw that he had a message. "We can help. We are tracking your phone. We know where you are. Stay low for 24 hours and you will be safe."

Amir was relieved. He finally saw the glow of the town coming up over the horizon. Looking at that dash clock it was 2200 hours. The city should be quiet at this time of night. Amir drove slowly through town but didn't stop. He hadn't seen a single soul. He turned left after heading through downtown. There was a sign for Highway 634, the highway he wanted to take. It would be safe to drive until dawn. After that, he would wipe the car down, ditch it, and continue on foot. He would be safe in 24 hours.

It wasn't hard for Amir to lay low for a day in the country. He stole a meal from a convenience store, a few Gatorades as well. It felt all too simple, which put him slightly on edge. He settled in at a small town and stayed out of sight for the most part. He meandered in and out of the downtown area, paying careful attention not to stay too long in one place. The hours passed quickly.

Eventually he reached the gas station at the end of town. He walked in. Looking at the clock on the wall it was 1800. He pocketed a few items, a bag of beef jerky and yet another blue Gatorade. He walked past the drinks one last time when another man walked in. This man seemed out of place for a small country town. He was dark in complexion, dark hair and eyes, and wore a tailored suit—minus the tie. The new man scanned the room and settled his eyes on Amir. Then the man left. It was obvious this man wanted Amir. It made him nervous. *That was fast,* he thought as he continued to walk through the store. He went to the window and saw the man standing by an AMG Mercedes outside.

Was this Jenkins' out? Did he have a backup plan in case he was killed or found out? Amir began to doubt everything. His took a drink of Gatorade to moisten his palate. He glanced back at the convenience store clerk who was busy watching the six o'clock news. *A lot of good she'll be if shit goes down.*

He followed the man's path out of the store and saw he was filling up on premium gas. Amir walked toward the vehicle. The man saw him approaching.

"Amir Qasmi?" he said, emotionless, cold, looking through his

Ray-Bans. "Get in the car," the man opened the rear driver's door for him to enter.

There was a phone sitting on the seat with a number already dialed. Amir pressed call.

"Amir Qasmi. I know who you are. You were ex-American military turned terrorist. I like that about you. What I don't like is that you assassinated my friend. It had taken me, well, quite some time to have a friend that close to the American leadership. You are now going to work for me, or, the man who let you in the car will kill you. It's that simple. If you choose to work, then he'll bring you to me. Your choice." The line went dead.

The front door of the car opened and the man entered, started the car, and pulled away. After several minutes, they were well out of town. "Do we have an answer Mr. Qasmi?" the man asked plainly with a thick accent.

"Take me to him," Amir responded, staring out the window, frustrated, but alive.

Washington, D.C.

It was restful sleep. Not once did he wake up with Sherman or his own death on his mind. He wasn't worried about Samantha, he wasn't worried about Dubs or how many things he had to do that day. For a moment, he had even forgotten about Amir.

He looked at the clock, 1100 hours. He checked his phone, no messages, no missed calls. He unlocked the phone and called Samantha.

"Hi," she said groaning and stretching in her bed after three rings.

"You sleep well?"

"Yeah, you? I almost hate to ask."

"I did actually. But I'm really hungry."

"You asking me to go with you?"

"I called you, didn't I?"

"Give me ten minutes. Then come get me."

Logan sprung from his bed and went into the bathroom. He brushed his teeth, staring at himself in the mirror. It was embarrassing, really, how giddy he felt, how bright his eyes were, how he couldn't get that damn smile off his face. He went back to his bed and turned on the TV hoping to pass ten minutes while he waited.

"The Saint Louis Rams have decided to move the franchise to Los Angeles following the terrorist scare. The owners stated that the team was in talks prior to the incident, but due to the revenue loss that will surely occur this year they decided it was the only option on the table," the sportscaster on ESPN stated.

Logan smiled, turned off the TV, and threw on some clothes. He left the hotel room not even checking if the door closed. Samantha's room was two floors down. He took the stairs, jumping down the last few on each landing.

Knock, knock, knock! Logan gently rapped at the door.

"That was only five minutes," Samantha said answering the door in her pajama shirt and shorts.

"You are beautiful," he took her in, letting himself fully commit to her for the first time. He had never really let his guard down with her. She had met him after Sherman. She never knew Logan before that life-shattering moment. The funny guy, the joker, the tenderhearted man they both always wanted him to be.

"You seem different," she said wrinkling her nose.

"I have been for a long time. Can I come in?" He smiled at her. She stepped sideways behind the door and gestured him to enter. He walked in the room, took the door from her hands, and grabbed the "do not disturb" sign. He placed it on the outside handle, and locked the deadbolt.

"Logan?"

He grabbed Samantha around the waist with both hands and brought her close. He looked deeply into her dark brown eyes. She saw it. Love. He kissed her. His inner terror was gone.

"We can get room service if we want. We don't need to leave this room," Logan said as he pulled away and looked at her eyes. She kissed him back.

I appreciate you taking the time to read my debut thriller. I'm assuming, if you've gotten this far, you enjoyed it. Please consider rating and reviewing the book at Amazon and Goodreads. It would mean the world to me. Thank you, and please know I'm working hard on another project to entertain you in the future. If you're eager to know more of the story, please read the following excerpt from Sins of the Father. You'll get a glimpse of what the continuation of the story entails . . . and it's going to be insane!

Chapter 1
THE CANDYMAN

Aden, Yemen

A child runs unseen down a narrow street, weaving through hundreds of people hiding from the scorching sun. The weather had been sweltering for weeks, but at least outside there was a breeze. The boy slowed, as the subtle smell of lemon and roasted nuts leapt into his nose. It was his favorite treat, a love cake, the only thing that could keep him from his mission. He inhaled deeply and scanned the area with his eyes. He searched past several vendors as they yelled while simultaneously wiping the sweat from their foreheads. Finally, he spotted the distraction to his left. His mouth watered as he imagined the sweet, sour treat crunching in his mouth.

Whap! A metal spatula slapped the table next to him and the vendor hollered for the young boy to move along. Instinctually, he ducked behind an adjacent food stand and crashed through a group of men drinking tea; giggling as he snuck away unseen. He turned down a steep and narrow alleyway. He was almost there, to an apartment a recluse called home; a ghost the children called the Candyman.

David Westbrook sat with light cascading in from the cracks at the front door. His eyes were glued to a jumble of numbers and letters as they flashed across the screen to his left. A larger, brighter monitor sat in front of him, and a third one displayed a three-dimensional map of the Middle East, extending as far east as China. On the map were hundreds of dots, some small and blue indicating limited activity, others large and red showing tremendous activity. He was pinging computers by the thousands, his algorithm working flawlessly as it began to create a picture of which computers were playing nice and which had ulterior motives.

"*El-khair!*" the young boy yelled as he burst through David's apartment door. The intense sunlight pierced the room, causing dust in the air to glow in the multicolored rays of light.

"Get out," David hollered, shielding his eyes, and shooing the boy to leave.

"*Biddi, Biddi!*" the boy exclaimed.

"You always want something but you never give me anything good," David responded, frustrated that the boy was once again bothering him during peak hours.

"*Beddak?*"

"Of course I want news, but you never deliver. I work alone Amal. Each time you tell me something, I have to follow up. It's how this works."

The young boy laughed and pointed at a box in the corner of the room. He held up two fingers, "*Ethnain.*"

"In English, Amal."

"Two for this."

"You tell me what you found and I'll decide."

The young boy, barely ten, always tried to negotiate his rates with the Candyman but it never successfully worked out. Nonetheless, he paused and rubbed his chin as if deep in thought.

"Okay Amal, leave now. I don't have all day," the impatient agent said as he spun his chair toward the desk and watched the numbers continue to scroll across the screen.

"It's good, it's good!" the boy said, shuffling toward the man.

Quickly, David sprung to his feet and stood well above the small boy from Yemen, his t-shirt sticking to his chest and abdomen. "Tell me now." The look David gave Amal was one meant for the men he often interrogated after hearing these "good" reports.

"I hear about a man in the mountains. Very powerful. Nobody knows his name but he's training hundreds to attack U.S."

"That's not even worth one," he said, holding up a finger.

"I know! That's not what I have to tell you. There's a man in the city. Today only. He will know. I hear a man on the street say he will be here."

"Where?"

"The port. A ship coming."

"Name?"

"Lady Phoenix."

"Okay. You can have one now, and two more—if this is all true," David said, softening his demeanor and rubbing the boy's head firmly. "Come back next week and I'll let you know."

Amal ran to the corner or the dark, lifeless room. He tore open a small box and grabbed a bag of blowpops.

"Amal. Grab me one," David said with his back to the boy. Once again, his full attention was on the data flashing across the screens.

"*Shukran,*" David said, smiling to Amal as they both unwrapped their candy. "You have a green! That's my favorite."

Amal lifted it toward the man, offering a trade.

"No, no. You've earned that. I'll see you next week my friend," David said and reached his large hand out, the boy took it and squeezed as hard as he could. David smiled at the effort.

Amal placed the candy in his mouth. The tart, sugary combination immediately made his mouth water and his eyes light up. He skipped out of the room, but only after giving David a high five. Once again, the room was completely dark, but this time the Candyman was focused on darker thoughts.

It was 1300 hours when David arrived at the port in Aden. He wore a small brown satchel over his right shoulder and held a digital monocular in his left. It only took him minutes to find the Lady Phoenix, which he quickly learned was heading for America in three days. He stood behind the tall legs of a loading crane as it lifted cargo containers onto the large ship, creaking under the stress of a particularly heavy load. Every ten minutes he would remove his Ray-Bans and lift the monocular to his eye, scanning the ship. Finally, after over two hours, he saw a group of five men.

They were as conspicuous as could be, all wearing yellow hardhats, all wearing overalls and thin white shirts, and all sporting beards of various lengths; except for one. His hardhat was white, pristine, and his clothes were meant for a lunch meeting at a five-star restaurant rather than the deck of a cargo ship. His gray pants and custom tailored white button-up seemed staunchly out of place.

As David walked toward the parking lot, he soon spotted his mark's car. It was the only luxury car in the lot, a black AMG Mercedes, parked perpendicular to the many other cars. David walked past a few port employees, nodded at them, and made a direct path to the Mercedes. As he approached, he reached into his bag and grabbed a small black device. He visually scanned the immediate area, as well as the horizon for any individuals who could be watching. By the time he reached the Mercedes, he was confident there was nobody providing security for the meeting on the boat.

David pressed the small device gently onto the door of the car. Within seconds, the doors unlocked and disengaged the security system. Quickly, he climbed into the spacious backseat and laid on the floor, the intense heat and thick, stagnant air immediately caused his heart to beat more rapidly.

He closed his eyes and focused on his dark, one room apartment, his data, and the map full of dots displayed on his screens. David ached to make sense of it all. He had thousands of data points. He knew all came together, but couldn't build the algorithm in his mind. His dual degrees in mathematics/electrical engineering and computer science from MIT should have helped, but without a fresh set of eyes looking over the information, it was tough to get perspective. It had been nearly four years since he heard an American voice. The data was too large to send, and too sensitive. He was forced to send small, encoded pieces back to the U.S., which were often overlooked due to the agency back home not having the full scope of the numbers. This is what led him to his unique form of interrogation. That's the only intel the suits back home listened to.

David lay uncomfortably still on the black carpet, his heart beating forcefully and rapidly. Sweat had saturated his thin clothing and began to moisten the floor of the car. He fought the urge to move, knowing the man he waited for was more likely to be coming with each second. Finally, he heard the actuators from the doors unlocking.

Bright sunlight entered the car as the driver's door opened. David could smell the man's cologne before he even entered. The man sighed heavily and dropped hard into the leather seat. He pushed the start button on the car, leaving the door open for a moment. David felt the fresh air wash over him and he silently took a deep breath. Cool air from the air conditioner reached his left arm, leg, and torso; a chill encompassed his body.

Thump, he heard the tight seal of the Mercedes' door close and slowly they pulled away, the sound of rubber over gravel gave David a rush.

David waited several minutes enjoying the comfortable air as his heart rate slowed to normal. He knew the drill. David reached quietly into his messenger bag and pulled out a black blade. He also removed a syringe full of his homemade "candy."

The car stopped for a traffic signal, and David shot up from the floor. Using his right hand, he grabbed the driver's chest and slammed him hard against the seatback. His left hand held the blade tight against the driver's throat.

"Don't move," he told the man calmly in Arabic.

"What am I supposed to do?" the man squealed as the light changed to green.

"Turn right and drive until it ends."

"I'll tell you nothing."

"I doubt that," David said as he bit down gently on the syringe between his teeth.

Quickly, the driver lurched forward, but David was faster, removing the knife from his neck and slamming him back into the seat. It was terrifying how both spindly and strong David's long arms were, as if they were hydraulic and carbon rather than human.

"Drive," David growled, as he noticed a streak of bright red running down the knife toward his hand, as he held it firmly against the driver's neck.

It took several minutes to reach the end of the road, but in that short time, blood had run down the blade handle onto David's hand; a metronome of viscous fluid dripped down to the floor of the car, becoming lost in the dark carpet. David was worried. His drug typically took thirty minutes for a full effect.

"Pull over," David said as he looked to the right and left, seeing nobody in the dark, lonely alleyway. This was one of several locations around the city that David had commandeered over the years. He found it much easier to have a variety of "facilities" enabling him to get to a location he knew was safe. He also knew his questions would never get answered without a certain amount of aggression. He tried leading with the nice guy approach on many occasions, but that only wasted time.

"Get out," he demanded and pulled the blade away when the driver's door opened. David got out and looked at the man for the first time up close. He was middle-aged, about five-foot-ten, and wore a thick, manicured beard. He also saw the crimson stains on the man's shirt had completely saturated his collar and advanced in a tapering streak to the level of his heart.

"Walk," David said, directing him with the knife toward a dark doorway of the building to their right. It was shadowed by its own height, the sun already descending behind the structure. The prisoner listened without hesitation.

Inside the room smelled of rust, despite the lack of steel. There were two wooden chairs and a small amber light hanging from the center of the room over plywood floors. As they walked deeper into the void, the wooden floor became peppered with dark spots, increasingly becoming larger and more dense as they approached the chairs.

"There," David said, pointing at the dark chair. The prisoner approached and the smell of iron filled his nose. His eyes became wide and he hesitated, thinking to run as he realized what the dark stains were.

"Please, no. I have children. I know nothing, I know nobody. I was at the port today for a friend. You must believe me!"

"I know you called someone in the car. Who was it?"

"A friend."

"Sit down," David said, glaring at the man and pointing the knife directly into his face.

"You'll kill me," the mark said with a trembling voice.

"Not if you talk. So, talk."

"I have no informa—"

David hit the man hard in the face with the handle of his knife, splitting the skin just under his right eye. Quickly, David took the syringe and jammed it into the man's arm, pressing the plunger down hard.

"You'll sing now," David said, wiping the spattering of blood off his dirty white shirt.

"Ha ha ha," the man began laughing as he plopped down into his chair. "I've done drugs before, sir. They gave me a lot of things for a moment like this."

"See, you're talking already. You can't help it, can you?"

"This is nothing. You won't make me talk. I've taken everything. Truth serum is useless, infidel."

"I'm not sure if you're just a bigger pussy than most, or if it's the loss of blood, but you're talking early. You'll die soon, either way."

"I talk for nobody! I told you in the car," he said and spat at David. David took off his shirt, revealing his lean body. He wound his moist shirt tightly and *whap!* He snapped the prisoner in the chest, splitting his skin. *Whap!* He did it again. *Whap, whap, whap!* He did it several more times leaving small wounds in the man's chest through his bloodied shirt.

"Stop!" the man yelled and covered his chest with both hands.

"What's your biggest secret?" David asked as he sat backward in the chair, leaning on the back of the seat playfully, his head resting on both hands.

"I slept with my wife's sister. Her son is mine. Nobody knows I give her money."

"Interesting," David said, laughing and sitting up, as the man sat staring at the floor, reviewing what had just come out of his mouth.

"It was a joke," the man finally said, looking up and stretching out his arms as he struggled with a smile.

"No, it wasn't. You see, the drug I gave you is my own cocktail so to speak. You haven't had any experience with this. I promise you."

"What?"

"Have you heard of the Candyman?" David asked, and waited for the reaction. He had a reputation, having been in the Middle East for over a decade, moving from one large city to the next. The terrorists had begun to hear rumors about a CIA operative who used atypical techniques.

The mark began to cry silently, several tears ran down his face as his mind drifted through horrific stories he heard over the years: the dismemberment, the burning, the waterboarding, hunting down family members and murdering loved ones. However, none of this was true. Most of the time, David let them loose after they talked. From there, the terrorist organization would likely do the torturing and killing as a retaliation for them speaking with the Candyman.

"So, talk."

"I was there to look at a ship."

"I know that much already."

"It was for a man from Saudi Arabia."

"Name?"

"I don't know."

"Tell me more than that," David said as he showed the black blade to the prisoner again who still stared at the floor. David lowered his head in a search to find the captive's eyes.

"That's all I know about it," he said, wiping his hands together.

"What do you know then?"

"An attack in the U.S."

"Where?"

"Los Angeles."

"When?"

"This month."

"Who's involved?"

"A dozen men."

"Do you have any names?"

"Only three."

David took out his bag and grabbed a notebook and a pen. "Write their names, and anything you know. Where they stay, what they plan to do, as much detail as you can."

Several minutes went by but the prisoner had written down two pages of information and given it to David. It consisted of three names, six addresses, and a tentative plan for suicide bombing several college campuses around Los Angeles. David looked the intel over with care before locking eyes with the prisoner who sat calmly in his chair. The prisoner was pale, his shoulders rounded forward, and he was taking slow, quick breaths. The left side of his shirt was covered in blood, and slowly dripped down to the floor, adding to the stains.

"Do you even have kids?" David asked gently.

"Only the one from my wife's sister."

"He's taken care of?"

"Yes."

"That's good." David stood up, took his shirt, wrapped it around the man's neck, and began to pull it tight. The prisoner didn't even fight.

David walked out into the night air and stretched his arms high above his head. Shirtless, he began his walk across town where he would make an encrypted phone call stateside. He knew this was something they'd want to hear immediately.

OTHER WORKS

Excerpts found on **www.michaelreidjr.com,** available for purchase at Amazon.com

| ABOUT THE AUTHOR |

Mike has worked with various individuals from government and military backgrounds, drawing from their conversations to develop his visceral stories. He has interviewed U.S. Marshals, FBI, retired and current military of all branches. He's had the opportunity to talk with pilots and captains of a wide variety of aircraft and vessels, as well as members of special forces, which allows him to go into great detail on how missions are run. He often speaks with police, firefighters, and EMTs to determine how certain situations would be investigated and responded to, as their protocols often change.

Mike's wide knowledge base helps drive his eclectic writing. He received his undergraduate degree in biology, with minors in both psychology and chemistry. He went on to Washington University in Saint Louis where he received his doctorate. He also spent time in religious studies and grew up in the church, which helped his unique writing style, allowing him to work across genres.

Outside of writing novels, he blogs professionally for Veritas Health, in their Spine and Sports sections.

His interests include writing, woodworking, and exercise, and has been known to work on cars and motorcycles.

CONTACT

Join Mike's email newsletter at his website for the latest information regarding new releases and upcoming work, as well as chances to win merchandise and new releases!

Web: **michaelreidjr.com**

Instagram: **@authormichaelreidjr**

Twitter: **@michaelreidjr1**

Facebook: **www.facebook.com/Authormichaelreidjr/**

| COLOPHON |

This book was designed and laid out by kalzub design (Racine, WI), April 2016; a.r. merlo, 2017 reprint.

The cover and back covers were designed by Mosbrook Design.

Interior text is set in Univers LT Std family and Twentieth Century MT family.